I0891226

A BROKEN BLADE

A BROKEN BLADE

MELISSA BLAIR

UNION SQUARE & CO.
NEW YORK

UNION
SQUARE
& CO.
NEW YORK

UNION SQUARE & CO. and the distinctive Union Square & Co. logo are trademarks of Hachette Book Group, Inc.

© 2021 Melissa Blair

All rights reserved. No part of this publication may be reproduced, stored in a retrieval system, or transmitted in any form or by any means (including electronic, mechanical, photocopying, recording, or otherwise) without prior written permission from the publisher.

ISBN 978-1-4549-4787-5 (trade paperback)
ISBN 978-1-4549-4788-2 (e-book)

Library of Congress Cataloging-in-Publication Data

Names: Blair, Melissa, 1995- author.
Title: A broken blade / Melissa Blair.
Description: New York City : Union Square & Co., [2021] | Originally self-published in 2021. | Summary: "Keera is a killer. As the king's Blade and his most gifted assassin, she is called upon to hunt down a mysterious figure called the Shadow who is moving against the Crown. She tracks the Shadow into the magical lands of the Fae, but the Faeland is not what it seems, and neither is the Shadow. Keera is shocked by what she discovers and can't help but wonder who her enemy truly is..."-- Provided by publisher.
Identifiers: LCCN 2022010411 (print) | LCCN 2022010412 (ebook) | ISBN 9781454947875 (paperback) | ISBN 9781454947882 (epub)
Subjects: BISAC: FICTION / Fantasy / Romance | FICTION / Romance / LGBTQ+ / General | LCGFT: Novels. | Fantasy fiction. | Romance fiction.
Classification: LCC PR9199.4.B557 B76 2022 (print) | LCC PR9199.4.B557 (ebook) | DDC 813/.6--dc23/eng/20220322
LC record available at https://lccn.loc.gov/2022010411
LC ebook record available at https://lccn.loc.gov/2022010412

Union Square & Co. books may be purchased in bulk for business, educational, or promotional use. For more information, please contact your local bookseller or the Hachette Book Group's Special Markets department at special.markets@hbgusa.com.

Printed in China

8 10 9

unionsquareandco.com

Cover art and design by Kim Dingwall
Interior design by Colleen Sheehan and Jordan Wannemacher
Map art by Karin Wittig

This book is dedicated to BookTok,
creators and viewers alike.
It wouldn't exist without you.

Love,
one of your own

Elverath

The Treaty of the Faeland
Aralinth
Caerth
Cereliat
The Dark Wood
The Burning Mountains
The Poison Fields
The Pool of Elvera
Myrelinth
Silstra
The Cliffs of Elandorr
Wolford
The Singing Wood
Belmoor
Volcar
The Barren Lands
The Frostlands
Exiles Res

The Fractured Isles
The Dead Wood
The Order
Koratha
Wenden
Mortal's
Landing
Calen's Rift
The Anticor Foothills
Blackpool
Ruins of
Faevra
N
W
E
S

Content Warning

This book is a fantasy romance that explores themes of alcoholism, addiction, colonialism, depression, and systemic violence. While it is not the focus of this book or depicted graphically on the page, some content may be triggering for readers who have experienced self-harm, assault, depression, or suicidal ideation.

Please read with care.

My body is made of scars,

some were done to me,

but most I did to myself.

Year [illegible] AC

The Halfling Decree

Henceforth the King shall only recognize two species as citizens of the Crown:

Mortals

&

Dark Fae

(as long as they reside in the Treaty of the Faeland)

From this day forward, all those of impure blood are considered wards of the Crown. All Halflings, those of Mortal and Elvish lineage, carry the same abomination as their impure ancestors. King Aemon has tirelessly fought to banish any surviving Elves from his Kingdom. Now that his mission is complete, he holds himself responsible for their unnatural offspring.

The citizenship of all Halflings is revoked, and they are now considered property of the Crown. All Halflings living in the Kingdom of Elverath must turn themselves in.

Refusal to submit to this order will result in death.

CHAPTER ONE

I had seventeen blades concealed along my person, each one more than capable of killing the man in front of me. The slivers of steel tucked into my leathers would land a deadly strike before he even saw my arm move. The twin blades I had crossed against my back would be slower, but he was Mortal. Human. He couldn't outrun me.

Any of my weapons would do, though I knew his life would end at the edge of the bloodred dagger holstered at my thigh. I only had to wrap my fingers around the bone hilt and levy the blow.

But I couldn't kill him until I had what I needed.

"Please," he whispered through swollen lips. A pleading look met my gaze, framed by the black eye I had given him the hour before. "I've told you everything I know!"

"You've been more obliging than most of the people I interrogate," I said truthfully. Many of my targets waited until I spilled half their blood before they would spill their secrets. This man had caved after the third strike. He barely squirmed when I restrained him to the chair.

"I would do anything for the king! Anything! Just let me go. Please." His last word came out as a pathetic whimper. I should have known this one was a crier.

"The king only requires one more thing of you before he extends his mercy," I replied. My right hand rested on the white hilt of my dagger.

"Anything." His voice cracked. Hot lines of tears poured down his cheeks as he rocked back and forth.

"A name." I took a step toward him. He flinched. His wide brown eyes darted from my face to my hand and back again.

"I already told you. He called himself the Shadow. He hid behind the hood of his cloak. That's all I know!" He leaned forward, fighting the ropes tied around his torso. Thick veins strained against his neck, pulsing almost as quickly as his breath. He knew what happened when the Blade was finished asking her questions.

"Not that name," I whispered. I didn't need any more information for the king. This name was just for me.

"What name? I'll give you any name you want," he said. Sweat pooled along the sparse hairs of his lip.

I needed to end this. I was being cruel.

"Your name," I answered.

He still stared at me, but his eyes lost focus as he slumped against the back of the chair. He swallowed. "Why?"

I hated these moments most. When a person's resolve melted away and they accepted their fate. Accepted that I would kill them. Surprise deaths were so much easier.

I lifted a gentle hand to his chin and pulled his gaze back to mine. My brown braid fell forward and tickled his cheek.

"How about a name for a name? You give me yours and I'll give you mine." It was all I could offer him. A sense of control in his final moment.

His brows raised as he blinked back at me. He gave me a single, slow nod.

"Mathias," he whispered. "My name is Mathias." His eyes traced my face waiting for mine. A flicker of curiosity replaced his dread.

"Mathias . . ." I said, unsheathing my dagger in one quick motion.

"My name is Keera." His throat was cut before the last word was said.

The Shadow. I didn't know when his name started being whispered across Elverath, but it was clear that he was building a reputation. And not just with the fish merchants of Mortal's Landing. I heard his moniker in hushed tones all over the kingdom. Everywhere I went, hunting enemies of the Crown, his name would crop up in overheard conversations in taverns or back alleys. Always with a fearful reverence that made me uneasy. It had been a long time since anyone had dared to move against the king—if that's even what this Shadow was doing.

I pulled out the cork of a wine bottle from the night before. I used my teeth, spitting it onto the floor of the coach that was pulling me into Koratha, the capital of Elverath. I gulped the bitter nectar as the coachman drove me toward the outer wall of the circular city. A soft muslin covered the windows, but I could still see the blurred bodies hanging from the stone wall. Mortals who had committed murder or treason. Halflings who had the gall to ignore an order. Anyone who had broken one of the decrees. Their bodies were strung up to rot. It was the king's preferred form of communication. A message to all those who wondered if they could defy his rule.

No Mortal was above the Crown, and Halflings were expendable.

I knew this all too well. It was my job to track down criminals and enemies of the Crown. Some of them were Mortal; most of them were Halflings trying to evade the king's service by hiding their Elvish blood. The ones who looked human enough could live for years without being found, but eventually their ruse was discovered. A nosy neighbor would become suspicious. Someone would notice their pinched ears or faster reflexes. Or worse yet, they would cut themselves and expose the amber color of their blood. It was the sign of abomination. Of being part Mortal, part Elf.

I trailed a finger along the edge of my dagger, knowing the same blood flowed in my veins. All Halflings were owned by the king, forced into his service. I served him best through death.

I hated being in the capital, but I couldn't put it off any longer. I had to have yet another audience with the king in which I told him his enemy had been punished but named this elusive Shadow. The fisherman I killed was the third person in as many months who had traded secrets with the masked menace. None of them had a name. None of them had seen his face. Part of me wanted to believe the Shadow was nothing but myth, but even I had crossed his path once. The Shadow was real, masquerading in a black cloak, concealing his identity from those who would kill him.

People like me.

The Shadow kept me from sleeping. I didn't even enjoy my wine at night because I couldn't stop puzzling over the man under the hood. As the king's Blade, I was the most skilled marksman and spy in the game. It should be my name, my cloak casting fear into the eyes of peasants and petty lords, but now they whispered of this anonymous figure.

Even the king was starting to notice the chatter. Lords and servants whispered about the Shadow all over the palace. Courtesans and maids debated who hid beneath that hood. Guards argued about the Shadow's motives. Everyone wondered whether the man draped in shadow was even Mortal at all. Maybe the Shadow was more treacherous than he seemed. Maybe he was a long-lost Elf seeking revenge on the king for killing off his kind. Maybe the Dark Fae in the west had finally decided to use their magic against the Crown. Or maybe he was a Halfling, forced to keep his face a secret or suffer the consequences of defying the decrees.

The truth was that no one knew the answer. Not even the army of spies the king kept well-trained and well-funded. As I was the head of that army, the king would notice I had once again returned empty-handed. My shoulders twitched. I preferred working outside of his view as much as possible. Having the eyes of the Crown on your head was dangerous. I should know as the person the Crown sends to retrieve those heads.

The coach drove through the city, reaching the innermost wall that protected the palace. It was a magnificent creation of white stone, built as if the rocks themselves had grown into three towers, carving out the chambers for those who inhabited it.

Fae. They had been the makers of this house millennia before. It had been the homestead of the Light Fae, a magical race that had long ago gone extinct. Each of the three towers was topped by stained-glass chambers with ceilings that were more than three stories high. The glass was wrapped by vines that grew thick in the light of the two suns. When the suns shone through the tops of the towers, hues of gold, violet, and silver would cascade onto the walls of the outer rims.

Half my wine bottle was gone by the time we reached the palace gates. I sighed when I heard their slow creaking as the guards pushed the iron doors forward. I wouldn't have time to finish my drink before I was expected in the throne room. Probably for the best—my head already throbbed from the night before.

A guard opened the door to the carriage, and I pulled my hood forward, shielding my face. He knew better than to offer his hand to assist my dismount. I may be the king's Blade, but I was certainly no lady. In Elverath, I wasn't even considered a woman. Those who bothered to address my kind called me the same as they did all women with Elvish blood—*female.*

Halflings had dirty blood, part-Mortal and part-animal in the eyes of the king. Calling us by our sexes was just another way he solidified the distinction between our kinds. Our enslavement was for the good of all; Halflings weren't even human. The guard stepped back from the door. No Mortal man would deign to touch a Halfling. Plus touching me was dangerous when I had been trained in over thirty ways to torture a man with my bare hands until he screamed for death.

He stepped back again as if sensing my thoughts. I smirked before jumping out of the carriage and landing on the dirt. The lacings of my leather boots were covered in mud from days spent on horseback, and my clothes were just as disheveled. I thought about retiring to my chambers to change, but one of the royal spies was waiting at the inner gate, obviously there to collect me.

She was a Shade, one of the elite forces of Halfling females the king trained to do his bidding. Who she was, I wasn't sure and didn't much care. Anyone could be hidden beneath that hood. She could've been someone I trained with at the Order or a recent graduate. Either way, I knew she wasn't a friend. I didn't have any. And if I did, I certainly wouldn't pick a Shade.

"The king is awaiting your presence," a cool voice said from beneath the hood when I slowed. I'd had more of the wine than I thought. My body still felt like it was being jostled around in the carriage.

"Are we not walking there now?" I bit back. I wasn't eager to meet with the king. He would inevitably rattle on about declining trade while my knee burned against the marble floor. I should have had more wine.

The Shade didn't respond but shifted her shoulders. I wondered if she was rolling her eyes at me. Again, I couldn't tell. The top of her hood was cut longer and contained a flexible rod to keep a shadow cast over her features. It was the same hood I wore and was specifically designed to keep our identities a secret. Same for the black tunic and trousers we both wore. When I trained at the Order, I was told the uniform was to protect us, make individual Shades more difficult to track. I thought it was a reminder that our identities didn't matter, only our service to the king. We were expendable, just like any other Halfling. Maybe even more so.

The only thing that distinguished the two of us was my added height and my cloak. Shades were only permitted a hood; a cloak had to be *earned*.

She drummed her fingers along her crossed arms. Her leg shook.

I sighed and I picked up my pace. Better to get the audience over with so I could retire for the night.

Two guards stood outside the throne room. They looked miniature next to the grand doors that reached for the pitched roof three stories above our heads. Though the white grain had yellowed over the centuries, the branches and leaves carved into the wood held large panes of painted glass. Another relic left by the Light Fae that had once roamed these halls.

"There she is!" My mouth dried at the king's deep voice booming off the pillars that lined the throne room. I took a stiff step onto the dais. I could feel his gaze boring into my hood, but I kept my eyes focused on the ornate foot of his gilded throne. I kneeled in front of him and did not rise. My stomach fluttered, though not from my wine.

"Pray tell, what news of Mortal's Landing?" he said. There was a cheery edge to his voice that made my pulse race. The king swiped a goblet from the tray beside him and raised it toward me. The rich scent of Elven wine filled the air. My head throbbed and the dryness scratched at my throat. Whatever I had drank the night before was horse piss compared to the king's collection of fine wines.

"Your assumption was correct, Your Majesty," I said. I was still kneeling on the cool floor, but I raised my head to look at him and pulled back my hood. His blond hair glinted in the light from the towering windows. The sunlight emphasized the two patches of silver above his ears. They were the only sign of aging that the king let show.

"The fish merchant the Shades discovered was indeed trading with criminals, one of which was the Shadow," I continued, shifting my weight onto my toes instead of my knee. "He was quite accommodating in the end. Gave me the names of everyone he was involved with. I will be sure to pass them on to the Arsenal for the Shades to take care of."

"From what I hear, the Arsenal hasn't heard from you in months." The king raised a thick brow.

I bowed my head. The gulp of air I swallowed felt thick.

"You selected the very best of the Shades to prevail over the rest. I trust the other mistresses have managed well in my absence." I dipped my head, hoping that would be enough to appease the king. As the Blade, I was the head of the Arsenal, and by extension, the Shades. But I found the day-to-day of it taxing. Why would I want to manage the hundreds of spies that were stationed across the continent? Or the training grounds across the channel, forging initiates into weapons for the Crown? The other members of the Arsenal were much better at it. Just like I was better at drinking and assassinations. It was more than a fair trade.

The king scoffed and peered down at me from the rim of his cup. Thick lashes framed green eyes that refused to blink. My breath stopped. I searched his face for a sign of what was about to come. A slight smirk or pursed lips. Fingers clenched against the goblet. But there were none. The king had mastered hiding beneath a mask long before I became his Blade.

"Rise," the king said through a gulp of his drink. I let out my breath and my shoulders dropped toward the floor. I stood in one swift motion, stepping back off the dais without a word. No one was allowed to stand taller than the king.

"Did you manage to get his name then? This Shadow figure I keep hearing about?" He placed his goblet back on the tray. His cheeks were flushed from the wine, but his face had lost that cheery glow from when I entered. My heart beat harder against my chest. The king was known for his sudden shifts in mood. And King Aemon the Corrupted was at his most dangerous when irritated.

"No, Your Majesty, I did not." My eyes wandered toward the gray lines etched into the tiles. It wasn't often that I returned to court with bad news. I had not been promoted to Blade by working in half measures.

"You mean you let him get away again?" It was not the king who asked this. The voice belonged to Crown Prince Damien, who sauntered in from the back doors leading to the royal chambers. His smirk was cocked to one side as he leaned against the wall. I glanced at him, noticing that he had cut his hair so that the blond curls he usually tied back had transformed to soft waves cut above the ear. A new haircut on the prince would send the young ladies at court into a frenzy for weeks. Damien knowingly raked a hand through it and raised his brow at me.

I bit my lips to keep from scowling.

"I never saw him, Your Highness," I replied, struggling to keep my voice even.

"Exactly. What use is a Blade if she has no one to cut?" His jade eyes shifted to my back.

I pulled my shoulders backward and met his gaze straight on. "My assignment was to apprehend and question the *fish merchant*, sire. A task I completed in half the time the king requested."

"About the Shadow . . ." Damien countered. "It was easily presumed that we want him dead. I think you're just too scared after losing against him in Volcar. Perhaps you have finally met your match?" He sauntered across the room and stood beside his father.

I clenched my jaw. I had been attacked by the Shadow during a scouting mission in the western city of Volcar. I had not expected it, which in itself was a kind of defeat, but he had not bested me. We fought for minutes before he abandoned the fight by jumping off a rooftop and onto a moving cart below. He escaped, which meant it was a draw at best. Though I did not draw with anyone.

"When we meet again, it will be the end of him," I said.

"Then let's make the assignment official. You are not to return to Koratha without this Shadow's head in a bag." Damien smiled wickedly at the command. My stomach lurched.

"If the Crown commands it," I answered. Even though I was repulsed by the thought of doing anything that pleased the prince, I wanted the Shadow. I wanted to beat him and make sure he realized it just before I stuck my blade through his belly. Any more failures and the king would take my head.

"The Crown does *not* command it," the king cut in, slamming his goblet on the arm of the throne. Droplets of wine launched into the air and pattered onto the marble floor.

"Father, don't be absurd—"

The king raised his hand and silenced his son. I smirked.

"This Shadow is a problem, but we have bigger problems, my Blade. Mistress Hildegard has informed me that she has reason to believe Lord Curringham is aligning himself with the Dark Fae." The king's cheeks were now completely red. His alliance with the Dark Fae was tenuous at best after several attempts at killing them off entirely. When the Blood Wars ended and their numbers had dwindled almost to the point of extinction, the Dark Fae had agreed to sign a treaty with the king. They wouldn't interfere with the Crown or the newfound kingdom of Elverath and, in return, they got to live out the rest of their immortal lives in the Faeland. Now that their last female had died, the Dark Fae could no longer pass on their magic. Their race was doomed to live out their immortal lives with the few Elves who had not met King Aemon's Blade.

"Both are our allies," Damien scoffed. "Surely, this Shadow is of more importance."

"They are *my* allies, but the only reason the Dark Fae have not rebelled against *my* kingdom is because they don't have the numbers. I don't plan on letting the bastards make deals with my own lords under my godsdamned nose!" the king huffed as he assessed his son.

"The Dark Fae would never move against you," Damien said, waving his hand. "You're their king."

The king raised a hand to his temple and shook his head. "You're a fool if you believe the Dark Fae have ever considered me their king." A cool calm settled into the room. It reminded me of the moment before a raid. Just before the violence started.

"What use do they have with a crown?" Damien said with a shrug. "Their powers have faded. Their race is doomed." He lifted a hand and studied his nail beds. His father scowled.

"You, my son, have already lived longer than any Mortal before me, but your decades are nothing compared to that of the Fae. I have lived centuries, but there are Fae still breathing who have lived near ten *thousand* years. As long as they live, they will *always* be a threat," the king said, his eyes turned to slits as they trailed over the prince.

"You destroyed the Elves easily enough. Without the full use of their powers, the Fae are the same," Damien insisted, though the color had drained from his face. He took a step away from his father's gold chair.

"We only suspect the Fae powers have continued to fade. We have no one to confirm it while the treaty holds," the king said, shaking his head. "And the Elves were defeated because they were an *abomination*. Non-magical children of the Fae were never meant to exist. They were unnatural. Vermin marked by the gods with their brown blood. Unnatural creatures are easy for the righteous to kill. The Fae will not be so easily wiped away," the king said in a clipped voice. He toyed with the large gold ring resting on his middle finger. It was carved with the crest of a burning sword. The one he had used during the Blood Wars against the Elves, a cursed species that stole the lands of Fae and men. The king was rewarded by the gods for purifying the land with a year of life for every Elf he killed. Or at least that was the story he had the minstrels tell at court.

The king caught me staring at his ring. I straightened and turned toward the prince.

"Lord Curringham is not a threat. He's the Lord of Flowers!" Damien chuckled, using the moniker he had given the lord as a cruel joke. The king's jaw hung slack, and his chest raised higher.

I was not about to correct a member of the royal household, but

Damien was wrong. Lord Curringham was perfectly positioned to be an ideal ally for the Fae. The king seemed to agree.

"Curringham might be an oaf," the king said, "but he yields the largest harvest of any man in the kingdom."

"He harvests corn and wheat," Damien mumbled, slumping into the chair beside his father.

"Yes. The very things that keep this kingdom fed," the king said, his knuckles turning white. "And now that the eastern orchards have failed, his are the only sources of *winvra* we have left." He picked up his goblet and chucked it across the room.

"Father," Damien said, sitting up straight. He finally noticed the irritation radiating from the king. His eyes danced between the throne and me. "Maybe we should have this conversation alone."

The king scoffed. "I'm sure my Blade is already aware that my son is too much of a fool to realize the very kingdom he expects to inherit may be primed to fall." I froze, feeling the cruel eyes of the prince boring into my flesh. I took a deep breath and stared directly in front of me. I could hear my heart pumping in my chest; Damien would make me pay for that comment later.

"The Dark Fae are too weak to attack the Crown," Damien insisted. His voice had turned into a quiet squeak beside his father's.

"The Dark Fae enact plans over *centuries*." The king slammed his fist against the armrest of the throne. "Do not be tricked by their complacency, boy. It is a ruse just like any other. The Dark Fae may be few, but they are not without the benefit of time. They've been waiting for years—lifetimes—for the Crown to show a sign of weakness. It does not bode well that the Shades have heard whispers of such an alliance now." The king grabbed the gold pendant on his chest and rubbed it between his fingers protectively.

"The Crown is as strong as ever!" Damien said, stretching his arms out beside him. He pulled them back when his father cast him a cold, disapproving look. I gripped my wrist behind my back and forced my jaw shut. The Crown was as rich as ever, but its people were hungry. With the right motivation, that unrest could spread like a fire across the entire kingdom.

"Do you think it's a coincidence that the Dark Fae begin to move just as the *winvra* begins to fail? For all we know, they are leeching the magic from the soil themselves," the king said, his fist shaking. *Winvra* was one of the few magical plants that still grew in Elverath. Most recognized it by its crimson vines and black leaves, but its true magic was held in its berries. Berries the color of night that could create all kinds of healing concoctions and bloodred fruit that could poison an entire table with a single drop of its juice. *Winvra* needed magic to grow, magic the Mortal realms across the sea did not have. But magic in Elverath had been fading for millennia and seemed to be fading even more quickly now.

The king leaned forward in his throne. His eyes were green slits staring at his son. "The entire kingdom would fall if Lord Curringham aligned himself with the Dark Fae. Explaining such politics to you at twenty was admissible, but you're coming to your third *century*. Maybe you should spend less time hosting parties and more time at your studies. Take a page from your brother's book," the king added. Damien's cheeks flushed and his lips pulled tightly against his teeth. Damien had little love for his brother Killian. It was why the younger prince was so rarely at home.

"Yes, Father," Damien said through clenched teeth.

"Good. This Shadow is becoming a nuisance, but we must address the larger threat. Ensure Lord Curringham's loyalty before another disaster strikes. Once the magic fades from his lands, we'll have nothing left to harvest. The Lord of Flowers could very well turn you into a prince of paupers, boy," the king finished.

Damien's fingers gripped his thigh so hard I thought the fabric might rip. His father's disappointment raised a shield of defiance in the prince that turned his eyes hard. The only thing he loathed more was being compared to his brother.

Damien bowed his head in penance. "Of course, Father."

The king shook his head before turning toward me. "I expect you to leave quickly, my Blade." I straightened and nodded. "I don't want to give those Fae any more time to work their evil over Curringham," the king said. "You leave on the morrow."

"I will be gone by dawn," I answered immediately. There was nothing for me in the capital apart from a hot bath and warm bed.

"Do you require the help of the Shades?" the king asked.

"No, Your Majesty. I prefer—"

"To work alone," the king finished for me. "So be it . . . But work quickly. First the Shadow and now the Fae. If anything else begins slipping through the cracks, I may have to find another Blade."

My breath stopped as an icy chill ran down my spine.

"And what of the lord?" I asked before making my exit.

"I would prefer if he remained alive. At least for now," the king said. A glint of red light from the setting suns sparkled in his eyes. "Knowing his allegiance is cracking could prove useful. If you find any proof of treason, you may kill as many Dark Fae as you like."

I nodded. "As you wish, Your Majesty."

CHAPTER TWO

I PULLED MY HOOD BACK over my face as soon as I'd left the throne room. Only a few people in the palace had truly seen my face. A good assassin knew how useful anonymity could be. Though the title of king's Blade was enough to strike fear in most and give pause to the stupidly fearless.

I marched in the direction of my chambers, hoping my bags had made it there by now. The scent of horse shit and stale ale clung to my clothes. I was in desperate need of a bath.

"Empty-handed again, Keera?" I would know that superior tone anywhere. There was only one person who made a point of using my name over my title.

"Lovely day, *Gerarda*," I said, emphasizing her full name only because I knew she despised it.

A petite halfling stood behind me, twirling her favorite throwing blade between her fingers. Her hood was pulled back slightly on her head, enough that I could see her face. A smug smile grew on her lips. Sun had tanned the high points of her cheeks and flat nose, leaving a tawny hue to her skin. A mark of her Elvish lineage.

Gerarda Vallaqar was also a spy and assassin for the king. We had trained together at the Order before she passed her Trials and became a Shade. By the time I graduated, she had already been promoted to the king's Dagger. It was the second highest position in the king's Arsenal.

The day I was promoted to the king's Blade, only three years after leaving the Order, had been glorious fun. Gerarda, expecting the nomination for herself after the death of my predecessor, had loudly gasped when the king called me forward. Dressed in the plain black garb and hood of the rest of the Shades, I had accepted my cloak, fastened at the neck by a silver sword. The cloak a symbol of the king's Arsenal, the fastener a symbol of my title within it.

Gerarda had left the throne room, her short black hair brushing against her shoulders as she raced away from the ceremony. If I hadn't been so nervous, I would've laughed. Gerarda was often inconsolably angry for such a tiny creature.

"The king might have to reconsider the order of his Arsenal if his Blade keeps failing him." The sweetness of her voice covered the poison of her meaning.

"That is for the king to decide. I am at his disposal," I said carefully. Trapping me to speak against the king would be the easiest way for the Dagger to become the Blade.

"Of course, this Shadow may dispose of you," she chided. I ignored her and started walking again. I did not have the patience for her quips, at least not without hard liquor.

"He does seem obsessed with us, doesn't he?" she called out after me.

I stopped. "What do you mean?"

"He struts around in a black cloak, keeps his face concealed underneath a hood. Maybe he didn't pick his name, but from what I've heard he certainly encourages it. The Shadow. The Shades. He's making a mockery of the Order." Her eyes widened, the thick line of ink along her lashes created the illusion of a crease. Gerarda always tried to blend in with the Mortals at court.

A cold wave of understanding crashed against my skin. In all the months of chasing down pieces of information on the Shadow, I had never taken a moment to think about what he was trying to *say*.

"He's not making a mockery of the Order," I realized aloud. "He's making a mockery of the Crown."

Gerarda studied me with crossed brows. My neck tensed as her gaze trailed down my body and back to my face. "Careful, Keera," she warned coolly. "Your drinking may be clouding your judgment more than you realize."

"My drinking is not an issue." I rubbed my temple, rolling my eyes under the cover of my hand.

"Maybe. Maybe not." Her voice was gentle. My brows stitched together. Gerarda was anything but gentle. "But the initiate I trained with would've never been shocked by what I said. She would've been the first to figure it out." She walked down the hall leaving me wanting nothing more than a drink.

I moved swiftly across the castle, taking the servant passageways between the royal wing on the west side and the Arsenal quarters on the east to avoid unpleasant encounters. The few servants I crossed paths with simply avoided my gaze and moved out of the way. They knew better than to address a member of the king's Arsenal, and those who didn't often found themselves without a tongue.

My chambers were on the side of the castle closest to the sea that bordered Koratha. From my balcony one could just make out the edges of an identical castle in miniature perched on an island off the coast. The Order. I had spent my childhood staring out of its windows, wondering what my life would be like as a Shade in Elverath. Now, whenever I found myself at the palace, I was forced to stare back at my past. No wonder I needed to drink.

I had just climbed the three flights of stairs when he appeared at my side, pretending to cough as if I didn't know he was there. Prince Damien had somehow crossed the castle quicker than I had.

Two women were standing at his side, ogling him, and giggling behind their silk fans. I didn't recognize either of them, but that wasn't unusual. Damien had a reputation for interchanging his women regularly. One had tightly coiled hair that floated above her ears. To anyone else, she appeared Mortal, perhaps a newcomer from the northern Mortal realms, but with my heightened senses I noticed the slightest pinch at the crest of her ear. She was part Elvish.

I looked away from her ear and met her gaze behind the fan. Her eyes were wide and the hand fanning her face quivered slightly. I could hear her heartbeat race. For her to be walking and laughing as she did meant that the prince did not know her secret. I would not be the one to let him know she was a Halfling.

"Did I forget something earlier, Your Highness?" I asked, hoping he didn't notice the brief exchange between me and his escort.

His mouth lifted at one side before he signaled for the women to leave us. I watched them walk down the hall, both looking back at the prince. I couldn't help but notice their dresses, which were identical apart from color. They had appeared typical from the front. Full skirts and sleeves, leaving an acceptable amount of bust for a lady at court, but their backs were bare, completely open from the curve of their shoulders to the base of their backs. It was beautiful but I also knew it was intentional.

"Lovely new fashion, isn't it?" Damien said, raising a thick brow at me. "I expect all the women will be wearing them this season."

"Then they will look even more beautiful than usual, sire," I answered coolly, unsure of where this conversation was going. He wouldn't forget what I witnessed in the throne room. Damien had all the king's ruthlessness and none of his tact.

Damien lifted his arm and lightly traced a finger from my shoulders down my back. His touch was a knife of pure ice, slicing my skin once again. "I would love to see you in one." His breath burned my ear.

I inched out of his grasp. "It would be inappropriate for the Blade to wear a dress, Your Highness. I am not expected to participate in the festivities of court."

"No, but I could have you wear one for me in private." His smirk had transformed into an evil grin. I felt my face flush at the suggestion, wondering if this was when he would cross that final line. He had spent decades threatening me with it.

I didn't move but I met his gaze head-on. There was no warmth in his eyes. The black rim around them seemed to thicken with his grin. He liked playing his wicked, little games.

"Perhaps when you return from Cereliath I'll have one waiting for you," he whispered, so close to my ear I could feel the brush of his lips. It sent a cold shiver down my spine. I reached for my dagger on instinct, but the prince had already turned toward his ladies.

I strode toward my chambers with my fingers still wrapped around the hilt of my dagger. I was usually able to ignore Damien's taunts, but lately it had become more difficult. Thankfully, the prince spent most of his time gallivanting across the kingdom from one lord or lady to another. A ceaseless trail of parties and women. He only came after me when he was home and bored.

My chambers looked the same as ever. A large four-poster bed sat in the middle of the bedroom bookended by two windows that faced the gardens below. The other wall was made entirely of glass, a window to the rolling waves along the beach. It magnified the view, so the water seemed to roll into the room. Koratha Palace was the only building in the kingdom with such features, thanks to the Light Fae who'd built it when their people ruled these lands. Some said the glass was imbued with magic; others believed it was a technology the Fae had developed. If that was true, the technology had been lost with their extinction however many centuries before.

The king had no interest in funding innovation. Instead, he ruled from the throne he built himself and forced those in his kingdom to farm and mine what was left of the magic. He traded with all the Mortal realms. The continents the humans had come from had no magic of their own, and they paid handsomely for just a taste of what Elverath had left.

The Light Fae had left a world of beauty behind, but that would not be the case for the king. If he ever died, if he were ever killed, his legacy would be one of death and destruction. Not that it mattered—the king believed he would live forever. At least, he said as much when in front of an audience. He claimed immortality like that of the Fae, but they needn't dye their hair to hide the gray.

My bags were already sitting at the foot of my bed and my weapons were splayed across the dresser waiting to be polished. Gwyn must have been called away. She was the only chambermaid I allowed in my rooms, let alone to touch my blades. I unsheathed the dagger from my thigh and unbuckled the holster. I placed the dagger gently beside the other weapons. The deep crimson of the blade stood out against the silver of all the others.

I undressed, lazily throwing my clothes onto the bench at the end of my bed, and walked into the bath. I turned the gold faucet to fill the large oval basin and sprinkled some essence of birch into the water. The room filled with the thick scent of wood and damp earth, the only thing that ever made me feel at home.

I caught a glimpse of myself in the looking glass that hung above the vanity. My dark brown hair was spilling from the braid I kept it in. My face was flecked with mud, the dark hue almost looked like freckles against my light brown skin. My eyes were still a striking silver—the color of blades and death—but all I noticed was the redness around them. Maybe Gerarda had been right. My endless nights of drinking were finally starting to show.

I hadn't always been a drinker. When I first graduated from the Order, I took my duty and my oath seriously. I roamed through cities and villages searching for secrets in whispered conversations. I traipsed across the kingdom on horseback, on foot, by sail. Whatever was needed to get the job done. All without touching a drop of ale or wine.

Eventually it got harder, the killing and the scheming. The broken promises.

Most Shades were dead in ten years, killed by some enemy of the Crown. The ones who survived would last twenty more if they were lucky, before their Mortal blood made them slow and weak.

But I wasn't like my sisters in the Order. For whatever reason, my Elvish blood ran stronger than theirs. My ears were long and pointed, unlike most Halflings who had something between Mortal and Elf. I stood tall among the Mortals at court, even among the Halflings. As a child, I wished I could say that I got my eyes from my father or my hair from my mother, but I was a foundling. No parents and no memories of what kind of life I had lived before.

I had long ago accepted that I would never know my true lineage. The only reason I had been taken into the Order at all, the only proof I had of my Mortal lineage, was my blood. Its amber color was the sign of Halflings. The mixed breeds of Elves and men.

All those of Elvish blood were an abomination in the eyes of the king. Any full-blooded Elves that still lived spent their days in hiding or had long ago left Elverath for other lands. I suspected most had moved into the Faeland west of the Burning Mountains.

So the only abominations left were the Halflings, though the king preferred to enslave us rather than kill us. Our bodies were of too much use to the Crown. Centuries after the Halfling Decree, most Halflings barely had a drop of Elvish blood. But a drop was all that was needed to make one's blood amber instead of red.

It didn't matter how much I hated it, how my skin recoiled every time the king's eyes landed on me. I carried the brand of his estate everywhere I went. With no parents to give me a name of my own, I carried the name bestowed upon all orphans.

Keera Kingsown.

I turned the faucet off and climbed into the bath. The hot water was biting; I could feel the grime and dirt loosening from my limbs and hair. Baths were hard to come by outside of the palace, especially when one was trying to avoid being seen. I leaned back and let my body fall into the water until I was completely submerged. I liked the way the water filled my ears and muted outside sound. I could no longer hear the waves rolling on the beach or the servants laughing as they pruned the garden. For just a moment, all I could hear was the beat of my heart vibrating through the water.

Eventually, I started to wash my body with the sponge and perfumed soaps Gwyn had restocked for me. The sponge's abrasive touch felt like it was cleansing away more than the dirt—if I only pressed harder, I might be able to wash away the blood on my hands.

Mathias's blood.

It always came back to that. The men crying for their lives, the Halflings fighting for their families. There had even been a few children. But I didn't let myself think about that without a barrel of wine nearby.

I washed my back thinking about the fish merchant. Whether he had a family who would miss him. A child whose mouth he had fed. Would they even have realized he was gone in the six days that had passed since I killed him? These were answers that I would never have, but the questions would never rest.

My back twinged where I pressed too hard with the sponge. Even after thirty years, the scars on my back were still sensitive. I could see the redness of them in the mirror. Harsh, curved lines carved into my back by Prince Damien. He had taken hours to paint the lesions along my skin, an Old Elvish rune no one could read. He had said it was a mark of my loyalty to the Crown.

Of course, that wasn't the only scar along my body. By now, most of my flesh was marked in some way. The small scar on my right hip from before I could remember. Its lines were too clean and perfect to have been unintentional, but I had no idea who the carver had been. Another answer I would never have.

The others I carved myself. They were the names that stretched across my shoulders, down my chest and arms. Tiny scrolls of the lives I had taken in the name of the Crown. Of the innocent and unarmed. Each one etched into my flesh so I carried their deaths with me always. In a sea of so many cuts, so many people, it was hard to tell where one name ended and the next began.

One name stood out from the rest. Etched in large letters along the forearm of my dueling hand. The rest of the skin around it was left untouched. I scrubbed at it with the sponge, glad when the suds rinsed away and it remained. I traced a finger along the ridges of the name over and over. It was one of the only things that could bring me a moment of peace.

"Keera? Are you here?" I heard Gwyn call from the bedchamber.

"In the bath," I answered, but Gwyn had already skipped into the room. I didn't try to cover my body from her. She was the sole person who knew of my scars and where they came from. She even carried some of her own gifts from the prince. It was a secret I didn't mind sharing with her. She had known of them since she was a wee Halfling and her mother was my chambermaid.

Gwyn's soft curls bounced as she approached the basin. The strands were a mix of bright red and auburn, just like her mother's. Her skin was pale from being kept inside. She always looked slightly ill because of it. Gwyn had not been able to leave the palace since her mother died.

"Sorry I couldn't finish earlier. I needed a moment in my room," Gwyn said shyly. I didn't need to ask why. I could tell from the red of her eyes and the tender way she walked that she had been with the prince. He loved tormenting the Halfling servants of the palace, but he especially liked Gwyn.

"Don't worry about it," I said, dunking my head to rinse out the soap. "There's something for you in the saddlebag."

I chuckled as Gwyn squealed and ran back into the bedchamber to fetch her gift. I tried to bring her back something every time I returned to Koratha so she could experience a little bit more of the world than she had been given.

"What is it?" Gwyn whispered, holding the small red pouch in her hands.

"You have to open it, Gwyn," I said gently.

She rolled her eyes. "The anticipation is half the fun, Keera. You should know this by now." I should, she said the same thing each time, but I never wanted to change our script. It was one of the few habits I kept.

She closed her eyes and opened the pouch, pulling out a ring. Where there should've been a stone, there was a cluster of gold lacing in the shape of a tear drop. "I've never seen such a ring," Gwyn said, turning the jewelry over in her fingers.

I smiled. "That's because it's not just a ring."

"It's not?" Gwyn eyes widened as she brought the ring to her nose to look at it more closely.

I shook my head as I stood and reached for a towel. I gestured for her to put it on as I wrapped the towel around me. "See this tiny button here?" I said, pulling her hand to the inner side of the ring.

"Not really, but I feel it," Gwyn said. She danced back and forth with excitement.

"Good. Now push it," I told her, dropping my hand from hers.

"Oh!" Gwyn gasped as the coiled lacing snapped into place around her finger, leaving her with a singular claw.

"Be careful. That blade may be tiny, but it's as sharp as they come," I warned. That single ring cost more than most of my daggers. Elven-made relics did not come cheap. "This way you can always have a weapon on you."

Gwyn twisted her hand to get a full view of the ring. "What am I supposed to do with a claw?"

I shrugged. "Scratch?"

"That won't kill anyone." Gwyn laughed. "Rawr!" She pretended to swipe me, but I grabbed her wrist.

"No, it won't kill anyone," I said seriously, not letting go of her hand. "But if you pierce the calf or thigh muscle, the cut will hurt. Enough for you to run. If you can't do that, pluck an eye out."

"Keera, that's disgusting!" Gwyn shrieked. Her face turned slightly green. Damien had never violated Gwyn, but I wanted her prepared in case he grew bored with beatings and mental torment. She deserved the chance to fight.

"Yes, it is," I said with a nod. "But so are men. I just want to know you're safe. Especially when I'm not here." Gwyn's mother had died three years before. At sixteen Gwyn had been so young. Too young to lose a mother and certainly too young to inherit her mother's debt.

"Thank you," she said, giving me a long hug. I tried not to tense when her hand grazed the scars on my back.

"I assume you want to sleep since you're leaving so soon?" Gwyn asked, walking with me back into the bedchamber. I nodded. The threat of a headache loomed over me, and I wanted to sleep before I felt compelled to find a different way to cure it.

"I'll take your weapons with me then. They'll be with your horse in the morning." Gwyn placed a large basket on the dresser.

"Thank you, Gwyn." I tried to smile but I was too tired. Gwyn gave me a soft smile as I climbed into bed and she started packing my weapons.

"Gwyn?" I asked, pulling back the heavy coverlet.

She turned back to face me. "Yes?"

"Leave the mage pen." I pointed to the nightstand beside the bed. She placed the gold handle on the table. I stared at the sharp point shaped like a quill. Gwyn gave me a knowing look and kissed my cheek, leaving me to sleep and carve yet another name into my skin.

CHAPTER THREE

As far as the Shades knew, Lord Curringham was staying at his residence in Cereliath—the House of Harvest. I could have traveled the entire way on horseback, but I preferred to take the canal system into Silstra and ride from there. It would shave a few days off the journey and meant that I had three days to laze about on a barge instead of getting sore from my saddle.

I kept to myself for most of the trip. I hadn't needed to sneak in with the shipment because the captain was an acquaintance of the Arsenal. He was well paid to keep our movements quiet and ask no questions. Regardless, I liked to keep a low profile. I boarded before the crew arrived and hid among the rolls of silks at the back of the barge. One never knew where the allegiances of paid men fell. The fewer who knew I was aboard the better.

The first day passed in a blur of sleep and drink from my wine sack. I swayed in the hammock gulping back the warm liquid and thinking of the Shadow. I needed to finish the mission in Cereliath as quickly as possible. Before the Shadow had time to strike again—or worse yet, before one of the other Shades brought him in.

The king would not stay forgiving for long. If he thought his Blade had dulled, he wouldn't subject me to a whetstone. He would discard me. Cast me away like the countless other weapons he'd tossed aside once their usefulness ran out. There would be an army of Shades lined up to replace me, starting with Gerarda.

I needed to be the one to bring the Shadow in. I couldn't leave any doubt in the king's mind of how valuable I could be. Not just for the sake of my head, but all those who counted on me keeping my title.

Every time I closed my eyes, I could see the outline of that hood. The dark clothes the Shadow wore and the long sword he wielded as we fought. He had been tall and well-muscled; trading blows with enough power behind them to strain my arms.

I drank in the hammock until I was too inebriated to remember my own name, let alone the Shadow.

I ran out of wine after the second night. The warm buzz dissipated and left my body shivering and sweaty. My head throbbed so badly I thought about ramming it into the rafter so it would hurt in a different place.

By the third day I was restless. I wanted to stretch my legs, taste fresh air, but I needed a drink. Every hour that passed felt like it would be the one to kill me, twist my stomach into knots so tight my head exploded. Only a drink would cure it. But my wineskin was empty, even though I kept opening the lid, hoping my lips would be met with the sweet taste of berry and tannin.

I couldn't remember the last time I had gone so long without a drink. Five years? Trying to remember set off a hammer against my skull. I hadn't had any liquor when I got caught in a snowstorm in the Frostlands. I had spent weeks bundled in an abandoned building, slowly tearing at the walls for something to burn and hoping to spot an animal through the white blaze that refused to clear. The only thing that had settled the craving was the hunger. By the third week, I had started eyeing my left arm, saliva dribbling down my chin. I only survived because a brumal bear crossed my path, and after three weeks of slowly starving, I had been mad enough to attack it.

The gargantuan, wintry beast put up a fight, smashing most of my weapons in a single strike, including the old hilt of my dagger. I finally managed to leap onto its back and stab it in the eye with a broken arrow, the only weapon I had left. Now the bear's bone served as the hilt to my dagger. Its fur coat had fetched a pretty sum at market too.

When I had finally made it back to Volcar, frostbitten and on the brink of starvation, I celebrated with a barrel of cheap ale. I couldn't remember a single day since where I didn't at least sip some kind of drink. A habit I had refused to notice.

Gerarda was right. I was slipping. It was why the Shadow had been able to stretch over the continent, inflating his reputation. His existence threatened my position with the king, jeopardized the small bit of power I had carved to shield those I could save. Hiding in the shadows would not protect him for long. I knew something of shadows, having trained to live within them. Shadows were largest just before the sunset, but lost their power when night inevitably fell. For Shadows don't truly exist in the dark.

It was time for me to bring the night.

Silstra was a city of merchants, beggars, and thieves. It sat at the mouth of three canals, the Sisters, that stretched across most of

Eleverath. Depending on which of the Sisters one sailed along, they would find themselves coming to port at any of Elverath's major cities. Because of this, Silstra was the main economic hub of the entire kingdom. Everything that was traded or sold across the country came through its waters.

Hence the merchants and the thieves. The beggars came because most of the harvest was sent through the city's ports. If this made its sellers amiable to charity I didn't know, but the hungry came to the food, nonetheless.

The city was built in two parts above the large dam. The west bank, where the rich merchants and lords would stay, was a city of stone. Grand houses that had multiple levels and plumbing circled around a small castle that was said to have been carved from a mountain. It had been a small city of Light Fae before the Mortals claimed it too.

The east bank was built by men and therefore much less grand. The lesser merchants had homes of brick that were patched and maintained from centuries of wear. The poor built shelters out of whatever scrap materials they could lay their hands on.

That is the part of the city I went to first.

The poor tended to have few secrets. *Secret* was just another word for power, and the poor certainly did not have any of that. The lucky ones who found more power than they were born with left the slums quicker than sewer rats on a stormy day. My gait was lighter there; I wasn't worried about crossing paths with anyone in the royal pockets. Even the Shades had few eyes in Silstra's lowest circles. It wasn't worth paying coin if the poor had no one to spy on.

"Keera!" Victoria shouted when I walked through the door of what used to be an inn but was now missing most of its roof. "I wasn't expecting you," she whispered as she pulled me in for an embrace. Her graying hair tickled my cheek. I smiled down at her. She had always been a short woman, but age had made her even shorter.

My eyes fell to the baby held at Victoria's hip. She always seemed to have a little one nearby. This one probably didn't have any parents.

Her blue eyes dropped to the simple tie at my neck. I had changed into a green traveling cloak before exiting the ship. The people here did not know me as the Blade, just Keera. My black cloak and silver fastener would draw too many unwanted eyes. Only Victoria knew the truth.

"I can't stay," I said, passing a pouch of gold coin into her hands. "I wish I could, but I have to find myself a horse strong enough to make it to Cereliath before dusk."

Her eyes lingered on the red lines surrounding my silver irises and the dampness of my forehead. Two days without a drink was taking its toll.

"Have some tea at least. Julian needs a feeding anyway," she said, tickling the fat baby's tummy until he giggled. He had a round face and soft arms with rolls that matched his legs. His ears were already beginning to pinch at the top. He was a Halfling.

"Is there still a doctor around to help him?" I sat down and drank from the mug Victoria laid in front of me.

"Aye, though he can't come 'round much. Still, he should be able to cut his ears in time." She kissed Julian on the head and popped a bottle into his mouth. Most Halflings were indistinguishable from humans apart from their ears. And if they were cut early enough, once they began to pinch, a gifted doctor or healer could stitch them in a way that made sure they grew round, looked more human. If it happened as an infant, most would never be able to tell.

"Have you had any trouble?" I asked after a large swig of my tea.

"No, not since you took care of things." Victoria's smile was tight and thin. I knew she wasn't comfortable with what had happened the last time I was in Silstra, but it had to be done, no matter how gruesome.

"Good." I put down my empty mug and stood. "I don't know when I'll be back. This mission could have me gone for another year, but I'll continue sending aid every month."

"You could spend your money on yourself, you know," Victoria teased, though I knew she would accept my coin. Too many mouths depended on her.

"It's not just my money." The king didn't notice if I funneled some of his reclaimed treasure to the poor—at least, not in the twenty some years I had been doing it. "Besides, you know as well as I do that an executioner has no one to spend her coin on."

"You're not an executioner, Keera," she said. Her eyes were wide and the hard line of her lips transformed into a soft pout. I turned away.

"No, you're right. An executioner has the comfort of knowing her victims had a trial," I said. The truth of my words pulled my shoulders toward the ground.

"We all have to do bad things, Keera. Things we don't want to do but have to in order to survive. Your hands are forced more than most, but not everyone decides to be kind. That should count for more than the bad." Victoria patted my shoulder. Gray curls framed her soft face, brushing against the wrinkles etched into her tanned skin. She was a kind woman, motherly. For a moment, I wondered if my own had been the same.

"I think you overestimate my kindness." There was no amount of good that could wash away the sea of blood I had filled.

CHAPTER FOUR

I HATED TRAVELING THROUGH the Dead Wood. Most travelers took the longer road along the riverbank, fearing the creatures that lurked in the sickly forest hungering for a taste of Mortal flesh. The stories never mentioned anything about the monsters having an affinity for the taste of Halflings. Not that it mattered. In thirty years of being the king's Blade, I had crossed through the Dead Wood many times, often by myself. I was always the closest thing to a monster skulking in the wood.

The decaying trees with their bent trunks and leafless branches no longer frightened me. Now I found refuge beside them, knowing that I would meet no strangers along the path and could nurse my wineskin freely. Dark sap spewed from tree roots. Scalding hot to the touch, it left the bark burnt and blackened like a fire had swept through the forest, so hot and so fast that no greenery could ever be reborn among the decay.

Once, the Dead Wood had lived under a different name. A name now forgotten by Halflings and Mortals. Trees of all kinds of magic had spanned across the north, home to creatures that had disappeared along with the Light Fae. The wood's magic was already fading by the time the Mortals landed. In the first centuries of King Aemon's reign, he cut most of the wood surrounding Cereliath, tilling the land into the farmlands that now fed Elverath's people and filled the king's pockets.

Minstrels traveled across the kingdom telling the story of the Dead Wood. The trees meeting the king's ax used the little magic they had left to warn their brethren to the south. How, the minstrels never said. Mortals only ever saw magic in two ways: profitable or evil. They had no interest in understanding further. The Dead Wood had been created from the latter. Knowing that the king would cut them too, the remaining trees retreated in on themselves. Twisting their trunks into unusable knots. Their magical leaves dropping in droves and scorching the ground. Sap oozing from their bark, leaving vicious burns on anyone who dared swing an ax.

The only safe way through the wood was along the narrow paths. One step off and a horse would be lamed, its passenger scorched. The king had killed hundreds of Halflings by forcing them to harvest the blackened trees to create the road. Their bodies lined the paths the king wanted cut through the wood. One path weaved through the trees and ended outside of the capital. The other was the road I traveled on now.

If the ghosts of those Halflings still lingered among the trees, I never saw them. Perhaps the ghosts who already haunted me kept them at bay.

By the time the trees thinned and gave way to the flat stretches of farmland, my body ached and my thighs burned from riding. I was also out of wine and still had a full day's ride into the city.

My horse trotted along the fields of wheat and corn. Occasionally, the sweet scent of berries would catch the breeze and I would come across a field of *winvra*. The tiny fruit grew in clusters, some black and some red. Some to heal and some to kill. The *winvra* grew along tall posts the Mortals had constructed, wrapping around them like ivy, ever reaching for the light of the suns. The fruit was the last magical plant that grew in the kingdom, the king's only way left to commodify the magic that had once run rampant in these lands.

Some of the orchards I passed were sparse and their berries shriveled. Their magic had begun to fade too. I watched as men measured the growth of the gray berries, picking samples to test back at their laboratory. Looking for answers for the king. It was a question the king had been pondering for centuries—why the magic of Elverath was fading. But no one could answer it for him. The best theory was that it was a kind of natural waning tied to the magic of the Fae. Many believed that when the last of the Dark Fae passed, all the magic would leech from Elverath entirely.

I didn't care about the magic. I only cared about the people who starved while the king balanced his *winvra* losses by selling more food to other realms. Elverath grew more than enough food to feed its people but sent away most of the harvest on long ships across the sea. The king and his lords kept their riches while the poor went hungry.

Bodies began to line the road as I reached the outer edge of the city. Some were dead, corpses baking under the suns feeding the scavenging birds, while others were almost dead. Limp hands reached out toward my horse; their owners too weak to beg. To earn enough to eat, one had to work the fields. The old and immobile were left to the mercy of passersby for a sampling of food or a spare nickel.

But as the *winvra* profits waned, so did the generosity of those who could afford to stock their table.

I could not help them dressed in my black cloak and silver clasp.

The king knew the hungry begged along every city of the kingdom. Knew their bones mixed into the earth of the roads, picked at by birds and crushed by hooves. He did not care. He did not offer them mercy. And neither could his Blade.

My teeth grated against one another as I rode into Cereliath, eyes staring straight ahead under my cloak. I focused on the tangled mane of my horse and tried not to taste the death in the air. I knew most of the hungry I passed were Mortals, but I also knew some were Halflings. Ones who looked human enough to hide among them and others who had been discarded by the lords who owned them. Left to die a slow death caked in dirt now that the king had extracted every ounce of labor from their bodies.

Perhaps it was a mercy to be a Shade. At least I knew whenever my long life ended it would not be a slow death, but one delivered by the end of a sharp blade.

Still my stomach churned as I counted the hordes of people the king was so willing to sacrifice. My hands clenched against the leather reins until my fingers tingled. My throat burned with the need for something to help cloud the faces of those who lay dying just outside the city walls. I knew they did not die by my hand. It was hunger that pierced their bellies, not my blade, but still I felt that itch along the smooth parts of my skin. Felt the urge to turn back and ask each of them their names before ending their pain myself.

But I couldn't.

When I reached my favorite inn, I asked the barmaid to send up two flagons of wine and drowned my urges in the tub.

Tailing Lord Curringham was tedious. Each morning I rose before the suns and stalked along the House of Harvest where Curringham lay sleeping until well after dawn. The House of Harvest was where all the harvest lords stayed in Cereliath. As the richest man among them, Curringham had his chambers on the topmost floor. The best view of the entire city and all the crops that surrounded it. I sat along its roof waiting for the lord to rise, watching as the dark skies were painted in long streaks of gold as the first sun rose. The sunlight was warm on my hand as I lifted my wineskin to my lips. Usually, half of it was gone before the servants came in to dress their lord.

The House of Harvest was erected from a single mountainous piece of sandstone. Like all houses built by the Fae, the stone was etched with intricate designs. The pattern of leaves wrapped around the stone pillars like vines scaling a wall. I used the grooves to climb onto the rooftop each morning, listening in the shadows as Curringham went about his day. Drudging conversations about trade arrangements. Discussions about the loss of potency with the latest crop of *winvra*. Boring reveries of his childhood in Caerth. But nothing that made me believe he was burgeoning an alliance with the Dark Fae.

"Lady Darolyn is waiting for you on the terrace, sire," a voice called from inside Curringham's office. It sounded like the assistant who followed Curringham everywhere he went.

"The girl from Volcar?" Curringham asked.

"No, sire. Lady Darolyn is from the northern continent. Her father owns one of the largest trade networks in the Mortal realms," his assistant reminded him. So Lady Darolyn was not a lady at all, but rich enough to buy the title during her stay.

"I'll be down shortly," Curringham said. He didn't sound excited to dine with the newest resident of the manor. Especially one who had garnered a reputation of being too eager to become a bride. Curringham, while handsome, showed little interest in finding a wife. Or even wooing the maidens of Cereliath with his rare smile and endless riches. Like everything else in the lord's life, he sought companionship like a transaction.

Every day at noon, his assistant would let a courtesan into Curringham's office for a rollick on his desk. In the three weeks I had been surveilling him, he never entertained the same woman twice and never more than a few minutes. Once they finished, he would dismiss them by tossing a small bag of coin and telling them to send a new girl on the morrow. I fought the urge to vomit each time he said it.

While the lord paced about his office and mumbled under his breath, I took another swig from my wineskin. I was looking forward to overhearing something other than Curringham's rapid breathing and obnoxious chewing for an hour. I waited to hear him leave his office before I lowered myself to the edge of the roof and onto the balcony below. Four floors was too far to jump quietly, so I caught hold of the thin pillar beside the landing and slid down the back of it to the ground. The midday shadows kept my movements hidden enough. If anyone caught a glimpse of my cloak, I moved too quick for them to track me through the maze of stone pillars.

The terrace was at the back of the manor, nestled along the moat that surrounded the house in a perfect circle. A feature Curringham had installed when he inherited his lordship from his father.

There was no roof above the terrace, so I stalked along the edge of the manor, my shoulders brushing up against the stone, looking for a place to spy on the lord and his guest. There was a small shed wedged between the manor and the riverbed. I slipped into the narrow crevice and waited for the lord to arrive.

His tall figure cut through the terrace in six strides. He had the same demanding gait of men born into wealth and the high chin of a man who had doubled the worth of his estate. His sandy hair looked blond under the suns, highlighting the paleness of his skin.

The complexion of a man who had never worked a field in his life yet harvested his coin on the backs of the Halflings he purchased from the Crown.

"Lady Darolyn," he said, kissing her neck in greeting.

"Lord Curringham," she replied, lowering her head as she curtsied, giving the lord a chance to glimpse her ample bosom. Curringham didn't even look.

Lady Darolyn was a beauty with her long neck and piercing green eyes. Her eyelashes fluttered as she and Curringham sat at the far end of the terrace, awaiting their meal. They were too far for me to read their lips, but with my Elvish ears I didn't strain to hear them.

"Have you been enjoying your stay in the kingdom, my lady?" Curringham asked, eyes searching for a servant. His knee bounced under the table.

"I have!" Lady Darolyn's high pitch sounded unnatural. She smoothed her red skirt, her fingers toying with the beaded belt along its edge. "The house may be the most beautiful in the entire kingdom." Her words had a roughness to them but that was the only sign of her accent.

Curringham's eyes flashed back to his guest. "Grander than the palace?" he asked, raising a brow.

Lady Darolyn exaggerated her nods, catching the lord's shift in attention. "The palace has a coldness about it that I didn't take to. There were not nearly as many guests as I expected and then when I arrived in Cereliath, I realized they were all here! Which makes sense—the manor is more comfortable, and its lords do the work to support the rest of the kingdom." Her eyes flicked up at Curringham as she sipped her drink. She blinked once, not breaking her gaze with the lord.

She would not be leaving Cereliath without a groom. And a rich one at that.

"Exactly!" Curringham shouted, turning his shoulders toward Lady Darolyn. He pressed his elbows into the tabletop and leaned in. The gold pendant he wore along his neck scratched the table. "The king often asks for my input on royal matters."

I scoffed at the lie.

"He is wise to seek council from the man who controls so much of the kingdom's *winvra*." Lady Darolyn ran her tongue along her lips. This time Curringham watched. She caught his glance and smirked.

"Have you tried it?" Curringham asked, leaning even closer.

"Won't it kill me?" she replied softly enough that I had to pause my breath to hear her.

"The red berries, yes." Curringham nodded. "One taste and you would drop to the ground and never wake again."

Lady Darolyn dragged a finger across her bottom lip. Curringham's eyes followed the movement.

If I ended up hearing them rollicking back on Curringham's desk, I would jump off the roof.

"And the black ones?" Lady Darolyn purred.

"The black ones can do all sorts of wondrous things . . ." Curringham played with his gold chain, peering at Lady Darolyn's full pout. "Their seeds can be mixed into ointments to heal the wounded or the sick. Their juice is bottled and used as a serum to keep the user young. But the best . . ."

Now, it was Lady Darolyn who was leaning in.

"The best way to enjoy them is to pluck the black berry right off its vine and eat it," Curringham said. He brought his fingers to his lips as if they held a berry between them.

"What does it do?" Lady Darolyn asked, her eyes were bright and her accent thicker than before.

Curringham cocked a brow. "The moment the berry passes your lips, your face will flush with heat." He cupped Lady Darolyn's face in his hand and traced his thumb along her cheek. "Then, your entire body will ignite. Hours will pass in euphoria so intense you might not even remember your own name, recognize where you are. But you won't care because the *winvra* feels *that* good. Just a single taste"—he slid his thumb over her lip in a slow swipe—"would be enough. Absolute ecstasy."

Lady Darolyn bit her lip, as if she could taste the berry's juice.

"How many times have you eaten it?" she asked. Her voice grated on her throat. She sipped her drink, slumping back in the chair.

"Never." Curringham leaned back, crossing his arms. He wore a proud smirk as his eyes took in the rise of Lady Darolyn's chest.

"Not once?" Lady Darolyn pushed, her dark brows knitting together as her head tilted to one side. The sunlight cast a warm glow along her brown skin, emphasizing the length of her neck.

"Lords who make a habit of tasting their crop soon find themselves without any," Curringham said. His lips were thin lines.

Her eyes widened. "It's addictive?"

"Very," Curringham answered. "Thankfully, *winvra* is too expensive for most to risk addiction." He smirked. It was a price that Curringham helped artificially inflate. And consequently fill his stores of gold.

"On my continent, people say that *winvra* is how your king sustains himself. A diet of berries to keep hold of his youth. It's a wonder how he staves off death and addiction," Lady Darolyn said, her eyes shifting toward the manor doors.

Curringham coughed. I thought he might ignore the accusation entirely, but he leaned closer to her. "The temporary thrills of *winvra* are not enough to tempt a man like the king. Or me. The king is not a fool. He would not share the secret to his longevity with the world, regardless of the profit."

I scoffed.

Lady Darolyn tilted her head. "But then how—"

"Balance," Curringham cut in. "They say there is a balance to the magic of this land. The Elves were greedy, they pushed the magic to its limits and even then, it wasn't enough. They wanted more. Unnatural creatures know no natural bounds.

"The king restored that balance during the Blood Wars that rid this kingdom of Elves. The gods blessed him for returning Elverath to its natural state, giving him a year of life for every Elf slain. His blessing still holds, and it seems he has passed that immortality on to his sons," Curringham finished.

Lady Darolyn nodded; her eyes wide. It was the same story that was told all over the kingdom. King Aemon and his burning sword bringing balance and prosperity to his domain for the end of time. I noticed that the stories never seemed to explain how the Halflings, unnatural creatures too, brought balance with their lives rather than their deaths.

Lady Darolyn tucked a strand of her dark waves behind her ear. Then she twirled the strand in her hands just above her chest. Her lips twitched as Curringham's gaze lowered again.

"When I was in the capital, a shipment of *winvra* was stolen. Does that happen often?" Her voice was light as her eyes fluttered. It was obvious to anyone that Lady Darolyn already knew the answer, but Curringham took a moment to process the question, his eyes still staring at her chest.

"No," he answered. His back straightened and his fingers flexed. It had been *his* shipment the thieves had lifted.

"Do they know who was responsible for the theft?" she asked, even though she knew that too. The entire kingdom knew who had managed to steal a crate of *winvra* from the king.

"Most believe it is the Shadow," Curringham spat. My body hardened at the name. There had been witnesses that night. Three of Curringham's own men, the ones who had not been slain, had named the Shadow as the thief. My eyes narrowed at Curringham's disbelief.

"You don't?" Lady Darolyn asked. Her brows brushed against her hairline. Apparently, that was not the answer she had been expecting either.

"The Shadow has been making friends with smugglers and merchants. I am kept up to date on his activities by the king." His gaze flicked back to Lady Darolyn's face. I rolled my eyes. Another lie. "If he was the one to steal the *winvra*, I would've expected it to end up in the black markets by now. But it hasn't. I have several spies who monitor it for me."

I made a note to check with the Arsenal about that. They had networks that would know if spare *winvra* was being bartered anywhere in the kingdom or the other realms. If Curringham's surveillance was true, that made the theft even more strange.

"If not the Shadow, then who?" Lady Darolyn asked. Her wide eyes and breathy voice seemed genuine for once.

"There's only one group who would take the *winvra* for reasons other than to sell it." Curringham tilted his head in the direction of the Burning Mountains. They were too far to see from the manor, but even foreigners knew what lay in the western lands of Elverath.

Lady Darolyn stared blankly west. Sudden recognition flooded over her features and her mouth hung open. "The Dark Fae," she said, her voice barely more than a whisper.

Curringham nodded, crossing his arms. He tucked his hand under his bicep pushing the muscle forward. "There are Dark Fae who still dare to disrespect the treaty, disregard the king's rule entirely. Sometimes they slip through the mountains in search of *winvra* to steal. Usually, they take it directly from the orchards, but their rebellious nature is growing."

"But how can you defend yourselves against them?" Lady Darolyn pressed. "They say some can kill just by looking at you and others can open up your mind and make you do unspeakable things . . ." She trailed off, too horrified to continue.

Lord Curringham puffed out his chest and adjusted his sleeves. "The Dark Fae are not as big of a threat as people believe. At least, not for powerful men like me or the king. Their powers had already begun to fade by the end of the Blood Wars and surely have all but faded now. I doubt one could make me do anything I didn't want to do, let alone kill me."

I leaned against the wall of the shed and folded my arms. If Curringham was aligning himself with the Dark Fae, would he speak so openly of them in front of a stranger? I took a step closer to the edge of the shed, eyes squinting in Curringham's direction.

"What about the shapeshifters or the stormcasters? Their magic laid entire armies to the ground," Lady Darolyn said, her arm stretching toward the sky. It shook slightly. I knew she was picturing a bolt of lightning cracking through the clouds and blasting the table where they sat. My lips twitched to the side. She wasn't wrong. The king had almost lost the first of the Blood Wars because of the powers of the Dark Fae.

Curringham let out a laugh. "No one has seen such magic in centuries. Even when the Fae were at the height of their powers, stormcasters and shapeshifters were rare. I doubt many still live, let alone find time to traipse into the kingdom for *winvra*." I didn't disagree with the lord. Fae magic hadn't been spotted by the Shades in over two hundred years.

"Rumor has it that all Fae magic faded away when their last female died. Now, they are nothing more than Elves—barely touched by magic at all," Curringham said. He toyed with the chain of his pendant. The pendant held a key, and he never took it off.

"But the Elves were skilled warriors," she said, her hand sliding across the table to rub his arm. "You wouldn't consider them a threat?" Her silk slipper pressed against his shoe.

Curringham threw back his head and laughed. Lady Darolyn's eyes shifted quickly from his hands to his face, her brows creased.

Curringham stood up and waved his arm across the terrace. "Look at this. Everything you see in front of you. This house. The food. The *winvra*. All of it once belonged to the Elves, but not now." Lady Darolyn scanned the horizon slowly, her mouth round and open.

"Minstrels sing of the Mortals conquering these lands. King Aemon building the first true throne and kingdom. Traitors say we stole it. The Elves thought we murdered it. I think it's infinitely simpler than that. We *won*. The Elves lost. If any still live, they're hiding in the Faeland on the brink of extinction while the kingdom of Elverath thrives." He pulled on the lapel of his jacket. "Do I think the Elves are a threat? The Fae? Absolutely not. I think they're losers, and to think of them as anything else is bad business," Curringham finished, sitting back in his chair.

I needed to inform the Arsenal immediately. This mission was no longer one for the Blade.

CHAPTER FIVE

I SENT A LETTER TO THE ARSENAL as soon as I returned to the inn. I would spend another fortnight in Cereliath while Mistress Hildegard sent a pair of Shades to replace me. As per the king's orders, Curringham would still need to be watched, but it seemed unlikely that he had even met a Dark Fae, let alone brokered an alliance with one.

It made for easy work. I still woke before the lord, hoisting myself onto his roof with an extra wineskin. I spent my days on the clay tiles of the roof shaded by the large tower in the middle of the manor. I stared up at it, taking large gulps of wine until I could hear the swish of liquid in my stomach. At the top of the tower was a giant sunstone, held by nothing it seemed. How the Fae had placed it there was beyond any Mortal's imagination. The answer was always the same.

Magic.

But what kind of magic? I had too much time to ponder the question spying on the lord. The days passed slowly, even with my wine. I was certain that Mistress Hildegard had been misinformed and the Dark Fae were not involved with Curringham at all. I would need to find the source of that information. They had cost me a month of my time. The king would not care that Curringham's loyalty had been assured. He would see it as another failure—perhaps the one that convinced him to wrap a noose around my neck and leave my body hanging along the walls of Koratha.

Wine quieted my worries.

Three nights later, I watched from my perch as Curringham extended his arm out for Lady Darolyn, helping her into a carriage. They were off to watch the traveling show perform in the market circle. I took a final gulp from my wineskin and stood up to follow them.

That was until I saw someone I didn't recognize arrive at the house. He had light brown skin, but the rest of his features were concealed under a navy traveling cloak. He moved quickly through the shadows, up the drive, and around the manor to a side entrance.

He was tall. Taller than me and most men. Without seeing his ears, I couldn't be certain, but there was something in the sureness of his steps that made me think he wasn't Mortal.

But was he a Halfling, or something else?

I scurried along the roof, too soft to make a sound and too quick to pull anyone's notice. He had slipped between the manor and the stables. I climbed down to the first tier of the manor, concealing myself in the crevice between the roof and the wall. No one would notice him leaning against the wooden pillar—he blended in with the dark shadows the lanterns cast, but I could see the outline of his torso and the tip of his boot. They were leather, slightly worn, but clean. There was a pattern embossed in the material, but I was too far to see anything more than that.

A young servant came out of the manor. He was dressed in a red tunic, well-tailored with a bronze sheath pinned to his chest. A symbol of a lord's assistant. I recognized him as Curringham's, always following him from room to room with papers. He delivered his sandwich at precisely noon every day. In a month of surveilling Lord Curringham, I had never heard him use his assistant's name.

But why would Curringham's assistant be meeting a stranger so late at night? And right after his lord had left. Perhaps he was acting as Curringham's messenger and alibi. The assistant took a step closer to the stables, leaning on the post his accomplice hid behind.

I leaned closer, careful not to make a sound.

"When?" Curringham's assistant said, as if to no one. He bent down and pretended to retie his boot.

"Tonight. Before dawn," the hooded figure answered. My shoulders relaxed slightly. The voice was not the dark, commanding voice of the Shadow. Whoever this man was, he wasn't the hooded menace. But that didn't mean he wasn't working for him.

"Same port as last time?" the assistant asked his boot.

So this had happened before. Now I just needed to know exactly what I was witnessing.

The stranger threw a small pouch on the ground as his answer. It landed with a soft clunk. The assistant swiped it off the ground and fitted it into his boot. At the same time, he pulled a bundle of papers from his belt. He stood up and leaned against the post, sliding the papers to whoever stood in the shadows.

I caught a glimpse of the blade holstered at the hooded man's belt as he reached for the papers. The hilt was not wrapped in leather or made of steel, but wood. Thick twists of branches formed the handle extending up along the stone blade. It was Elven made.

They were almost unheard of in the kingdom. And those that did exist were displayed over the hearths of rich men, not strapped at the side of some unknown traveler. No Mortal miscreant would carry such a weapon. No Halfling could afford it. Whoever stood beneath that hood came from the other side of the Burning Mountains.

Without another word, the stranger disappeared back into the shadows along the carriage path. I started to follow him but froze at the edge of the roof. Too many questions were spinning in my head. Why had someone from the Faeland come to visit Curringham's assistant? Did this mean that the lord had struck an alliance with the Dark Fae after all? Was the person beneath that cloak Fae? An Elf? A Halfling?

I needed answers. And I knew my best chance to get them would be from the young assistant rather than whoever had disappeared into the night. For the first time as the Blade, I wished I had a partner. She could watch the boy at the manor while I went after whoever he had met with.

But I worked alone. I sat down on the roof and waited for the assistant to sneak out of the manor and lead me to whatever was waiting at the ports.

Curringham's assistant didn't come back outside until an hour before sunrise. I walked behind him, too far back for his Mortal senses to notice, but he never left my sight. He walked down to the older ports, where the poor begged for passage in exchange for work and criminals would slip through crates of stolen goods.

He looked out of place in his well-tailored tunic and clean boots among the decrepit docks. Tattered sails hung loosely along the boats. The docks themselves were worn; entire planks of wood rotted away. No one here would spare the coin to replace them.

The assistant walked onto a small ship named *Auriela*, a beautiful name for a pitiful vessel. I leaped off the dock just as it was pulling out and hid behind one of several large crates. I opened the lid and was surprised to find it was stocked with food. Flour and cured meats. Jam and grain.

Why would the Dark Fae be trading in staple goods?

I listened closely. There were only two heartbeats on board, the steady tempo of the assistant and a quieter one, presumably the captain.

I pulled my hood forward to ensure it covered my face and then I moved.

I crept into the small steering cabin first, the frail old man driving the boat was standing beside the wooden wheel. I wasn't sure if he would be strong enough to swim back to the docks this far downstream, but a chance was better than the sureness of my blade. He didn't have time to shout before I hoisted him out of the room and into the gray water. I sighed in relief when I saw his head emerge. His frail arms started paddling toward the docks.

The assistant didn't even notice the splash, giving me time to grab some rigging. He turned as I lifted my arms to strike his face and wrapped the ropes around his torso. He started to shout but I slipped one of the small blades from its slot in the leathers along my sleeve and held it to his throat.

"You only live while no one knows I'm here," I whispered coldly.

He stopped, looking at my face even though he could not see it. I sat him atop a crate and tied the rope to an anchor beside the mast.

"You scream, I kill you. Understand?"

He nodded.

"Good. I saw you speaking with that male. I want to know why."

"I bought myself some Elven armor—" I stuffed part of his tunic into his mouth as he let out a blood curdling shriek. I had pulled out one of his fingernails with the pliers from my boot.

"Lying will only bring you pain. Want to try answering that again?" I pinched another nail with the pliers.

He nodded. I slowly pulled out the gag from his mouth.

"They wanted to know who the lord was meeting." He coughed. "And how often."

"*They*?" I had only seen one.

"Sometimes it's someone different. I never really see their faces, but the other one was . . ." He bit his lip as if to keep the words from spilling out of his mouth.

I cocked my head to the side. "Fae?"

He shrugged.

"And the one from today?" My eyes narrowed on his. His pupils were dilated so much that his eyes looked black. I could smell the adrenaline pumping through his veins.

"Halfling, I think." He coughed again. His eyes stared down at his hand and the blood dripping from his finger. "I only saw him once without a hood, but his ears were normal." He leaned back on the crate, putting as much distance between us as possible.

I pushed my hand harder against his throat. "What else did you tell them?"

"Not much. Sometimes I give them papers. Contracts. Harvest records. Usually, they just want to know which lords are in the city and who calls on them." There were many reasons the Dark Fae could target Cereliath. Most hinged on disrupting food distribution. Just as the king had worried.

"Did they say why they wanted to know?" I doubted either of them would have been dumb enough to reveal their plans, but it was worth asking all the same.

"No. I didn't ask." His voice quivered, but he lifted his chin.

"You didn't wonder?" I pushed.

"I didn't care," he spat. I raised my brows, but he couldn't see my surprise under the hood.

"People are hungry," he continued. "Bodies line the city, so thin and frail that the birds don't even come for them. They just lay there and rot." His jaw pulsed against his ragged breaths.

"And the male tonight? He's going to stop that, is he?" I crossed my arms, still holding the thick rope that bound the boy's limbs at his sides. He knew better than to move.

"He is. Him and the Shadow." He didn't even try to mask the anger in his voice.

"The Shadow?" I echoed.

He gave a stiff nod.

"How do you know this male works with the Shadow?" I asked, pulling him closer. "Have you met him?"

He shook his head. "I don't know. They don't use names. But the crates"—he kicked the box he sat on with his heel—"are full of food. Food to feed the hungry. Mortals. Halflings. They don't care. Anyone with an empty belly."

"And the Shadow has claimed to do this?" My mouth pinched. I had not heard of the Shadow's charity.

"Not outright," he said with a shrug. "Yet the people whisper his name all over the city. Every sack of goods that gets delivered is met with prayers of thanks to the Shadow. No one else has come forward to claim the deeds because no one else knows it's happening." His lips formed a soft smile.

"Curringham doesn't know?" I asked.

The boy scoffed. "Curringham doesn't care what happens to the poor. He spends all his time in Cereliath ignoring the people, locking himself in the manor pretending that everyone outside its walls is fed. His own city is even worse. There, half the people go without food each night. Babies die because their mothers don't eat enough to make milk. Children as young as six work the fields outside of the lord's house to feed their families." His nose crinkled and he bit his lip.

I loosened my grip on the rigging. My stomach churned like the waves underneath the boat. I could smell the death of the city; its scent was burned into my nostrils. I closed my eyes and saw flashes of the bodies that lined the road into Cereliath, too weak even to beg. Too weak to hope.

I swallowed the memories back down. My hands clenched around the rigging as I opened my eyes to study the boy in front of me. It didn't matter that I understood his anger. It didn't matter that I agreed with it. I was still the Blade.

"You approached the Fae then?" I asked through clenched teeth.

He shook his head. "They came to me. After a few visits I realized they were the only ones trying to help. Who was I to judge them when my own lord turned his back on his people?" He turned his head toward the docks, toward the House of Harvest. I knew from the glare in his eyes that he would burn the whole manor down if he could.

"When did you start working for them?" I asked. His attention snapped back to me.

"I don't work for them—" I pushed my blade against his throat again. "This spring," he choked against the steel.

"Betraying your lord is betraying the Crown," I reminded him. He nodded, his eyes lingering on the silver blade at my neck. When he looked back up at my hood, there was a hardness in them that had not been there before.

"My lord betrayed me when my baby brother starved in his bed last winter," he snapped, thrashing against his bindings for the first time. I knocked him back and pressed the sharp edge harder against his throat. A thin line of red appeared along the steel.

"No matter your reasons, treason cannot go unpunished," I said. The words tasted like acid in my throat. I swallowed the pain and tried to ignore what he had said about his brother.

"Funny how we can feed the poor and it's called treason, while the Crown lets its people starve and it's the king's divine right."

I didn't answer.

"If we don't fight, who will hold the king responsible?" he asked. I froze at the words, an echo of something I had said so long ago. A promise I tried so hard to forget.

I studied his face. His eyes were kind and round, dark like his hair and skin. He couldn't be more than twenty. So young but already filled with such anger. It was unfair what this kingdom seemed to do to those with kind hearts. They were the first to die or the first to rot.

I took a deep breath and asked, "What is your name?"

"Rylan Porter," he said with a self-assured air, as if he could sense what was coming.

"Rylan Porter," I repeated, picking up the anchor with one hand and the rope twisted around his limbs in the other. "The king's Blade extends you this mercy." I threw him off the boat with the anchor, unsheathing a throwing knife from my belt. I struck his eye before the weight pulled him under.

At least I didn't let him drown.

CHAPTER SIX

I DOCKED THE BOAT at one of the richer ports and paid the dock manager enough coin to keep his mouth shut. I told him a contact would come to collect the crates. I knew someone who ran a refuge in Cereliath. A friend of Victoria's. She would make sure the food got into the hands of those who needed it.

I skulked back through the city to the House of Harvest to spy on Curringham. I crept through the shadows and around the hungry who slept on the streets. The lord slept in later than normal and did not seem to care when a servant informed him that Rylan had not arrived that morning.

"Fetch another" was all he said.

By midday I was certain that Curringham knew nothing of the Fae or that his old assistant now lay at the bottom of the canal. When his new courtesan arrived at noon, I packed up my wineskins and headed back to the inn to sleep.

I slid down one of the stone pillars and jumped onto the wall dividing the gardens from the carriage entrance. Tall trees lined the stone, their thick branches the perfect place to hide as I scurried along the wall back toward the market.

When I reached the inn, I ordered a flagon of wine to my chambers and hot water for the bath. I sat in the tub until the candles burned low, staring at Rylan's name. I carved the tiny scrawl along the crook of my elbow. Its red lines would fade along the swirl of flame. His name completed the design along my left arm.

Amber blood pooled on my skin, turning brown as it clotted on top of the cut. I dipped my arm into the cool water and watched as the blood dissipated into the basin.

I leaned my head back against the edge of the tub and stared at the ceiling. Goosebumps erupted across my skin as the cold water stirred. I would have gotten out and dressed, but Rylan's words kept echoing in my skull. Crashing in my mind again and again, too hard and too loud for me to ignore.

Who will hold the king responsible?

His words sent me back thirty years as I traced the only name on my forearm. The one I couldn't bear to say.

The memories washed over me like the rush of high tide. I was in my room at the Order. The tiny space was all I had to call my own in the decades I spent training on the island. Moonlight shone across the bed where I lay awake hours after the initiates were meant to be asleep. *She* lay beside me. As she always did. Her blond hair tickled my face as we whispered about our distaste for the king. For the Crown.

I had asked her the same question. *Who will hold the king responsible?*

Her answer still haunted me all these years later.

We will.

"Would you like any wine, miss?" The barmaid's cheery voice grated against my skull. I held up the cup of wine I had brought down from my chambers for her to refill. Her eyes widened for a moment before she poured the red liquid into my cup. She paused when the cup was halfway full. I glared at her. She left the flagon on the table, scurrying back to the kitchen to fetch me my food.

It was hours since my bath. How many I wasn't sure, but the suns were still up, casting a golden light across the floor. My arms were stiff from the frigid water as I lifted the drink to my lips. My stomach growled as I gulped, eager for solid food, but the wine soothed the pulsing ache in my skull.

The barmaid returned with a plate of food, her face pink and her eyes hidden behind her long hair. She didn't say anything as she placed a bowl of steaming soup in front of me. The scent of lush spices and hearty squash swirled through the air. The inn might be a tawdry establishment, the favored post of scoundrels and rogues, but the food was some of the best in the city. A small comfort to make up for the poorly stuffed mattresses it offered.

I slurped my soup from a wooden spoon and sampled the array of cheeses and meats she had brought. My stomach settled; the food was rich and heavy in my mouth. I couldn't remember the last time I had sat for a meal.

I slowed down and savored it while the fire in the hearth burned low. My replacement Shades would be here within the week; until then I would keep surveilling the House of Harvest to see if the mystery male from the Faeland returned for Rylan.

Not likely, I thought to myself.

The Dark Fae were ancient. Their eldest were over eight thousand years old. It didn't matter who had been hidden beneath that cloak.

It was a fool's wish to hope they would return to the manor. Those who lived for millennia knew a bit of self-preservation. I'm sure they knew that the boy was dead, and that Rylan's killer would be waiting for them to make a mistake.

Which meant I was at a dead end. Unless I could think of some way to entice them—but I had nothing to offer. Their contact was dead. And even if I hadn't killed Rylan, his usefulness ran out the moment I spotted him talking with a male carrying an Elvish blade.

"There's another shipment coming in next week," I heard someone whisper across the almost empty room. Something in the voice sounded desperate. I slowly put down my fork and swallowed a mouthful of cheese. I leaned back in my chair, placing my hands on my stomach, and shifted my shoulders in the direction of the voice.

It belonged to a large man, hunched over a small table. His hands were huge and calloused from hard labor. His skin was tanned and weather-beaten, accentuating the fairness of his hair. Beside him was his opposite; a tiny man whose feet hovered above the floor as he sat on the cushioned seat of his chair. He had a crooked nose and wide eyes that tracked across the room.

I had never seen either of these men before.

"So you say. The last one never arrived," the small man said. His lips barely moved, and his face was turned away from his comrade. I doubted anyone but me and his friend knew he had said anything at all.

"Probably had trouble along the way," replied the larger man. He raised a brow and bent his chin. To him, trouble meant dead.

Like Rylan and his missing shipment.

"We don't even have a place to store any of it. I told you to tell him no." The wide-eyed man twitched. He tried to cover it by lifting a dainty hand to scratch the scar along his nose.

"We'll make do. People are hungry, and winter is near. Do you want a repeat of what happened last year?" He slammed his large hand into the table, sending it into a wobbling frenzy. The tiny man's hand shot forward to steady it. His head snapped back over his shoulder to see if anyone was watching.

I faked a yawn, stretching one arm out as I took a swig from my goblet. I leaned back in the chair and hung my neck like I was resting. I heard the tiny man turn back toward his friend.

"But if we can't hide it, someone will find it and then what good will it do?"

"We could ask *him* to help," the large man said, matching his friend's hushed tone. "He might have a second location we could use."

I peered at the men from beneath my hood. The tiny man was waving his feet underneath the table and shaking his head. "Why are you so eager to trust a man you've never met?"

My ears twitched and I had to stop myself from sitting up.

"That's not true," the big man said. "We've met."

There was an edge to his answer and in the defensive shrug he paired with it. Perhaps I wouldn't need Rylan as bait after all.

"You can't meet a man if you've never seen his face." The tiny one leaned forward across the table. "You have no idea what he looks like or what his name is."

I didn't need to hear the man's response to know who they were talking about.

The Shadow.

I stood without thinking, cutting across the room to where the men sat in five paces. "You're speaking of the Shadow," I said. It wasn't a question.

The small man froze against his chair while the larger one reared back as if to attack, but I moved faster. I lifted the table off the floor and smacked it down against his knee. He fell forward, and

I grabbed his head with my hand. A thin razor blade peeked from between my fingers. The large man blinked at the glint of the metal. I unsheathed my dagger and pointed it at his small companion.

"You move, you die," I warned.

The small man nodded. The large man's eyes danced between my blade and my hood. I pressed the steel to his chest. "Got it?" I asked, giving him a hard shove into his chair.

"Yes," he breathed. He spotted the fastener at my neck and sweat began to pool along his brow. I could see his heartbeat pulsing at his thick neck.

"I know you are talking about the Shadow," I said again.

"We weren't talking about—" I interrupted the small man with a soft prick of the dagger. He squealed and leaped back in his chair hard enough that it hit the wall.

"I don't care." I rolled my eyes at the tiny ball whimpering on the chair. "I'm not going to out you to the king . . . I have a message for you to give the Shadow the next time you see him."

"We can't kill him!" the small man exclaimed, peering through his fingers. Thin red lines surrounded his wide eyes.

I scoffed and shook my head.

"I don't need you to kill him," I said, lowering my dagger. He cautiously lifted his tiny head. "Just tell him something for me," I finished.

"What?" The big oaf puffed out his chest. He studied me, eyes following my dark brown plait until it disappeared into my hood. They stopped at the silver sword, not meeting my gaze.

I smirked even though they couldn't see it.

"Tell him the king's Blade requests a rematch."

CHAPTER SEVEN

DAYS PASSED and no one appeared at the House of Harvest. I spent twenty hours a day perched on the roof of the manor, hiding from the suns and the people below. No conspirator with an Elvish blade. No Shadow. No one out of the ordinary at all.

I took a swig of my drink. The second sun was disappearing beneath the horizon, a cool breeze fluttered against the heat of my skin. I needed to stop the Shadow. One more attack against the Crown and I knew the king would dispose of me.

I didn't care about my head. Part of me longed for the relief of a noose, but this was about more than me. I only killed those I had to. Those the king named. Anyone I could spare, I did. I funneled money through the refuges to keep Halflings hidden and fed. I knew Gerarda would not do the same if she was promoted to Blade. She would slay whoever she needed to complete her missions. To serve her king.

I was cursed with the blood I spilled. But I spilled less than others would.

Less than the king thought I did. It was a measly penance in the face of the lives I did take, the lives I ruined. But it was something. I wouldn't let the Shadow destroy the little change I had managed to make.

Not until I fulfill my promise, I thought. I brought the wineskin to my lips and drank from it until that thought washed away. What good was wine if it didn't keep me from thinking of my failures?

I heard Curringham's servant leave the lord in his bed. The oil lamp that painted soft orange lines along his window went out. A few minutes later, I heard the familiar rise and fall of the lord's snores.

I stood up too quickly. My hands reached out to keep me from falling as the roof spun underneath my feet. My wineskins sat empty beside me. I needed to get to bed quickly before a pounding ache started to split my skull.

A flash of movement caught my eye. A servant dashed out the side entrance and continued down the stone carriage way. That alone wasn't odd, but the same servant had just entered the manor three minutes prior and now his clothes were disheveled and his stature six inches taller.

The impostor moved quickly, peering back over his shoulder as if he expected someone to be following him. If he had been smart enough to look *up*, he might have seen me.

I tracked him as I jumped onto Curringham's balcony and then to the one below it. I launched myself onto the stone wall, my arms winding to keep my balance. The impostor had to show up *after* I'd finished my wine.

He looked back twice as I followed him along the wall. The trees kept me hidden, but there was something off about his gait. His chest was not pounding, and his steps were too sure for how clumsily his arms flailed at his sides. I couldn't make out any features on his face, but I was certain this man did not work in the manor.

This was a ruse. And an obvious one at that.

I reached the end of the wall and paused. My eyes followed the man as he crossed the laneway and started toward the inner city.

This was a trap.

And whoever was waiting for me at the end of it likely didn't have a belly full of wine. I sloshed with every step I took, off-balance. I was slow. Too slow for a fight.

I gritted my teeth as the man disappeared into the shadowed laneway of the business sector. I wanted—no, needed—to know who was setting the bait. If it was the Shadow, I couldn't risk losing the opportunity.

It was him or me. The rest didn't matter.

I jumped off the wall and ran in the direction the impostor had gone. My legs were sluggish. My fingers ached as I hoisted myself on top of the row of businesses. It didn't take long to find him again; his pace had slowed. His gaze shifted in every direction like he was trying to find me lurking among the crowd. Bumping into carts and passersby. He was making himself easy to track.

The wine stirred in my belly. I lifted a fist to my mouth, swallowing the urge to vomit. My foot slipped off the roof. I fell on my back, sliding toward the edge. My arms reached for something to grab onto. I grasped a small chimney and pulled myself back onto the roof. I crawled along the tiles and peered over the pitch.

No one was looking up or whispering. I could just make out the silhouette of the impostor, head turned back over his shoulder. The fall sobered me a little. My body was hot but focused. I did not slip again as I leaped from roof to roof following the mystery man below.

Eventually, we crossed the entire city and came upon an abandoned temple. I watched the man pull chains from the door—no lock held them together—and open it just wide enough to slip inside. There was a window above the door. Its glass was broken, leaving only a camber hole in the wall. I pulled two pointed blades from my belt and secured my hood. I ran full speed along the church and leaped. I pushed off the doorframe for extra height and anchored myself to the wall with a blade. I lifted my arm and secured the second, using it to lift myself up into the windowsill.

I peered inside. The temple was one large room. Moonlight from the tall windows sliced through clouds of dust. The man had gone. Disappeared out of one of the busted windows without a trace. A light breeze swirled against a purple banner that hung on the pulpit. It was faded and ripped, but I could still see the sigil of a long arrow stitched in gold.

I leaned into the wall on my perch. I knew this wasn't a coincidence. The man had been so obvious traipsing through town, only to disappear the moment we were out of sight and earshot. Few people walked by this part of the city and now that the suns were set, the dock workers had already gone home. It was the perfect time for an attack.

Someone was coming out to play.

I pulled the twin blades from my back and jumped. I landed on the pulpit with a soft thud.

"I heard you wanted a rematch," a deep voice spoke from the corner of the temple. My back tensed. I recognized the voice from our fight in Volcar.

The Shadow was cloaked in black just as I was. His tall frame leaned casually against a pillar. His arms were crossed, not even holding the sword that was sheathed behind his head. I couldn't see his face beneath that hood, but somehow, I knew he was smiling.

Mocking me.

I saw the similarities then. The ones Gerarda had noticed. His hood was fashioned exactly like a Shade's. Like mine. His cloak was made of different material, somehow darker than my own. He even wore black trousers and a tunic.

I would have to ask about his tailor before I killed him.

"Glad to hear my message was received," I said. I twirled my left blade, feeling the weight of it on my wrist.

"It would be impolite to ignore a request from the king's Blade," he said with a shrug. I cracked my neck, waiting for him to take a step toward me.

"You're eager to die?" I paused my breath to listen for accomplices hiding in the shadows, but I could only hear his heartbeat and mine. My nose wrinkled when I realized mine was beating faster than his.

He let out a chuckle as if he could read my thoughts.

"Are you sure you *can* kill me?" he asked, slowly pulling his sword out of its holster.

He took a single step toward me.

"Are you so sure I won't?" I challenged, lifting my blades.

"May the worthy win," he said.

Then he charged.

Six steps into his run, he leaped. Arms above his head, he drove his sword toward me. I rolled out of the way, dodging his swing. I spun on the ball of my foot. My blade swept his legs.

He lunged backward, but I nicked his boot. A thin slice in the leather, not deep enough to cut his skin. I stood as he swung again.

I ducked and jabbed with my blades. He jumped back.

I stepped closer, shortening the room he had to swing his sword. Every strike would be a risk with me so close.

He swung and I blocked it. His sword hung in midair between the cross of my blades. We stood frozen, our breaths melding together. He was bigger—much bigger—than me.

He swung again. I darted to the side, making two quick swipes with my blades.

He jumped over them. He was quick for someone so big.

"It's been more than a minute and you have yet to draw blood," he teased.

"Again, you're so eager to die," I said. Each breath burned my throat and my head throbbed.

"Death is the only certainty in this life," he said, changing his sword hand as we circled each other. I stepped back. "I expected more from the king's Blade. I was dodging blows like that as an apprentice."

I snarled. I launched myself at him with full force, but he matched every swing, every strike.

It was like a dance as we moved across the floor. Circling each other's bodies. Dodging life-ending blows and fielding our own.

He swung. I tripped and his blade fell only inches from my neck.

I could see the fog of my breath on the steel.

I dodged a second swing and widened the space between us. He rushed forward, his sword crashing down toward me.

I ducked under his arm and ran toward one of the benches. I could hear his ragged breath behind me.

I jumped off the back of a pew, flipping through the air above the Shadow's head. He turned too slowly. I kicked his wrist, and his sword flew across the room.

He didn't reach for his weapon but moved toward me. He grabbed my wrist and twisted the blade out of my hand. I swung the other at his neck. He caught my forearm mid-swing. I flinched. I could feel the bruise already forming where his fingers met my skin.

He kneed me in the stomach. Hard. The air flew from my lungs. My blade fell behind me. The Shadow was already running for his sword.

I pulled a throwing blade from my sleeve and launched it at him. It tore through the skin of his hand. In the dark, I couldn't make out the color of the blood.

I didn't care. I had drawn first blood.

"Any requests for how I kill you?" I taunted, catching my breath.

He froze.

"No. But I would like to know *why* you want to kill me," he said. His hood faced me, but his shoulders were turned toward his sword.

"The king commands it," I said simply, readying myself to attack when he moved.

"You don't dream of *not* serving the king?" His voice was dark and even. The hairs on my neck prickled along my skin. Did he know how many times I had stood in front of the king imagining one of my daggers in his chest?

"That's the thing about crowns," I whispered. "When one head falls, they're placed on another."

He paused. I couldn't see his face, but I could feel his eyes studying me. My breath stopped.

"Only if you leave a crown to claim," he answered after a moment. He bent down, fingers only inches from his sword.

I lunged from the floor and kicked the sword out of reach. He swung his leg. I jumped but landed wrong on my ankle. My legs were unsteady from the wine. I fell just as the Shadow straightened.

I pushed off the floor, my hands above my head. I landed on my feet.

He lunged at me without a weapon.

I didn't have time to grab my dagger. I ducked.

He punched again. I stepped to the side. I swung my arm. He dodged it. We traded blows back and forth. With the wine, we were evenly matched.

I studied his gait. His steps were even and his shoulders were straight. He didn't seem to favor a side or a knee.

He lunged forward. I moved left. But he expected that, feinting his lunge and pushing me into the pillar. The plaster cracked against my skull. Black spots flooded my vision. When they cleared, I caught a glimpse of his dark eyes before his hood fell forward covering them in shadow. They were wide, studying my face.

My face.

My hood was pinched between my head and the pillar. I had lost my anonymity and the fight in one blow. But why hadn't he made the final strike?

"It's not possible," he whispered. To himself or to me, I wasn't sure.

"What are you talking about?" I spat. My head throbbed, and I could feel blood matting against my hair. The slice of his blade would cure it just as well as any drink. What was he waiting for?

"You can't feel it?" he asked, completely ignoring me.

I opened my mouth to repeat my answer, this time not holding back on the cursing, but he stopped me.

His lips were on mine.

I was too stunned to move. He tasted sweet and fresh, like the glacial waters of the Burning Mountains. He pressed into the kiss and a shock of electric current churned through my body. I could tell by the way his hand tightened on my waist that the Shadow felt it too.

The Shadow.

The person I was meant to be killing.

My mind cleared as I moved to deepen the kiss. I ran my tongue along his teeth and felt a sharp prick.

Fangs.

I pulled him closer. The scent of birchwood and dew filled the air. I nipped at his lip, slowly unsheathing the dagger at my hip.

His hand held my neck as he bit me back. Tugged at my hair.

I let out a soft moan as I slammed the dagger into his chest.

The Shadow moved so fast his arm was a blur. One moment his lips were bruising mine, and the next his fingers were wrapped around my wrist. He held my arm in the air, the dagger suspended just above my head. His other arm was pinned against my torso holding me against the pillar.

"You make a habit of kissing people before you kill them?" I spoke. I thrashed against his hold, but he was strong. Stronger than me. I tried to catch a glimpse of his face under his hood, but it was too dark.

"It won't happen again," he murmured against my cheek.

I took a quick breath, anticipating a deadly strike. But it didn't come. He leaped back, leaving me against the pillar, and disappeared through a broken window.

CHAPTER EIGHT

I HAD NO CHOICE but to leave Cereliath the next morning. Two Shades appeared at dawn waiting for a brief. Even though we were alone in the room they rented, I kept my hood on. It shielded my eyes from the light and numbed the pain pulsing behind them. Each breath tasted of the vomit I had spewed the night before. Once beside the pillar after the Shadow disappeared, then again as I stumbled back to the inn.

My mouth was parched, and my lips cracked as I spoke to the Shades. I craved the taste of wine. Anything to curb the ache of my body, numb the shame of my defeat. But I refused the barmaid when she asked if we wanted a flagon.

I didn't deserve my vice. It had almost cost me my life. It *had* cost me the Shadow.

My tongue would not taste a drop of wine until I held the Shadow's head in my hands.

But for that I needed time. Time to find him. Lure the Shadow into the light long enough to stick my blade through his chest. Or neck. Or eye. I didn't care as long as he was stopped. As long as my place as Blade was secured once again.

"Anything else to report, Mistress?" one of the Shades asked. Her dark eyes peered up at my hood, but I was distracted by the long scar that crept from her tunic up her neck. She was young, and from the paleness of her skin and the curve of her ears, mostly Mortal. I doubted she was older than twenty.

So young and already so scarred. I shifted my shoulders. The names along my skin scratched against my tunic.

"No," I lied and walked out of the room. What was I going to tell the Shades? That I had killed Curringham's assistant and fought the Shadow but had nothing to show for it? I would keep those secrets until I had to reveal them. Until the king started asking questions.

Somehow, I doubted an unexpected kiss would be an excuse in the king's eyes.

I didn't understand why the Shadow had done it. Was it a distraction tactic? Unlikely. He'd had the upper hand. Perhaps it was a game to him. I had crossed paths with many men who liked to play out sick fantasies. Every Halfling female had.

Prince Damien's face flashed across my mind.

I smirked. He was cruel enough, but I could never imagine the crown prince hiding himself from the world. He was too proud to keep his actions a secret.

I galloped out of the city until I reached the edge of the Dead Wood. I didn't want to see the faces of all those hungry people again. To know which ones had died, their bodies left to rot under the suns.

Sweat pooled along my brow as I let my horse stop and rest. I took a sip from my wineskin and let the warm water flow over my tongue. It quenched the thirst but not the craving. As soon as I began riding again, I heaved over the side of my horse. His black eyes stared at me as I wiped the sick from my mouth.

It was going to be a long ride back to the capital.

"Good day, Keera," Gerarda said. She was waiting for me with two Shades outside of Koratha. Her frame looked even tinier in front of the towering wall behind her. I counted seven bodies hanging against the white stone. Thin lines of red and amber trailed under their feet.

"Dare I ask how you knew to wait for me here?" I cocked a brow. I usually came into the capital by the ports, not horseback.

"Some of us are spies, Keera," she said, her lips twitching to one side. I didn't miss the dig or the use of my name in front of the Shades.

"I didn't realize we spied on each other, *Gerarda*," I said, watching that sideways smirk fall.

"The mistress would like to speak with you," she said, completely ignoring my insinuation. She tucked her short black hair behind an ear and shrugged.

My brows knit together.

"Now?" I asked, gesturing to my filthy clothes. I wore the scent of horse shit, vomit, and sweat. The only thing I wanted more than a drink was a bath.

Gerarda shot me a wicked grin and nodded.

"Which one?" I asked even though I knew who she meant.

"The Bow," Gerarda answered, using Hildegard's proper title with a glance back at the Shades. Gerarda saved her disrespect for me.

"Very well," I said. I tapped the side of my horse and started to trot along the curved wall of the capital.

"Wait!" Gerarda called after me. She spun on the tips of her toes and took a dainty step toward my horse. "I am to escort you there." She motioned for the Shades to take hold of the reins.

"I do not need a babysitter," I spat, jumping off the saddle. Without a word, the two Shades mounted the horse together and rode toward the first gates.

"Think of it more as a guide," Gerarda said, rolling her eyes. When I didn't move to follow her, she turned back around. "Keera, she would like to speak to *both* of us. And for the record, I don't appreciate being sent to fetch anyone. Least of all you." Her arms were locked at her sides, fists balled inside her leather gloves.

At least we both weren't happy about this.

She spun around, her Arsenal cloak leaving a trail of black behind her. I kept my distance as we traveled along the outer wall of the city toward the sea. We walked in silence until I could taste the brine in the air. My ears focused on the familiar hum of waves crashing against the rocks that surrounded the coast. Gulls flew in lazy circles above our heads, swooping down into the water to hunt. My boots stepped into the wet sand of low tide as we reached the blunt end of the wall.

There it was.

The Order.

The mirror image of the king's palace, only smaller, placed on its own tiny island like a child's play set. Though the island was no place for children. It was where the strongest female Halflings were sent to train as initiates. And then, if they were strong enough, as Shades.

I had not stepped foot on that island in over two years. My stomach churned violently with each step I left in the sand. The Order was the backdrop of too many of my nightmares. I thought about running toward the palace instead. There, I would find my chambers, my bath. Gwyn. I could pull rank and tell Hildegard that she could meet me there.

But I didn't. I tramped behind Gerarda, wiping my brow with the inside of my sleeve. Summer was fading, but the suns were still hot, and my body was wrecked from a fortnight without a drink. My knees ached every time my foot sunk too low in the sand.

I heard Gerarda's footsteps clink against the glass and looked up. She was standing on the only way to access the island: The Forbidden Bridge. A long glass arch that suspended over the channel between the palace grounds and the island. Only Shades were allowed to use it—not that it mattered. The bridge was not completed but ended high above the swirling water and three hundred feet from the island's shore.

The gap was filled with several small posts made of the same stone as the Order. They protruded out of the waves at different heights, scattered across the chasm. Only someone skilled enough to maneuver across them would find themselves on the island's shores.

Gerarda moved first. She leaped onto the closest pillar, somersaulting in midair. The flair was for my benefit. She jumped deftly from one pillar to the next, some only as wide as her foot, but she never faltered. She pranced across the gap like a dancer. Within seconds she crossed to the other side.

I did not have Gerarda's grace. I bolted toward the end of the bridge, pushing off the edge into a long leap. My legs cycled under me, propelling me forward. I landed on a middle pillar and ran across the posts. With long strides, I pushed off one to the next in an exaggerated run. I launched myself off the last one, twisting in the air and landing with my feet cemented to the ground.

Gerarda popped her jaw to one side and crossed her arms. We both lowered our hoods before starting toward the front entrance of the Order. This was the only place a Shade could shed her shadow.

We marched up the large staircase and then another. Hildegard's study was in the middle tower. I had to stop halfway up. My hands gripped my knees as I fought the urge to vomit. My eyes squeezed shut, trying to dampen the throbbing ache behind them. I thought after a fortnight the withdrawal would have lessened, but beads of sweat still poured out of my skin. My parched throat ached for something other than water to douse the pain.

Gerarda sniffed loudly. Her foot tapped at the top of the stone staircase. Behind her stood a statue of an Elvish warrior. The statue was dressed in leathers stitched with each of the elements across her limbs and torso. I instinctively pulled at my sleeve knowing the same pattern was carved into my skin. My hidden rebellion against the Crown was not safe to reveal to anyone, even to those I had spent my life training beside. No one could know I didn't fear that lost part of myself, the Elvish part, like I had been told to. Instead I reclaimed it in my own way with every name I etched into my skin.

I caught my breath and slowly climbed the remaining stairs. Gerarda's eyes paused on the red circles around my eyes and my clammy skin. She bit both her lips, setting them into a straight line. I waited for a snarky retort, but she said nothing.

Gerarda knocked on the Bow's door twice.

"Come in," a voice commanded from inside the room.

Hildegard stood at her desk with her arms held behind her back. She'd held the same stance whenever I had gotten in trouble as an initiate. I had spent a lot of time in the mistress's office then. Her gray hair was pinned back in a low bun, tugging at the wrinkles that framed her eyes. She was only fifteen years older than me, but she looked like an old woman, whereas I could disguise myself as a young maiden of twenty.

I gave a slight bow before I took my usual seat. Gerarda did not sit but stood beside the small window, facing us and the door all at once. Ever the perfect soldier, especially in front of her favorite teacher. Gerarda had always been a kiss-ass.

"Glad to see you back on the island, Keera," Hildegard said. Her nose twitched as a breeze from the window blew my scent toward her. I scowled. She was the one who insisted on the urgent meeting.

"We've kept your office clean for you," she added, gesturing to the door across the hall. I had never stepped foot inside it, and I never would.

"No need," I said. "I've spent enough time in these halls. Besides, I would only get in your way. We wouldn't want that; you do such a wonderful job with the initiates." My voice was thick with sarcasm, but it was true. Hildegard was a strict mistress, but a fair one. Any Halflings in her charge were safe.

"Not like it's your job or anything," Gerarda mumbled from the window. She mimicked Hildegard's stance. Back straight as an arrow with her hands resting behind her.

"As the Blade, my job is to run the Arsenal as I see fit, Gerarda," I replied coolly. "The Bow and the Arrow have never complained about their duties training the Shades. Have you?" I raised a brow to Hildegard. My eyes locked on the silver bow she wore as a broach on her tunic.

"No," she answered.

"I admit I haven't seen the Shield in some time, but does she complain of her duties when you're in bed together?" I asked Hildegard again. She pursed her lips, green eyes narrowing slightly, and shook her head.

"Just as I thought. That leaves you then, Gerarda," I said, turning toward her. "Are you making an official complaint? Is being the Dagger and organizing missions too much for you?" I raised a brow and flashed a smile.

"Absolutely not," Gerarda said through clenched teeth.

"Then no need to speak of it," I said, waving my hand. "Today. Or in front of the king." My last words were flung at Gerarda. She at least had the decency to look at her boots. I had not forgotten the king's lecture the last time I was in the capital.

"Enough with the pleasantries," Hildegard said, her face hard. "There was an attack in Volcar. We haven't identified the culprits, but we lost four Shades." I sucked in a breath. Attacks against the Shades had always been a part of life at the Order, but lately it was getting worse.

"Add that to the three we lost in Mortal's Landing, and the group that never came back from the Fool's Trap, our numbers have severely waned," Hildegard said, chewing the inside of her cheek. She took a deep breath before she continued. "The king believes it's time to call the Trials." Her eyes dropped to the parchment on her desk.

I clenched a fist against the arm of my chair.

"So soon?" I said. "The last ones were only two years ago." The Trials were what every initiate trained for. A series of five challenges created to test each initiate in the most brutal of ways. Only those who passed all five became Shades.

Hildegard gave a grim nod.

"How many are you calling to take them?" I demanded. The Arsenal selected the initiates they thought were ready before each set of Trials. Since I had been Blade, I left that responsibility to the other mistresses.

"The king believes that anyone with eight years' experience is trained well enough," Hildegard answered. Her voice was calm. Too calm.

My jaw clamped shut. I picked up the vase on her desk and chucked it across the room. Gerarda and Hildegard didn't flinch as it shattered against the wall.

"Eight years?" I scoffed, pacing back and forth in front of her desk. "Eight years is barely enough to master basic skills. If you call initiates with so little experience, you're calling them to die." My chest heaved as I stared at Hildegard.

Her eyes were soft, but her jaw was set. She crossed her arms in front of her chest.

"I am at the king's command," she said. "We all are."

"Fuck the king!" I shouted.

Gerarda's attention snapped toward me, eyes wide with warning. Hildegard walked over to the door and shut it.

"The Shadow has the king on edge," Hildegard said. "He thinks these attacks are connected and he's worried about his numbers. His army has dwindled, and there are fewer Shades now than there used to be—"

"Maybe if he didn't insist on *hanging* every Halfling he decided was a traitor for no reason, he would have more bodies to fill his service!" I snapped. I waved my arm across her desk, accidentally hitting a bottle of ink. The dark liquid spread across a loose page of parchment.

"Keera, that's enough," Gerarda hissed, helping Hildegard with the ink.

I shook my head. Every ragged breath pulsed against my skull. My skin was raw, burning with rage at the king's indifference. He didn't care how many Halflings died in the Trials. He didn't care that they would serve him better with more training.

He wanted more Shades. Whatever the cost.

"He already makes us hunt them," I spat. "Search all over the kingdom for Halflings hiding their children. Do you know how many parents I've slain just to bring their daughters to this cursed island? And for what? So she can die before ever passing her Trials? Or be struck down on her very first mission because she doesn't know how to protect herself? Has the king learned *nothing* from last time?"

"Apparently not," Hildegard whispered. For the last Trials, the king had insisted that all initiates with ten years' experience be called forward. Half the graduates were dead within a year.

"This is madness," I said, crumpling back into my chair.

"And yet these are our orders." Hildegard sighed. "There's no changing the king's mind. I've already tried." She bit her lip and looked out the window. I could see the glassy sheen covering her eyes.

"If only you had come back with the Shadow's head," Gerarda muttered, picking up the broken pieces of glass off the floor.

"I was sent to Cereliath to surveil *Lord Curringham*," I said. "Which, by the way, was a waste of time." Gerarda's fingers clamped against a large piece of vase. She didn't know about the assistant and the Shadow; I certainly wasn't going to tell her.

"Regardless," Gerarda said, "the king is in a state over this Shadow. Until the menace is stopped, he won't change his mind about the Trials."

"So I will end the Shadow once and for all. *Before* the Trials are held," I said simply. "Please tell me we have time."

"The king is adamant," Hildegard said. My stomach dropped through the floor. "But I told him the initiates will need time to prepare. I think I can convince him to hold off the Trials until the winter solstice."

"Five months?" It wasn't a lot of time, but I would make it work. "I'm not being a judge," I said, crossing my arms. I had only ever judged one set of Trials as the Blade. I refused to ever do it again.

"That is between you and the king," Hildegard answered. A shadow flashed across her eyes, and I knew she was thinking of the last time I had stood as judge. She found me passed out in a mucking stall wearing the same clothes I had on the night of the final trial. I had hopped from pub to pub all month long, leaving only when the patrons kicked me out. Hildegard pulled me from a pile of manure and nursed me back to a functioning state of mind.

I never attended a set of Trials again.

"I will be there," Gerarda said. The pride in her voice made the contents of my stomach gurgle up my throat. "But I agree with Keera. Let her go after the Shadow. If the Trials can be stopped, that's for the best."

My mouth hung open as I stared at her. The Dagger didn't look at me but gave a stiff nod.

"Where will you begin your search? Back in Cereliath?" Hildegard asked, looking at the map hanging on her wall. It was marked with a hundred pins. The locations of all the Shades on mission. She took out a pin and readied it above the parchment.

"No," I answered. "The Faeland."

Gerarda gasped while Hildegard slammed her pin into the wood frame. It snapped in two and fell to the floor.

"That's a death wish," Gerarda whispered. "No one returns from the Burning Mountains."

"The king will never allow that," Hildegard said, facing me again. "He won't break the treaty on a hunch."

"He will," I replied, slapping my hands on my thighs as I stood. "He wants the Shadow more than anything. And his patience with me is running thin. I will not survive another failure."

Gerarda placed her hands on the desk. "He would never dispose of you," she whispered. "You're his shining glory."

"We all know I have not shined for a long time. Too long." I bowed my head. It was the best apology they would get. "I've put myself in this position. If the choice must be risking my life in the Faeland to protect them"—I pointed out the window to the initiates training below—"or waiting for the king to dispose of me, let me make that choice."

I stared at Hildegard, refusing to blink until she relented. A long moment passed and then she nodded.

"Then it's settled." Hildegard clapped her hands. "We will buy you as much time as we can, Keera. But you need to end the Shadow."

"I will," I said and walked out the door.

The sea breeze cooled my rage. My lungs filled with the salty air, loosening my chest with each breath. Every time I was forced to return to the island, I was shocked by how unchanged it was. Walking along the grounds was like walking through time. The same giant stones pierced through the sea in a circle around the island, keeping sailors from landing on its shores. The same targets were laid across the field next to the same obstacle course that I trained on as an initiate.

I watched at the top of the hill as initiates practiced below. Even they looked like those I had trained with. The same black garb and tight plaits. A mixture of pinched ears and round ones. It didn't matter that their faces changed over the years; each initiate still had the same amber blood in her veins. The blood that marked her as the king's.

These initiates were young. Not just in age but in skill. They only stood thirty feet back from their target yet some of their arrows still missed. One initiate struggled more than others. Her arms were tight and her bowstring slack. A pile of arrows lay on the ground halfway between her and the target.

I walked over to the young Halfling, watching her elbow jut upward as she launched another arrow. It flew only fifteen feet before cascading to the ground.

I approached her slowly. She lowered her bow and turned to me, eyes widening at the silver sword glinting in the sunlight at my neck.

She tucked her face behind her bow. "Hel-lo."

I tried to give her a gentle smile. "What's your name?"

She quivered so hard I thought she might snap her weapon. "Fy-Fyrel."

"Fyrel," I said as gently as I could. "Your grip is wrong, that's why you can't align your arm properly." I gestured to the bow. It shook in her hands. "Pretend to nock an arrow."

Her fingers clenched against the grip too far up along the leather. I cupped my hand over hers, loosening each of her fingers one by one. I studied her stance once more and tilted her hand ever so slightly to the left.

"Try like that," I said.

She pulled back the bowstring, her arm perfectly aligned this time.

"I did it!" she shouted. Her wide eyes stared at the length of her arm.

I nodded at the circle. "Try hitting the target."

Fyrel nocked an arrow and took a deep breath. She pulled back on the string, adjusting her grip as I'd showed her. She let go and her arrow flew across the field. The arrowhead pierced the inner rim of the target around the small red dot.

"I've never hit the target before!" she shouted, wrapping her arms around me.

I knelt to the ground, leveling my gaze with hers. "What is your best skill? Your favorite one to do?"

"Sword fighting," she answered immediately.

I called one of the other girls over. A petite Halfling with dark hair and thick brows. She was the best archer of the group.

"What's your name?" I asked her.

"Saraq," she said.

"Do you two know each other?" I asked. They nodded shyly.

"Good," I said. "Fyrel here needs help with her archery, and I know you're the best in your year." I smiled at Saraq, she nodded proudly. "And Fyrel is the better swordsman. I want you two to train together from here on out. Use each other to hone your skills."

The two girls locked eyes and turned back to me. They nodded in unison just as the bell tower rang for the dinner call. The two initiates gave a short bow before they raced each other up the hill where their food was waiting.

"That was kind of you," Hildegard said. I peered over my shoulder. I hadn't heard her approach the training session.

"It's easier," I said, letting my shoulders fall, "when you have someone at your side."

Hildegard sighed. Her eyes followed the initiates up the hill, and I knew she was wondering when the king would make her call them to their deaths. "You would know," she said after a moment.

I turned toward the cliff's edge, watching the waves crash against the stone. I didn't want to talk about that. About *her*. I bit my lip and waited for Hildegard to say something else.

"Tell me what happened in Cereliath." She was always quick to read my moods.

I sighed. "I danced with a Shadow." It was more than I should admit, but I knew Hildegard wouldn't tell the king. She knew one foul mood of his could mark any of us for death. Even his Blade.

Her brows lifted.

"But you could not catch it?" she asked, walking toward the cliff 's edge. I followed beside her.

"No." I kicked a stone with my boot. "I was not at my best that night." The words scraped along my throat, but I swallowed down the shame.

"Ah," Hildegard said, crossing her arms behind her back once more. "I assume that's why you showed up here looking like you're on the brink of death?"

"Yes." No point denying it. Hildegard's eyes traced the red veins in mine and the dark circles that hung like cloaks under them.

"How long?" she asked.

"Thirteen days." It was such a short amount of time, but with the craving, time stretched. Every minute without a drink felt like an hour. Or ten.

She smiled softly and pulled something out of her pocket. It was a vial of black liquid.

"Take this," she said, placing it in the palm of my hand. She clasped my fingers around the bottle, pressing my thumb over the cap. I brought the vial to my nose and sloshed the dark liquid.

"Is this—"

"*Winvra* elixir, yes," Hildegard said. "Just one drop every day should help you through the worst of it. It will numb the pain until you can handle it on your own."

"I can't accept this," I whispered, handing it back to her. It was too expensive. I wasn't even sure how Hildegard got hold of it.

"Yes, you can," she said, ignoring my hand in front of her. She gripped my shoulder, and my neck tensed as her thumb pressed against one of my scars. "This will help you, Keera. Help you end the Shadow and save the initiates from a fate worse than the ones already written for them. Take it. Use it. And come back with your mission complete."

My mouth hung open. No words escaped my lips because I couldn't think of any that meant as much as the potion she had given me. I pulled her into my arms, wrapping them tightly against her back. She looked at me with wide eyes before settling into the embrace.

"I won't fail them," I said with one last look at the white walls of the place that had once been my home.

Not again.

CHAPTER NINE

The palace grounds were full. Not of people, but tables and food. Ribbons hung in limp strips from the garden trees. One drifted down and landed on my shoulder as I stalked toward the east entrance of the palace. I walked around broken glass that lined the path and stepped in rotten pieces of crushed fruit. I sighed and rubbed the red berries off on the grass.

"Keera, you missed the festivities." My back stiffened as Prince Damien stepped in front of me.

"I didn't realize the king was holding a celebration," I said, straightening to my full height. Damien was leaning against the stone wall, his wrinkled shirt untied at the neck.

He pointed at me with one finger while holding a goblet. Dark liquid splashed over the edge. "We both know the only party my father is interested in throwing is his Crowning." His words slurred and his eyes refocused each time he blinked. I doubted the prince had gone to bed at all.

"Of course, Your Highness," I said, bowing my head. Every ten years the king would celebrate the inauguration of his kingdom with an entire summer of events. For weeks the palace would be bursting with excitement over the tourneys, feasts, and music. Thankfully, I didn't have to suffer through that again until the summer after next.

Damien hiccupped and stood up with a jolt. "This party was all me," he said, swaying as he took a step toward me. "I planned it for my baby brother. He was *delighted*, I'm sure." Even drunk, Damien couldn't keep that smug grin off his face. His brother hated parties more than Damien liked throwing them.

He gripped my shoulder with his hand and my teeth gritted together. I knew he could feel the ridges of his marks stretching over my back. He stroked my face with a sticky finger, still clutching his cup of wine. "You would've looked lovely in one of those backless dresses," he whispered, his fingers tracing down my spine. I bit my tongue until I could taste blood.

"You would have all the lords drooling at the sight of you. The forbidden fruit," he said, his face folded into my hood so that I felt the flick of his tongue on my ear. "Such a beautiful piece of fruit at that but"—he clawed at the widest scars—"rotten."

My skin seared like it was being split again under Damien's touch. I closed my eyes and held my breath, hoping that would douse the fiery rage pulsing through my veins. My hand fisted around the hilt of my dagger, but I didn't pull it from its guard. I refused to play into Damien's game.

"I'm sorry to have missed it, sire," I answered coolly.

Damien's head reared back, his wide eyes studying me. I kept my face flat knowing the slightest hint of a smirk could send him into a brutal rage. One that he wouldn't take out on me, but Gwyn. His cold eyes stayed on mine, squinting as if he watched the suns. After a moment, his lips cut into a grin.

"Yes, it is a shame," he said, stepping back and taking a large swig of his wine. "That mouth would have been a delight at the Bastard Ball."

I couldn't help tilting my head, brows stitching together.

"You haven't heard?" Damien said, sliding against the wall once again. "It started as a joke, but the name stuck. Maybe I'll throw one again the next time my brother deigns to visit us." His jaw pulsed before he took another gulp of wine.

I pasted a smile on my face. "Very clever, sire," I said with a stiff nod. Damien waved his cup in front of his pursed lips. He hated that his brother had been born at all, let alone to a Fae. Damien had been at his mother's bedside, the king's first wife, when she died at the age of a hundred and seven. Three days later, Killian had been born by the king's Fae mistress.

"I should've called it the Halfling Ball," Damien mumbled into his cup, finishing the drink. I nodded, but Damien was no longer listening. Three ladies had appeared at the end of the hall. The prince's hungry eyes stalked the sway of their skirts. He tossed his goblet to the ground and strode after them without another word.

I picked up the cup and placed it on the table. Damien had nothing but contempt for his brother. I didn't understand. Killian showed no interest in the throne and spent years away from his father and brother. I stared down the hall where Damien had wandered.

Halfling.

Was that why he hated his brother? I shook my head and marched up the staircase toward my chambers. The king had sought to sire a child with the Fae to cement the peace with the Faeland. Or so he'd said. Regardless, Killian was born, and his mother died in childbirth.

While technically the second prince was a bastard, he was not a Halfling.

Killian had been born Mortal, no added strength or height. His ears were round, and his skin as pale his father's. Even his blood ran red. Mortals and Fae had pure blood—red blood—and therefore made pure offspring. The only thing different about the prince was his lengthened lifespan, something he and his brother inherited from the king.

I collapsed onto my bed without bathing. I was too tired to draw a bath, and I could feel a craving scraping at my throat. I pulled out the stopper of my elixir and tasted a drop, letting the sweetness carry me into a dreamless sleep.

The king waited a full day to call an audience with me. Two guards opened the grand doors to the throne room, sunlight from the large windows warmed the hood of my cloak. I stepped into the room and found each of the three chairs filled. The king sat in the middle on his throne, his sons flanking him on either side. My breath hitched. I hadn't been expecting a full audience.

I lowered my hood and knelt before the throne. I could feel the king's eyes staring through my skull and Damien's down the linen blouse I wore under my cloak.

"Rise," the king said in an unusual act of mercy for my knees. This was either going to go well or very, very poorly.

"What did you learn in Cereliath?" the king asked through clenched teeth.

Poorly then.

"Not as much as I'd hoped, Your Majesty," I said with a bow. "I tailed Lord Curringham for over a month. I found nothing that leads me to believe he was dealing with the Dark Fae or"—I took a breath—"that he was aware his assistant was doing so."

"His assistant?" Damien raised a brow. He slouched over his chair, leaning on one armrest with a leg cast over the other. Killian sat straight up but his brows were raised.

"Yes, Your Highness," I continued, refusing to look at Damien. It had been a risk telling the king about the boy. A risk I hoped paid off. "The young man had been in Lord Curringham's service for over a year. I saw him meeting with a conspirator who he believed to be working for the Shadow."

"The Shadow?" the king echoed. His fingers clasped the arm of his throne tight enough his knuckles turned white.

"Yes, Your Majesty," I said. "The man kept his face hidden beneath his traveling cloak so I could not identify him. When I interrogated the assistant, he said he only dealt with two people—one he believed to be the Shadow and the other his accomplice." Not entirely true, but the king didn't have anyone who could verify it. I had left the only witness at the bottom of a canal.

"Are you telling me the Shadow and the Dark Fae are working together?" the king bellowed. He slammed a fist on his throne. His heavy breaths shook his beard as his eyes disappeared behind his flushed cheeks.

I shook my head. "The boy wasn't sure. Rylan never saw much of him, but he said he moved too quickly to be Mortal."

"Rylan?" It was Prince Killian's soft voice. I stilled. Killian barely spoke at court, least of all to me.

"The boy's name, Your Highness," I said, blinking up at the prince. He leaned forward in his chair, his head tilted to the side.

"I don't care about some dead traitor's name!" the king shouted, slamming his other fist. "What was the Shadow doing in Cereliath?"

I broke my gaze from Killian and faced the king. "The conspirator was moving a shipment of food through the city. I believe the other person the assistant met with may have been the Shadow or someone working for him."

"Why?" Killian asked, raising a honey-colored brow. He pushed a stray lock of hair out of his face.

"The boy believed it to be true," I answered, lifting a shoulder. "So do many of the peasants in Cereliath. The poor are hungry, and someone has been feeding them. They believe it's the Shadow." Killian gave a slow nod. I could see his eyes swirling, processing the information in his quiet way.

"The only people starving in Cereliath are those who refuse to work," the king said.

Or those who can't, I thought, gritting my teeth.

Damien rubbed his face, throwing his arm over the back of his chair.

Killian's head snapped back toward me. "This only proves that the boy was working with the Shadow. Not that the Shadow is connected to the Dark Fae."

The king leaned forward, his thick brows lifting with the corners of his mouth. "Do you find this to be true, my Blade?" he asked, licking his lips.

I paused. "I didn't find any *direct* evidence of the Dark Fae while I was in Cereliath. The boy was adamant he had never dealt with them." Another lie. Rylan hadn't been able to confirm one way or the other.

"So the true threat is this Shadow menace," Damien said, smirking at his brother. "Did I not say as much the last time you were in this throne room?" He turned to face me with the same cocky grin on his face.

The king slumped back in his throne and levied a cold stare at his eldest son.

"I would like to hear your indirect evidence," Killian interrupted. His rosy lips were parted in a testing smile.

"Your Highness?" I asked, tilting my head toward the prince.

"You said you didn't find any *direct* evidence," he said, with a small wave of his hand. "I would like to hear what your indirect evidence is."

The king nodded while Damien rolled his eyes.

"The conspirator that spoke with Rylan was carrying a blade," I said. "It was Elven-made and too fine a weapon for a mere criminal to carry." Killian's lips twitched. "And," I continued, "the Shadow fights too well. Whoever he is, he is too strong to be Mortal. And if he was a Halfling from Elverath he would not be trained in combat." The king believed male Halflings were too dangerous to arm so he put them to work instead. He left his army to those he could trust—Mortal men—and those he could control—the Shades.

"You fought the Shadow again?" Damien cut in, sitting up in his chair. His jade eyes were murderous.

Sweat pooled at the small of my back and my heart hammered against my chest. If I wanted to convince the king to send me after the Shadow, I could not tell him I failed to beat him again.

"I was referencing our duel in Volcar," I answered coolly. "As far as I know, the Shadow was never in Cereliath during my stay." Damien collapsed back in his chair. Killian studied me, his eyes roamed along my face and limbs. It wasn't the predatory stare of his brother, but a curious one. I thought he was going to say something, but he leaned back and looked out the window instead.

"You think the Shadow is Fae?" The king's words were hot and dangerous.

"I considered it, Your Majesty," I said, lowering my head. "But it would be very difficult for a Dark Fae to roam through Elverath without alerting the notice of the Shades. Or catching the notice of the people." The Dark Fae were easily marked by the violet color of their eyes.

"I think it's more likely that he's a Halfling," I continued. "One that grew up in the Faeland perhaps. Or . . ."

"An Elf," Killian whispered for me. I nodded as a cold hush fell about the throne room. Few dared to mention Elves in front of the king. I could hear the king's teeth grinding as I held my breath.

"I don't care what he is," Damien said, daring to break the silence. "A traitor is a traitor, and he needs to be killed." He drummed his fingers along the armrest, looking to his father for approval. The king's face remained still, his eyes tracing over Damien. He nodded once and turned toward Killian.

"I agree," Killian said. He was clenching and unclenching a fist on his chair.

"With the Blade or your brother?" the king asked, waving his arm from me to Damien.

"Both," Killian replied. "If there were a Dark Fae traipsing across Elverath, the Shades would know. Either way, this Shadow is becoming too large a threat to ignore."

The king gave a stiff nod.

"It's time for the Shadow to be brought to justice." The king's eyes flashed down to where I stood. "Prepare yourself for a hunt, my Blade. I don't want you to return until you've unmasked this Shadow, preferably by bringing me his head."

"Gladly, Your Majesty," I said with a bow.

"Didn't I say this last time?" Damien mumbled. He tossed his legs over the side of his chair again, his bored expression returning.

The king's eyes were hard as he stared at me. "I trust you to finish this as you see fit. But know, where you are headed, I cannot send anyone after you if things go awry."

I nodded. I had expected nothing less.

"And if you can't give me the Shadow's life," the king continued, his mouth set in a straight line, "then you will give me yours."

My back stiffened. My cloak tightened around my neck as my pulse raced. I pulled it away from the skin—it felt too much like a noose.

"An Elf could only hide across the Burning Mountains," Killian said, his face soft beside his father's stony countenance. "Which Fae city will you target?" he asked with a quick glance at his father.

"Aralinth."

The city of eternal spring.

CHAPTER TEN

I had never been to Aralinth. The Dark Fae kept their city well-protected from those who served the king. Anytime the Crown had business with the Fae, they would meet the royal emissaries in Caerth. The little trade that occurred between the Faeland and the kingdom was also done east of the Burning Mountains.

Few in Elverath had ever seen a Dark Fae, yet legends of their powers were still told across the kingdom. The way they could wrap their opponents in darkness, blinding them until they landed a fatal blow. How they could speak to their comrades without moving their lips, placing thoughts directly into minds. How they could transform any liquid into a tasteless, scentless poison that would cause the most potent agony before bringing a victim to their death.

I hoped the rumors of their magic fading were true. I didn't know how long I would survive in the Faeland if they weren't.

I swallowed the fear as I walked away from the throne room. The decision was made. I was going to the Faeland in search of the Shadow. If I had to take out the rest of the Dark Fae before I slid my blade across his throat, so be it. The Order was counting on me. The Halflings were counting on me.

And what did I have to lose? I would either die in the Faeland at the hands of their magic or return to the king empty-handed and he would dispose of me. Journeying to the capital city of the Fae was dangerous—perhaps the most dangerous thing I'd ever done—but it was also my only option.

Droplets of sweat formed along my brow as I walked across the palace. A familiar ache scratched my throat until it burned. My hand fell to my side, grasping for a wineskin that wasn't there. I plucked the small vial out of my front pocket instead, pulling the glass top from its neck. I lifted the thin rod to my mouth and watched a tiny drop of ebony fall onto my tongue. It tasted sweet, sweeter than any fruit or wine I'd ever had.

Instantly, my shoulders relaxed and my heartbeat slowed. The burning in my throat settled enough that I could think of more than just how badly I wanted a drink. Still, I didn't trust myself to stay too long in my chambers alone. I had spent too many solitary nights in those rooms drinking wine. It would be easy to fall into old habits and send a chambermaid to fetch a flagon or two.

I looked for distraction in the gardens. The suns were high in the sky, too hot for the ladies of the palace to stroll along the blossoms and too early in the day for the servants to be done with their work. It was the perfect time to be alone and think.

I sat under an old maple tree, its trunk sturdy against my back. I closed my eyes and let the warmth from the suns wash over me. The scent of fresh blooms wafted through the air. I could hear the soft murmur of chambermaids chatting as they laundered clothes outside of the kitchens. Their voices were carried on the same breeze that swept over the sea and through the hanging clothes. I let the peace wash over me and eventually lull me to sleep.

"Keera," a voice called. I blinked as I looked up. All I saw was a black silhouette against the light of the suns behind them. "I thought you'd be back in your chambers by now."

I rubbed my eyes and smiled. I didn't need to see her face to recognize Gwyn.

"I didn't know you were waiting for me," I said, standing up and brushing the dirt off my trousers. "I haven't seen you since I've been back."

"I know, sorry," she said. Her eyes stared down at my boots while her cheeks turned pink. "I was . . . Prince Damien . . . He kept me in his rooms until the last of his guests left. I wasn't let out until last night after you had gone to bed." She raised her head and grabbed her elbow behind her back. I noticed the redness along her lashes. I bit my lip to keep from cursing the prince's name.

"Why?" I asked. Damien was cruel but also easily bored. It wasn't like him to keep Gwyn for days at a time.

Gwyn shrugged, rubbing the toe of her boot into the ground. "He didn't do anything. Not really. I think he just liked showing me he could." Bright red marks lined her wrists. The prick had restrained her.

"Walk with me?" I asked. I held my arm out to her. She grabbed it with a wide smile, and I noticed the gold ring on her finger. The one I had given her the last time I was in the capital.

She caught my gaze and twiddled her fingers along my arm. "I didn't have to use it," she whispered. I nodded and tried to return her smile but couldn't. A cold wave crashed through my body. I dreaded what the prince might do to Gwyn one day, how far he would take things. My worst fear was returning to the capital and finding Gwyn's body hanging from the prince's balcony.

"How was Cereliath?" she asked, pulling me from my thoughts.

"Boring," I said as we moved out of the garden and toward the beach.

Gwyn let go of my arm as I stepped onto the sand. She couldn't go any further.

"Sorry," I said when I realized. I hadn't been thinking about her tether.

"It's all right," Gwyn said, her voice quieter than before. "Though I do wish I could walk along the beach again." She watched the waves with wide eyes. Not the way she had as a child, full of wonder splashing in the rising tide, but the forlorn way sea widows watched the sea. Drowning in the memories of something that once was, filled with pain and the slightest bit of hope. A hope that was strangled by her tether.

Gwyn was bound to the palace as part of a life debt. Not one she made, but an ancestor of hers long ago. She was tied to the palace grounds by some long-lost magic and would remain so as long as the king lived. Just as her mother and grandmother before her. I remember the day her mother died, three years before. I had been standing beside Gwyn when her mother took that final rattling breath. A tear rolled down Gwyn's cheek when it happened. She howled as the tether took hold, searing its mark along her ankle like a brand.

We walked back along the outskirts of the garden through the lush trees and thick blossoms. Gwyn told me of the gossip from the party. A wife of a lord had been found rollicking with a Halfling in an empty chamber. She had been disgraced. He had been swiftly put to death.

We reached the walls of the castle and Gwyn dropped my arm. She had duties to attend to but promised to dine with me before the suns set. I reached out for her as she walked down the hall, but she didn't turn around. My hand fell limp at my side as a somber feeling took root in my stomach.

Damien tormented her. My chest tightened, knowing on some level he did it because of me. Ever since he carved the scars into my back, he hungered for other ways to cut me. He had watched as I grew fond of Gwyn, letting her mother bring her to my chambers as she worked. Sometimes baby Gwyn would stay for hours in that room, listening to stories of my travels. As soon as the tether took hold, he started playing his games with her. Taking some sick satisfaction from knowing that every way he hurt her, he hurt me too.

Gwyn knew why the prince favored her more than the other Halflings, but she never held it against me. It was a kindness I couldn't ever repay.

Looking back at the beach, an idea struck me. The suns were past their midpoint in the sky, the shadows along the garden terrace had already begun to stretch. I would have to be quick to get it done before Gwyn met me for dinner.

I crossed through the garden and stepped onto the library terrace. Hidden in an alcove of the castle was a small door I knew the servants kept gardening equipment in. I needed a bucket. A big one.

What I found was even better. A rusted wheelbarrow. Old as it was, it would get the job done. I moved the host of rakes and hoes piled beside it and pulled it out of the small closet. It creaked when I wheeled it, but I threw a shovel into its basin anyway. I didn't care if I annoyed the servants.

I turned back around the corner onto the terrace, deftly navigating the wheelbarrow through the stone pillars. Just as I passed the last pillar, someone stepped out from behind it and slammed into me.

"I'm sorry," said a soft voice.

"For not having eyes?" I snapped. The blood drained from my face when I realized who it was.

Prince Killian grinned at me, his soft green eyes glimmering in the sunlight. He held a book in his hand.

"I apologize, Your Highness," I said with a quick bow. I pulled my hood back so he could see my face.

"It's *I* who should apologize," he said with a crooked grin. "I do have eyes. I should make it a habit of using them."

I froze, unsure of what to say.

"Keera, it's truly fine," he said, still smiling. "I'm actually glad I ran into you. I wanted to give you this." He pushed the book toward me.

"A book?" I asked. My brows crossed as I peered at the leather-bound cover. It was embossed with three golden leaves, their stems twisted together into one branch.

"It's a collection of historical essays," he explained, tracing the Elvish lettering along its spine. "It covers some Elvish history, some Fae. I thought it might be useful for you to read since you plan on spending time in the Faeland."

I took the book from his hands. It was heavier than I anticipated.

"Thank you, sire," I said, still surprised. "Though I'm not sure I will have much time for reading on my journey. Or if it will help."

Killian nodded, biting the inside of his cheek. "I haven't seen much of war or conflict for myself. Elverath's battles were won long before I was born, but I have made a point to learn about the wars of men—and Elves. Understanding one's enemy is key to defeating them. Perhaps it will help you defeat the Shadow."

I opened the book at its middle. An image of a Fae holding two babes at her breast was sketched into the paper. My fingers traced over her voluminous curls and strong chin. Her eyes were molten gold.

She was a Light Fae.

"Is that the key to preventing wars, then?" I said, my eyes still focused on the sketch. "Use knowledge of your enemy to defeat them before the battle even begins?"

Killian's lips twitched to one side as our eyes met. "That is one advantage," he said softly.

"And the other?" I asked, snapping the book shut.

"It can also help you realize if an enemy is truly your enemy at all," he said. His eyes bore into mine without blinking. I raised a brow, but he did not say anything else.

"How long do you plan to stay?" I asked, breaking our stare to place the book in the bag under my cloak.

Killian cleared his throat. "I leave for Volcar the day after tomorrow. I only returned at my father's request." He rubbed his neck, and I spotted a small ink stain on his sleeve. Killian was always in the library when at home. Reading most of the day, writing for the rest.

"I have stolen too much of your time already," he said with a small duck of his head. "I will let you get back to your work." He peered down at the wheelbarrow, a smile playing at his lips as he raised a brow back at me. It was amazing how similar his strong features were to his brother's yet the princes looked nothing alike.

"I'm fetching some sand," I said, gesturing to the wheelbarrow, feeling the need to explain myself.

"Sand?" He chewed his lip, but there was a lightness in his eyes that eased my shoulders.

"Yes." I nodded, unsure if I should elaborate.

The prince stepped back toward the library with a short laugh.

"We're all entitled to our secrets, Keera," he called over his shoulder, disappearing between the stacks of books and scrolls.

I had just finished the surprise when Gwyn walked in.

"What did you do?" she squealed, her hands covering her mouth as she danced back and forth on her tiptoes. She had done the same when she was a small child anytime I brought her something from my travels.

My entire bedchamber was lined with sand from the beach. I'd pushed the dresser into the bath, so nothing blocked the view of the sea along the long glass wall. Two towels were placed in front of it with a basket and pitcher of water.

"We're having a picnic on the beach," I said, unable to contain my smile. My chest was always lighter trying to bring some cheer to Gwyn's day.

Her eyes were wide as she stepped out of her slippers. She walked toward the makeshift beach, stopping at its edge. She held her foot out for a moment, suspended over the sand, slowly lowering her toes onto the beach. A giggle broke from her lips, and she scrunched her feet into the sand, swinging her hips back and forth.

"It feels glorious!" she said before running across the room and jumping on top of me. I almost fell onto the basket before I could steady myself. "Thank you so much, Keera." She laughed as I twirled her around. I would bring barrows of sand to her every day if it meant her laughs would never dwindle.

"I'm glad you like it," I said, sitting down on one of the towels. Gwyn continued to walk along the room, twirling and playing in the sand. It reminded me of when she'd followed her mother around the castle as she did her chores, dancing and laughing from dawn to dusk.

"Look under your pillow," I told her when she finally sat down on her towel.

She pulled out a parcel sealed with a fine ribbon. The outline of two crossed sheaves of wheat was pressed into the wax, the symbol of the House of Harvest.

"What is it?" she asked in her usual way.

I raised a brow and shook my head. "You have to open it, Gwyn," I said, refusing to let our script drop.

She giggled as she pulled off the seal and opened the box. Inside was a glass bottle of perfume. The flute was made of gold and encrusted with a small ruby on top. The red reminded me of her hair.

"I love it," she said, studying the blue liquid swirling in the glass. "But what is it?"

I laughed. "Perfume," I said, "the fancy kind that ladies wear. I bought it because I thought it smelled like Volcar when it snows."

Gwyn spritzed some on her wrist and sniffed. "This is what snow smells like?" she asked, her eyes as round as her open mouth. She closed them, and I knew she was picturing the snowcapped volcanic city I had described to her so many times before.

"It must be beautiful," she said, taking another whiff of her wrist. "Something this lovely has to be."

"It certainly can be," I said, leaning back into the sand on my elbows. "But it can also be vicious when a storm hits. Deadly."

"Kind of like you," Gwyn said, spritzing me with the bottle. I waved my hands in front of my face as I laughed. The scent wafted around the room, filling our nostrils with snow as our toes dug into the sand.

We lounged for hours as we ate the picnic dinner I'd nicked from the kitchens. Gwyn had me tell her more about Volcar and its large snowcapped mountain that could erupt into a firestorm of coal and ash. Gwyn loved hearing my stories, and I never grew tired of telling her them. She didn't care about the missions or the people I hunted. She only ever asked about the cities. The trees. The way people spoke or laughed. What they ate. There had been many nights when I was alone, cold and miserable, that I thought of Gwyn and how amazed she would be to see even the most ordinary view. It helped me remember there were those who did with much less than me. People who would suffer if I didn't return with my mission completed.

"How long do you think you'll be gone this time?" Gwyn asked, plopping a chocolate-covered berry into her mouth.

I shrugged. "I don't know. Months. Maybe longer." Even at full haste it would take three weeks to reach Aralinth.

"Do you think you'll kill him? The Shadow?" She licked the chocolate off her lips.

"I don't have a choice." My shoulders sagged as I let out a breath.

"That's too bad. I kind of liked knowing there was someone out there working against the king," she said, pressing her toes against the cool glass.

"Gwyn, you can't say such things," I whispered harshly. Anyone could be listening to us in the capital.

"I would never say that to anyone but you," she said in a quieter voice. "Can you blame me, Keera, for wishing him dead?" Her mouth was set in an unnatural straight line.

I shook my head. The king's death meant her freedom. I couldn't begrudge Gwyn for wishing for such a thing, even though it was a foolish dream.

"You need to be careful." I grabbed her hand. She squeezed mine back and lay down with her head in my lap. I tucked a stray curl behind her ear and stroked her hair. She closed her eyes, the dark circles under them almost disappeared in the cool moonlight. At nineteen she already looked older than I did, fine lines marking her forehead like the callouses on her palms. Gwyn's blood was amber, though she was mostly Mortal. I doubted she would live any longer than the average woman. Perhaps even less depending on how the prince kept tormenting her.

My body felt heavy and hollow at the thought of her short life of servitude. I'd been alive for more than six decades. I'd lost people before, watched Mortals and Halflings younger than me grow old while I aged so slowly that I seemed not to age at all. Each death slashed through a heartstring, leaving a brutal hole that would never be filled. It didn't make it easier to lose someone, only harder to bring myself to care again. After Gwyn, I doubted I would be able to care at all. If my heart didn't stop beating altogether, it would be ruined for all else.

"Keera," Gwyn said, her eyes fluttering open and focusing on the crash of the waves. I stopped stroking her hair. "You need to be careful too."

I swallowed. "I will."

"Good." She grabbed my hand, holding it against her shoulder as she smiled. "I can't have you dying before you bring me a gift from Aralinth."

CHAPTER ELEVEN

I WAS AT THE ORDER. I could smell the salt rising from the waves in wafts of mist.

Crash. Quiet. Crash. Quiet. Crash.

It was the melody I'd fallen asleep to those first decades of my life. No matter how tired or angry I was, the waves could always rock me to sleep.

But I wasn't sleeping now. I was walking along the cliff's edge, the Order towering above me, brilliantly white as the suns bore down upon it. It was a hot, midsummer day. I was stopped, cooling off in the spray blowing along the cliff's edge. I peered down below where jagged rocks cut through the water and into the air like arrows cast through their target.

One wrong step and I would fall to be skewered by their pointed edges or crushed under the weight of the sea.

Crash. Quiet. Crash. Quiet. Crash.

It was like a siren's song luring me into the depths. Daring me to jump.

"Keera, you can't," a voice called from behind me.

I turned and she was standing there. Dressed as she always was. Black pants and a sleeveless top of the same color. The uniform of an initiate.

She had never received her hood.

"The waves are calling to me," I whispered. "I want to jump."

"You can't, Keera," she repeated.

"Why?"

"You promised," she said simply. Her blond hair was down, strands of it blowing across her face in the wind. She was just as beautiful as always.

"I tried," I choked, falling to my knees. "You have no idea how many times I tried. I can't do it alone," I whispered.

"But, Keera," she said, taking a step toward me. She held my head in her hands, but I couldn't feel them. "You don't have to be alone."

A tear rolled down her cheek. I stood up and wiped it away with a gentle caress of my thumb.

"You're not here." The words clanged against the dark pit inside me. "I have no one."

"You promised," she said, taking a step back. "You have more than your ghosts, Keera."

She dashed past me before I realized what she intended. Before I could reach out and stop her.

I watched as she ran toward the cliff's edge, leaping into the air knowing there was nothing to land on, nothing to catch her. Knowing that I wouldn't reach her in time.

I reached out anyway, my heart pulling itself from my chest, as I watched her fall toward the rocky chasm below.

I screamed her name.

And then I woke.

The dreams plagued my journey across Elverath. It had been so long since I'd dreamed at all. I'd spent years falling asleep in a drunken oblivion that kept the dreams at bay. Now, they'd returned with a vengeance that woke me each night, ragged and sweating.

The elixir Hildegard had given me was working. My throat still burned each morning, craving the taste of wine, but with the *winvra* it was manageable. My stomach didn't churn anymore, happy to have something other than alcohol run down my throat. I could feel the strength in my limbs returning. My body didn't ache from the days on horseback. The dark circles that had lined my eyes were fading too.

I hadn't realized how weak I'd become. No wonder the Shadow had bested me. Thoughts of him plagued me too as I rode from Silstra to Caerth. Every night, I would lie next to a fire nestled into a hillside, staring up at the sky. I didn't notice the moons or the stars. All I could see was the Shadow. His tall frame towering above me, his lips on mine.

I replayed that scene in my head over and over. Trying to understand why he hadn't killed me. He had been so close, yet I was alive. The ghost of his lips burned my skin everywhere he had touched me, haunting me each night.

Why had he kissed me? It didn't make sense. And the current that flooded my body the moment his lips touched mine . . . I knew he had felt it too. No matter how many times I replayed the night, I was only left with more questions and no answers.

Maybe when I unmasked the Shadow and removed his head from his neck, I would finally get the answers I needed.

I smelled Caerth before I reached it. The scent of *winvra* and smoke wafted over the hillside and blew through my clothes. The fields of wheat I'd been riding through for days faded into bountiful orchards and farmhouses that got larger and grander with every step toward the small city.

Mobs of peasants lined the outer city, crumpled in the dirt with bowls sitting in front of their withering bodies. Most of them were old, their bodies broken from decades of labor in the field. The younger ones were missing limbs. The ones who could walk did so with the help of canes.

I tapped my horse and sent him into a canter. I didn't want to look at people I couldn't help. My black cloak choked me as I rode into the city, the silver sword leaving its imprint along my neck. There was a Shade waiting for me at my usual inn. Her dark hood was pulled forward, her hips flanked by two long blades. Every passerby gave her a wide birth as they walked along the street. My eyes scanned the road; I didn't see her partner. She must've been fetching supplies in one of the nearby shops.

"Mistress," she said with a bow as I jumped off my horse.

"A message?" I asked, holding out my hand. It was the only reason Shades were ever waiting for me.

She pulled a thin envelope from her bag. "The bird was sent to Cereliath since there are no Shades posted here. If you have nothing for us in return, we will start back to Cereliath immediately."

I tore the seal of the letter and recognized the thin script as Hildegard's. At the bottom of the parchment was a stamp of a bow. I read through the letter twice before answering the Shade. The Shadow had struck in Volcar. He stole two transports of grain and set fire to a farmhouse full of Halflings. The king and Prince Damien would stay in Koratha until the Shadow was vanquished.

"Did any of the Halflings survive?" I asked the Shade.

She shook her head. "They used an accelerant. The entire house was turned to ash within an hour."

"When did this happen?" I asked, crumpling the letter in my hands.

"The night before you left the capital. We are to return to Cereliath and leave with the Shades posted there for Volcar immediately," she said as her partner appeared beside her. The second Shade bowed but remained silent.

"Very well," I said quietly. "When you reach Cereliath, send a bird to Hildegard. Let her know that I will still travel into the Faeland. If I don't find anything, I'll take the southern pass and meet you all in Volcar."

They nodded and left without another word.

I tied my horse to a post and carried my bags inside the inn. I laid some coin on the desk in front of the innkeeper. He was a middle-aged man, short enough that I could see where his hair had thinned to nothing on his scalp.

"The same room as last time?" he croaked, eyeing the silver sword at my neck. He swallowed hard as he swiped the coins from the desk.

I cut across the hall and marched up the stairs, ignoring the scent of fresh wine and cooked meat drifting from the kitchens. I pulled out the vial and placed a single drop of black liquid on my tongue before my throat could even begin to burn. I had better things to be thinking of than wine.

Like the Shadow and where he had really taken those Halflings.

I didn't know much about the Shadow, but I knew enough to know that he hadn't murdered twelve Halflings in their sleep. If there was no sign of them left, it was because they were no longer there.

They weren't dead, but free.

The real question was why create the scene at all? I thought about what the Shades had said. They would make haste for Volcar. I wondered how many Shades Hildegard had reassigned to the western city. The entire weight of the Order coming to search for the Shadow.

I threw the letter into the hearth and watched it burn.

They wouldn't find the Shadow in Volcar. In all the months he had been working against the Crown, he had never left a trace. Sometimes it was days before his thefts were discovered, and even then, the only thing that tied him to it were the whispers of his name in alleys and taverns nearby. He had never made a spectacle of himself. Not once.

This wasn't a show of strength. It was a diversion.

The Shadow wanted our eyes on Volcar so he could wreak havoc someplace else. I needed to discover where that someplace was before he laid another attack against the king. My hands gripped the mantel of the fireplace as I watched the flames dance among the logs.

Until now, the Shadow had always been one step ahead. I'd trailed his movements across the kingdom, collecting bits of information long after he had walked back into the shadows, and waited for him to reappear to start my search again.

I smirked at the flames. That had been good enough when I spent my nights drowning in wine. Now, I had all the time in the world to ruminate on the Shadow's plans. For the first time, I felt like *I* was leading the dance between us.

I didn't know if the Shadow would be waiting for me in Aralinth, but I was confident he didn't want me there.

All the more reason to go.

There was only one northern pass into the Faeland. It cut through the Burning Mountains, the range that split the Faeland from the rest of the kingdom. I restocked my stores in Caerth and rode toward the foothills at first light. White clouds covered the peaks, blending into the snow that already began to pile among the highest mountains.

Thankfully, Wiseman's Way weaved through the cliffs, avoiding any elevation too high to pull a trading cart through. Even with the flat ground, it took days to cross the mountains. The first three were easy rides, the even fields outside Caerth gave way to the thick forest that lined the base of the range. The tallest of the trees were an ancient kind of birch. Their white trunks only grew close to the Faeland. The nearby peasants said their roots needed magic to survive.

From afar, the forest looked like it was consumed in flame as the blazing leaves fluttered in the wind. The sight is what gave the mountains their name, but inside the forest, the trees didn't look like fire. Instead, their crimson leaves reminded me of blood. Dark red veins lined the rounded leaves that fell onto the trail. In the sunlight, some of them even looked amber. It sent a chill down my spine.

I knew when I reached the midway point through the mountains because the forest changed. The tall birches still grew, but their trunks were larger, wider than my horse. Their branches weaved together in a canopy of gold instead of red. The underbrush changed too. Plants of every size and color sprouted between the birches. Trees that only existed in the Faeland shot through the brush, some of their trunks twisted together in an everlasting embrace.

The forest was rich with magic. I had officially crossed into the Faeland.

My twin blades were holstered at the side of my horse rather than my back. I wore my bow and quiver instead, readying it each time I heard a noise. I wasn't worried about running into Fae this far from Aralinth, but there were creatures in this wood that did not exist in the kingdom. Magical beings that walked unseen among the forest, their skin changing to match the fronds and thicket. If the stories were to be believed, some could even shift their skins altogether.

Changing into deer or foxes, luring a horse into a false sense of security only to rip its neck open as soon as night fell.

I couldn't sleep well in the forest. My skin crawled with every touch of breeze, sensing something in the air that barely existed in the kingdom. Magic. It was palpable. I could taste the tang of it on my lips. Even my horse grew unsteady at night. His ears flicked back and forth, listening to whatever lurked in the dark.

I would lie awake for hours next to the fire. Whatever sleep I did manage was chased away by my nightmares. They were getting worse. I didn't know if that was because I hadn't touched a drink in a month or because the magic set me on edge.

The book Prince Killian had given me turned out to be a good distraction. I was slow reading the Elvish scroll but found the words interesting enough. Some of the stories were ones I'd heard before: Elvish accounts of the Blood Wars, King Aemon's descent into Elverath and the destruction he had caused the Elves who lived there. The essays lacked the royal ministrations of the history I had learned. I recognized the king that existed in those pages, a brutal man with a hunger for power. So different than the version that was told across the kingdom. Of a man who sought to purify the lands from all abomination. Elves and Halflings alike.

Is that what the prince wanted me to realize? That the Fae—and the Elves they hid—had good reason to move against the king? I'd never doubted their distaste for the Crown. In fact, I shared it. But they got to live their lives almost entirely free of the king's influence. They were not chained to serve the throne. Forced to work fields to feed Mortals and fill their coffers. Forced to hunt their own to please a conqueror.

No, that was the reality they had left to the Halflings. As much as the king abused us, the Fae had let it happen. They had taken their fraction of the lands they once ruled and left the Halflings behind. I wasn't empathetic to their struggles against the Crown. From where I stood, they had won.

My sixth night in the mountains was longer than any other. Only one moon shone in the sky, casting a dim light over the trees that played tricks with my eyes. The wind whispered through the leaves loud enough that my arm flinched against my dagger with every snap of a twig. I wanted a drink to numb my fears and lull me into a deep, dreamless sleep.

But that was all. Wanted. My throat didn't burn with yearning for a taste of wine. My brow had not sweat in days. Even thinking about the sweet scent of fresh wine did not ignite a craving. I let out a deep breath. A rogue piece of burnt wood turned orange against my exhale, rolling back into the fire.

My hand held the vial of *winvra* elixir, the liquid over halfway gone. I swirled it in the glass, lit by the flames dancing beside me. I realized it wasn't black but a deep violet that clung to the sides of the vial. I put it back in my pocket without taking any. Better to save it for when the cravings returned.

I tossed all night with little sleep. I saddled my horse hours before dawn, not that he minded. I could tell by the uneven speed of his gait that he wanted out of the Burning Wood as much as I did. Hours later, the suns rose over the tree line. We were far enough from the mountains that I could see the sunlight climbing over the forest and up the peaks behind me. In the morning light, it looked as if the mountains themselves were dipped in gold.

I thought of the king and knew if he ever beheld such a sight, he would see peaks gilded just for him. No wonder the Fae were so protective of their land; its beauty was unmatched by all the rest of Elverath.

I turned back around and saw that my horse had broken over a hillside. Nested in a valley below was Aralinth. Its gold-capped palace sat at the center of its city. An Elder birch bigger than any that grew in the forest. Its trunk stood as tall as the king's palace and its branches scraped the sky with blades of gold.

It was a sight no one in the kingdom had ever seen and returned to tell tales of its grandeur.

I would be the first.

CHAPTER TWELVE

FEW PEOPLE STARED as I rode into the city. My cloak and pin were packed away in my bags, replaced by the simple garb of a traveler.

My charcoal cloak trailed behind my horse as I rode into the city. The houses were built of stone, some of them attached, some large enough to fill with many families. Like the Fae-built cities in the kingdom, Aralinth was built as a circle. Straight lanes that led to the city palace were intersected by curving alleys.

It was easy to notice at the edge of the city with so few people walking along the streets. Most of the houses sat empty, still brilliant and white, with large drapes hanging over furniture. Some were completely vacant like they'd never been lived in at all.

The city was only a fraction of what it once was. I wandered along until the houses grew smaller and people filled the streets. A cascade of florals poured down from the roofs as I searched for an inn. Their vines tangled together in large twists, scaling up the white walls, connecting each dwelling in a canopy of fresh blooms.

I took a deep breath of the scent. The air felt lighter in my lungs, tasted better than any garden in the kingdom. I came across a small inn with a dark blue rose hanging above its door. The sign was painted just like the blooms that blanketed the streets. The sweet scent of dew hung from their petals.

Dew roses. A blossom that only grew within the magical cities of the Fae.

I tied my horse out front and opened the door. My mouth watered at the smells that filled the room. Lush spices, salt, and cooked meat. My stomach growled loudly.

"Sounds like someone's hungry," a voice called in Elvish from a nearby room. I turned and lowered my hood.

I nodded to the young innkeeper standing before me. Or at least she looked young. There were no lines around her dark eyes, her brown skin plump and dewy. She was an Elf. I doubted she'd be the only one I'd meet in the Faeland. I never believed the king had killed all the Elves. And seven hundred years was a long time. How many Elves had survived only to have families of their own hidden in the Faeland?

Perhaps the Shadow was one of them.

"We just pulled a deer roast out of the oven," she said, her brows knitting together as she studied my face. "Do you want some?" she asked.

"Yes, I am very hungry," I said in broken Elvish. In truth, my Elvish was impeccable, but I needed to play the part of newcomer escapee.

Her brow split open with wide eyes as she caught my accent. I tucked a piece of hair behind my ear, making sure she saw the sharp point.

"I'll be right back," she said, switching to the King's Tongue.

I dropped myself into one of the cushioned chairs. There was no one seated in the dining room, but I could hear laughter erupting from the kitchens. Moments later, she returned with a steaming plate of meat and vegetables. I thanked her and dove into the meal. It had been a week since I dined in Caerth, and that food had not been half as tasty.

"Wine?" she asked after I cleaned my plate. Her long, dark hair was kept back in twists. She pushed them over her shoulder as she held a flagon of wine. I placed a hand over my goblet and shook my head, mouth full of food. She smiled and walked back over to the front desk.

I drank some of the water she'd brought with the meal and watched as people passed the windows. Most of them were Elves, which was against the treaty, but nothing less than I expected. Or the king for that matter. I doubted he cared how many Elves hid in the Faeland as long as their numbers were too diminished to pose a threat. From what I had seen of the city so far, Aralinth barely had enough to fill its market, let alone an army.

The door opened again, and a tall figure stepped through the frame. I couldn't see their face but noticed their pointed ears protruding from brown waves. Intricate little braids lay over their mane like lace. They exchanged quick words with the Elf at the desk and dropped something on it before exiting out the front door, never turning toward me.

The innkeeper stared at the desk with wide eyes. I swallowed a gulp of water just as her gaze cut to me. I put the goblet down on the table and slowly lifted my hand to the dagger at my hip. I recognized the cautious look in her eyes, the stilted gait as she walked over to the table.

I'd been made.

"This is for you," she said, all the warmness in her voice had disappeared. She dropped the letter onto my plate and shuffled back to the kitchens. I turned the thick parchment over and studied the wax seal. It was a perfect violet circle. In the middle was the imprint of an Elder birch leaf lined in gold.

I swallowed a breath before I opened it. There was only one place the letter could have come from.

I lifted the seal and pulled a thick piece of paper out from the envelope. The scroll was intricate and detailed. Swirls of ink formed a single name at the top of the page.

Keera.

Fuck.

The Fae had known I was here the moment I'd arrived in Aralinth. Perhaps the moment I'd arrived in the Faeland. Why was I not surrounded by guards bringing me to the palace? I had broken the treaty coming into their lands without permission. The king's protection only went so far. If they wanted to kill me, there was no one to stop them. No one would come to avenge my death either.

My eyes scanned the rest of the page; it shook in my hands.

It was an invitation.

Lord Feron invites you to dine at Sil'abar.

I was to arrive at the palace the next day dressed for a ball. Lord Feron had thwarted my plan to stay hidden with the stroke of a pen.

I could no longer hide from the Dark Fae; I would have to dance with them instead.

Since my arrival in Aralinth was no longer a secret, I didn't see the point in staying at the small inn. Not that the innkeeper would have let me. She didn't come back out of the kitchen to collect her coin for the meal. I left it on the table instead.

If the Dark Fae knew I was in town, I might as well rent the most luxurious suite available.

The inn was tucked beside a lavish garden at the center of the city. I chose it for the gilded balconies that had a direct view to Sil'abar, the tree palace. The inn had an Old Elvish name I didn't know how to read let alone pronounce, but I sauntered through the front entryway and tossed a heavy bag of gold on the counter.

The servant behind the desk flinched, staring at the pouch. I noticed the blunt curve of his ear. The stitching was bumpy and uneven. A botched attempt at curbing the Halfling's ears. So the Fae were hiding Halflings in their lands as well.

My eyes lingered over his tall frame and blond hair. His back was straight. The skin at his neck and wrists was unmarked. No scars from beatings or restraints.

I rented the suite on the top floor. It had a long balcony that stretched across the entire front of the building. If the Fae wanted to watch me, I would watch them too. A lush bouquet of dew roses sat on the table in the sitting room. I picked out one of the flowers and inhaled its fresh scent as the Halfling placed my bags in the bedroom.

"How long have you been in the Faeland?" I asked him, twirling the flower under my nose.

He stiffened. I could hear his breath stop.

"I'm not going to report you," I said, scenting his panic. "I don't care. I just want to know if you came here willingly or if you were forced into these lands." I tucked the flower behind my ear and leaned on the table.

He jerked his head. "You think Lord Feron shackles Halflings like the king?"

I gripped the edge of the table, drumming my fingers along the thick wood. "I take it from your answer that he does not."

"No," he said, walking toward the door. I thought that was all he would say but his hand hovered over the handle. "Lord Feron treats all Halflings with respect. We're not servants here."

"*All* Halflings?" I said, raising a brow. How many had taken refuge in the Faeland?

He smirked to one side. "Welcome to Aralinth," he said, closing the large door behind him.

I went out in search of a tailor. Since my plan had rested on staying out of sight from the Fae, I had not brought anything fine enough to dine with Lord Feron. I stalked the streets in my familiar black garb.

The main business district was west of the palace, a few streets over from my inn. The laneways were full of people, but they parted quickly as I walked between the rows of shops. Everyone stopped to stare at the black hood and cloak. Some pointed at the silver fastener and whispered into their neighbor's ear.

Despite the caution, no one barred me from entering any establishment. I perused a large apothecary where herbs hung from the windows as elixirs brewed over the hearth. I showed the owner the contents of the elixir Hildegard had given me. She gasped as she placed the vial in her hand, holding it like the slightest touch might break it.

"I have a vial or two," she said in Elvish. "Though it will cost you."

I pulled my bag forward, ready to pay whatever she needed. I left the shop lighter than before, the second vial of *winvra* elixir safely tucked into my pocket.

The shops reminded me of Cereliath. Each one was connected in a row, carved out of a giant gray stone that lined the street. Its twin stood on the other side, housing another row of shops. I assumed the roofs were made of stone as well, but I couldn't tell. The canopy of blooms that hung along the streets continued inside. Long vines twisted along the walls, flowers sprouting wherever sunlight touched the stone.

Aralinth was called the city of roses. Its magic held the land in a perpetual spring. The flowers had millennia to sprawl across the city, their blooms never withered.

The third shop I visited was a tailor. I eyed the beautiful robes in the window. Gowns of fine silk and rich colors hung on mannequins made from petals. The skirts were long layers of sheer fabric that turned into tight twists along the bodice in the shape of leaves or waves. Sheer sleeves cascaded from their beaded necklines, so long they almost skimmed the floor.

I bit my lip. Neither would hide my scars.

It was hard to dress as an assassin. Not only did I need to hide the names written on my skin, but the dress had to conceal at least three weapons and still look fantastic. I had already been caught off guard by Lord Feron; I was not going to show up outdressed.

"Do you need help finding anything?" a voice called from across the shop. I turned to see the tailor carrying a young child on her hip. Her ears were long and pointed but the child's ears were slightly rounded. A Halfling born and raised in the Faeland.

"Do you do custom orders?" I asked, crossing the room in three strides.

Her dark eyes squinted, trying to glimpse my face under the hood. "Yes," she said slowly. "When do you need it by."

"Tomorrow," I answered. She caught the pouch of gold I threw at her with a flash of her arm and nodded.

CHAPTER THIRTEEN

I SHOULDN'T HAVE BEEN SURPRISED when a carriage appeared outside the inn to collect me. Two black horses pulled the ornate carriage, steered by a coachman. My eyes lingered on his long, rounded ears and red hair. He gave a tight smile and opened the door. After only one night in Aralinth, it was evident that more Halflings lived in the city than Fae or Elves. Far more than I ever imagined would dare to cross the mountains. Or have the chance to try.

It set me on edge.

I wanted as many Halflings safe from the king as possible. If they found solace in the Faeland, I wouldn't expose them. Even if it was against the treaty. My stomach churned. The only reason the Dark Fae wouldn't care about the Blade seeing how flagrantly they broke the treaty was if they didn't plan on me returning at all.

They had me trapped.

I slipped into the coach and watched as Aralinth passed by the windows. I was still amazed by the flower canopy and trees that grew all over the city. The blooms seemed to embrace the buildings, plants growing up walls and over rooftops, building cascades of flowering vines and branches.

It was as if the city itself were alive.

The palace was just as beautiful. *Sil'abar*—the White Tree—the invitation had called it. The white trunk stood as wide as the king's palace, thick bark serving as the palace walls. Its branches stretched over half the city. Golden leaves fluttered above as large as houses. It was an Elder birch, just like the ones that grew in the Burning Mountains. Their giant twin.

The carriage came to a halt at the end of the stone drive. The Halfling jumped off and opened the door without looking at me. I stepped down, staring at the entrance in awe. Two guards stood on either side. There were no doors for them to open. Instead, the living wood split, leaving a wide crack at the base of the tree. The guards did not try to stop me as I walked past, though their eyes tracked each step.

There were no windows in the palace; warm orbs of light lit my path. *Faelight*. Magical balls of sunlight that hovered in the air, casting rays against the grain of the walls and floor. I reached out to touch one, but it floated away, as if caught on a breeze. The faelights led to the end of the hallway where two more guards were standing. This time they flanked a set of grand doors carved with three Elder birch leaves, their stems woven together.

The guards opened the doors, each pulling one forward with two hands. The gust of air blew against my skirts, carrying a whirl of voices from the room. "Lord Feron is expecting you," one of the guards said, his arm pointing toward the railing of the landing.

I nodded and straightened my back. I savored a deep breath and couldn't help but wonder if it was my last. Perhaps I would walk down those steps and the Fae guards would descend upon me. The daggers I had holstered to my thighs would do little against them.

If I died, at least it would be quick.

I stepped out onto the landing; the large doors groaned behind me as they closed. I took another step and stood at the top of a staircase. Everyone in the room below turned at the same time, their eyes watching me as I descended. My hands clenched around the layers and layers of sheer fabric that made my skirt. Each one was dyed a different color—blues, grays, and violets—but piled together my dress was as dark as nightshade. The tiny faebeads stitched into each layer glowed liked stars in the night sky.

The tailor had made my garment just as I'd envisioned it. Its long sleeves accentuated the length of my arms. The high neck split down the middle of the bodice in a thin line of skin that trailed to my navel. It didn't show much, but it emphasized the toned contours of my stomach that had returned after weeks without a drink.

My favorite piece was the crown veil. It curved around my forehead in twisted vines covered in gold thorns. Ribbons of black cascaded from the thorns, covering my hair in a long braid. Dew roses I'd picked from a nearby garden were placed between the strands of silk-covered hair, completely hiding my natural color. A large stripe of black ink cut across my face, covering my cheeks and brows.

I'd be remembered. But anyone here would have trouble recognizing me when the night was over.

I took the final step, landing on the ballroom floor. Some still watched me, but many of the Fae had turned away. Their violet eyes finding interest somewhere else. I craned my neck as I searched the room. No windows to escape from, only one set of doors that were too big to slip away unnoticed. I would have to leave the same way I came. If I left at all.

A tall Fae approached me. He was dressed in a light blue robe. The silk sash tied at his waist held a silver scabbard. The faelight shone along his deep skin like moonlight across the night sky. A deceivingly youthful glow. His hair, set in long twists down his back, did not contain a single gray hair. His most striking feature was the one that marked all Dark Fae—his violet eyes. They were shaded by his own ink mask, but where mine was black, his was a vibrant shade of gold.

He gave me a slight nod. I returned it with a small bow.

"Lord Feron, I presume?" I said with a small smile. My hand instinctively grabbed for a weapon, but they were covered in sheets of tulle.

He nodded with a wide smile. "I am honored to be dining with Aemon's Blade. Welcome, Keera Kingsown."

"I'm honored to be here as well, Lord Feron," I answered back. "But you may call me Keera." My ears would chafe if I had to hear my title at the turn of every conversation. Or that godsdamned last name.

"Only if you call me Feron," he said with a soft chuckle. My brows raised before I could stop them. I could never imagine the lords of Elverath so easily discarding their titles. "Would you like some wine?" Feron pointed to a servant carrying a tray of fine glass goblets.

I stilled. The rich scent wafted over to us; my throat itched. "Perhaps with dinner," I said.

"Very well." Feron took a goblet for himself. "Let me introduce you to our guests."

The next hour passed in a blur of faces. Some Fae, some Elves, most Halflings. All wore tight smiles as they asked about the kingdom and the king. I evaded most questions easily. No one seemed truly concerned about what was happening in Elverath. As if the people on the other side of the Burning Mountains did not even exist.

I took a sip from the glass of water Feron had fetched me. He interacted with everyone with a wide smile and open arms. He was never rushed, meandering from one group to the next with me on his arm. He asked after their families, their friends, as if he knew them. He even referred to his servants by name.

I stood, holding the glass in front of my lips, studying him. I couldn't imagine the king behaving so warmly at court. I tried to find a crack in his mask, a pinched brow or tense neck, but there was nothing. Feron was completely at ease.

Unlike me.

"You are quieter than I expected," Feron said as the last group of people crossed the room in search of refills of their wine.

"I've never been to the Faeland before. As you know," I added, raising a brow. "I thought it best to observe."

Feron tilted his head to the side, smiling down at me. "And have your observations met your expectations?"

I tensed, unsure how to answer his question.

"I expected you to put a knife in my head," I said honestly.

Feron's eyes widened. A cool silence settled between us, hanging in the air. I stood tall, refusing to blink until Feron broke into a fit of laughter.

"Keera, we may be old," he said, clapping his hands, "but we have not resorted to killing dinner guests for entertainment just yet." He smiled so wide two dimples appeared on each of his cheeks.

A wave of heat washed over my skin. I smiled, hoping he couldn't see it in my face. "So the killing will come after dinner, then?" I pushed, placing my water glass on a passing tray.

Feron's laugh stopped in his throat. His full lips were set in a straight line as he addressed me. "If I wanted you dead, Keera, you never would have set foot in this city." A shiver ran down my spine as his violet eyes pierced through me. "I have no plans to kill you.

Tonight, or tomorrow. I expect the same of you," he said, his eyes flickering to my skirts. My skin crawled against the concealed blades along my thigh.

I swallowed a thick gulp of air.

"You break the treaty so freely and I'm to think you'll allow me to leave? To tell the king?" I crossed my arms and hoped I looked more dangerous than I felt.

"If anyone has broken the treaty, it is you," Feron said, crossing his thick arms to match my stance.

I ignored his point.

"The Fae are meant to turn any Halflings over to the Crown," I pushed.

Feron's lips twitched. "You expect me to kill you because you have met my citizens?"

"Halflings are owned by the king," I said automatically. The moment the words left my lips the names on my skin seared under my dress.

Feron lifted his chin as his brows pinched along his wide nose. "Then let the king collect them." The cheery lilt in his voice was gone. His tone was nothing but serious.

I blinked twice. "You *want* me to tell the king?" The blood drained from my face.

Feron let me stew, taking a sip of his wine. "No, I do not," he said. "But it does not matter if you do. The king will not cross into the Faeland."

"The king is a proud man," I said before I could stop myself.

Feron smirked. "I am aware of Aemon's pride. But let me ask you this, Keera. Has the king ever been concerned about Halflings coming to hide in the Faeland?"

I shook my head.

"I am not surprised. I am sure it is more than the king led you to believe. But the truth is that Aemon is fully aware Halflings live freely in these lands. Just as I am fully aware that he will not take the trouble to claim them as long as I do not expose his secret." He gulped back the last of his drink and placed it gently on a table beside him. The green gemstone hugging his fingers reflected faelight across my face.

"Why tell me this?" I asked, thoughts swirling in my head. What kind of game was Feron playing?

He offered me his arm and I took it cautiously. "I am not playing a game, Keera," he said with a sideways glance as we walked toward the tall doors across the room. "I only think it is fair that you know as much as the man who claims to own you."

His words shook through my body and left me feeling cold and empty. I didn't like the way his violet eyes trailed over me, like he was reading the run of thoughts inside my head. Using his magic on me. The floor spun under me; my head felt faint.

"Keera?" Feron grabbed my elbow sensing the spike of my heartbeat.

"Is there a room where I could freshen up?" I asked, holding my stomach.

"Of course." Feron nodded. He walked me to a wall that looked like the ribbed edges of a tree. No door. No opening to walk through. I turned back toward him just as his arm stretched out, placing a palm against the grain.

My skin prickled, something in the air shifted. The next moment, the wall split open. A dark hallway waiting on the other side.

Feron reached out and grabbed one of the faelights. "This will lead you there," he said, blowing it away like a dandelion seed. It hovered through the hole and stopped, as if waiting for me to follow. I stepped across the bent wood and let the light lead me to a room in the heart of the tree palace.

The faelight led me to a grand room with a privy and bath. Water cascaded down one wall, pooling at a groove in the floor before draining through a thin line in the wood. Flower petals swirled in the running water, almost sparkling in the light from the orb. Now that I was alone, I could hear the low hum of the walls. Too faint for any Mortal to hear, but it was there. Like the steady pump of a heart through every part of the palace.

Sil'abar wasn't just a palace. It was alive.

I dampened a cloth in the waterfall and cooled the skin along my chest. I was a fool to let myself be so rattled in front of an enemy. But was that even what Feron was? He had not attacked me even when he knew I was in his city. He had not called his guards on me for the blades hidden in my dress.

He was the king's enemy, but did that make him mine?

I stepped back into the hall, trailing after the soft faelight. My skirt caught on a bent root sticking out of the ground. I pulled at it once, launching myself forward as it gave way. I bounced off something hard and fell to the ground. The heavy skirt made it too hard to balance.

"I thought the king's Blade would have better reflexes than that." A figure towered in front of me. Three faelights swirled above his head, drenching the hall in warm sunlight. I looked up and saw a pair of dark violet eyes watching me. He was tall, even for a Fae, his face partly hidden in the sheet of black hair that fell past his chest.

"I was distracted," I said, a moment too late. The Fae didn't say anything but crossed his arms, the soft light emphasizing the warmth of his golden-brown skin. I helped myself up, smoothing my skirts with my hands. He didn't move, even though he was close enough for me to smell the hints of birchwood and dew wafting off his skin.

"What are you planning to spy on in an empty hallway?" he asked, raising a thick brow. His lip snarled as he leaned over to peer behind me.

"I wasn't spying," I said, crossing my own arms. "Lord Feron knows where I am. I doubt there's anywhere in the city he can't track me."

His eyes snapped back to me. "True, but I doubt you care."

Who was this prick?

I shook my head and tried to step around him. He held his stance for a moment, but I didn't waver. I just stared back at him, studying the sharp angles of his face, until he leaned into the wall and let me pass.

"Just so you know," he called after me, "not all of us are as welcoming as Feron. Don't get caught in places you shouldn't be again."

CHAPTER FOURTEEN

I stepped back into the ballroom as the tall doors opened and we were corralled into a dining room. A long wooden table stood in the middle of the space; its legs sprouted from the floor like roots. The top was decorated with dozens of bouquets of dew roses surrounded by tiny orbs of light.

"Feron has requested that you sit with him," a Halfling reported as soon as I stepped into the dining hall. I followed her to the end of the table where an empty seat sat on Feron's left.

"I hope you do not mind having your meal with me," Feron said. He pulled the chair back with one hand and gestured for me to sit.

"The honor is mine, my lord," I said respectfully. I glanced down the table looking for the angry Fae I had crossed in the hall, but he wasn't seated. My gaze was pulled away as the most glorious music started playing behind Feron's chair. A group of Elves and Halflings were holding instruments I'd never seen. Some strummed golden strings that glowed as they played. Others blew into tiny flutes that sung angelic melodies. I couldn't keep my eyes away.

"You enjoy our music, Keera?" Feron asked, taking a bite of grilled fish.

"It has a kind of beauty that cannot be replicated," I said honestly.

I glanced across the table where the chair to the lord's right sat empty. "Are you expecting someone else?"

"Ah, Riven. He is attending to something. He will join us later," Feron said. He held a glass of wine in the air and the rest of the table followed. My eyes darted to my glass, expecting to see it topped with red liquid, but it held water instead.

Feron started speaking with a Fae down the table and the rest of dinner passed with little contribution from me. I preferred it that way, listening to the conversation. What people were planning to do for the harvest season, whose children had started tutoring or apprenticing. I doubted anyone would say anything of importance with me in the room, but every piece of information was vital when I knew so little of the goings-on in Aralinth.

I finished the fish and set my spoon on the plate for the servants to take. I felt Feron's gaze on me and turned toward him, unblinking as his eyes trailed over my face. "You have beautiful eyes," he remarked softly. "I have not seen anyone with eyes like yours in a long time."

"I've never met anyone with eyes like mine," I replied honestly. My brows furrowed at how easily the words slipped out.

"I would not expect you have," Feron said. I waited for him to elaborate but he turned toward a Halfling couple on the other side of the table. We were eating dessert before he spoke to me again.

"Tell me of your parents," Feron said. "Where were they from?"

"I don't know." I put down my spoon. "As far as I remember, I have no parents. I have no memories before I was taken into the Order."

"None?" Feron pushed. His hand reached out and brushed my fingers. They felt warm against my skin.

I thought of the scar at my hip. I had it the day they found me. The lines were precise and even, carved into a symbol no one at the Order had ever seen. Someone had cut the marks into me. Maybe it had been my parents or whoever had left me alone.

A warm sensation crawled up my spine. I didn't understand where the heat was radiating from, but my body relaxed as it coursed through me. My skin prickled along my neck and a tangy taste settled on my tongue.

Magic. Feron was using his powers on me.

Fuck off, I thought. Feron didn't seem to react, but the warm sensation faded away.

"You are very young," Feron said after a minute, his dark brows knitted together as he scanned my face.

"Thank you." I wasn't sure what else to say.

"How old were you when you were taken to the Order?" There was a lightness to Feron's voice that I didn't trust. It was too sweet. Too eager. But I felt compelled to answer anyway.

"They say I was eight," I said, taking a spoonful of mousse. "But with no parents and no memories, I don't know if that's accurate."

"You have been the king's Blade for quite some time. Longer than any of the others. Yet you are still so young. You must not have attended the Order for very long," Feron remarked, his fingers drumming along the side of his goblet.

I could feel the magic working over me again but didn't fight it. I didn't see the harm in answering these questions. I'd save my will for any secrets he tried to pry away.

"I trained under Mistress Carston first and then Mistress Hildegard. I spent almost thirty years there before I was called to take the Trials," I answered, hoping it was enough to appease his curiosity.

Feron was quiet for some time, studying me. "There are no Elves left in Koratha, not for two hundred years. Your Elvish blood runs very strong if you have seen sixty-some turns." His eyes trailed along the length of my ears beneath my veil. I fought the urge to reach up and cover them.

"It seems that way."

"Were you found near the Burning Mountains?" Feron asked. I followed his train of thought. Perhaps I'd been sired by an Elf from the Faeland.

I shook my head.

"I was found in Calen's Rift. I doubt an Elf would've traveled so close to Mortal's Landing." The eastern city was where the Blood Wars had begun. Their hatred for the Elves was older than the decrees outlawing their kind altogether. It was why the Elves had left to begin with. Even today many Halflings were found beaten and stabbed in the streets of Mortal's Landing and the villages surrounding it.

"*In* the Rift?" Feron repeated, his brows lifting.

I nodded. "They say I fell. I was found on a ledge inside of the Rift near Wenden. I had no memory of how I got there."

Feron brought his cup to his lips but did not drink. Instead, his finger tapped against the side of the goblet, swirling the wine inside. "I was there the day the Rift was formed," Feron said in a soft voice. His eyes settled on the table, wide and unfocused.

"You saw Calen create the Rift?" I asked in awe. The chasm was wider than the capital city of Elverath. A jagged cut so deep that many believed the bottom didn't exist, just a never-ending tunnel of shadow.

"Create the Rift?" Feron said, his gaze snapping back to me. "What version of history do they tell over the mountains?"

I leaned back in my chair. I'd never considered the tale I heard in the kingdom had not been one of truth. "That Calen was a powerful Light Fae," I said, trying to remember the details. "He created the Rift after his love was buried without him." The story had been well-loved in the Order, whispered among the initiates late into the night.

Feron shook his head.

"Everything you said was wrong." He chuckled. He leaned back in his chair and sipped his drink. "Calen was an Elf. Not Fae."

I shook my head. "How could an Elf create such a thing? They have no magic."

Feron gave me a knowing smile that sent a warm rush through my skin. Another touch of his magic. "Elves do not have the ability to *wield* magic, but that does not mean they do not *have* magic."

I blinked.

"Everywhere you look is magic. It pulses through every plant in this city, every creature in the forest hills. In us." Feron sipped his wine.

I didn't understand how an Elf could conjure such a feat. "Calen cursed the land?"

"No. Curses are the stories of men who fear us, Keera," Feron said, his eyes flicking to me. "They do not exist. Blood oaths, however, are a powerful form of magic." I froze, my spoon suspended halfway to my mouth as I waited for him to explain.

"The Rift burst over five millennia ago, at a time when my people were fighting creatures much too terrifying to have a name in the King's Tongue. We dispatched an army to end the horror. I was one of the soldiers, as were Calen and Laurdril. Both were Elves, only a few centuries old, and caught up in the throes of young love." Feron smirked as he sipped his wine again.

"The night before the raid, Calen soothed Laurdril's nerves by making a blood oath. He pricked his finger and placed the blood along his lover's brow, promising that he would never let a creature hurt him. The next day, the creatures surrounded us. Smog brewed from their nostrils, blinding us. We fought them off for hours, Calen taking more than any other. He tore into their flesh with his ax until nothing but dark, scaled bodies lay beside him.

"In a moment of triumph, he put down his ax to embrace his lover. At that same moment, one of the creatures pierced Laurdril's back with its tail and he fell to the ground. Calen fell beside his lover, holding him as Laurdril took his last breath. I watched as the magic tried to claim Calen for breaking his oath, but he fought it. Roots tore from the ground, wrapping around his legs, but he cut them back with his ax. Anything to stay by his lover's side." I leaned forward as Feron stared at the grain of the table.

"Eventually, the magic shook the ground so violently it split, and both Calen and Laurdril fell into its depths. Together even in death." Feron finished his wine. I was spared having to follow his tale by the loud groan of the wood doors opening. The entire table gasped at the transformation of the ballroom. There were no longer any chairs or tall tables, and the center of the room held a large platform. Thousands of faelights filled the room, casting vibrant colors along the walls and floor. Feron stood, leading the party into the ballroom. I followed at the edge of the crowd, anchoring myself to a spot along the wall.

My eyes caught sight of a tall Fae at the bottom of the staircase I'd come down earlier. He was dressed in a long black tunic, tied at his waist with a bronze belt and Elvish dagger. It was the same Fae I had run into earlier. His violet eyes locked with mine as he stalked across the room.

Feron materialized at my side. "Keera, this is my nephew, Riventh Numenthira."

"Riven," the Fae said with a sidelong gaze to Feron.

"Nephew?" I asked. I didn't know Feron to have any living kin.

"In the sense that all the Fae are related," Riven said with a bow. I rolled my eyes. The pleasantries were moot after what he'd said in the hall.

Riven's jaw pulsed. "It's a pleasure to meet the Blade," he added, taking my hand and giving it a small kiss. I ripped my hand away. His eyes were as dark as nightshade as he looked up at me. I caught a glimpse of his fangs as he pulled his lips back into a tight smile.

He turned to face Feron. "I need to speak with you."

Feron studied his nephew for a moment and nodded.

"Let me find someone to entertain Keera while we talk," Feron said, gently patting my shoulder.

I flinched. "That's not necessary—"

"Nikolai!" Feron called to someone across the room. Nikolai ended his conversation with the pretty Halfling he was speaking to and sauntered over to where we were standing.

"Feron." He bowed with a dramatic flourish of his hand. He wore a striking robe of scarlet with no weapon that I could see. It complemented the rich bronze of his skin and the tight curls that blended with the shadow along his cheek. I couldn't help noticing the rough cut along his ears; they'd been stitched round. He was a Halfling.

Nikolai gave me a brilliant smile so wide a line appeared across his brow.

"Keera, the guest of honor!" he cooed, leaning in to kiss my neck in greeting like the lords of the kingdom. When he stood straight again, he gave me a wink. His forwardness was shocking, but I couldn't help but smile.

"Nikolai, do not scare her," Feron cut in. "I need you to entertain Keera while Riven and I speak in my chambers."

"Of course!" Nikolai said, exchanging a look with Riven. "You don't have to convince me to befriend such a marvelous creature."

Feron gave Nikolai a small smile. Riven crossed his arms. The nephew didn't have his uncle's charm.

Nikolai grabbed my hands and stretched out his arms. His eyes scanned my body, starting at the edge of my skirt and rising slowly. He paused over the deep cut of my bodice before eventually meeting my gaze. "You really are breathtaking," he said, pulling me closer to him. "I've been lusting after you since I watched you walk down that staircase. I *adore* a dramatic entrance."

My mouth fell open. "That's a bold claim to make for someone not wearing a weapon," I said, only half joking.

Nikolai shrugged and gave me a devilish grin. "I have *other* weapons at my disposal. Some I find to be much more effective."

I rolled my eyes. "I'm sure."

"I can think of one in particular . . ." His eyes looked downward.

I scoffed and motioned to slap his shoulder, but he caught my hand. The music started, and he wrapped his other arm around my waist, leading us into a slow waltz. He couldn't have timed it better if he'd planned it.

"Are you always this irritating?" I asked.

He broke out his wide grin again. "I think you mean charming."

"I don't."

"So just my naturally seductive demeanor, then?" he countered with a smirk.

"Are all males in the Faeland this forward?" I asked before catching myself. I closed my eyes and felt the heat rush over my cheeks.

Nikolai raised a brow. "If you think I'm offended by you calling me a male, I'm not."

"But in the kingdom—"

Nikolai squeezed my hand. "I've spent some time in the kingdom." My eyes flicked to his cut ears. "I know how they treat those of Elvish blood. It's despicable, and you won't find any in this room that disagree." He spun me twice. "But the Mortals' rigid obsession with the sexes, I never understood."

I tilted my head. "Why?"

Nikolai shifted his shoulders as we danced. He leaned in closer. "Apart from the fact that the practice is inaccurate, the Elverin don't see ourselves that way. The practice is sillier to us than rude."

"Elverin?" I asked. I'd never heard the word before.

Nikolai smirked. "Elves and Fae. Halflings too. We don't draw lines between us as easily as the king does."

I opened my mouth to ask another question, but Nikolai dipped me so low, his face was level with my chest. When he lifted me back up, I hoped he could see the irritation burning in my eyes.

He did, but it only made him smile wider.

"I hope you're not planning on cutting me down, Keera," Nikolai said, twirling me again before he swept us back into the dance. Other couples drifted across the floor beside us, twirling and laughing.

"I would never bring a weapon to dinner," I said. "Lord Feron trusted that I would come unarmed. So I have." I tried to match his light air, but it was difficult when Nikolai spun me around again.

"Liar," he taunted with a smug grin.

I lifted my brows in a challenge.

Nikolai pulled me closer to him. His chin was right beside my ear as he whispered, "I would bet my horse that you have at least three weapons hidden on your person. I would expect nothing less from the king's Blade." He looked down. "I bet you could hide a treasure trove of items under that skirt. Though I'm sure nothing would compare to your—"

I squeezed his shoulder until he winced. "I wouldn't finish that sentence, or you will come to know just how deadly I am, Nikolai." I was no longer joking.

"I do love the way you say my name. So much malice. So much

passion." He smirked wide enough that I could see his fangs. "But we both know you're not going to kill me."

"Why not?" I asked, playing along, wary of the tension building between us.

"Because you've had your chance and didn't take it." There was something knowing in his smile. A dare to guess his meaning.

I tried to picture his face with a hood, covered in shadow, only the line of his chin showing. He was the same height as the Shadow. But Nikolai craved attention. He loved that everyone's eyes were on us as we danced around the room. Could someone who hungered for the world's attention really be the hooded menace I'd come to kill?

"What are you trying to say?" I asked as the music came to a halt.

Nikolai gave a bow just as exaggerated as the one he'd given Feron. "You're smart, Keera. I know you'll figure it out."

CHAPTER FIFTEEN

"You promised."

The words rattled through me, turning my bones to ice. I turned slowly, scared of what I might see.

"You promised," she said again. She was sitting in the middle of the room on a wooden chair. No fire raged in the hearth behind her, no candles lit the room.

It was just us and the gray moonlight that cut across her beautiful face. The faint scar looked silver across her eye and cheek. It pulled tight as she frowned at me.

"You promised."

"Will you stop saying that?" I screamed, running my hands through my hair. "I know I promised. And I failed."

"Failure always precedes success," she said with a faint lift of her brow. It was what Hildegard had always said during our training.

"Sometimes failure precedes death," I spat. I couldn't look at her. It

ripped at my chest until I couldn't breathe. Every heartbeat shook against my rib cage so violently I thought one might snap and pierce it altogether.

That would be less painful.

"Then die," she whispered.

My eyes snapped back to where she sat. Her face was calm, but amber blood soaked her tunic. It pooled down the front of her, but she did not move her hands to stop it. I watched in horror, unable to move, as her neck went limp.

Honey-colored eyes stared up at me.

"Don't leave a crown to claim." Her last words rattled from her chest before her eyes went cold.

My lungs set themselves on fire as I screamed.

And screamed.

And screamed.

I was sick of dreaming of her. Not dreams, nightmares. Every time I closed my eyes, I saw her face. She called out to me over and over again until I gave up on sleep entirely. I left a pool of sweat in my bed and dressed for some fresh air. The first sun was only beginning to peer over the hillside, the golden leaves of Sil'abar gleamed above the city.

I watched the leaves flutter silently, high above my head. The streets were empty. No one stirred in the early hours after a party. I sat on a garden bench surrounded by lush blooms of every color. Their petals just starting to widen with the heat of the sun, each laced with dew.

I couldn't enjoy the beauty of the garden. All I could hear were those words ringing in my head.

You promised.

As if I hadn't carried that broken promise with me everywhere I went. She didn't need to plague my dreams reminding me of how I failed. How I failed her. My fingers traced the name along my forearm through my linen sleeve. Again, and again.

"Long night?" I looked up to see a Halfling standing in front of me. She was dressed in one of those sheer gowns I had seen at the tailors. The gold ink along her face had started to fade.

"I couldn't sleep," I said, shifting on the bench. In my rush for fresh air, I had left my cloak and hood behind. I felt exposed with her dark eyes lingering on my face.

"I hope you were having fun at least," she said, perching herself on the bench beside me. She pulled her long black waves behind her neck.

I shook my head and slid away from her.

"Have you found what you're looking for?" she asked, crossing her legs and soaking in the sunlight.

"What?" I stood up. My hand gripped the hilt of my blade. At least I'd remembered to arm myself. My brows pinched together. It was brave of her to approach if she knew I was the Blade.

Her lips cracked into a sly smile. "No need to pull that out," she said with a lazy wave of her hand. She closed her eyes and leaned back in the sun. "Aralinth is a small city; there are no strangers here. Anyone can see that you're new. And you're a Halfling, which means that you crossed the mountains searching for something. Most of us came as refugees in search of safety. I would know." She pulled back the long drape of her sleeve. Her wrist was burned with the image of a crown.

"You were a royal courtesan," I said. The king's courtesans were Halflings forced to fill the pleasure houses. Technically, the houses were against the decrees, but they turned a profit for the king. And supplied him with more Halflings to own.

I let go of my dagger. She'd seen more violence than most. I would not add to it. "How did you escape?"

She pulled down her sleeve. "I was sent with a group to Cereliath for the Harvest. The lord who bought me fell asleep before he received his . . . services. I took his money and his cloak and walked out the front door." She laughed, twirling a strand of hair in her fingers. "I don't think they expected any of us to leave. All those years I spent dreaming of running away, plotting an escape, and when it finally happened, no one noticed."

"They never sent anyone after you?" I asked, sitting back down beside her.

Her dark eyes cut to mine. Her shoulders slumped as she leaned toward me. "I don't think they looked. The prince was there that night."

She didn't need to say anything more. My fingers scratched along the edge of the bench as the scars on my back itched. Halflings often disappeared when Prince Damien was around.

"You didn't stay in Cereliath?" I asked as the shutters of a nearby shop swung open.

She shrugged. "I was not made to work the fields, and with my brand I was too easily discovered." Her eyes shifted to me for the briefest of seconds. Heat flooded my cheeks. I had caught many Halfling runaways in my time as Blade. Most never got the chance to return to their posts.

"I would rather die than go back," she continued, "so I spent that lord's coin to buy transport to Caerth. Then I packed up as much food as I could carry and walked into the Faeland." She turned on the bench looking away from Sil'abar to the golden forest on the other side. It was too far to see, but somewhere among the trees and hills was the entrance to Wiseman's Way.

"You made it into the Faeland on foot? Weren't you scared?" The journey had taken me a week on horseback. I couldn't imagine how long it would take an untested hiker.

She let out a laugh. It rang through the garden like a bell and sent a pair of birds scurrying into the branches of the White Tree. "More scared than I'd ever been in my life. I'm sure you've heard the stories of what lurks in that wood. Or in the Faeland for that matter." I had. Everyone in Elverath knew that you didn't cross into the Faeland and expect to survive.

"Then why go?" So many Halflings managed to hide in the kingdom well enough. Apart from her brand, she could pass as Mortal.

"I was desperate," she said with a heavy breath. She gazed at me with glassy eyes. "If I was going to die at least it would be on my terms. At least I'd be—"

"Free," I finished for her.

She nodded and a knowing silence fell between us. I leaned back on the bench and stared at the canopy of blooms that hung above our heads. Shades of green intermingled with bursts of pastels, set against the backdrop of the golden leaves of Sil'abar. I could live for millennia and never tire of the view. No wonder the Elves and Fae loved it here.

I studied the Halfling, the long lines of her arms and high angles of her cheeks. I could tell she knew I watched her, but she didn't stop me. Instead, she pulled a peach from somewhere beneath the silks of her skirt and bit into it.

There was little difference between the Shades and the courtesans. Each of us were chosen as children, trained to please the king with our bodies. Mine had been made into a weapon, serving the Crown with every life I took. Courtesans were forged into weapons of their own kind, serving the king with every petty lord they were forced to take to bed.

I'd never met either kind who'd escaped. At least, none who lived to speak of it.

"Do you ever think of going back?" I cut through the silence.

She took another bite of her peach, wiping the juice off her full lips with the back of her hand. "Sometimes," she said with a shrug. "Not in any real way, but if I ever went back I would . . ." She trailed off.

I perched on the edge of the bench. When her eyes cut back to mine they were cold and murderous.

"I would kill the king," she finished in a whisper, her dark hair falling in front of her face as she leaned forward. "Haven't you ever thought the same?"

You promised.

"Yes," I whispered. The tightness in my chest broke as I said the words aloud. "Yes, I have." It was the first time I'd ever admitted that to anyone. I expected an adrenaline-fueled panic, the familiar nausea that swept over me whenever I let my thoughts crack through the decades of defenses I'd built around me. Maybe they had become brittle without the wine because I could feel my walls cracking and it didn't scare me.

"I don't know your name," I realized, pulling myself out of my daze.

"Dynara," she answered, standing up off the bench. She was almost the same height as me. She walked in the direction of the inn but turned back around. The sunlight glistening off the gold ink still left on her cheeks.

"Keera," she called, running a hand through her hair.

I raised my brow. "You knew who I was all along?"

Her sly smile returned, and she nodded. "I remember how lonely it feels. Serving the king. Trying to find something that matters before you die for him." I crossed my arms, shielding myself from her piercing stare. I felt exposed again.

"But that's what he wants," she continued. "That's how it works. Convincing us that we're alone, when the truth is we are surrounded by people trying to break free too."

"You want to help me kill the king?" I scoffed.

She didn't laugh. Her lips fell to a straight line, and she took a step toward me. "I'm afraid my skill set won't help as much as yours, but there are people who may be willing to help you. If you're willing to look in unexpected places."

My stomach fluttered. "I could never ask Halflings who've escaped the king to take up arms against him." I wouldn't be responsible for any more of their deaths. Not for a lost cause.

Dynara shrugged. "Maybe that decision has already been made," she said coolly. "I know who you've come here for. I don't know if you came on your own accord or at the king's command, but I know you came out of desperation. Why else make a journey you didn't expect to survive? But maybe you'll find more than survival here. Maybe you'll find redemption."

CHAPTER SIXTEEN

Dynara's words scratched the inside of my skull. Had this been the reason for the dreams? It had been years since I gave up on my promise to kill the king, to end his reign and the Crown altogether. I had silenced the guilt in barrels of wine. Two decades passed in oblivion. Now I couldn't stop thinking about that promise. About trying again.

But the Shadow? Why Dynara thought he would help was beyond me. I had spent the better part of a year chasing leads, trying to pull back that hood and kill whoever hid beneath it. Why would the Shadow trust me? How did I even know he wanted the king dead?

Only if you leave a crown to claim.

They were his words. I didn't think much of it then, but it made sense. He wasn't just trying to keep the people of Elverath fed. He was working to take down the king. Though he wouldn't get far stealing cargo and food. He needed to attack the king where it hurt.

In his pockets.

I paced back and forth in my room until a line formed in the lush carpet. It was ludicrous. Offering an alliance to the person I came to the Faeland to kill.

Gwyn flashed across my mind. Then the initiates at the Order. The blurry faces of the hungry in Cereliath the king had all but executed. I didn't know when they would die along that road, but their blood was on the king's hands. Just as my hands dripped with the blood of the names carved into my skin.

Killing the Shadow only bought the Halflings time from the king's rage. A few years would pass, more magic would fade, and they would not be safe from his wrath. Didn't I owe it to them to at least try to end it, once and for all?

You promised.

Maybe her dreams weren't meant to be a torment, but a push. She had echoed the Shadow's words—*only if you leave a crown to claim*—did she think an alliance would work?

Only one way to find out, I thought to myself.

I needed to find the Shadow.

I started with Nikolai. I wasn't convinced he was the Shadow, but I was still thinking of his parting words. I was trained to remember faces at the merest glance, and I knew I'd never seen Nikolai before Feron's ball. Yet he alluded to an encounter I didn't remember.

Unless he'd never shown his face.

He was the best lead I had. The *only* lead I had.

I took three days to learn his routine. Nikolai stayed in a luxurious apartment across from the palace. The only thing I learned about him was he didn't just love flirting, but he also loved fucking. Every evening there was another visitor at his door, sometimes two. They would spend the night eating delectable cuisine and drinking the finest wines. There had been Fae, Elves, and Halflings. Most of them females.

How did someone with such a long string of lovers keep their identity a secret?

I didn't have much of a plan. I needed to speak to Nikolai alone. On the fourth night, I waited for his suitor to arrive. I recognized the Elf from Feron's dinner. Her deep skin glowed under the moons, accentuating the layers of light blue fabric she wore.

I stood behind the trunk of a large tree near the entrance. I'd been waiting, hidden under the branches, ever since the guards switched shifts. They were too distracted watching the pretty Elf to notice me sneaking in the door. I pressed my back against the wall and waited for her to walk by.

I held a tiny bobble in my hands. It was made of blown glass and had a sharp needle protruding from it. One prick and she would be asleep for hours. She never even turned around when I jabbed her neck. She fell backward into me. I caught her limp body in my arms and set her gently on a small bench.

I climbed the stairs to the fourth floor. There was only one door in the middle of the hallway, painted gold against the white stone walls. I thought about kicking the door in, but I couldn't picture his suitor doing the same.

I knocked.

"Come in," a voice called from inside.

He was sitting at the edge of a grand bed, the nightshade of his clothing stark against the white silk of the sheets. His hood was drawn over his face, but I knew he was watching my every movement. Each step. Each breath.

The Shadow.

"He's not here," he said. His voice was a dark rasp that cooled my blood.

"Who?" I said, trying to cover my surprise.

He stood, casting a tall shadow over my face. "I wasn't going to let you kill Nikolai."

"Why do you assume I was coming here to kill him?" I asked, taking a step back. I needed space to get my bearings. I hadn't expected the Shadow to appear. Let alone armed. "Maybe I was just jealous of all his pretty lovers."

"He'd be ecstatic to hear that," the Shadow said flatly. He pulled the long sword out of the holster along his back. "What of the Elf? Did you kill her?" He raised his blade toward me.

I pulled out a long, curved blade from my belt.

"No," I said. "She's sleeping."

He pounced, swinging his blade. I stepped to the side as the steel clanged against the stone floor. I rolled over the back of the sofa. He slashed, ripping into the fabric.

I swung my own blade. He jumped back, crashing into the bed.

I swung again before he steadied himself. He blocked it.

He circled the sofa. Sword high as I moved back. I feigned another swing and kicked his knee. He tumbled over the sofa, landing on his feet.

My cloak snagged on the foot of the table. I yanked it loose.

I took a step closer to the Shadow, then stopped. I didn't need my cloak and hood. He had already seen my face.

I reached up to my neck and let them fall to the ground.

"You look better with the cloak," he taunted.

"I'm sure you look better without your head," I bit back. He laughed, craning his neck as he trailed my movements.

"If you're not Nikolai, why do you care if I kill him?" I asked.

"He's a friend," the Shadow answered. The moonlight from the window glowed against the inky black of his cloak.

“I didn’t realize shadows had friends,” I said, moving in front of the window.

He leaped over the couch. “More than blades.”

The Shadow lifted his sword and waited. Inviting me to strike again. I still had more questions.

“Friends are weaknesses a Blade cannot afford.” I swung again. He blocked it with his sword. I turned, slashing at his torso. He took a step back, evading the blow before offering one of his own.

Strike. Dodge. Strike. Turn.

We fell into a steady tempo. The clash of our steel marking the beat as we danced around each other. He moved quick, but I was quicker. With each strike I pushed him back until his heels hit the wall.

“You don’t seem to be trying very hard to kill me,” his dark voice rasped between blows.

I switched hands, aiming a strike at his chest. He evaded a full blow, but the tip of my blade cut the dark fabric of his tunic. I grinned at the slice I left across his sleeve.

“That’s because I don’t want to kill you,” I said before I dropped, swiping his leg. He jumped, so I rammed the hilt of my sword into his knee. He flew forward and fell to the floor. I pulled a small, hooked blade from my boot as he turned to face me.

I leaped off the ground, twisting over his head. I lowered my arm just enough that my hook caught his hood. I pulled it down as I landed behind him, holding my sword at his throat.

Dark violet eyes looked up at me. Swirling pools of rage, covered by dark brows and an angled face.

A face I knew.

The Shadow was Dark Fae.

The Shadow was Riven.

CHAPTER SEVENTEEN

"NICE TRICK," Riven spat. His head was tilted upward, leaning back against me as I held the edge of my blade to his skin. I looked down at his eyes, his violet eyes.

"The Dark Fae are making a move against the Crown?" I couldn't keep the shock from my voice. I knew the Shadow was connected to the Faeland, but I assumed only an Elf or a Halfling would've been motivated enough to attack the king. The Dark Fae had lived for seven centuries under King Aemon's rule and never made a move against him. Why wait until the fate of their race was already decided to rebel?

"No, they're not." Riven coughed, inching backward. I pressed the blade farther into his flesh. Not hard enough to cut him, but enough that he would be a fool to try and move.

I scoffed. "You expect me to believe it's just you? One rogue against an entire kingdom?" I already knew he had accomplices. The other hooded figure from Cereliath, for starters.

Riven clamped his teeth so hard I could hear it. I pushed my blade harder.

"If you don't answer me, I'll kill you now." It was an empty threat, but he didn't know that.

"I don't work alone," he relented. "But none of them are Dark Fae. They don't want to break the accords with the king."

My eyes narrowed. "Then why do you?"

"Because I don't think my duty is only to the residents of the *Faelinth*. As long as there are Halflings in chains, then I will fight the Crown. Kill them all if needed." Riven's voice was harsh and venomous. I loosened my blade a fraction.

Riven dropped the sword in his hand, its hilt reverberated off the floor.

"Why not just *rescue* Halflings?" I asked. "Many will die if the king goes to war."

"Who do think brought all the Halflings here? Or the others in the rest of the *Faelinth*? I have been saving families one by one for decades. It's not enough."

He was right. There were always more mouths to feed, more people to protect. And those were only the Halflings with enough Mortal blood to allow them to hide. Those easily identified spent their lives in service to the Crown. Laying their lives down at the king's leisure.

Just like the Shades.

The Arsenal.

Just like me.

"There's no way you have an army large enough to launch an assault against Elverath," I whispered, tilting my head down at him.

"Not yet," Riven choked against the steel.

I pressed my blade, angling it slightly, so I did not cut him but pushed against his trachea. "You're not in a position to hide anything," I reminded him.

"I will not spill my secrets to the king's Blade. My death isn't worth it," he said.

"So dramatic." I rolled my eyes. "The way I see it, you only have two options. Stay silent and let me kill you. Then, there's no one to protect your dear Nikolai or anyone else I discover has helped you." I felt his shoulders tense. I'd hit a nerve.

"*Or* you can tell me everything and I *might* kill you," I finished.

Riven choked in disbelief. "Might?"

"You doubt me?" I said in a mocking tone of concern. I liked toying with him while he was on his knees, my blade against his throat. It almost made up for his rudeness at Sil'abar.

"I doubt the king's Blade has any use for me alive." He paused. "I reckon the king may kill you if you return to Elverath without my head."

"Probably," I admitted.

"You don't seem concerned?" Riven's voice was ragged and dark. He was growing tired of my ruse.

Good.

I shrugged. "Are you planning to kill the king?"

Riven made a show of clenching his jaw. Stubborn violet eyes stared up at me.

"I'm not asking for details," I said. "I just want to know, is that the goal of all of this—ending the king?"

Riven didn't respond. I held his gaze, his heavy breaths mixed with my staggering heartbeat. I'd hoped for this more than I'd let myself admit.

"No," Riven finally spoke. "We're not just going to end the king. We're going to end the Crown."

I let go of his hair and pulled my dagger from its holster. I stepped in front of him, my sword still pressed against his throat before bringing the dagger to his chest.

"Then to answer your question," I said slowly, "I'm not concerned with the king killing me."

I dropped the sword and let it clatter to the floor. I pulled at Riven's arm until he stood, the threat of my dagger still pressed against his chest.

"Why not?" Riven asked, looking down at the red steel pricking his leathers

"Because I'm going to help you kill him."

Riven's breath stopped. His chest didn't rise to meet the pointed blade of my dagger. His eyes seemed to darken as he stared into my own. My skin prickled with an electric charge that left me on edge. I felt the urge to run and scream and fight all at once. What kind of Fae trick was this between us?

"This is an odd way to broker an alliance." Riven broke his silence with a glance down at the dagger. "Allies or death?"

"Isn't that the beginning of any truce?" I countered.

Riven huffed, his jaw bulging as he studied me. "If this is your way of distracting me before you kill me, it's rather unprecedented."

"Would you rather I kiss you?" I said, raising a brow. "Or is that trick only fun when *you* do it?"

Riven sneered exposing his fangs. Apparently, it wasn't the time for jokes.

"I want to kill the king," I repeated.

Riven shook his head. "Has being Blade finally bored you?"

"I've wanted to kill the king for . . . a long time," I said. "Probably longer than you."

"Why?" Riven pushed.

In a show of good faith, I dropped my dagger and sheathed it in its holster. I met his gaze and waited for him to strike. He didn't.

"My reasons are my own. As are yours. That doesn't change the fact we want the same thing." I stood there waiting. He would either strike, and only one of us would leave, or he wouldn't, and both of us would leave. As accomplices.

"Why should I trust you?" Riven crossed his arms, his eyes never leaving my hands.

"Besides the fact I didn't kill you when I could've?" I raised a brow, pointing to my blade on the floor. Riven only clenched his teeth and waited.

"You can't trust me." I sighed. "Not really. And I can't trust you. But I can trust that there's a better chance of us succeeding working together than us trying apart." I picked my cloak and hood back up from the floor and refastened them around my neck.

"You're willing to risk everything. Your title—not to mention your life—on an alliance with the Fae you've spent months hunting?" Riven asked, a hard line forming between his brows.

"My title and life were forfeit the moment I chose not to strike you down." I grabbed my blade from the floor. Riven's fingers curled around the dagger he wore at his side. "Returning to the palace without your head is risking my life. I might as well risk it on something worthy."

"Why now?" Riven stooped to pick up his own sword. He held it at his side for a long moment before holstering it behind his back.

"I tried to take him down myself in those first years I was Blade. I failed . . ." My throat tightened. "It's not something one person can achieve on their own, I've tried." I could taste the bitterness on my tongue.

Riven studied me as he rubbed the back of his neck. Thoughts swirled behind his violet eyes.

"This is not a decision I can make on my own," Riven said, his fists clenched at his sides.

"Understandable." I nodded. "I will give you the night to discuss this with whoever you need. I will wait for you at the inn near the—"

"I know where you're staying," Riven spat.

"Then you know where to find me."

CHAPTER EIGHTEEN

I WAS BEING FOLLOWED. Someone trailed me along the roof of the apartment and then onto the shops. Their feet were heavy against the vines and stone. There was another tail, a male wearing a blue traveler's cloak, walking in front of me. He used the reflections in the shop windows and a mirrored eye piece to trail me from ahead.

I didn't care that they followed. If Riven was sincere, they wouldn't touch me. If not, I would easily take them down.

I didn't go straight to the inn. Instead, I dined in one of the taverns near the palace garden. It was dark but clean and smelled of fresh spice and ale. The Halfling owners scurried from patron to patron to ask them about their day and meal. Eventually, the wife made it to me.

"How's the roast, my dear?" she asked, refilling my water glass.

"Lovely," I replied.

She took my empty plate. "Any dessert for you, miss?"

"Sure, but could you deliver it to my room across the way?" I pointed to the inn.

She nodded.

"Excellent," I said. "Do you think you could follow these instructions?" I tossed the note I had scrawled on the table, along with a healthy sampling of gold coins. Aralinth was a small city with inhabitants that lived for centuries. I was willing to risk my purse that she knew every resident well enough that she would know exactly whose name was written on that note.

She scooped up the gold and the note, reading it twice over before she nodded. "What time will you be requiring the call?" Her lips pursed as she bit her cheek.

"Give it an hour."

The tails followed me back to the inn. When I got to my room, I pulled the large curtains open along the wide windows. Anyone posted on the rooftops opposite the inn would have a direct line of sight into my room. First lesson in spy craft: it was easier to control a narrative if I let the watcher believe he had all the information.

I drew a bath. It sat in the middle of a large room, marked off from the rest of the suite by a wall of sea glass. Bright blue hues scattered across the white tile floor from the faelights. Whoever Riven had sent to watch me would be able to see enough through the glass to tell that someone was inside but not much more. I undressed, knowing the tail on the rooftop could only see the blurred outline of my body.

Thirty minutes later, a knock rattled against the door. I smiled into the water.

"Come in," I called. I heard the door open and click shut.

Dynara stood in the doorway dressed as a chambermaid. She was carrying a load of towels.

She raised a brow at the sight of me in the tub. Even in the soapy water, I knew she could see everything I tried so hard to cover up. Her smile faltered as she noticed the scars on my arms. Her eyes trailed up to my shoulders before she turned away. I stood, reaching out for a towel, shielding her from the ghastly wounds on my back.

Dynara's eyes met mine. Her lips pinched, but she didn't say anything. She only gave me a stiff nod. She carried scars of her own. She wouldn't judge me for the ones I'd given myself.

She passed me another towel for my hair, and I dropped it on the floor. We both ducked under the sink. She ripped the pins out of her hair. A cascade of brunette waves fell past her shoulders. From a distance she looked enough like me.

Dynara wrapped a towel around herself, pulling her robe down far enough that her shoulders were bare. I quickly dried off and pulled on a matching set of robes that I had stolen on the way to my room. When we stood, it was as if we had switched places. I was now the maid and she the assassin.

"Thank you," I said, still a bit surprised that she had come with only a note to convince her.

"Make the king wish for death before you give it to him," she said, brushing her fingers through her hair.

I left, carrying out the used towels and concealing my bag beneath them.

When I reached the outer hallway, I dipped into an empty closet and changed. I pulled my weapons out from the bag and holstered them along my body. The last thing I put on was my cloak and hood. I stepped into a stairwell at the far corner of the building and slipped into the dark alleyway.

I marked the two tails easily enough. One was perched on the roof across from the inn. The other was dressed in blue sitting by the tavern. If Riven meant for his scouts to watch me all night, they would have to work in shifts. When they traded off, I would follow them and see if they led me back to the Shadow.

CHAPTER NINETEEN

THREE HOURS LATER, I watched as the Halfling posted above the apothecary was relieved by another of Riven's scouts. I lurked in the alley, my cloak melting into the moonless night. I had been disappearing into darkness long before Riven brought his Shadow to life.

The Halfling I followed was young. I couldn't see his face in the shadows, but he sauntered across the city with a confidence that only came with youth. He cut a direct route under the canopy of closed blooms, then down a back alley without checking for trouble ahead or behind him. He had grown too comfortable on that roof, convinced himself that his target was asleep in her bed.

It was a mistake I found most only made once. If it didn't cost them their lives the first time.

Riven's scouts needed to be more disciplined if we had any chance of reaching the king unseen. I would speak to him about better guards. This one was utterly clueless that I had tailed him from the moment he left his post.

We walked to the outskirts of Aralinth, where the buildings started to shrink and darken. Dwellings that had fallen into disarray as the population of the city dwindled. It was not a place I would expect to find one of the Fae, but it was the perfect location to keep your plans out of the watchful eye of one's uncle. Perhaps Riven had been telling the truth and the rest of the Fae had no part in his schemes.

He finally turned into a decrepit tavern. Dark curtains were staked into the stone at each window. The one closest to us had a loose corner that drifted gently in the breeze. No light shone through the gap, from the road the tavern appeared entirely empty.

But my ears could hear the murmur of conversation through the rain that had started to fall in thick sheets. The drops pelted the dirt path to the stables, leaving divots in the ground. The perfect cover to overhear whatever plans Riven was devising.

I needed to know if he planned to join me or kill me.

I followed the Halfling to the stables in crouched strides, making sure he didn't catch sight of my cloak. Instead of crossing through the stalls, I leaped onto the open gate and pulled myself onto the roof.

The stone was slick from the rain, but solid enough to hold my weight. I slowly crossed to the back of the building, testing each step to ensure the Halfling didn't hear an unexplained creak from above. I perched above a window, my head leaning over the edge of the roof.

I could hear heartbeats—at least three people were inside. Maybe four.

"Has she left the inn?" someone asked. The voice sounded female.

"No. She took a bath and went to bed. Airrin and Hax are watching her now." The report must have come from the Halfling I followed. He said nothing more, and I heard a door open and close before anyone else spoke again.

"Do you trust her offer is legitimate?" I recognized the voice as Nikolai's.

Someone grunted in response. I rolled my eyes, knowing the grunt was Riven.

"And if it is not?" the female voice asked.

"Then we're probably dead," Nikolai retorted. He sounded bored. "She could be calling in reinforcements right now. She saw your face. She knows your name. She has all the power now, Riv."

"I don't need the reminder," Riven answered. Even from the roof, I could tell he spoke through clenched teeth.

"Maybe not." It was the female voice again. "If she has not sent word yet, it might not be too late. The scouts said she only stopped to eat before going to bed. We could still—"

"Have her over for tea?" Riven chided darkly.

"I was going to say we still have time to kill her," the female mumbled. I gritted my teeth as I reached for my dagger. I'd like to see them try.

"Dark," Nikolai scoffed. I agreed with him. "Shall I be the one to stab her in her sleep, then?" he added. Maybe I didn't agree with him.

"Yes, Nik." The female voice was thick with sarcasm. "*You* are the one we send in to assassinate the king's Blade."

"It wouldn't be the first time I've been accused of murdering someone in their bed," Nikolai replied. I could hear the smirk in his tone.

"Do you not think it is time you grow out of such childishness?" the female voice said.

"It was obviously a joke—though there was this close call in Myrelinth . . ." Nikolai trailed off. "Besides, we can't kill her. I thought you needed more information for your *theory*."

"Feron's theory," Riven cut through their bickering.

What theory? I thought before Riven continued.

"And that was before she showed up in the *Faelinth* and found out who I was. We need to decide. I would prefer it if the decision was unanimous."

"Can we eat first?" Nikolai asked. "I'm starving."

Riven growled. Nikolai chuckled, completely unperturbed.

I leaned over and caught Nikolai's reflection in the open glass shutter. He was leaning back in his chair, foot resting on a knee with both hands laced behind his head.

"Let me get this straight," Nikolai said. "If we reject the alliance, she kills us. If we accept the alliance, she *probably* kills us?"

"Yes," Riven answered bluntly.

"Seems like we have our answer." Nikolai dropped the front of his chair back on the ground.

"Why are those the only two options?" the female voice countered. "I still think we could kill her."

"We can't kill her," Riven said.

"Why not?" the female voice asked. I tightened my grip on the roof. Whoever she was, she was testing my nerves.

"First of all," Riven said. "Whether she has been in contact with the Shades or not, they must know she's here. If she goes missing, we'll be giving the king a reason to send his armies into the Faeland."

"Don't want that," Nikolai added. It sounded like his mouth was full of food.

"Second," Riven continued, "she would kill Nikolai in a matter of seconds."

Nikolai's reflection shrugged. "Fair enough."

"And I doubt I have enough luck to evade her a third time. I held my own in Cereliath, but her skill is greater."

You bet it is, I thought.

"She would not best me," the female voice boasted. I heard the clang of steel as she unsheathed some weapon.

"Syrra." Riven's voice was softer than before. "You may be willing to gamble with your life, but I'm not."

"Then we are at an impasse, my friend," the female voice, Syrra, replied. "I do not trust someone who has spent her life killing Halflings to charm her king." I bit my lip to keep from cursing. Maybe they *should* send this Syrra after me. I would enjoy teaching her just how charming I could be.

"I don't like it either," Riven said. "But if her offer is genuine, we have a better chance succeeding with the Blade than without her."

"How can we trust her?" Syrra pushed.

"We can't." It was Nikolai who answered, seemingly done eating. "We can speak in circles all night, but the truth is—she has us cornered. We played right into her hand. There's no denying that now—"

"Which is exactly why we cannot—" Syrra started but Nikolai cut her off.

"Which is exactly why we *need* her. She has direct access to the king and the Shades. She's the head of the entire Arsenal. She clearly has a talent for strategy and the king doesn't know she's switched allegiances."

"*If* she's switched sides," Syrra mumbled. I bit the inside of my cheek.

"Just because we're allies doesn't mean we have to tell her *everything*," Nikolai said, almost too quietly for me to hear. I stilled. The rain pattered against my neck as I lowered my head to hear better.

"What are you suggesting, Nik?" Riven asked. He took a step forward, and I could glimpse the profile of his tall frame in the glass.

"Do you reckon she has told you everything?" Nikolai asked. "Or that she plans to?"

Of course I haven't. Riven would be a fool to think I had.

"I doubt it," Riven said. Good. I hated working with idiots.

"Exactly." Nikolai nodded. "Agree to the alliance, but only if she agrees that we keep some level of autonomy." I shivered against the cold rain. My cloak was soaked; it pulled at my shoulders.

"And if she betrays us?" Riven asked, his reflection walking toward the hearth. I was jealous of the dry warmth that glowed against his legs.

"Then you and Syrra will have your chance to murder her after all," Nikolai replied casually, as if he was talking about what they planned to make for dinner. I took that as my cue. I didn't want to give them any more time to reinvent their plan and try to kill me after all.

I gripped the edge of the roof and flipped my body into the open window. The glass smashed against the wall. I landed in the middle of the floor in a soft crouch, wearing a smirk.

"Oh, Nikolai," I said as I stood up, brandishing my sword. I gave him a teasing wink. "And here I thought we were going to be friends."

CHAPTER TWENTY

NIKOLAI STOOD UP SO FAST his chair fell over. The person beside him had deep brown skin and black hair that fell down her back, laced with intricate braids. She crouched, holding two circular blades—one in each hand. I eyed the weapons, my stomach fluttering with curiosity.

Riven leaned against the mantel of the fireplace, his eyes hardened into thin slits. He didn't even unsheathe the sword on his back.

"Stand down, you two," he commanded. "If she wanted us dead, you already would be."

I cocked a brow in response.

"One Halfling taking on the three of us?" Nikolai took out a small knife from his belt. It was puny. Even if he did stab me with it, his aim would need to be precise for his cut to be lethal. "I don't think so." He waved his little weapon.

I sliced the air with my sword, twirling it over my wrist. "You didn't know I was here until I came through that window. I could've killed you before you even had the chance to scream."

Nikolai dropped his arm. His eyes flicked to Riven, who nodded.

"If you do not want us dead, why not walk through the door?" Syrra asked, refusing to lower her blades. I watched her cautiously. I'd never trained with those weapons but knew they were only wielded by the most skilled Elvish warriors. The scars that trailed down her arms were proof of that. Intricate branches that stretched down her limbs flourished with leaves I didn't recognize. Elvish warriors only received a marking in recognition of a great feat. Syrra had several.

"The truth?" I said, tapping the point of my sword with my finger. I smirked at her as a tiny drop of blood dripped from my skin.

Syrra's black eyes never left mine, but her broad shoulders tensed. "I have no interest in lies."

"When I climbed onto the roof, I hadn't decided yet," I said. "If I was going to come in, I mean. Then I overheard your *riveting* conversation. You reached a decision. There was no reason to put off introductions. The window smashing was for Nikolai's benefit." I feigned a swipe in his direction. He stepped back, holding his knife pathetically out in front of him.

"Me?" Nikolai choked.

I shrugged. "I figured you'd appreciate the dramatic entrance," I said, echoing his words from Feron's dinner.

The room was silent as they stared at me until Nikolai broke into a fit of hearty laughter. Syrra shot him a look while Riven shook his head.

"I knew I liked you," Nikolai said between ragged breaths. His previous fear melted away as he patted my shoulder. My skin recoiled under the touch, but he didn't notice.

"You don't know me," I said. I knew he couldn't feel my scars through the thickness of my cloak, but I hated the heaviness of his palm.

Nikolai removed his hand to pull at his cuff. Something told me it was for added flair rather than comfort. "You were so *delightful* at dinner, Keera. You mean to say that was all just an act?"

I shot him a sideways look. "Only as much as you were acting."

"That was no act, Keera," Nikolai replied, his devilish grin returning. "I meant everything I said that night. You looked absolutely *delicious*." His eyes trailed over my soaked clothes. "If you get over this sudden need to prod me with weapons, I'll gladly show you just how honest I can be."

"Enough." Riven held up his hand.

"Come on, Riv," Nikolai crooned. "I was just getting to know our guest here."

"She doesn't want to hear it any more than I do." Riven's voice was hard, just like his eyes that had not left my skin since I barged in.

Nikolai shot Syrra a pleading look, but she just shrugged, refusing to look away from me either. "They'll warm up to you," Nikolai mumbled beside me.

I didn't care. We didn't need to like each other to kill the king.

"How much did you hear?" Riven asked, his jaw tense as he leaned against the mantel.

I sat in an empty chair next to the wooden table. I lifted my leg on top of my knee and pinned my hands against my head. Another flair for Nikolai that I knew would irritate Riven. I needed him on edge. People revealed the most when they felt unsettled.

"I arrived somewhere between her"—I pointed to Syrra with my chin—"wanting to kill me and you telling them that you weren't strong enough to do it." I couldn't hold back my smirk.

Riven's crossed arms flexed. "I never said that."

I cocked my head, crossing my arms to match his.

"You did *kind of* say that," Nikolai said, tilting his head. Riven's eyes finally cut away from me, glaring at him. Nikolai shrugged, a grin twitching at his lips. I was warming up to him.

"You heard everything?" Syrra asked, lowering her weapons, though she refused to sheathe them.

"Yes." I nodded. Syrra pulled back her shoulders, the muscles along her neck twitched.

"What are you here for?" Riven snapped. His hands balled into fists.

"I'm here to listen to your plan to end the Crown," I said. "I assume you have one?"

Riven scoffed. "You needed to hear it right now?"

"Yes, it's why I followed your scout here," I said. "You need to train them better, by the way. A novice could have tracked him here." Syrra's fists clenched. I got the feeling she had brought this up before.

"So tell me the plan," I continued, "and I'll tell you how to fix it."

Riven's jaw bulged, but he nodded.

"And if it does not need amendments?" Syrra pronounced every syllable slowly, holding her anger in a tight cage. Her full lips were drawn straight and a small dimple appeared beside her mouth.

"If you were confident in your plans, Riven would've never considered the alliance in the first place. You're either lacking manpower or lacking ideas. Probably both." Syrra rolled her eyes at me. "Either way, you *need* me."

I stared Riven down. This was the true choice. Once he told me his plans, they couldn't turn back. Or Syrra would have to take her chances on killing me. I didn't move. This was my only shot.

Riven took the seat across from me. His large frame hunched over the table. He pointed at the two empty spots, his eyes darting between his comrades. Nikolai picked up his chair from where it still lay on the ground. Syrra didn't move, refusing to look away from me. Small crinkles appeared along the thin bridge of her long nose.

"Syrra," Riven murmured. "Sit."

She held my eye for another moment, making sure I saw her hand resting on the handle of her blade before taking her seat.

"Like I told you," Riven said, laying his fist on the table, "we don't think it's enough to kill the king. We want to take down the entire institution. Make sure there is no way anyone else can take power and enslave the Halflings again."

His eyes flicked to mine. All I could do was nod. My stomach churned too much to speak.

"Nik"—Riven tipped his head toward him—"you're the mastermind. Explain it to her."

Nikolai took a deep breath, smoothing the front of his shirt. I noticed the Elvish dagger holster at his belt. I had seen the braided, wooden handle before—in Cereliath. Nikolai had been the hooded figure trading secrets with Curringham's assistant. When his eyes met mine, all his flirtation was gone. They were focused. Calculating.

"We want to destabilize trade to the capital," Nikolai started. "Food, mainly. Fan the flames of anger that are already present against the king. Show the king to be merciless and useless, especially to the Halflings. Help people. Feed them. If enough of them feel like there's hope, they will join us." I nodded, and Nikolai broke into the specifics of his plan.

I listened without interrupting. They had been responsible for more of the Crown's issues than I believed. Working for two years before Riven had to take up his false identity to have someone to blame it on. Nikolai didn't get into the details of their contacts or how widespread their networks were, but it was clear they had infiltrated most of Elverath's cities.

They had been sending supplies and Halflings through Silstra and Cereliath—sometimes all the way from Mortal's Landing. The supplies I knew about—the barge in Cereliath had been stocked with food—but I was surprised to hear they were moving so many Halflings.

They were more prepared than I thought. Their plan was ludicrous, but it was a shot.

More than I'd ever had before.

"What do you think?" Riven asked, his voice rough. He chewed on his lip while I chewed on my thoughts. I had to be careful with them. Gentle.

Not exactly my strong suit.

"I think it's a plan," I said as diplomatically as I could.

"A plan?" Syrra snarled. "That is all you have to say?" Maybe I'd been *too* gentle.

"How many people do you have?" I asked. I would need *some* details to help strategize.

"With us? Thirty," Riven answered sheepishly. Most of his contacts must be paid off. Smugglers and crooked Mortals willing to look the other way. There were enough of them. I spent most of my life hunting such kinds of people.

"That's not enough," I said, chewing the inside of my cheek. "How many people could you rally? Here, and in the kingdom?"

"If we had a month?" Riven said, pausing to think. "Two hundred or so. But that would mean rescuing Halflings would need to stop. No refugees could be smuggled into Aralinth if I pulled them out."

"Isn't the point to free the Halflings?" I pushed back. This wouldn't be the only time we had to weigh the cost of lives.

"You think we need to reprioritize?" Nikolai cut in. He wrapped his arm around the back of Syrra's chair. She didn't move against it, but I caught a look between them.

Unexpected, I thought. Nikolai didn't seem to be her type. If she ever stopped thinking about bloodshed long enough to have a type.

"We need to go bigger," I said. Riven's dark brows pressed against his hairline. "Even if no one got killed or captured, which is unlikely, attacking trade transports isn't big enough. Thirty men? We'd be lucky if we stopped half as many transports."

"It's been working so far," Syrra said.

"When you were trying to *weaken* the Crown." I leaned forward. "Small moves over time to protect your anonymity. If we're going to bring the Crown to its knees, we have to be willing to show our hand."

"You don't think attacking trade is the right move?" Nikolai asked.

I shook my head. "We can't just attack it. We need to *stop* it."

"What are you suggesting?" Riven asked. For the first time, the hard set of his jaw seemed to soften. He leaned on the table until the wood creaked beneath the weight of him.

"Why attack the ships when you can attack the dam?" I answered with a small smirk.

Three pairs of wide eyes sat across from me. Nikolai whistled.

"You want to blow up Silstra?" Riven whispered.

Syrra rubbed her brow. "It would completely flood each of the canals. Probably destroy every port between Koratha and Volcar." Her eyes flicked to me. "People will die."

I shrugged. "Probably."

Riven slammed his fist on the table. "Absolutely not."

I sighed. "Then we're doomed to fail before we start." Hurting the king's people wouldn't be enough. Aemon didn't care about peasants. He cared about his pockets.

Riven leaned back in his chair, his violet eyes piercing through me. "We'll find another way."

I stood, pressing my hands into the table. "You said you wanted to kill the king—take down the *Crown*—did you really believe you could do that without any bloodshed?"

Riven crossed his arms. I could see his jaw pulse in the warm light from the hearth.

"The king won't care about lost lives if this comes to war," I urged. "He won't care to lessen the bloodshed. Only that we're snuffed out quickly. We need to attack him hard enough to make him worry. Blowing up the dam does that."

I paused while Riven shook his head. "We'll attack at night," I continued. "The ports and fields should be empty. This is the best way to hurt the Crown, with the fewest lives lost. You need to get comfortable with that. And quick." I crossed my arms, my eyes scanning across each of their faces. My heart pounded against my ribs, but I was right. I'd been balancing the scales of life and death for decades.

"We attack at night," Riven agreed after a long silence. Even Syrra nodded. My shoulders fell and my heart slowed.

Syrra crossed her brow. "How would we create a large enough—"

"I can get it done," Nikolai said with a stern nod. I raised my brows at him. "I'm more than just a pretty face, darling," he added, breaking into a grin.

"It would only cause chaos," Riven said. "We would only disconnect the smaller cities, make *them* more vulnerable, but the capital would be safe. The king has enough stores to feed his people for a year."

I ran my tongue along my fangs. Riven seemed to know quite a bit about Koratha for someone who lived on the other side of the continent. I tilted my head, wondering who his contacts were.

Riven shot me a look. "The people in the capital will be the last to go hungry."

"Maybe not," I said, trying to remember the Arsenal reports about the stores. I'd been on my second bottle of wine when I read them. "When the *winvra* started failing, the king began trading more food with the Mortal realms. He sold the good crop and has been feeding the capital on the reserves. The last I heard, three of the granaries had been compromised."

Silence fell across the room.

"What about everyone else?" Nikolai asked. "How will they eat if we push the harvest lands into a drought?"

"The cities should have enough rations to get through the winter," I said. "But we need to start shipping food south immediately. Then get as many as you can spare to Silstra. It'll be chaotic when the dam explodes, and we can use that to our advantage. Dress the horse transports in the royal colors; take the food straight from the source without them even realizing it."

"The Shades won't notice?" Nikolai countered.

"They will," I said. "But we'll be gone before they do."

"There is no guarantee that people will join our cause," Syrra warned after a long silence.

"No, there's not," I agreed. "But let's focus on blowing up the dam. It'll be a big job. Too big, probably. I'm not convinced Nikolai can do it."

Nikolai shot me a tense sneer. "If you want to blow up half of Silstra, I'd be nicer to me, Keera."

"That wasn't at all convincing," I replied flatly.

Riven snorted, shaking his head. "Nik will get it done," he said. "He's one of the finest mechanics in the *Faelinth*. Also, he has to or we're dead."

"Thanks for the support," Nikolai mumbled, crossing his legs.

I stood, slapping my thighs with my hands. I had too much energy coursing through my body. My legs were shaking. I needed to start moving, doing something to channel the energy and regain my focus.

"If we want to blow up the dam, we'll need explosives," I said, walking over to the hearth. The fire warmed my legs as my cloak dripped on the floor.

Nikolai tilted his head. "Cereliath used explosives to build their irrigation canals. Whatever they have left should be more than enough."

"I agree," I said, fanning my fingers in front of the flames. "But we'll need the key to get them."

"And where would that be?" Syrra asked, crossing her arms.

"Around Lord Curringham's neck," I answered.

CHAPTER TWENTY-ONE

Syrra and Nikolai left to prepare for the journey to Cereliath. The door shut behind them, and I could feel Riven's cold stare on my back.

His footsteps barely made a sound as he walked across the room and stood behind me. I could feel the warmth of his chest through my cloak. I stilled. He took another step, and his breath scattered goosebumps across the skin of my neck. We hadn't been this close since that kiss in Cereliath. I rubbed my fingers along my lips. They were warm and swollen like they had been the night he left me in that temple.

"Why did you kiss me?" The words fell out of my mouth in a whisper. "I've played that night in my head again and again, but it makes no sense. You could've ended me right there." I turned around, lifting my eyes to his. Without the hood, I could see the sharp hollows of his cheeks and the strength of his jaw. His hair hung down his chest like sheets of ravensilk, the top pulled back into a small braid. Even stripped of his cloak and hood, his features were still made of shadow. I'd never seen anyone like him.

Riven didn't break the stare. His eyes turned to violet flames with the reflection of the fire. "It was a mistake," he said. "It never should've happened." He flexed his jaw and didn't say anything else.

"It wasn't to distract me?" I pushed, stretching onto my toes. "Seduce me to get closer to the king?"

Riven shook his head. "It had nothing to do with any of that."

"But what—"

He cut me off. "You're making me regret *not* killing you." He scowled. My eyes dropped to the handle of his sword peeking out behind his shoulder. If this was a test to see who would cave first, I wasn't going to lose.

Riven bit the inside of his cheek. "We're not talking about this," he said, walking toward the window I had smashed in.

"Why not?" I asked, crossing my arms.

"I don't trust you," he said simply, stooping down to pick up a large piece of broken glass.

I stepped back toward the hearth. "That makes two of us," I mumbled, untying my cloak and placing it on a hook over the fire. Water spread across the stone floor.

"Why would *you* doubt *me*?" he asked, tossing the glass into a waste bin. The hand at his side was knotted into a fist. "I wasn't the one killing Halflings. My allegiance shouldn't be in question."

I cocked a brow. I'd found the most self-righteous Fae in the entire kingdom to ally myself with. "Why now?" I asked, my words filled with ice.

Riven froze. His brow furrowed in my direction, violet flames dancing in his eyes again. "What do you mean?" he asked slowly, like he was issuing a threat.

"Why now?" I repeated. "You're Fae so you must be older than I am. Do you count your years in centuries, or have you moved to millennia now?" Riven didn't say anything; he just leaned against the wall with his arms folded together.

"How many lifetimes has it taken for you to decide to help the Halflings? My kin have been forced to serve the king for seven *hundred* years while the Fae did nothing. Still, they do nothing—apart from you." My words came out in ragged breaths. I clenched my hands to keep from shaking. "Your work so far is admirable; I don't deny it. I'm grateful to anyone who spends their time getting Halflings to safety, especially after seeing the lives they have here. But you don't get to judge me for the sixty years I took to cross the king. Not when you've had lifetimes to come to the same decision."

I turned back to the flames, too angry to even look at him. I heard him take a step toward me and then stop. A thick silence fell between us. Only the flicker of the fire filled the air. Even the rain had stopped.

"Fair enough," he said. "But you say you tried to kill the king before. You must've had opportunities. Why is Aemon still alive?" He stood next to the hearth facing me. He leaned against the mantel. The only warmth in his eyes came from the fire. His stare pierced through me, leaving a chill along my skin.

"Only if you leave a crown to claim," I whispered. Riven's breath stalled as he crossed his arms. "You said that in Cereliath. You know killing the king is not enough."

"Perhaps not, but you could—"

I held up my hand. My fingers brushed his wrist, sending an electric current up my arm. I pulled away, staring at the tips of my fingers. Riven shifted his shoulders, pulling me back to my thought. "Killing the king but leaving the Crown would be worse than letting Aemon live out his reign."

Riven raised a thick brow. His lips were set in a straight line, but he didn't speak.

"What have you heard about the crown prince?" I asked.

Riven's eyes squinted as he shrugged. "He's a vain man more interested in power than the intricacies of ruling a kingdom."

"That's true," I said, nodding my head. "But he's also reckless and cruel. King Aemon doesn't care about the deaths of Halflings or peasants, but there's always a reason for it. The prince kills Halflings for sport. There's no telling what he would do if he ever claimed the throne."

Riven's neck tensed as he swallowed. "Surely some of that is an exaggeration."

I slammed my hand against the mantel. "He keeps Halflings locked in his chambers, torturing them, making them feel worthless. Sometimes he cuts them. Sometimes he leaves marks on their skin that take weeks to heal. Sometimes he doesn't touch them at all but leaves them tied to a wall for days." My chest heaved with each word. I was speaking of Damien's tendencies, but in my mind all I saw was Gwyn.

Riven's hands fell to his sides. The hollow of his cheek widened as he chewed the inside. "I had no idea it was that bad," he said, his eyes dropping to the hearth. The scars on my back scratched against the tunic. I knew I could show him just how cruel the prince truly was. They were ugly enough to convince anyone of my vitriol for the king and his son. But I couldn't. I'd carried them too long on my own. Exposing them to the world felt wrong. I wouldn't do it, even to buy Riven's trust.

I would earn it some other way.

Riven stared at me for what felt like years. His eyes trailed over the lines of my face so slowly I barely saw them move. I shifted my feet, uncomfortable under his intense gaze but unable to turn away.

"We will kill the prince, too," Riven said with a stiff nod. "Both of them if we have to." I didn't doubt the earnestness in his eyes.

The door opened and I broke away from Riven's stare.

"What, Collin?" Riven called over his shoulder. The Halfling I followed here stood in the doorway. His blond curls were still damp with rain and clung to the freckles along his cheeks. Riven's shoulders tensed as he walked across the room. Collin whispered in his ear, too quickly for me to parse the Elvish. Riven's head pulled back. "Where is she?" he demanded, his dark voice filling the room.

"The east side of the city," Collin answered. "Looking for *her*." His eyes cut to me.

This was not good.

"Who?" I asked, reaching for my cloak.

"The Dagger," Riven spat. "She's here."

No. Not good at all.

Despite the warmth on my back, an icy chill ran down my spine. "Why is she here?" I asked Collin. I pulled the cloak off the hook and wrapped the heavy black fabric around my neck. It pulled against my throat, but I didn't care. If Gerarda was here, that could only mean bad news.

"I expected you would know better than us," Collin replied coolly. He raised a brow and shared a look with Riven.

"I don't know why she's here," I said, heat rushing to my cheeks. "She was stationed in Koratha when I left."

"If this is some trick—" Collin started.

"It's not." I pulled the damp fabric around my shoulders. "I have no idea why the Dagger is here. Let me go find her and send her back to the kingdom before she learns too much."

"No." It was not a statement; it was a command. I turned toward Riven, ready to strike.

"No?" I repeated.

"You will not speak to her," Riven continued, stalking toward me. "You won't even see her. I might believe you have your reasons to want the king gone, but I won't give you an opportunity to expose us. Or lead us into a trap."

"She won't leave until she finds me or has reason to believe I've left." I knew Gerarda. She wouldn't abandon her mission until she knew her target had fled. I needed to talk to her. "I promise you don't want the Dagger poking around your city for very long; she won't be nearly as gracious as me."

Twelve hours. That's how long we had until the Dagger started showing Aralinth how she'd earned her title. Maybe less if someone gave her reason to attack.

"You are not meeting her in our city," Riven repeated.

I gritted my teeth. "Then we have to lure her out."

Collin scoffed. "Lure her where?"

"Back through the mountains," I said, waving my arm in the direction of the kingdom. "I assume you don't want her expanding her search to the rest of the Faeland?"

Riven shook his head. Collin's cheeks turned red with whatever words he wouldn't say in front of me.

"Then Caerth's the only option." I rested my hands along my belt. "We'll have to give her reason to go back to through the pass. Make it seem like I've headed back to the capital."

"And if she catches up with you?" Collin asked, his honey-colored eyes turning to thin slits.

I shrugged. "We'll manage that on the road. The important thing is getting the head start." I looked at Riven. Collin didn't trust me, but he'd follow Riven's orders.

"Then we leave tonight," Riven said. "We'll ride with Syrra and

Nik across the pass, drawing the Dagger away from the city. The rest of the Elverin will stay here and wait for our signal that it's safe to cross." He cut a look to Collin who nodded and left the room.

"I need my blades," I said, pointing to the outside door.

Riven grabbed his own cloak off a hook on the wall. He slowly fastened the neck with a tight knot of Elvish rope. "I'm coming with you," he said, walking out the door.

CHAPTER TWENTY-TWO

We crossed the city in silence. Riven moved through the shadows just as easily as I did, scanning the streets for a sign of the Dagger. I followed behind him and kept my eyes on the roofs. We crept up to the back of the inn, and I slipped Riven the key from my pocket.

"Wait for me in my room," I whispered. "I know you know which one it is."

Riven scoffed.

"I need to let the staff know I'm headed back to Caerth," I said, crossing my arms. "We need to leave a trail for Gerarda to find if we expect her to follow it."

I could hear the grind of Riven's teeth as he loomed over me. He nodded. "If you're not upstairs in one minute, I will come and find you."

I agreed, watching him cross the alley in a dark blur. I followed him, turning to enter through the main doors instead of the back. The same Halfling who had checked me in on my first day was standing behind the counter.

"Good evening," he greeted me with a polite nod.

"Lovely," I said, sliding a pouch of gold coin toward him. "I must leave for the capital right away. I wanted to make sure my bill was paid. I leave tonight."

He swiped up the bag, his eyes widened at the weight of it. "Absolutely," he choked. "I shall get your change right away."

"No need," I said, patting the top of the desk. "Whatever is overpaid is for you." I'd spotted the Halfling coming from the pubs each morning. Hopefully he wasn't shy explaining where he'd gotten all that gold for drinks.

I gave him a tight smile before scurrying up the staircase.

Riven was standing beside the armoire when I walked in. Two orbs of golden faelight were the only sources of light in the room. They lit one side of Riven's face and casted the other in shadow. I paused, realizing I understood him less since I pulled down his hood. The Shadow was familiar, but the tall, brooding Fae in my room was a stranger.

My eyes shifted to the rumpled sheets on the bed. Dynara, my double, was gone.

"I forgot to tell you she was in here," I said, still staring at the bed. "Did you scare her?"

"No. The opposite actually. Is she . . ." He trailed off, too reserved to finish his thought.

"From a brothel?" I asked, crossing my arms. I didn't know what Dynara had said, but it had put Riven on edge.

He coughed. "We don't call them that here."

"She was, in a past life," I said, rushing to the large table where my extra blades were laid. "I needed someone to keep your scouts distracted. It was an easy solution to find a lookalike."

"You hired a courtesan?" Riven whispered. His violet eyes wide and unfocused as he noticed the unmade bed.

"I'm the king's Blade," I scoffed, throwing open one of my bags. "I kill people. Lots of people, and you're surprised that I have connections with courtesans?"

"I'm surprised you have connections with anyone," he said evenly. I could feel the weight of his stare on my back. My skin shivered with how easily he tore at my words. How accurate his assessment of me was, even in a fleeting comment. I wasn't used to being marked, especially by a target.

But Riven wasn't a target anymore, was he?

I doubted our alliance would be enough to forge a friendship between us. Not that I wanted that. But where did that leave us? I didn't think it was possible for rivals to truly become allies.

Accomplices?

"You have a mage pen?" Riven asked, stirring me from my thoughts. He held the gold knife between his fingers. It looked so much smaller in his hand than mine. I pulled my cloak tighter around my body, purposely not looking at the pen.

"Yes," I said, haphazardly throwing clothes into one of my saddlebags.

"How?" His voice was soft with wonder. "They're very rare to come by, even for the Fae."

"I stole it," I said with a shrug. I didn't have time to weave a creative lie.

His eyes widened with curiosity when he realized it was truth.

"From whom?" He twirled the pen in his fingers, studying the tiny, sharp point of it. A point that would never dull no matter how it aged or what it cut.

"Does it matter?" I shot back. Thinking about that night was something I tried to avoid, especially without a stiff drink.

"What's wrong?" The curious edge to his voice had evaporated, and all that was left was the analytical mask he'd worn ever since I pulled back his hood. Just how many faces did Riven have?

I stopped packing. I steadied myself with a deep breath, ignoring the burning at my throat. "There are things you do as a Shade," I said, "and even more as the Blade, that tear at you. Rip you into pieces until you don't recognize yourself anymore. I don't like talking about them, so don't ask me about that pen again."

Riven placed the mage pen back on the table. "What did—"

I sighed, throwing the last of my clothes into the bag. "If we don't stop having this conversation, I *will* stab you." I tossed him a bag. He caught it with lightning speed.

Riven opened his mouth to speak again, but no words followed. Instead, he pulled the saddlebag onto his shoulder and reached for the second. I packed the rest and pulled my cloak over them.

"We need to go," I whispered, extinguishing the faelights in the water basin. Riven opened the door, his long arm holding it open for me. We cut through the inn without being seen and Riven followed me into the night.

Neither of us spoke as we stepped into the narrow alley. I crept down the path. Riven followed behind me close enough that I could feel the rise and fall of his breath. The alley cut across one of the main streets, well-lit from the faelights that hovered below the bloomed canopy. I crouched low, peering out to see if the way was clear. Riven took a step forward, but I reached out, feeling the hardness of his chest through his shirt. He tensed under my palm, and I dropped my hand. Violet eyes met my own and I pointed to the rooftops.

If Gerarda was surveilling the city, she would take the high ground.

Riven looked up, scanning the roofs, and nodded. He reached above my head. His chest stopped only a few inches from my face. I braced my hand against it to keep him from touching me. He didn't move back or speak as I tilted my head up toward his face. His strong jaw and sharp cheekbones were silver blades in the moonlight. His scent wafted around me, warm and earthy with a hint of something familiar that I couldn't place.

His eyes were closed and his hand was wrapped into a tangle of vines that hung from the green canopy. Where the plant touched his skin I could see the slightest shift of light pulsing through the vine, like its tendrils were basking in the light of the suns despite the blanket of darkness that covered the sky.

Magic.

Riven was using magic. Besides Feron's attempts to comfort me into admitting the truth, I'd never seen a Fae use their power before. Compared to the stories of shapeshifting or lightning strikes, this was mild, but I was awestruck all the same. What was Riven doing with that plant? What other powers did he have?

Riven opened his eyes slowly. His irises had a vibrant glow before settling to their usual dark violet. His breath hitched when he realized how close our faces were. I pushed the thoughts of the last time we'd been this close from my mind. Riven's mouth twitched, and for a moment I wondered if that kiss in Cereliath had been more than a mistake.

"She's waiting for you in the pub," Riven whispered hoarsely, cutting through the tension that had settled between us.

"Did the vines tell you that?" I was only half joking.

"In a manner of speaking." Riven stepped out of the alley, disappearing into the shadows. I rolled my eyes and followed him. When we reached the western outskirts of the city, his pace finally slowed enough for me to walk beside him.

"You're not going to explain the thing with the vines?" I said, raising a brow.

Riven looked over his shoulder, eyes scanning the roofs, before turning back to me. He pointed to a small crevice between two abandoned dwellings and pushed me against the wall.

He grabbed my wrist. His grip was firm but gentle as he pulled a vine from the canopy over our heads. He braided the vine around my fingers before placing his own through mine. "Every living thing can speak to one another," he whispered as he called his magic forward. "Just as Elves speak to Fae, or animals speak to each other."

I let out a breath in disbelief.

"Plants are the best communicators," he said, ignoring me completely. "They rely on it. Speaking to each other is part of their survival." Drops of suspended rain sprinkled from the petals above as he shook the vine. They spattered against his cloak.

"You're saying you can speak to the plants?" I asked in wonder.

Riven nodded and the vines wrapped between our hands started to glow. I could feel heat anywhere the plant touched my skin and something else. Something like . . .

"Sadness?" I thought aloud. Riven's eyes opened immediately, and the glow stopped.

"You could feel that?" he asked, letting go of my hand as the vine swung along the wall.

"Was I not supposed to?" I blinked. What had the hand-holding been for?

"Some warmth from the magic yes," he said. "But reading the

plant is something only the gifted should be able to do." Riven's jaw clenched, his brows stitching themselves together. This was becoming the expression he usually wore around me.

"I didn't read the plant. It didn't say anything to me."

"They don't actually speak to you," Riven said, his words tense and short. "Not in words. It's more like a feeling. With practice, a Fae can learn to sense one plant from another. Eventually, we can use them to sense others nearby."

"The plants can sense Gerarda?" My mouth hung open. This was how Feron had known I was in Aralinth. I wondered how far these powers could be tested.

"Not exactly, more her essence. That she's new," Riven explained, his loose hand waving in the air. "Feron makes sure I can sense every resident of Aralinth, so newcomers are easy to identify."

I leaned my head back against the wall. "So Gerarda is sitting next to a plant?"

Riven's eyes flicked down the street and back along the roofs again. We were spending too long answering my questions, but I couldn't find the will to move without answers. "Everyone is next to a plant in Aralinth," he said. I looked up to the canopy of vines and closed blossoms above our heads but Riven looked down.

My eyes widened. "The ground?"

Riven nodded slowly. "Their underground network is much wider. Most of the buildings were formed with tunnel systems for the plants to grow through the walls."

That's why Feron didn't send scouts to watch my every move. He could track me from the comfort of his palace.

The Fae were more powerful than I'd thought.

"The king believes the Fae magic has completely faded," I whispered.

Riven's mouth was a straight line. "The king is mostly right. Many of our powers have faded. What we still have access to is usually . . . restricted somehow. Especially mine."

I tilted my head. "What kind of—"

"I need to make sure she's still there. We've been stopped too long," Riven said, cutting off my question. He wrapped his wrist with the vine again. Part of me wanted to reach out and feel the sensation of the magic once more, but I didn't.

"What are your expectations for this?" Riven's husky voice cut through the rain that had started again. The rain would provide good cover for us as we raced to beat Gerarda to the mountain pass. I wondered if that was another product of Fae magic. Did Riven have the ability to call forth rain? Had the stories told across the kingdom held some truth?

"Expectations?" I shot him a sideways glance. We had left the last of the inhabited dwellings behind. Only empty stone houses lined our path now. The blinds staked along their windows clapped in the heavy wind, so we had to speak louder.

"For this alliance," Riven said. We were standing under the stables of the pub. He leaned against the post I'd climbed up earlier. His head almost grazed the rafter as he glared at me. He wanted an answer.

I dropped my saddlebags onto the ground. I rubbed my shoulder, a stinging rush of blood returned to where the strap had cut off circulation. "They depend on yours," I said as I stared back. It was the truth. I was taking a gamble just as much as he was.

I could see him weighing our options in his mind, his violet eyes were on my skin, but unfocused. Like he wasn't seeing me at all.

"Are you willing to put all your cards on the table?" he asked, his attention cutting back to me again. "Tell me everything I ask you?"

"Absolutely not." I held too many secrets. Most of which would cost people their lives if Riven betrayed me. And the rest were secrets I'd never spoken aloud. If that was the cost of the alliance, it wasn't one I was ready to pay.

"Would *you* agree to that?" I asked, hanging my cloak along a stall door to dry.

"No," he said, shaking his head. "But an alliance between two parties that don't trust each other is doomed to fail."

I smoothed the wrinkles along the black fabric of my cloak. Fat drops of water fell on my muddy boots. I couldn't disagree.

"So what are you proposing?" I asked, facing him. I wanted this alliance to work, needed it to. But our chance of defeating the king was slim. I wouldn't forfeit the lives of people I had spent decades protecting on hope alone.

"We tell each other what we *need* to know," Riven said, emphasizing his point with a jut of his strong chin. "Not anything more, but not anything less." He crossed his arms and pushed off the post. His large frame cast a shadow over my face as he took a step toward me, but I didn't move.

"I don't make promises," I said, staring at him. "If I agree to your terms, we have an agreement. I'll hold up my end, but I don't swear oaths and I don't make promises."

Riven's brow lifted as he squinted down at me. I thought he would protest, but he only shrugged.

"How would we know if the other is being dishonest?" I asked.

Riven shrugged again. "We'll just have to—"

"Trust each other?" I cut in. I couldn't hide the sarcasm from my voice.

Riven loosed a heavy breath. "*Hope* that our shared distaste for the king is enough to keep us honest."

"And if it's not?" I asked, kicking the mud off my toes.

"Then one of us is a traitor. To the Halflings, and to themselves." It was more than just a statement; it was a dare. Riven wanted me to prove him right. That I was nothing more than a Halfling who had crossed her own kin.

I wasn't merely untrustworthy to him.

I was irredeemable.

I ran my tongue along my teeth. Riven could hold whatever opinion of me he wanted as long as he helped blow up that dam. All I cared about was freeing the Halflings. If agreeing to tell him the bare minimum cleared the path to Silstra, then so be it. Riven's opinion was his own problem.

I held out my hand.

"Need to know," I said, shaking Riven's large hand just as Nikolai and Syrra appeared. They were armed and packed.

If a revolution was coming, it started now.

CHAPTER TWENTY-THREE

Riven left the rest of his Elverin with Collin. I tried to listen to their conversation, but Syrra brought me outside to ready the horses. I couldn't hear more than muffled bickering over the noise of the steeds and the rain. When Riven barged out of the door, his brow was creased, and I swore the shadows swirled around him. I scented the rage pouring off his skin as his heart raced.

Collin was evidently not a fan of the alliance. Or me.

Riven mounted his horse without a word. I followed behind Nikolai as Syrra carried the tail. We headed southwest, leaving Aralinth behind. Balls of faelight suspended in the giant branches of Sil'abar grew faint until they were nothing more than stars in the night sky.

No one spoke when we reached a grove. The moons hung in the sky, lighting our path that ended at the edge of the forest. Tall trees with black leaves were encased by thick brush. Heavy vines wrapped around the branches like serpents, so wide a blade would have trouble hacking them away.

Whatever path had existed here was overgrown. I pulled on the reins of the horse they had given me, bringing the brown mare to a halt.

"There is no need to stop," Syrra called from behind me. "We must make haste."

I snapped my head back, pointing to the blocked path. How could she not see it? Her Elvish eyesight should be as good as mine.

"Watch," she said, nodding toward Riven. I turned back in the saddle. Riven and Nikolai had not stopped. I watched Riven's horse step into the brambles. It was too thick—the horse would maim itself in the brush—but that didn't happen.

As soon as its hoof touched the lush greenery, it disappeared. Like a glass tableau, it shattered, revealing a well-traveled path through the wood. The forest receded, the tall trees and thick vines cleared enough for two carts to travel side by side. The branches and vines braided across the treetops, weaving a canopy so thick overhead no moonlight filtered through at all.

Syrra pulled her horse beside mine. "It is called a glamour."

"Magic," I whispered. "Did Riven do that?" I watched his cloak disappear into the darkness. Nikolai followed without looking back.

"No, this glamour is tied to the land. It uses its magic," she answered, her black eyes studying me. "Once you know the truth it hides, a glamour loses its effect on you. You now hold a secret of the *Faelinth.* I hope you are worthy of that trust." She gave one last evaluating stare before clicking her tongue and catching up with the others.

I paused, feeling the weight of her words on my back. Another secret I had to carry. I would—I had no reason to betray the Fae—

but I couldn't help but wonder how many more secrets I would hold before my work was done. My fingers shook in the cold rain as the familiar burning crawled up my throat. I wanted to drown myself in wine until I forgot about the secrets entirely, until the weight of them could be taken off for good.

Instead, I pulled the vial out of my pocket and let two drops of *winvra* coat my tongue. The sweet, tangy juice warmed my skin and numbed the pain in my throat. The craving settled to a mild ache in my stomach, and I trotted into the black.

I took first watch the next night. We hadn't stopped since we'd left Aralinth, traveling through the night and the entire next day. We curved through the wood to the south of the city and back up toward the pass. Too tired to speak, we rode in silence until our backs ached, not stopping until our bodies were numb.

We wanted to put as much distance as possible between us and Gerarda. She could already be heading back to Elverath, only a few hours behind us. I knew Gerarda would ride fast and long once she left Aralinth. Every minute we weren't resting needed to be spent on the trail.

I let the others warm their bedrolls by the fire and sat with my back against the trunk of a tree. Its leaves were pinkish in the firelight and its bright yellow vines seemed to glow. It bore no fruit that I could see but smelled of flowers all the same. I kept my exhaustion at bay by whittling sticks to sharp points with my knife. They'd make useful skewers or traps on the road, but mostly it distracted me from the weight pressing on my eyelids.

The forest was quieter than when I'd crossed before. The wind whistled a faint song through the leaves that must have put the creatures to sleep. Even with my heightened hearing, I didn't sense anything lurking around our camp. I nestled closer to the tree, leaning my head back as I cut into a thin branch.

Something moved. I raised my head at the noise, hands wrapped around my blade. But I didn't need to bother. It was only Riven standing up from his bedroll. I watched him stretch, arms wide, his neck craning to one side. He snapped around as if he sensed me watching.

I started whittling the twig again, ignoring him. He marched away from the camp until his footfalls were too faint to hear. When he came back, he held out a water sack, freshly filled, and took a seat beside me.

"Did you poison it?" I asked.

Riven snorted. He grabbed it back and took a large gulp. "Don't give me any ideas," he said darkly, holding it out once more.

I took a small sip, the water cool and fresh on my tongue. I took another. Riven's eyes fell to my lips as I handed the sack back. I dried them with the back of my hand. Riven's gaze flicked to the fire. The hazy outlines of two bodies were just visible through the flames. Syrra slept so still, with her hand resting on the circular blade beside her, ready to attack. Nikolai shivered as he snored softly, half of his body stretched out from beneath his coverlet.

"What are you doing?" Riven asked. He took another gulp of the water. "You're supposed to be on watch."

I shot him a hard glance before carving out another thin slice of wood. "I'm making skewers. To snare and cook with. And since my hearing is just as good as yours, you should know that nothing is sneaking up on us while I'm awake."

I thought he would rebuff what I said, add a sneering comment. Instead, he picked up one of the sticks. I passed him a knife from the bag beside me. We sat in silence, falling into a steady rhythm of slicing our blades through the wood. We finished our skewers at the same time.

"You can't know that," Riven said after a long silence. I pinched my brows together. "That your hearing is as good as mine. I'm Fae. You're a Halfling."

"And?" I threw the finished skewer into the pile and picked up another stick.

Riven leaned against the base of the tree, closing his eyes in a slow blink. "Fae are stronger than Halflings. Faster. Our hearing is better too."

I wanted to scoff and ignore him, but I didn't. The past two days had been filled with awkward silence. Whispered conversations between him and the others. I wasn't only the odd person out, but the one with the most to prove. My skin itched beneath my tunic. If I refused to reveal my scars as proof of my commitment to our mission, then perhaps I could gain his trust with a little bit of truth at a time.

"I was tested at the Order," I said, unsure if he would care. Riven didn't interrupt so I continued. "When they found me. I had no idea who I was. *What* I was. No parents to be found, no memories. The face and ears of an Elf. They almost killed me right there, but then someone pricked my arm with a knife and my blood ran amber." I stared into the fire until the blur of orange faded into the memory of that day. I'd been shackled by a king's guard until the Arsenal came to assess me.

"Halfling blood," Riven murmured, pulling me out of the reverie.

I nodded, dropping the stick into my lap. "But that wasn't enough for them," I whispered. "They tested me against other Halfling children whose lineage they could trace. Females and males. After a while even full-grown Halflings. But I was always stronger, faster.

Every test they gave me, I passed." My throat swelled, stifling my voice. They'd only been the first tests I would pass. The others would be tests cast in blood.

Riven set his arms on his knees as he whittled the last stick. "They thought you were Elven born?" he guessed.

I nodded. "Most did. A couple even thought I was Fae, despite my blood. But my ears are longer than yours, aren't they? More like the eastern Wood Elves, I was told. So that's the conclusion they came to in the end. I was born from Elf and Halfling." I tucked my knife back into the roll of blades beside me.

"What about you?" Riven asked, turning his head toward me. "What do you think?"

I took in a deep breath. Without anything distracting my fingers the exhaustion crashed through me. "I don't think it matters," I said with a shrug. "Halfling blood is Halfling blood. I'm no different than any other. Not under the decree."

"You're here," Riven said, chucking the knife on top of the roll. His arm stretched across my chest, casting his scent of dew and birchwood into the air. "You're more free than any Halfling I've ever met." He did not try to hide the venom in his words.

I scoffed. The names etched into my skin burned, begging to be unmasked. I rubbed my arm through my tunic and sighed. Only those who'd never been through the Order would think a Shade was free.

"I'm not as free as you think," I said, too tired to add any fight behind the words. "And the freedoms I do have come at a cost most never pay."

I could feel Riven's eyes on my face, watching me as I tilted my head back, trying not to fall asleep.

"Enough about me," I said through a yawn. "Do I get to know anything about you?"

Riven paused, his eyes flicking back and forth between me and the stick he twirled in his hand. "What do you want to know?"

"How old are you?" The question had been bothering me since we struck our deal in Aralinth. I'd never heard of Riven. His stories were not told in the kingdom. He was either too young or too inconsequential to have any legends of his own. I'd spent too much time wondering which one it was.

"Older than a Mortal." I raised a brow, keeping my eyes closed. "Older than you," he added.

"I was born after the last Fae female died," I said, rolling the back of my head along the rough bark to look at him. "I already knew that." Only two Fae could produce another Fae. The children of Fae and Elves were always Elves—they had no magic. If children between Fae and Mortals ever happened, their names were lost to history. Except for Killian. But if the king was to be believed, he'd been blessed with eternal life for ending the Elves. Yet hundreds of Elves still lived in the Faeland, so maybe the king was not as human as he claimed.

"Are you as old as your uncle?" I asked. Even though the Fae didn't age, I already knew Feron was older. His emotions were muted in a way that Riven's weren't. It reminded me of the easy nature of old Mortals. No longer quick to anger like those of youth.

"No," Riven said. "Feron is one of the oldest of our kind now." Each word fell out of his mouth in heavy syllables as if he couldn't decide whether to answer my question.

"At least tell me if you're older than Nikolai," I said. It was clear after only two days that Riven and Nikolai were close. The way they flipped between easy laughter and scalding remarks reminded me of brothers.

Riven weighed his answer before standing up and turning toward me. “Nik is older,” he said. He crossed his arms and took a step away from me.

“How much older?” I pushed. I would just as easily believe that Nikolai was eighteen as eighteen hundred.

Riven’s eyes bore into my own before breaking into a smirk. “Need to know,” he said, reminding me of our deal. That was all the information I was getting out of him tonight.

“I can’t sleep,” he said. “I’ll take the rest of your watch.”

He walked away, leaving me beneath the tree. I’d known Riven for days, joined together for every hour, but I still knew nothing about him. Beneath the Shadow’s hood had been a Fae wearing a mask, a mask he seemed reluctant to take off.

The journey through Wiseman’s Way was tedious. The winding pass curved around the mountains while a cold breeze fell from their peaks. My fingers stiffened against the reins as the forest thinned the higher we climbed. We rode our horses until they refused to walk any farther. I helped make camp while Syrra and Nikolai fed an elixir to each horse to help them heal and ride strong again on the morrow. They whispered together in Elvish, too quick for me to catch. Riven didn’t speak at all. If the others were bothered by this, they didn’t show it.

It took three days to reach the eastern side of the range. The slight decline slowed our horses along the narrow path. We were forced to ride in single file between the rocks that had slid down the mountains. Riven stopped his horse beside a pile of large stones. He steered his ride into them, and they vanished.

I blinked. One moment there had been a pile of rocks, the next a thin trail off the main pass leading to a crevice in the rock face. It was a cavern, glamoured by the Fae. No one would stumble across it, unless they knew the cave was hidden behind the rocks.

Gerarda wouldn't either.

We settled into the small cave for the night. Riven took the horses deeper into the mountain where a small spring pooled along the rock face. They could rest there while we waited for Gerarda to catch up to us along the path. I set my bedroll next to a small crevice along the cave wall. I let myself be dragged into oblivion as soon as my head crashed against the thin roll.

I woke hours later to the three of them bickering around a small fire. I lay still, listening but not turning to face them.

"Three of us are more than enough." Syrra's hushed voice sounded annoyed.

"Perhaps, but it's still a risk," Riven said. I could tell by the impatience in both their voices that this conversation had been going on for a while.

"It is worth it if it means we will not be caught unawares in Caerth or Cereliath," Syrra shot back.

"I understand that," Riven snapped.

"I hear she's tiny. I doubt it would take three of us," Nikolai said louder than the others.

They were talking about Gerarda.

I sat up, shooting Riven a stern look where he rested against the wall of the cavern. Syrra sat next to him, glaring at me.

"You're not killing the Dagger," I said bluntly. I rubbed my hands over my face and through my hair. I thought our last conversation had resolved the issue.

"And why not?" Riven asked sarcastically.

"Because even if you manage to kill her," I said, crossing my arms, "there are at least six Shades waiting for her in Caerth. They won't be easy to quell if their mistress doesn't return. And if we're forced to kill them as well, the Arsenal will know something is up before we even make it to Silstra. The entire point is to evade the king's notice for as long as possible."

"And what if the Dagger finds the cave?" Syrra asked, throwing a pebble into the fire.

"She won't," I answered, stretching my arms behind my head. "You told me Feron glamoured this cave himself. It will not fail us. And if it does, if she discovers our alliance, I will strike her down myself." I didn't break my stare with Syrra as I said the words. I wanted her to know I meant it. I didn't *want* to kill Gerarda, but I would.

"She's right," Riven said after a moment. "We can't afford to draw attention to ourselves." He lay down to sleep, refusing to look at any of us.

But I wasn't done. He could hate me all he liked, but whatever distaste he had for the Shades needed to be stifled before we reached the kingdom.

"Good," I said, tossing a pebble at the wall above Riven's head. "I wouldn't want you to be a hypocrite."

"I'm not a hypocrite," Riven spat, taking the bait. He sat up, his dark eyes devouring me like a wolf after its prey. But I could be a wolf too.

"Really?" I pursed my lips. "Didn't you tell me you wanted to save the Halflings? That you saw them as your *kin*?"

Riven nodded, his scowl made his high cheeks even more severe. His violet eyes swirled with rage as his chest breathed heavy.

"The Shades are Halflings too," I said, standing up. Heat flushed my skin and my stomach churned as I looked at Riven's disgusted face. "You don't get to judge them for being the monsters the king turned them into. The Shades weren't born as weapons. They weren't born as killers. They were born as *children*. Stolen. Ripped from their parents and placed on that godsforsaken island." My hands turned to fists at my side. My voiced cracked as I continued, but I refused to break away from Riven's gaze. "They were children faced with a simple choice: survival or death. You have no right to judge them on how they survived it. If you want to liberate the Halflings, you liberate them all."

Riven's brow furrowed. He didn't look at Nikolai and Syrra who sat frozen in their bedrolls. He just turned over and went to sleep.

CHAPTER
TWENTY-FOUR

I WOKE TO SYRRA CLEANING one of her blades and the others packing their bags. I leaped up out of my bedroll. Gerarda must have passed while I was asleep. I reached for my dagger at my hip, but its holster lay on the ground beside me where I had placed it the night before.

Syrra kept wiping her blade, murmuring to herself before she addressed me. "Calm down, child," she said softly. "We did not hurt the Dagger."

My eyes narrowed at the weapon on her lap. "You didn't?"

"It is good practice to tend to a blade before one starts a journey. That is all I am doing." Syrra dragged out each word with another wipe along the steel. "The Dagger passed only an hour into my watch. I tracked her down the path. She camped for a few hours and then continued on. We are a half day's ride behind her now."

"She'll reach Caerth by the morrow," Riven cut in, buckling a saddlebag.

"Should we wait another day? Just to make sure we don't catch up to her," Nikolai asked, one of his legs shook as he strapped a bag to his horse. "This is all for nothing if we run into each other in Caerth."

I shook my head. "We don't need to travel with the same haste as before, but we need to travel. The Harvest draws closer every day. We can't afford to lose another." The leaves of the forest had already begun to turn, though the colors were different here. Black leaves turned gray and the burning crimson of the Elder birches shifted to dark amber.

"You're certain she won't dally in Caerth?" Syrra asked for the third time.

"No. She thinks I'm back in the kingdom. Whatever it is she came to tell me, she can do so using our networks. She already thinks I'm headed back to Koratha; she'll only spend the night. Knowing her, she'll stay just long enough to hear a report from the Shades and catch a few hours' sleep. She'll leave with them at first light." Gerarda prided herself on her quick travel, often forcing her Shades to ride eighteen hours a day during assignments.

"She won't leave the Shades in Caerth? To watch for who may follow her out of the *Faelinth*?" Riven asked, coming from the back of the cavern with the last horse.

"Gerarda travels with three pairs of Shades. There weren't any stationed in Caerth when I came through, so I suspect she'll leave one pair behind to surveil the city. They will not be a threat to us."

Riven froze, the reins falling from his hand. "You mean to kill them?" he asked. His eyes turned to slits as he stared at me.

I shook my head, trying to hide the disgust from my voice. "No, the entire point is to *not* alert anyone to where we are or where we're headed. When we reach Caerth, I will seek the Shades out. I can learn why Gerarda was in the Faeland and send them off with a message from me."

"You want to meet with the Shades in Caerth?" Riven repeated. He dropped a saddle onto the back of his horse and buckled it with a strong tug.

"Yes," I said, preparing myself for a fight. "Managing them is smarter than hiding from them."

"Absolutely not," Riven said, slicing his hand through the air. The black steed beside him swung its head away from his hand.

"I thought this was an alliance?" I said, my blood simmering beneath my skin. "So far you've fought me every chance you've had."

"And I'll keep fighting you as long as you're trying to get us killed!" Riven bellowed, his anger bouncing against the walls of the cave.

"We've been trapped in this godsforsaken cave for three *miserable* days!" I yelled back, throwing my arms into the air. "If I wanted to kill you, why would I suffer through that?"

"Even *I* wanted to kill you after the second day," Nikolai muttered under his breath. Riven flashed him his fangs.

"Enough," Syrra interrupted, holstering her blades. I took the moment to strap my own dagger back on my hip. The next time Riven decided to fight me, he would be met with steel. "We allied with Keera *because* she is the Blade. Keeping her from using such sway only disadvantages our mission."

"So we're settled," I said, slipping the dual blades into the holster along my back. "Two out of three is better than nothing. Riven, you're outvoted."

"Hold on." Syrra raised her hand toward me. I could see where her scars met her hand. Brown leaves that faded into the sand-colored lines of her palm. She might be the only Elven warrior left in existence. My skin itched with the desire to pull up my sleeves and bare my own. Her proud scars alongside whatever mine were. I tugged my sleeve lower along my wrist. Syrra wouldn't understand why I carved the names, how I'd tried to reclaim something I'd never even known. She would scoff at my mockery of her order, the sanctity of her skill.

I may be better than a Mortal in her eyes, but I would never be an Elf.

"I agree that sending the Shades away is preferable to disguising ourselves," Syrra said evenly, "but that does not mean I trust you, child." She crossed her arms as she faced me. Her mouth was drawn into its usual straight line.

I shrugged. I didn't trust them either. The only show of good faith they'd demonstrated so far had been *not* killing someone.

"Nikolai can come then," I offered. "Make sure I don't get up to anything I shouldn't be." My eyes shot daggers at Riven who was saddling the last horse. His shoulder blades were pinched together. He didn't like the suggestion, but he didn't reject it.

"Me?" Nikolai said, placing his hands on his chest. "What am I supposed to do?"

"Nothing," I said, my attention turning to him. "Don't speak. Don't even breathe if you don't have to."

Nikolai huffed.

"I mean it, Nikolai," I said, loading the rest of my blades into my belt. "The only reason you're coming is because Riven thinks I need to be supervised. You're the only one who can pass as Mortal."

"Do I get a weapon?" Nikolai asked with a crook of his brow.

I raised an eyebrow back at him. "Do you know how to use one?"

"Not really," he said with a shrug. "But I don't want your friends to know that."

"The Shades are not my friends," I said automatically. "Shades don't have friends."

"And why is that?" Nikolai asked. He was studying his nail beds, but I could see his nonchalance was an act. Probably for Riven's benefit.

"Because friendships get you killed."

The suns set as we reached the outskirts of Caerth. We only passed a few wooden dwellings before Syrra turned her horse toward the safe house at the south edge of the city. Nikolai and I would continue to the market in search of the Shades. Each of our hoods were pulled forward, shielding our faces from any curious townsfolk.

The others wore different shades of traveling cloaks, but I wore my black cloak and silver fastener. Both felt tighter around my neck now that we were in the kingdom. I coughed, pulling the silver sword off my throat with my hand. Riven's back was straight in his saddle, his knuckles bulged from gripping the reins so tightly. He nodded at Nikolai before leveling me with a deadly glare.

"If you do anything that results in his death, I'll hunt you to the edge of the realm." Riven's eyes were dangerous storms, churning as he held his anger back. I could see the worry in the violet clouds, worry that this would be the last time he saw his friend.

I turned to Nikolai, expecting to see a surly smile, but instead I saw Gwyn. The worry I felt each time I left her alone at the palace within the clutches of the prince. I blinked and Gwyn was gone. Instead, Nikolai had transformed into *her*. She disappeared in an instant, fading back into my dreams where she belonged.

I snapped my head to Riven, willing the memories to stay locked inside the vault I kept in the darkest reaches of my mind. It had been so long since I'd let myself think of her face, felt the burn of her absence.

I swallowed, flinching as the pain rose to my eyes. I don't know if it was the need for a distraction or the concern on Riven's face, but something called me to pull out the bloodred dagger at my thigh.

Without thinking, I pulled the blade across the tip of my fourth finger, deep enough that amber blood began to pool. I reached over to Nikolai, mounted on his horse beside me, and wiped the blood across his forehead.

"If he dies by my hand, then I shall die too." Feron hadn't mentioned a specific phrase or oath when he told the story of Calen and his lover. Only that the magic of the vow was carried in the blood itself.

"Can she do that?" Riven asked, turning to Syrra. Her wide eyes trailed over my face and settled on my cut hand.

"She has Elvish blood," she murmured, tilting her head. "The Halflings do not hone their magic because the practice is kept from them, but they too have magic in their veins." Syrra's eyes flicked to Riven. He crossed his arms, his gaze falling back to me.

"The blood oath will hold," Syrra reasoned with a stiff nod.

I raised a brow at Riven. He refused to say anything else and started down the street toward the safe house. Syrra followed him, her eyes not leaving my hand until her horse turned down the path.

I turned to Nikolai. He was dabbing his forehead with a silk handkerchief from his pocket. "This can't be sanitary," he mumbled.

"I'd say I'm sorry," I whispered, leaning closer to his horse, "but I'll probably need to use that trick again before the month is out."

Nikolai pulled back his head in a laugh, his hood falling behind him. He winked before pulling it back up, casting his face in shadow.

I smiled back, hoping *my* blood would be the only blood spilled in Caerth.

My eyes burned as we approached the small wooden desk of the tavern. The walls were polished, but the stench of piped tobacco clung to the wood, nonetheless. I could feel the stale aroma soaking into my clothes as Nikolai coughed behind me.

The Piper's Pub was too fitting of a name. I never stayed at the inn while traveling through Caerth. Its reputation for a poorly stocked bar was enough to have kept me away. But it was also known for being cheap. And where most saw it as an inn for grifters, Gerarda saw it as the most responsible way to spend the Crown's coin.

I knew this was the only place she'd allow the Shades to stay.

"I don't need to see your faces, but if you insist on keeping your hoods on then I need payment up front." A rough voice called from the other side of the desk. I peered over the edge as two brown eyes blinked up at me. The woman's back was bent with age and her legs shook violently as she stepped up onto a stool, popping her head out from behind the desk.

Nikolai began to laugh, but I pressed my heel into his toe.

"I'm looking for the Shades that have been staying with you," I told the old woman. Her eyes widened but then settled onto the silver sword fastened at my neck. In the clouds of smoke, it was the shiniest surface in the room.

"They have yet to return, Mistress." Her words came out in a quick roll. Her hard voice faded away to a quiet creak.

"Did they say when you should expect them?"

The woman shook her head.

I looked back at Nikolai, who shrugged. We would have to wait. Riven would hate it, but the Shades knew me well enough that I wouldn't chase after them. Especially after a week-long trip through the mountain pass. I couldn't risk alerting them that anything had changed.

We would have to regroup with Riven in the morning.

"I need two rooms then." I slid a small pouch of coin across the counter. The woman swiped the bag, quick for her age. "When the Shades arrive, tell them to wait for me down here at first light."

The woman nodded and passed a key to me and another to Nikolai.

"Shall I send up a flagon of wine?" The woman eyes didn't meet my own, but instead lingered at the silver blade fastening my cloak.

The heat in my throat reignited and my hand stiffened in a fist around the iron key. It had been days since I took my elixir. My heart hammered hard enough against my chest that I could hear it. There was nothing I wanted more than some wine, but I knew after weeks of abstaining, my thirst wouldn't end with a single flagon.

Nikolai laid a gentle hand on my shoulder and my attention snapped back to the woman and her question.

"That won't be necessary," Nikolai said from under his hood.

My throat still burned, but my shoulders relaxed at his words. Before I could think better of it, I dashed up the stairs and into my room. I leaned against the door, pulling at the clasp along my neck. I whipped out the vial of black liquid and placed a thick drop on my tongue.

I heard Nikolai walk up the hall and pause. I closed my eyes, waiting for him to knock, but he never did. Eventually, I heard him unlock the door across the hall and close it behind him. I slumped onto the floor; I'd let Nikolai glimpse my need. He was too observant not to guess, a guess that he would tell Riven.

Maybe he was drafting a message to him at that very moment: *Don't do something stupid . . . But we're spending the night. And apparently the Blade has a craving for the Bottle.* I could even picture his overly flourished scrawl as he crafted his joke. One that Riven would not find funny at all.

I crawled to the bed and collapsed on top of it. I had no clothes to change into, but I didn't care. The only thing I saw when I looked up at the pitched roof was Riven's scowl. The one he'd have when he realized that he'd hitched himself not only to a killer, but a drunk. The thought of it stung deep in my chest.

My mind no longer craved the drink, but my body did. It had been so long since it had faded into that dark oblivion. A place too dark to see the ghosts of those I'd killed. Too cold to feel the sting of that truth.

But that's all it had ever done. With every bottle I swallowed, I created moments of nothingness, where I could breathe just a little more freely. I had chased those moments for decades, trying to forget who ordered the deaths of those I'd killed. Forgetting my promise to end the king.

This alliance was the closest I'd ever gotten to achieving it. No flagon was worth risking our chance, no matter how small, to end the king's reign. We would either succeed and the Halflings would be free, or we would die.

I was fine with either outcome.

CHAPTER TWENTY-FIVE

NIKOLAI TALKED IN HIS SLEEP. Fortunately for Riven, he didn't reveal anything interesting. He only mumbled a few words in Elvish every couple of breaths. Though from the words I did catch, he seemed to be having a good time. I kicked his bed and smirked when he jumped, holding the sheet over his bare chest.

He really would be easy to kill. Even the most novice Shade could do it.

"The suns are about to rise," I said in Elvish. I propped myself on the edge of his bed.

"How did you get in here?" Nikolai asked, pulling off his head wrap.

"I'm the king's Blade. You don't think I can pick a lock?" I replied in Elvish again. In truth, I'd come through the window. Sleep had abandoned me well before dawn and I'd decided to watch the stars fade away from the roof. And keep an eye out for the Shades.

Nikolai's sleepy modesty faded away with a single yawn. He stretched his arms above his head so that the bed sheet fell to his hips. He peered at me with one eye and smirked before standing up, completely naked.

I rolled my eyes. Nikolai chuckled and reached for his trousers, which were draped along the chair.

"It's nothing I haven't seen before." I tried for a bored tone, knowing it would annoy Nikolai most.

He popped his head out of his shirt with wide eyes. "Your Elvish is very good," he said, switching to the King's Tongue.

"Why wouldn't it be?" I grabbed Nikolai's boots and tossed them at him.

Nikolai cocked his head curiously. "You were raised in the Order. I didn't realize there was opportunity for learning Elvish there."

"There was for me." I thought about telling him exactly how I'd learned it, but I knew the truth would only upset him. It was too early in the day for that conversation.

"You all don't need to speak the King's Tongue for my benefit," I added as Nikolai tied his boots.

"It's not for your benefit," he said. Even facing the floor, I could see his brows knitting together before retying his laces. "It's Riven's call. He thinks we're less conspicuous if we speak in Mortal tongue. It's become a habit."

I nodded. Nikolai's lips were pinched into a thin line. There was something more to the decision he wasn't going to tell me. I let my curiosity go. We didn't have time for it anyway.

"Let's go." I opened the door, waiting for Nikolai to catch up behind me. "Hood," I reminded him before he left the room. Mine was already drawn over my face. The ends of my cloak trailed the tips of each step as we descended the staircase.

The innkeeper was there, waiting for us. Dark circles had appeared under her wrinkled eyes. She had not yet been to bed.

"They never arrived," I said. It wasn't a question, but the old woman nodded all the same.

"Have their rooms been emptied?" I asked.

"No, Mistress." Her voice cracked. "Their spare clothes are still hanging in their room."

My shoulders tensed. I shot a quick look to Nikolai, but he was already walking out the door.

"If they return, tell them they're not allowed to leave this tavern until I speak with them," I shouted behind me, following Nikolai to the stables.

We saddled the horses without saying a word, refusing the help of the stable boy who had been sleeping in one of the empty pens. I hurled my body onto my brown mare and galloped down the street, trailing after Nikolai. I let my horse steer us through the city as my eyes darted along the rooftops, searching for a sign of the Shades.

Nothing.

My stomach lurched. There were only two reasons why they would not return to their post. They were dead. Or someone else was.

Nikolai led us to a small house on the south side of the city. Its roof was faded, and the front window was cracked like many of the other dwellings it was nestled between. Syrra appeared outside as soon as we approached.

"What happened?" My voice was harsh, but I didn't care.

"There was a scout in the middle of the night," she said, her arms tucked behind her back. She stole a glance at Nikolai, who shook his head in exasperation. "It seems the rest of our group ran into some trouble on the road."

"The Shades?" I asked, gripping the reins so tightly my knuckles ached.

Syrra nodded.

"Where is Riven?" I demanded.

"He went back with the scout. I was to wait here for you." Syrra's eyes darted to Nikolai again. I didn't need to live centuries to understand the look between them.

"You mean you were told to keep me distracted." I seethed through clenched teeth. My heart raced inside my chest; my vision clouded.

Syrra didn't bother to protest. We both knew it was the truth.

"Where is Riven now?" I demanded again.

"He is an hour's ride toward the mountains." She motioned to her horse that was already saddled. She'd known there would be no stopping me once I found out where the Shades were.

"Not the way I ride." I kicked my horse into a running start and flew toward the flaming red trees of the Burning Mountains.

The Elverin we'd left behind in Aralinth were camped beside a small creek just a few strides from the main path. Two Halflings jumped in front of me as I approached. I pulled tightly on the reins, but my horse reared and kicked one of them in his chest.

"You deserve it," I spat, jumping off the horse and passing the reins to the other Halfling. Her eyes were angry slits, but she took them without complaint.

The rest of them had formed a wall between me and whoever stood on the other side of it.

"Riven!" I roared, pulling the dual blades from my back. "If you're still alive, you have three seconds to call off your hounds before I put them down." I swung a blade above my head and crouched. One more second and I would begin with the Halfling on my right.

"Let her pass," Riven commanded. I'd recognize that cold disdain anywhere.

The group pulled back. Riven was standing next to a small fire with one of the Shades bound and gagged beside him. Her eye was already black, and a thick line of blood marked her mouth. Her blond braid was stained amber.

"Put down your weapons," Riven demanded. His voice was icy and hard, but it only ignited a raging fire inside my chest.

"What is the meaning of this?" I lifted my blades in front of me and bent my legs. The slightest move and I would pounce.

"There was an attack—"

"Where is her partner?" I didn't see the second Shade. If she'd escaped, our plan was doomed.

"She's dead." A cheerful voice cut through the crowd. My eyes scanned through the bodies until they landed on the smug smile of a sandy-haired Halfling. Collin.

Nikolai and Syrra finally caught up. Syrra launched herself off her horse before it even stopped, pulling out her circular blades and placing herself between me and Riven.

"What's going on?" Nikolai's tone was too casual as he slipped off his horse.

"Riven was just about to tell me why his scouts *killed* a Shade," I said, gritting my teeth.

Nikolai gulped. His eyes shifted to Riven.

"Like I said"—Riven's dark eyes cut to Nikolai—"there was an attack. The Shades ambushed the caravan last night."

The Shade tied next to the fire began to thrash against her bindings. Her angry words were unintelligible with the thick rag stuffed down her throat.

"There were only two of them," I bellowed, pointing to the tiny bundle of a girl in front of me. "If the Shades did attack them, then they did something to provoke it."

Riven's eyes flicked to Collin who was staring at the ground.

I pointed my blade at the young Halfling. "Speak," I commanded.

Collin looked to Riven who nodded. I took a step closer, so the tip of my blade was only a few inches from his chest.

"We were camping in the woods. I was on watch with Tarvelle." Collin pointed his chin in the direction of a tall Elf with deep brown skin and green eyes. "We were filling canisters from the creek when the Shades attacked us."

I shook my head and tilted my blade toward Collin's heart. I heard it begin to race, pumping against his chest in fast, ragged beats. "Why did they attack you?"

Collin shrugged. "Because we were easy prey? I don't pretend to know why killers kill." The sneer Collin shot my way didn't go unnoticed.

I jabbed my blade at Collin's throat. He fell back, a small drop of amber blood pooling along his skin as he hit the ground. I pulled back my blade and holstered both behind my head. Collin's eyes shifted to Riven and back to me. When Riven didn't rise to defend him, he turned back toward the crowd, scurrying to safety on his hands and knees.

If Collin wasn't going to answer my questions, I knew someone who would. I walked over to the Shade whose eyes were stalking me. I knelt in front of her, so our eyes were at the same level.

"Do you know who I am?" I asked gently. She nodded. Her pupils were so wide her eyes looked black, lined with red from the punches she had taken. I could tell from the deep bruising that the blows had happened after she'd been restrained. Shades protected their heads at all costs; they were our greatest weapon.

I shot a look at Riven, prepared to hurl every curse I knew toward him, but his eyes were soft and guilty.

"That stopped when I arrived." His voice was as hard as his clenched fists. I knew that he wouldn't allow the same to happen again.

I turned back toward the young Shade. I pulled softly where her braid was caught in a piece of rope. "I'm going to remove your gag now," I whispered. "I need you *not* to scream."

She nodded again.

I pulled out one rag and another behind it. Complete overkill on the part of her captor, though I assume that was the point. Collin had wanted some retribution before he killed her too.

"What's your name?" I asked.

The Shade shifted her jaw up and down in stiff jolts before she answered. "Alys." The word was raw and labored.

"And your partner's?" I asked as gently as I could.

"Elinar."

"Why did you and Elinar attack the Halflings?" My eyes darted back to Collin, whose arms were crossed along his chest, raising with each heavy breath.

"He was speaking ill of you," Alys answered.

My eyes widened. "Of *me*?"

She nodded. "He said it was stupid to believe anything the Blade said . . . that they shouldn't trust someone who spent her life killing her own kin." Her eyes dropped down to the ground.

I placed a gentle finger under her chin and lifted her gaze back to mine. "What else did he say?"

"That you were luring them all to their deaths. And that if they were smart, they should kill you in your sleep." She sliced Collin with her eyes and spat in his direction. I was tempted to smile at her guile, but a wave of dread burrowed into my chest so hard that each breath left my lungs raw.

"So you attacked because he was going to kill me?" My eye twinged where hers was bruised. She was hurt because of her devotion to me, and I hadn't even known her name. My hands were iron fists, clenched so tightly that I dented the skin of my palm. I didn't care. It was nothing compared to Alys's wounds or Elinar's fate.

"We assumed you must be in the midst of some plan to lure the Shadow out of hiding. He was threatening that plan. Elinar—" Alys broke off as tears poured down her face. I reached out to Nikolai knowing he would have a handkerchief. He passed me a small square of silk without saying a word.

After a moment, Alys started again. "Elinar and I were in the woods to bathe and pick some burning leaves for a healing ointment. The group appeared on the trail, and we hid to surveil them. But we'd only brought two weapons between us. It was not enough to disarm them."

I closed my eyes, trying to keep my face neutral. It was against protocol for Shades to travel anywhere with so little to protect them, but Alys was young. I wouldn't be surprised if she had graduated with the last group of initiates. With only two years on, she hadn't seen enough of the world to grow wary at every turn.

And now she would never get the chance.

I pulled out a small case from the inner pocket of my tunic. Inside were seven glass darts filled with a flaming red liquid. One spot was empty from the sleeping draught I'd used in Aralinth. I pulled one out and pinched the tiny vial between my fingers.

"You're safe now," I murmured, bringing the dart against Alys's arm. Her brows furrowed. Her eyes widened even further, dancing back and forth between my hand and my face. I grazed her cheek with my thumb. "Shh . . . This will help you sleep. I won't hurt you and you won't feel any more pain."

It was all I could offer her.

When her breaths settled, I raised my hand to her arm again.

"Okay," she said. I pushed the dart against the sleeve of her tunic until it pricked her skin. Within seconds her body slumped against my shoulder. The dart would keep her unconscious for most of the day.

But she wouldn't live that long.

I lowered Alys's unconscious body to the ground, careful to make sure that nothing pressed too hard against her swollen cheek or bloodied ribs. A loose strand of hair covered her face. I tucked it behind her ear. Despite the bruising, she looked peaceful and even younger in her sleep. Long lashes framed her unlined eyes and tickled the soft freckles along her nose.

The handkerchief she had used to wipe away her tears was still clutched between her fingers. I pulled it free and tossed it into the fire. Someone behind me gasped, but I didn't have the patience to argue with Nikolai over fine silks. There were matters to be discussed.

"Where is Elinar's body?" I asked Riven, standing to my full height. His dark eyes were studying the unconscious Shade at my feet. I could see the thoughts swirling behind his furrowed brow.

"She was left by the creek," Riven said in a low rasp. His eyes were locked on Alys's face.

"Send two of your best to retrieve her. If they touch her with anything other than the gentlest of hands, I will slit their throats." His violet gaze shifted to me for the briefest moment before he nodded to two Halflings dressed in green cloaks.

"Do as she says," he instructed. They moved instantly, cutting through the crowd toward the creek behind us.

"I would send the rest of them away," I said, more calmly than I felt.

"I'm not going to fight you." Riven's shoulders tensed, but his hand drifted toward his sword.

"I don't want to fight. But what I have to say isn't something you want heard by the group." I crossed my arms. If he insisted on having this argument in front of everyone, I would. But I'd rather the likes of Collin leave us alone.

The two Riven had sent to fetch Elinar's body returned. They laid her beside the fire next to Alys. Her face was unmarked, but her tunic was soaked in blood. The handle of a small Elvish blade protruded from her chest. At least her death had been a quick one.

Something about her launched Riven into action.

"Collin, you and your unit will continue on to Cereliath. Don't stop in Caerth. Travel light and travel quick. You know where to wait for us." Riven's tone was unyielding.

Collin opened his mouth to reply but closed it with a single look at Riven's crossed arms and daring eyes. He nodded and marched toward the wagons.

"Tarvelle," Riven called to the tall Elf who had stabbed Elinar. "You'll take the rest into Caerth. Wait two days and start sending out teams to the trade routes we'll be targeting. Syrra can brief you while you ready the horses." Tarvelle accepted his orders with a slight bow. Syrra was already waiting for him by a group of mares, whispering the locations in Elvish.

I waited in silence as the groups dispersed. My tongue burned like the flames beside me, waiting for the opportunity to lash out. Finally, the only people who were left were Riven, Syrra, and Nikolai.

I pulled out a small blade I kept holstered in the belt along my hip. It was shorter than most of my weapons but was one of the sharpest. It would make for a painless death. Quick enough that a victim would not wake from her slumber as the steel pierced her flesh.

I handed the blade to Riven.

"What's this?" he asked, holding the blade in his palm.

"She cannot live—she knows too much. The person responsible for that should be the one to end her life." My voice was hoarse. The fiery rage in my stomach burned low, leaving only smoke in my lungs. My throat ached and my eyes stung with each word. Alys had been dead from the moment Collin had opened his mouth.

"My Elverin did not attack the Shades. I won't take responsibility for Collin's act of self-defense, no matter how unfortunate the circumstances." Riven's nose wrinkled to its sharp hook, his lip pulling into a thin line.

"Collin would never have been attacked if he didn't feel *entitled* to openly disregard your commands," I snapped back. "The Elverin were meant to wait for instructions in Aralinth. They left against your orders."

Riven's fingers wrapped around the small handle hard enough that I could see veins pulse in his hand. He looked at Nikolai and Syrra, but neither of them spoke. "I will speak to Collin when we arrive in Cereliath," Riven offered quietly.

"Collin is an idiot, but this was *not* his fault," I said. Riven opened his mouth to protest, but I cut him off. "You made your disdain for *me* and this alliance clear to everyone who follows you. And then you left Aralinth without giving them *any* reassurance that you thought this plan would work. Without any insight as to why you agreed to this alliance in the first place. Your only concern was to make sure I, and everyone else, knew how much you *despised* it. Message received."

I turned toward the flames, hoping the heat would reignite some of my rage, but it didn't come. My throat was raw, and my chest ached as I tried to ignore the two young Shades lying at my feet. One dead, one about to be.

All my emotions drained out of me; I was just an empty shell. "I expect you to have reservations about me," I said softly. "About our plan. I know none of you trust me. But we won't succeed if every scout, every Halfling with an attitude, feels like they can question your orders. Be insecure in private—I don't care. But in front of *them*"—I pointed toward the path where the caravan had disappeared—"you need to be steadfast. Unwavering. You need to *lead* them, Riven, or it'll be the ruin of more than just these two lives."

"You expect me to stab her in her sleep?" Riven choked. I turned back to him. His hand holding the knife was shaking.

"Would waking her to die in fear bring you comfort?" There was no malice in my voice. I knew there was never any comfort in taking the life of an innocent. It was time for Riven to learn the same.

Syrra stepped toward the fire, unsheathing a dagger of her own.

"I can do it." Her lips drooped as she looked for Riven's approval.

"No." I held up a hand in front of Syrra. "Passing the blade to someone else will not relieve any of the pain; it will only add to it," I said, closing the distance between us. I placed a hand on Riven's shoulder. "You will carry her death on your conscience until your last breath, regardless. The *least* you could do is ensure no one else carries that burden with you. Give her the honor of only haunting one soul and not two."

Riven leaned into my hand, dark violet eyes boring into mine. Tears pooled at the corner of one eye, but they didn't fall. Instead, Riven took a deep breath and blinked. When he opened his eyes, they were focused and resolved.

"Let me know when it's done," I said, leaving him to kill her.

CHAPTER TWENTY-SIX

RIVEN EMERGED FROM THE WOODS twenty minutes later. His long hair blew against his face in the breeze, but he didn't lift a hand to move it. He rode his horse with unfocused eyes, his back stiff, and his limbs rigid.

Nikolai and Syrra followed him, already on mounts of their own. Nikolai's eyes tracked Riven's back. His usual smirk was gone as he gnawed on his bottom lip. I didn't say anything as he passed.

"I'll meet you back at the safe house," I told Syrra as she brought her horse to a halt.

Her dark eyes studied me for a long moment.

"Only someone who has carried that burden many times over would recognize it was a lesson he needed to learn." Her lips barely moved as she spoke. Her eyes broke from my face and focused on the backs of Riven and Nikolai, who'd become ants along the trail.

"We will wait for you back at the safe house. Do not linger long."

Syrra clucked her tongue once and her horse cantered away, leaving me alone with the Shades.

Each step back to the fire was a struggle. My boots turned to iron, almost too heavy to walk in. My breaths were ragged by the time I reached them. The blade I'd given Riven stuck out from Alys's chest, matching the knife that had ended her partner's life. Elinar's face was untouched, as if she'd been sleeping too. Her black hair was pulled back behind the sharp points of her ears and fell in a loose spiral beside her. Where her braid ended, Alys's blond plait began, trailing back up to her soft face.

They were tied together in death, as they had been in life.

Had they been friends despite everything the Order preached? Alys's sobs for her partner rang in my ears, my throat raw like I'd cried them too. Memories I'd spent so long trying to forget scratched at my chest until my eyes stung. My body was a shell filled with nothing but loss. It was all I knew. And all I gave.

Perhaps it had been a kindness to end Alys's life instead of forcing her to live in the world without Elinar at her side. Friends or not, they were all each other had. All each other knew. Life after a loss like that didn't feel like a life at all.

I built a single pyre, large enough for the girls to lie side by side. I picked up Elinar first. Her body was light and feeble in my hands. I hadn't realized how short she was until then, how fragile. Alys was next.

I fixed their braids back in the connected swirl and joined their hands. The knives were still buried in their chests, but I didn't remove them. If there was any chance of revenge after death, I wanted them armed. Every Shade knew her life would end in violence. It was an honor to know death came in one hard blow rather than the sum of a thousand pricks.

I hummed a sad melody I didn't know the words to. Low, soft tones like the rumble of night rain. I stopped halfway through, unsure of how the song finished, and lit a piece of driftwood in place of a torch. I lit the pyre in five places just like I'd seen Hildegard do for the fallen Shades whose bodies made it back to the Order. I stood, staring at the flames, and didn't move until their bodies were nothing but ash.

Whatever strength I had shattered when I watched those girls burn away. I'd left Koratha in search of the Shadow to save initiates from an early grave. I'd made the alliance with Riven to save *all* the Half-lings. But not even a full day in the kingdom and two Shades were dead. How many more Halflings would die before the king was killed? How much more blood could my hands carry?

In the smoke of the pyre, I saw the shadowed faces of all the lives I'd taken. Most were innocent Halflings who called out to their names etched into my skin. My flesh seared with the hundreds of deaths replaying in my head.

Their pleas for mercy reverberated through my skull. The wails of parents knowing their children were being taken. Or worse, killed by my blade too. All the deaths the king had ordered. All the lives I'd been forced to take in his name.

I fell to my knees, warm ash coating my trousers as I screamed. I wanted to swear to the woods, to whichever creatures hid among the trees, that I would never kill again. But I couldn't. That was all I'd been trained to do. My days taking lives in the name of the king were over, but my days of killing were not.

My shoulders bowed under the weight of that truth. My steps

scuffed the dirt as I walked to my horse and slumped over the saddle. I could only manage a soft tap with the stirrup, but she set a trot back to Caerth without need for reins.

I reached the edge of the city just as the suns began to set. I didn't turn down the narrow street that led to the safe house where Riven and the others were waiting. Instead, I kept on the main road in search of a pub.

I stumbled into the first building that smelled of cheap ale and spilled wine. The floor was tacky as I meandered to a table and waited for the barmaid to find me. A young woman with curly black hair and rouged cheeks materialized beside the table. Her skirt brushed against my leg. It left an ashy mark on her apron.

I doubted it was the worst thing she'd ever had on her clothes.

"I'll take your strongest drink." I slammed a small pouch of silver coins on the table. "And keep them coming."

She stared at the coin for a moment before she swiped it away. She reappeared with an ale so dark it looked like night turned to drink. I held the vial of *winvra* elixir in my hand. I pictured myself tasting the sweet liquid and marching out the door, but my legs couldn't carry the weight of the pain anymore. They needed rest. They needed oblivion.

I seized the goblet and swallowed it in one gulp.

I woke up in a bed. A hard one, but better than the sticky floor of the pub I remembered crumpling onto. The room was dark and small. I felt the familiar pull of my tunic along my scars and the weight of blankets. My boots were off, but my long socks were still on.

I lifted my head and my skull split open. Someone lit an oil lamp across the room. I blocked the light with my hand and saw the outline of a person as I squinted. I wanted to ask who was there, but a large belch bellowed from my stomach instead.

"There is a bucket beside you."

Syrra.

I threw my body over the edge of the bed and vomited into the slop bucket. It was already partly full.

"What happened?" I was too nauseous to care that I couldn't remember.

"You binged half the ale in Caerth." Syrra crossed her legs.

I felt like I binged half the ale in Elverath. I wiped my mouth. "Are we at the safe house?" The curtains were drawn, and I didn't sense any sunlight behind them. We could be anywhere in the city.

"No," Syrra answered.

I rubbed my temples. "Why not?"

"I figured you would not want Riven to see you in a state like this. Or Nikolai."

I opened my mouth to respond. No words came. What reason did Syrra have to show me any kindness? I certainly hadn't tried to win her favor.

I vomited again. Syrra passed me a damp towel.

"Why?" I only had the strength for short sentences.

Syrra stood from her chair and stared into the small flame of the oil lamp. I almost retched again before she spoke.

"I know the pain you feel," she said, still staring at the light.

I wiped the cloth across my lips again. "You can't."

"No?" Syrra scoffed. "I have lived for millennia, *ikwenira*. Long before your king came to these shores. Before the magic started leeching from the ground. When my people were free and at peace. Spent their days training and laughing and loving under the suns." Something caught in Syrra's voice, and she coughed.

"I watched it all fade away. I watched my people die. Watched my *family* die fighting the king you serve, knowing I was too powerless to stop it. I carried that guilt with me for a long time. I choked it down with more than drink too. Anything to spare me from that pain. Spare me from the memories. The decisions I made. And the ones I could not take back." Syrra poured a cup of water from the dresser and shoved it toward me.

"I do not pretend to know the details of your pain, but I know the weight of it. I will not judge you for how you lighten the load." Her dark eyes stared down at me. There was no friendliness in them, none of the warmth that shone when she looked at Riven or Nikolai. But there was no condemnation either.

The tension in my shoulders relaxed and I leaned against the headboard.

"What if the pain is too much? What if it crushes me?" I whispered. They were questions I'd only ever asked myself.

"It won't," she said simply.

I raised a brow at the certainty in her tone.

"If the pain was too much, you would have ended it by now." Her eyes cut through me, and I wondered if she had glimpsed what lay beneath my clothes. I pulled the bed cover higher up my chest.

Her words pricked my eyes until they stung. I blinked back the truth. "I don't deserve that kind of relief."

"The weight you bear is not your punishment, Keera. It is your heart. One day it will stop bleeding." Syrra's fist gripped her shirt over her own chest. Over her own stitched heart.

"I don't have a heart anymore," I said quietly. "It turned to stone the day I passed my Trials."

"What I saw today," Syrra said, "was someone who still cares. Someone who cares a lot. You might be in pain, but you still have purpose."

I winced. "To be the Blade?"

"To be whatever you need to be to get the job done." She made it sound so simple.

I leaned my head against the wall and stared at the dark rafters until the grain started to swirl.

"I'm too broken to get the job done." My head hung against my shoulders and my eyes pinched shut. My scars felt sharp, not like the knife that had cut them, but the jagged edges of broken glass. I was made of pieces, sharp edges that tore into me with every move I made. Every breath I took.

"A broken blade can be mended." Syrra's voice was heavy. For the first time I could hear the lifetimes behind her words.

"How?" I asked. My voice cracked again, eager for an answer.

Syrra lips twitched. She held out her hand to help me out of bed. "Killing the king is a good place to start."

CHAPTER TWENTY-SEVEN

THE MORNING AIR WAS CRISP, carrying the scent of wet earth as the first fallen leaves began to decay. Even at their highest, the suns no longer heated my back to the point of scorching. Most of the day, I kept my cloak wrapped tightly around my neck to stymie the chilly breeze that was our constant companion along the road.

Autumn was coming fast. The equinox was just over two weeks away and would start the Harvest celebrations. Silstra would mark the day by sending full barges of grain and vegetables down the Three Sisters—Eleverath's sustenance for the winter. The dam would need to be blown by then for our plan to have a chance at succeeding. A fact that wasn't lost on the group. We spent most days keeping a steady trot along the road. Conversation was minimal and always among the three of them.

Nikolai enjoyed my company, if only because I was someone

other than the two people he seemed to have spent his entire life with. Entire *lifetimes* for all I knew.

By the fifth day, we reached a village too small to have a name. There wasn't much to the town besides a large farm where most of the men and the Halflings worked. The sprinkling of houses was worn, shingles missing from roofs, and cracked panes of glass served as windows. Not that it mattered, since the windows were so thickly caked in dust, they'd stopped being windows long ago.

Riven and I left the others to set up camp. We would resupply the bags with enough food for the rest of our journey to Cereliath. I insisted on going because I wanted to check on a small refuge Victoria had set up in the village a few years before. Riven insisted on coming to watch over me.

We walked in silence from the small grove of trees where Syrra and Nikolai would ready the camp. It was a long walk into the village, but our horses needed rest more than we did. Riven stalked behind my intentional, slow pace. I could feel him growing more annoyed with each step. I smirked. If he was intent on making my journey miserable, we could both play that game.

We found the market soon enough, a collection of merchant carts lining the only street. I purchased vegetables that were already limp, and Riven bartered with a butcher over his lack of stock. I pretended to be distracted by a jeweler cart while they argued.

One of the other merchants told Riven the tavern had cured meats and would be willing to sell them for the right price. Riven gave the middle-aged woman a terse nod from under his hood and marched toward the tavern door.

I took the opportunity and fled down the street to where Victoria had told me the refuge was.

It wasn't much. In fact, if I hadn't known it was there, I might have missed it entirely. The shack leaned against the building beside it. Scrap wood and stained linens constructed the roof. Through the summer months it would've been enough to protect visitors from the suns, but there would be no way to keep in heat come winter.

The rose imprinted on the stone pathway was chipped and so weather-beaten that no one outside of our underground service would even recognize it as a refuge. Probably for the best. I walked through a gap in the wall that I assumed once held a door. The floor was hardpacked earth, and a small stove stood in the corner circled by four chairs.

No beds. No food.

Someone sat in one of the chairs, her toes pointing toward the flame of the oven. Her long, curved ears poked out from her white hair, so thin I could see the pink flesh of her scalp. She craned her neck when I moved through the door. Her eyes were heavy-lidded and framed by wrinkles so deep they looked like scars. Perhaps they were.

"Hello," I said cautiously, unsure if she could hear me. "I'm looking for the keeper of this house."

The Halfling didn't say anything. She nodded slowly without raising her head and reached for the cane leaning beside her chair. I thought for a moment she would try to stand up, legs buckling under the weight of her, but all she did was shake the cane.

A bell tied to the bottom of it rung. Soft, but distinctive amidst the dust and emptiness of the village.

Someone popped out from behind the shack, red hair pinned back against her head. She was younger, possibly even Mortal, her pale skin red along the bridge of her nose. Like the pale Mortals who flushed after too long in the suns.

"Wrae? What is—" She stopped, noticing me in the room. "Can I help you?" she asked, standing straight. Her eyes darted to the doorway behind me.

"I'm looking for the keeper of this house," I said again.

"You found her," she answered slowly, raising the basket of clean linen higher on her hip.

I smiled and flashed her the rose pendant I kept hidden under my tunic. She glanced at it and instantly relaxed.

"Oh, good," she whispered in relief. "I thought you were one of those Shades for a minute."

"Have they been here?" I asked.

"Yes," she said. "Though they were only passing through. I don't think they were looking for Halflings."

Gerarda would've taken this road back to the capital.

I tried to keep my tone light. "How long ago was that?"

"Six days, I think." She placed the basket down on the chair and began folding. "They didn't do much. Spent a night at the inn, ate some food, before heading back to the city."

"Cereliath?"

"Aye," she said.

"How many?" I asked, already knowing the answer.

"Four," the woman said. I nodded. Gerarda must've been at the inn waiting for the Shades to refill their stores.

I looked back at the Halfling, Wrae. She was asleep in her chair, her head bobbing against her chest as she wheezed.

"Do you have any others to care for?" I asked.

"Not at the moment," she told me. "Usually, I spend the funds getting them somewhere bigger. Cereliath or even Silstra. Easier to hide in crowds."

"And her?" I asked, nodding to where Wrae slept.

The woman smiled. "She's actually indentured to the farmer up the road. But she's too old to be useful. He doesn't care that she's here. Keeps the responsibility out of his hair and I can make sure no one gets any ideas about what to do with her," she added darkly. Many Halflings were disposed of when their owners decided they cost more to keep than they were worth. Some were barred from their houses. Others were found with a knife in their side.

She offered her hand in greeting. "My name's Emeline, by the way."

I shook it but did not offer a name of my own.

"I don't get a lot of visitors," she said, starting to fold her laundry again. "Though I don't get many needing my help either, so that's to be expected."

I pulled out a small pouch of gold. It was less than I usually gave; I needed to restock my stores when we reached Cereliath. It was all I had left.

"You may be getting more," I told her, tossing the pouch into her linen basket. She hid it in the layers of folded sheets. "We're trying to move as many Halflings west as we can, so if more come through, try to get them to Caerth."

"Caerth?" she whispered. "It's not much bigger than here. They'll be hard to hide."

"They won't be staying."

Emeline's blue eyes widened as she realized my meaning. Most Mortals never traveled outside of their city of birth, let alone into the lands of the Dark Fae.

"Will they be safe?" she asked in a frightened whisper.

"Safer than they are under the king."

Wrae woke with a start, her cane dropped as her chair shifted and fell to the floor with a loud ring of the bell.

"I'll take that as my leave," I told them. "Be ready."

I slipped out of the tiny shack and back onto the street. I didn't walk two paces before Riven marched out of an alley and grabbed my arm.

"What are you doing?" he whispered so harshly against my ear that I could feel the heat of his voice instead of just hear it.

"Trying to remember why I haven't stabbed you yet," I answered.

His fingers curled tightly around my arm, pressing hard enough that they pushed against my bone. I snarled at him. He stepped back in shock and dropped his hand. I rarely showed my fangs. Those in the Order who had them were trained to keep them hidden. Fangs were a sign of being unclean.

"I'm not going to let you lurk around with strangers and not expect an answer," he bit back, flashing his own pointed canines. Thankfully, we were out of sight from any of the villagers.

I scoffed. "What happened to *need to know*?"

"I *need* to know you haven't just betrayed us." His voice was a low growl.

I shook my head and shoved past him. I knew he wouldn't cause a scene in the middle of the village. This conversation could wait until we were back on the road. I felt his eyes penetrating the back of my skull as we marched through the village without saying another word.

The moment we were out of sight of the dwellings, he jumped in front of me, blocking my way.

"Who was that woman?" he asked, his voice full of venom.

I raised a brow. "You saw her?"

"Yes." His violet eyes traced my face. He was so close that I could feel the soft rush of air each time he exhaled. "I also saw you give her something. A message for the king?"

"What will it take for you to believe me?" I yelled, pulling at my hair with my hands. "I want the king dead. Even more than you do." How could he doubt that now? After what had happened in Caerth? Those Shades had died for no good reason. The guilt pricked me like thorns, leaving scratches that festered and oozed each time I choked the feeling down. I couldn't do it anymore. I had let too many thorns lash my skin. I wouldn't take the brunt any longer. I needed to tend to my wounds so my body would stop rotting from the inside out.

Riven turned away, ready to flee now that the tension between us was too heated. It'd been a trick he'd used many times as the Shadow, but I had already forced down that hood. His days of running from me were over. I grabbed his arm.

"No," I said, whipping his wrist toward the ground. "I won't keep running in circles and taking your taunts and snide remarks. We're all alone. No Nikolai here to calm you down or Syrra to run interference. What pisses you off more—that I *bested* you or that you *need* me?"

His violet eyes flashed as he took a step closer to me.

"I don't care that you beat me," he said, dark and slow like he was luring me into a trap. "I don't like that after years of serving the king, years of doing his bidding with no remorse and no guilt for the people you hurt, you just *decided* you were done. Threw off that black cloak of yours and swapped sides. Is that supposed to impress me? Am I supposed to thank you for helping us? What happens when this is all over? Will you answer for *your* crimes?" His breath was hot on my cheek, the rapid rise and fall of his chest beat against my own.

"That's what you think?" I snapped, refusing to retreat. "That I've been happy serving the king all this time? Do you think I enjoy my life, knowing it's paid for in blood? The blood of Halflings! The blood of *my* kin." Riven bit his bottom lip, the points of his fangs threatening to draw blood. His sharp cheeks were so close I thought they might cut me, but I didn't back down from the loathing in his eyes.

"You want to know who that woman is?" I asked him, too angry to wait for an answer. "She runs a refuge here. She helps hide Halflings from the king. From the Shades. I came to see her because I fund her work."

Riven's gaze trailed along my face as if trying to read the truth in what I said. "You know of the Rose Road?" he whispered incredulously.

So he knew about the refuges? I couldn't help the smug grin tugging on my lips.

"Know about it?" I shook my head, not breaking his gaze as I pulled out the bronze pendant that hung around my neck. "I founded it."

Riven studied my face, his gaze lingering on my bottom lip. For a moment, I was reminded of that second duel of ours. My body pinned against the wall with his, knowing I was moments away from death, only to feel the brush of his lips on mine. My breath stilled in anticipation. Would he do it again? Would I let him?

After a long moment, he took a step back, his eyes dropping to the ground. "I didn't know," he said softly.

"You didn't ask." I tucked the pendant back inside my shirt.

He looked up at me, his lips pursed. "You're right." He turned around and started back along the path.

"And for the record," I said, unsure why I felt the need to prove myself further. Why I cared about his opinion of me. Riven didn't turn around but stopped, waiting for me to speak. "I've never taken a life I didn't *need* to take. If the Crown falls and you want to put me on trial for the lives I did end, I won't stop you. Every life I couldn't spare, I carry with me. You don't need to tell me I'll answer for them one day. I already know."

I pushed past him, uninterested in speaking any more about his hate for me. Mine was enough for the both of us.

CHAPTER TWENTY-EIGHT

RIVEN TRAILED BEHIND ME the rest of the way. I didn't slow my pace or turn around to see how far his cloak lagged behind. The well-worn path from the village began to veer toward the King's Road, leading to Cereliath. I treaded off the path and onto the soft grass of the glade. A gentle wind blew through my hair and swirled along the edges of my cloak. I inhaled the faint scents of *winvra* and wheat that it carried.

The suns had well passed their midpoint in the sky; dusk would soon be upon us. My stomach rumbled loudly. I stepped into the small grove where Nikolai and Syrra were waiting. The forest was green, beautiful, but felt lacking after my time in the Faeland. I missed the metallic leaves and unusual combinations of colors along the brush.

I stumbled upon the half-made camp. A pile of wood lay in the middle of a small clearing. Our bags were dropped in their usual circle around the would-be hearth, but Nikolai and Syrra were nowhere to be found.

I leaned down, reaching for something to eat from my bag, when I noticed it. Three of our horses were tied along the trees but the fourth's reins hung loose. One of Syrra's circular blades lay beside its hoof.

Syrra would never discard her weapon so carelessly.

They'd been taken.

I pulled my cloak over my shoulders and crouched to the ground. I closed my eyes and listened as intently as I could. I heard the steady rhythm of Riven's heartbeat still crossing through the glade. To the west I heard running water, a spring from the cool, fresh scent in the air. Not far to the east, I heard faint murmuring.

I opened my eyes and headed east, listening for voices and heartbeats every few steps. The sounds grew louder as I hunted, curving through tree trunks like a wildcat stalking her prey. I noticed footprints in a patch of wet earth. They were new and slick but trampled over again and again. At least ten captors.

I crawled along the base of a small ridge. There was a large stone set among the trees and hidden behind thick brush. I leaned my back against the rock and listened.

"One Halfling—and an Elf!" a gruff voice shouted. "No one in the capital will believe it. Imagine the dinners that creature will buy." Several voices broke into a chorus of laughter. I tested the strength of a root wrapping around the stone. It didn't break. In one motion, I hoisted myself on top of the rock, peering over the edge at the scene below. There were over a dozen men, some burly and tall, others short and thin, standing around a fire. At the far side of their camp was a brown carriage. The outer wall of Koratha was painted on its doors, six miniature bodies hanging from the stone.

Traffickers.

Nikolai and Syrra were bound in ropes near the carriage. Nikolai was twisting his body, fighting the ropes that kept his hands tied behind his back. Syrra was tied too, but her body lay crumpled beside him. Dread ran through me like a blade. I watched her body to see if she moved, but Syrra was perfectly still.

I moved on instinct, pulling my twin blades from behind my back. I leaped off the rock, cutting the first man down before he could look up.

I perched on his shoulders as he bled. I counted fourteen more.

I stepped onto the ground as the first man fell. The second man turned around and caught my blade by the throat.

Make that thirteen.

Riven appeared at my side. He charged at a large man standing by the fire. Riven growled as he ran, giving up our position, but it didn't matter. I'd already taken my third kill. If they were traffickers, they weren't very good ones. Most weren't even properly armed.

How had they captured Syrra? Nikolai was understandable, but the Elvish warrior must have been incapacitated or worse. I looked to where Nikolai and Syrra were tied. He was conscious, trying to shout through his gag, but Syrra's limp body slumped against him. I spotted a red dart sticking out of her neck and relief flooded my body.

Sleeping draught.

These traffickers were better equipped than they seemed.

"About time," I shouted when the burly man fell with a hole in his belly. He and Riven had traded several blows before Riven had gotten an opening.

"Wouldn't want to outshine you," Riven called back. He was circling two men wielding double axes against his sword.

I smirked, holstering my blades along my back. A short man with weathered skin charged at me. I leaped, somersaulting over his head.

I threw blades into the throats of two riders still mounted on their steeds. They fell before I landed on the ground.

I swiped my leg at the man who charged me. He tripped. I grabbed my dagger, plunging it into his heart before he hit the dirt. Blood spurted from his throat as he gave one final cough.

Nine more left.

I ran toward the four men standing over Nikolai and Syrra. They stood, holding rusted swords, waiting for me to make a move. One was shaking so badly, his blade looked like it was made of linen rather than steel.

"Scared?" I taunted, holstering my dagger, and pulling out my own sword. The blade glinted in the sunlight.

Each man ran toward me at once. I dodged the first one, grabbing the hood of his cloak. I slammed him into the man that followed. They fell on top of each other, and I struck my blade through both men in one blow.

Nikolai was lying there, gagged and motionless. His eyes stared behind me.

I grinned as I turned my blade and buried it into the chest of the man behind my back. I didn't even turn around. A little reminder for Nikolai as to what I could really do. His wide eyes met mine and I gave him a quick wink.

The fourth man had stopped, holding his blade behind his head. He launched it at me, the hilt rolling over the blade in the air.

If Syrra and Nikolai weren't tied behind me, I would have merely dodged it, but I needed to make sure it landed away from them.

I dropped my weapon and jumped. I soared over the blade's path and tracked it from above, grabbing the hilt when it rose to meet my hand.

With a double-handed grip, I landed in a crouch and shot his blade back at him. It hit his chest with enough force that he was pinned against the carriage, six feet from where he'd stood.

I caught a flash of movement to my left. Riven had taken out both of his opponents and only one man was left standing. He held a blade in his hand, but it rested at his side. He held up a hand to Riven in peace.

Nikolai grunted through his gag, swinging his legs back and forth across the earth. Riven ran to him and pulled the gag from his mouth.

I reached for my dagger as I watched the last man, making sure he didn't move. He dropped his sword.

He raised his arms above his head. "I don't want to kill anyone."

"It's true, Keera," Nikolai said as Riven untied his hands and legs. "He argued with the tall one over there." Nikolai gestured to the burly man Riven had taken down. "He just wanted our money. Fought with the others when they attacked."

"I wish you no harm," the man added. "I'm just hungry." His blue eyes were pleading, but then they dropped to my neck. To the silver sword that marked me as the Blade. Understanding registered over the man's face, his arms dropping slightly.

I looked at Nikolai and Syrra. Both their faces had been uncovered when they were tied. I turned to Riven, his hood had been knocked down in the fight. The man had seen us all.

My blood cooled. My body stiffened. I took a deep breath and tried to focus on the mission. On the lives we would save.

It didn't change the fact that he was another life I would have to take.

"What is your name?" I asked the man, walking toward him.

Relief washed over his face, and he lowered his arms. He put out a hand for me to shake.

"Gareth," he answered.

I shook his hand, getting one last look at his face. Blue eyes and a jagged scar on his cheek. Then I drew my dagger across his throat.

"We need to leave. Now," I ordered to the three behind me. Refusing to turn around to witness their horror as I stalked back to the horses and our still half-made camp. We couldn't risk staying the night. Nikolai carried Syrra to his horse, hoisting her up on the saddle with him while Riven steered her steed. I didn't turn around until we stopped to make camp again, long after the moons had risen over our heads, Gareth's blood on my fingers shining in their light.

CHAPTER TWENTY-NINE

I LEFT THE OTHERS TO SET UP camp on their own and found a creek to wash the blood off my hands. I cut Gareth's name into the flesh along my ribs. His life finished the crest of one of the waves that framed my chest. I found a strip of linen in my saddlebag to bandage the cut even though it had already stopped bleeding.

I lingered at the edge of the creek, listening to the water wash the blood downstream. I wasn't eager to return to camp. They'd glimpsed the true nature of the Blade—*my* true nature. I knew whatever progress I'd made with Riven had been washed away just like Gareth's blood. I just hoped if they saw me as a monster, they saw me as a necessary one.

I returned to find Syrra and Nikolai bickering over which rabbit should be roasted first.

No one said anything when I sat down on my bedroll. Relief pulled me into the thin cushion. I didn't want to have to defend my choice to murder that man. I just sat and watched the smoke disappear into the branches above us. The leaves had already begun to fall, exposing the sea of stars that flooded the sky.

"Keera deserves first choice," Nikolai said once the rabbits were cooked and the tea made.

"It's fine," I answered. I didn't have the patience for his charm.

"It's a thank-you, Keera," Nikolai insisted softly, pointing a skewer at me. "You better move your ass and take it before I *throw* the rabbit at you." He lifted the rabbit Syrra was in the middle of carving and pretended to throw it. I laughed, but Syrra shot him a deadly look. I'd already learned not to get between that Elf and her food.

"Thanks," I said as I walked over.

"Thank *you* for saving us today," Syrra said, her face stripped of all sarcasm. On her neck was a paste to help drain the rest of the sleeping draught, though she would be lethargic for days.

I shrugged. "You would've done the same."

"I am ashamed to say I would have hesitated," Syrra admitted. Her dark eyes met mine; there wasn't any laughter in them. "Leaving you to perish would have seemed like a solution in the moment. From what Riven and Nikolai have told me, you did not even hesitate to weigh your options. I will not forget that, nor the life debt I owe you." She handed me a leaf of rabbit, including a large piece of leg. That alone was enough for me to know she was serious.

A shift had happened.

"I reckon *I* would've helped," Nikolai said with a sideways grin to Syrra. "But even if I had, there's no way I could've taken on fifteen men by myself. And certainly not as spectacularly as you did." Nikolai winked at me.

"Riven helped," I reminded them, taking a bite of my rabbit. Whatever Syrra had managed to add to it made the meat so much sweeter. I took another mouthful, my stomach rumbling in satisfaction.

"Not very much from what I hear," Syrra added between bites of her rabbit.

"I killed three of them!" Riven said. I thought he was offended but he shot Syrra a rare smile. It cut through my chest with its warmth. Riven was handsome when he wasn't brooding. "And I don't hear anyone thanking me for their lives," he added, throwing another log onto the fire.

"You killed three in the time it took for her to fell . . . ten?" Nikolai shot a glance to me.

"Eleven." I didn't hide my smirk.

Nikolai barked a laugh. "You were just there for moral support, Riv."

Riven crossed his arms and tried to hide his laughter.

"I prefer to think of him as an apprentice," I quipped. Riven's violet eyes darted to me, anger swirling behind them. He wanted to murder me, but I refused to look away. I'd meant what I said earlier that day. I would no longer entertain his judgment of me.

After a moment, Riven gave me the smallest grin and nodded.

"You're not half as bad as I thought you were," Nikolai admitted through his laughter. "I'm realizing you really could've killed us that day you barged through the window."

"Easily," I agreed, stripping a leg clean.

"Do all the Shades fight as you do?" Syrra asked. Her dark eyes studied me as if trying to learn where I hid my tricks. Always a warrior. In that way we were the same.

"We all receive the same training," I answered diplomatically, tossing the leg bone into the fire.

"That's a no then," Nikolai said with a wry grin.

"Any Shade could kill Nik if that's what you're asking," I replied with a smug smile of my own. Nikolai brought a hand to his forehead and slumped backward from his bruised ego. He peered through one eye to make sure I was smiling. I tossed a bit of rabbit at him.

"Do not waste the food," Syrra cut in. Her voice was light, but her eyes were serious. Nikolai choked on his laugh.

"And me?" Riven asked. "Could a Shade take me down?" He was standing against one of the trees. His expression was playful, but his jaw was hard. In the firelight, his eyes were pools of mulberry flame watching my every move; my skin prickled under his gaze. I was beginning to enjoy the feeling of it.

"You would beat a Shade, maybe even two," I said honestly. "If you ever get approached by three or more, I recommend you run. Fast."

Riven let out a small laugh before grabbing his food. He never fed himself until everyone else had served themselves. Even me.

"How many Shades could you take on?" Syrra asked, grabbing another piece of rabbit.

"As many as I'll have to," I answered. Two Shades had already lost their lives because of our alliance. I wasn't blind to the fact that many more would be killed before we reached the king. My only goal was to keep that total as low as possible.

Syrra gave me an understanding nod. I didn't look to Riven but could feel him studying me from where he stood.

"That took a dark turn," Nikolai said. He stretched along one side of the fire and kicked off his boots. "So, Keera, what's the most impressive kill you've ever made?"

I scoffed. "That's how you lighten the mood?"

Nikolai gave a lazy shrug. "As good a time as any. We all want to know."

I laughed, but when I looked up, three pairs of eyes were staring back at me. Waiting.

"I took down a brumal bear once," I offered. "With nothing but a broken arrow."

"You're lying," Nikolai replied, tossing a rabbit bone into the fire. It hissed and crackled in the flames.

"Straight through the eye." I unclipped the holster at my thigh and tossed it over to him. He gasped when he unsheathed it.

"Bloodsteel?" he asked in awe. He grazed his fingers along the dark red blade.

I nodded. "The damn bear broke the original hilt, so I replaced it with its bone." Nikolai traced the outline of the white handle, focusing on where the blacksmith had carved a paw print into its base. He passed the blade to Syrra. Her gentle fingers studied it in delicate appreciation.

"Bears aside," Nikolai said, his eyes lingering on the bloodsteel blade. "Who is your proudest kill?"

I froze. I wasn't proud of any of my kills. Killing was something I had to do, something I was very good at doing. But it had never been something I took pride in. Gareth's face flashed in my mind. I hadn't *wanted* to kill him. I regretted that I'd *needed* to. But there was no pride in that. No achievement or satisfaction. If anything, each one of my kills had chipped my pride away until there was nothing left. Until I felt less like a person and more like a killer. But that still hadn't made me proud.

"I know it," Riven whispered, pulling me from my thoughts. He had staked himself next to a tree, leaning on the wide trunk.

I looked up at him, confused.

"Last year in Silstra," he started, walking closer to the fire. Closer to me.

He sat down beside my bedroll and poked the fire with a stick.

"A gang of traffickers had been rounding up Halflings," he continued. "Taking them from the slums and whorehouses. There had been too many for anyone to stop them. No one wanted to risk their lives over a few Halflings."

Eighteen Halflings, I thought.

"Keetes's men?" Syrra cut in, her eyes wide in disbelief. "*Sixty-four* men were found hanging from the dams that night. You are saying it was all one person?" She looked at Riven.

He nodded.

"You?" Syrra asked, her eyes landing on me. "How did you do it? Find and move that many men in one night?"

I didn't respond. It had been a long night, and in truth, I didn't remember most of it. Just running, cloaked in darkness, taking the men one by one until they all were hanging from the canal walls. I threw the last of them over the edge just as the first sun was rising.

I had no idea how Riven had figured it out. I searched his face for answers, but he only shrugged.

"I knew the person responsible had to be someone dedicated to helping Halflings. Regardless of the risk," Riven said without looking at me. "When you showed me that pendant in the village, I knew it was you. Who else could've done it? Who else *would've* done it?" His eyes cut to me. All the anger they usually held for me was gone. Their violet hue was soft, welcoming even. Riven's brow crinkled as he traced the lines of my face, like he was seeing me for the first time.

"I should've realized sooner that it was you. I let my own assumptions cloud my judgment," Riven finished. It was as close to an apology as I was going to get.

He reached out and patted my knee. I felt that same shock of something between us that ignited each time we touched. It shivered through my skin and into my blood. Riven pulled his hand back, turning it over to study his fingers. Whatever it was that kept happening between us, Riven didn't understand it either.

The scene was just like the afternoon attack. Their carriage. Two horses standing next to where their riders had fallen with my blades in their throats. One of their boots still hung from a stirrup. The bodies Riven and I killed still lay where they fell, but Riven was nowhere to be found. Nor Syrra or Nikolai.

They were just gone.

Gareth stood in front of me, hands raised. I felt my hand moving toward my dagger, readying for the kill. I would have to do it again. I always had to do it again. The killing never ended.

But then it wasn't Gareth standing there at all.

It was her.

Blond hair set in soft waves fluttered in a breeze I couldn't feel. The sun radiated off her, bright as the smile she was giving me. Warm and wide, framed by rosy lips the same color her cheeks blushed when I looked at her.

I smiled back, reaching my hand out to touch her. Just once. Just one more time.

She stopped smiling. Now tears streamed down her cheeks, and the suns were covered by thick, gray clouds. Her honey-colored eyes swam in a pool of tears that flowed down her face.

"You promised," she whispered, reaching out to me.

You promised.

You promised.

You promised.

No. I would not do this again. Why did she keep coming for me? Keep making me relive it over and over?

"Don't make me do this," I pleaded.

"You promised," she sobbed and fell to her knees.

"I never promised this," I told her, as I had so many times before.

I walked over to her without wanting to. My body was not my own. It was powered by the will of my dream. Of my memory.

She looked up at me. Heartbreaking and beautiful.

"You promised, Keera," she whispered.

I ran my dagger through her heart. It was the only thing I could do to silence her.

I woke on the dirt, dim light cast over my face from the dying fire. Someone's arms were wrapped around me. They were whispering something in my ear.

"It's okay. You're okay." It was Riven. His voice was softer than I'd ever heard it. His hand stroked my hair as he whispered more calming words.

I relaxed into him, too exhausted from the dream to care what he thought of it or how close his hands were to the scars on my back. Adrenaline coursed through me, leaving my breaths ragged as I tried to remember none of it was real. It wasn't real.

Riven pulled his head back to look at me, holding my cheek in the palm of his hand. "You were scaring the horses," he murmured.

"I didn't mean to," I answered dumbly. "Usually, they're not that bad. The dreams."

His fingers stiffened against my cheek. I expected to see anger in his eyes, but his stare was soft. His full lips frowned as his jaw flexed. Concern. My breath caught. It had been so long since someone had cared enough to worry about my nightmares.

"It's okay," Riven whispered, his lips brushing against my ear. He rubbed his thumb across my cheek and then stopped as if realizing he'd done it. He dropped his hand from my face, but I could still feel his warmth beside me.

"Do you have them often?" he asked softly, his eyes meeting mine.

I shrugged against the hard ground.

"Need to know," I murmured. Riven bit his lip, holding back a retort. He nodded and didn't ask the question again. I took a deep breath, the tightness in my chest beginning to loosen. When I breathed again, all I could smell was Riven.

"I thought you didn't make promises?" he asked after my breathing had slowed to its regular rhythm. I froze. What had I said in my sleep?

"I don't," I whispered after several breaths. "Not anymore."

"Because of the nightmares?" His brow furrowed as he wiped away the wetness on my cheek. I'd been crying.

I shook my head. "Because one broken promise haunting me is enough," I said, refusing to meet his gaze. I rolled back onto the softness of my bedroll.

He didn't ask any more questions. He just lay beside me until I drifted back to sleep. Just before that familiar blanket of nothingness crept over me, I felt the brush of something warm against my hand. We lay side by side like that, barely touching, until morning.

CHAPTER THIRTY

I WOKE TO THE SMELL of burning wood and cooked meat. Syrra was kneeling beside the fire, turning a fresh rabbit over on a spittle she'd fashioned from fallen branches. Her hands moved deftly as she spun the meat, stoked the fire, and finished brewing the tea all at once. Riven and Nikolai were nowhere to be found, but I had the impression that she'd sent them off.

"You can wake me," I told her, packing the bedrolls. "I don't mind doing my share of the work."

"When I feel like you are not carrying your weight, I will let you know." She smiled and there was a lightness in her eyes that had never been there before. At least not when she was looking at me.

"How long have you known Riven?" I asked. I'd been wondering about it since we left Aralinth, but I never felt like she would answer the question. Even now, I was worried she'd throw a burning stick at me.

"A long time," she answered, turning the rabbit over so its cut belly was tickled by the flames. "We both trained in Myrelinth together. Spent many days cutting each other with knives and beating the other to a pulp." Syrra grinned widely, her eyes glittering as she reveled in some distant memory.

"You're the same age then?" I asked, crossing my brow. I knew Syrra and Riven could be the same age; Elves and Fae lived for thousands of years before they died. But Syrra had always seemed older somehow, more like Feron. Never in a rush and never rattled.

She studied me for a long while before she answered the question. "I am older," she said simply.

"How much older?" I asked.

Syrra was distracted suddenly by the fire, grabbing her poker to settle it. I kept watching her.

"I am old enough that years pass like days," she answered vaguely. I leaned back, unable to comprehend the lifetimes she'd lived. My days as the Blade were long. Each minute serving the king pulled against me, stretching out the hours. If Syrra's days were anything like that, I prayed I had enough Mortal blood in me that I would not be cursed with immortality.

"Did you always want to be a warrior?" I asked, changing the subject. My gaze trailed along the swirling scars carved into her arm. Every branch and leaf marked a mastery of skill or great feat.

Syrra traced the scars along her wrist, smiling at the curved lines of her branches. "I was born a fighter. As soon as I was old enough to hold a dagger, my parents could not keep me from practicing dawn until dusk. I was given an apprenticeship earlier than most."

I'd never wanted to spar with someone so badly. I could spend days with Syrra having her teach me everything she knew. "And Riven?" I asked.

"He was a late bloomer," she said with a wry smile.

"Who?" Nikolai called from across the field. Riven was beside him. They both carried rabbits.

"It is no concern of yours," Syrra replied, flicking a red coal at him. Nikolai caught it in his hand without breaking her stare. I could hear the sizzle against his skin as he crushed it, but there was barely a mark when he opened his palm. I tilted my head. His Elvish lineage must be strong for his skin not to burn.

"We brought food, Syr." Nikolai shook the rope in his hand that held two rabbits. "It's only fair you tell us. It's Riven, isn't it? I thought we said we wouldn't make fun of him for never kissing someone until he was twenty."

Riven tried to smack the back of Nikolai's head, but Nikolai ducked. Syrra just shook her head.

"Sorry, Riv," Nikolai teased. "But obviously they couldn't be talking about me." He winked. Syrra rolled her eyes as she coaxed the flames. I coughed to hide my laugh.

"Twenty?" I repeated, giving Riven a sidelong glance. He was handsome; it was hard to believe that the Elverin of Aralinth had let him go so long without their company.

"I was *nineteen*," he corrected.

"By two hours," Syrra mumbled into the pot of tea.

"Fine," Riven admitted. "I wasn't as daring with the *ikwenira* as Nikolai. And Syrra had a habit of stealing the ones I managed to talk to." He cut her a sideways glance.

"You were terrible at talking to women," Syrra said with a smug look. "You still are." Nikolai sat down beside her, throwing an arm over her shoulder as he passed her another rabbit.

"And you two never . . . ?" I asked, pointing to Nikolai and Syrra. They were so close, always whispering together in Elvish or sitting together around the fire.

"Absolutely not," Syrra said. Her lips pulled back like she had tasted something bitter.

Nikolai dropped his rabbits and broke into a fit of laughter. "What gave you that impression?" he asked through his wheezes.

"You seem so close. I thought there was something between you," I said with a shrug.

"Nikolai is my nephew," Syrra replied. I thought she might vomit into her tea.

I tied the last of the bedrolls and piled them together. When Nikolai stopped laughing, I shot him a confused look.

"Your father was a Mortal?" I asked.

"No." Nikolai's brows knotted together. "He was Fae."

I blinked in confusion. "So *your* sister was a Halfling?" I asked Syrra.

"No, she was an Elf," Syrra answered. She reached out and touched my forehead with the back of her hand. Her lips tugged downward.

Riven was the first to realize the source of my confusion. "Nikolai is an Elf," he explained. "Not a Halfling."

Syrra's and Nikolai's brows both lifted at the same time. Now that I knew of the family connection, I could see it in the shape of their eyes and cheekbones.

"But your name is a Mortal name?" I thought aloud. "And your ears are cut?" I crossed my arms as I realized I'd only assumed he was a Halfling because of the scars along his ears.

Nikolai's smile faded. "My parents were caught during the last of the Blood Purges. Word hadn't reached them to head to the *Faelinth*. My father died protecting our clan. My mother escaped with me. I was only a babe, but she was caught outside of Volcar. One of the king's soldiers took pity on me and left me at an orphanage in the city. My ears were cut and I was given a new name to pass as Mortal. I was four when Syrra found me and took me home."

I didn't respond. The Blood Purges were how King Aemon took his throne. Well-organized attacks on unsuspecting Elves. By the time the Fae intervened, most of the clans had been killed off and Aemon had already claimed his crown.

"You never took your Elvish name?" I asked, reaching out a hand to Nikolai.

"I don't remember it," Nikolai said, squeezing my hand. "But even if I did, I wouldn't change it. It's a reminder of what happened to our people. What is still happening to our people." He cast his eyes eastward. The Elves saw the Halflings as their own. Kin they hoped would one day return to them, but I didn't know if I agreed. The Halflings were a lost people. No culture of their own. Even if we freed them, I knew some would refuse to see the Elves as their kin.

"Come now, Keera," Nikolai said after eating in silence. He offered his hand as he stood, but I ignored it and stood up myself. "The quicker we leave, the sooner I get to spend the evening falling in love with the maidens of Cereliath."

"No interest in the men of Cereliath?" I teased. It had certainly been an interest of his in Aralinth.

Nikolai rolled his eyes. "Mortals are so rigid in the way they see the world. I don't have time for the shame of their men. At least the maidens are fun."

"You'll spend your evening *terrorizing* the maidens," I said with a smirk. "It's your coin that will entice them, not your claims of love. And if you do bed a woman, I'll be sure that she was not a maiden to begin with."

Syrra barked a laugh. Riven had a curious smirk on his face as I mounted my horse.

"True enough, Keera dear," Nikolai said, chuckling into the mane of his steed. "The day I fall in love will be the day I'm a changed man."

"*If* you fall in love," I countered, tempted to stick out my tongue.

"There's the cynical side we've missed all morning." Nikolai laughed as he cantered ahead of the group.

Somehow the day passed more quickly than the ones before.

We arrived in Cereliath with only a day to spare. I looked up at the beautiful sandstone manor, turned russet in the light of the setting suns. Tomorrow it would be teaming with lords and their guests celebrating the start of the harvest. Lord Curringham would be the host with the key to the storehouses slung around his neck like always.

Riven and I left Syrra and Nikolai in the outskirts of the city. They would check in with Collin's crew and try to find rooms for us. Even the dingiest places were full when the House of Harvest hosted a ball.

I was in search of a tailor to make a dress. The event was only a day away. I knew every seamstress and tailor would be booked. It would take a fortune to get mine rushed ahead of all the other orders.

"I need to stop at the merchant house first," I told Riven as we passed our horses to one of the stable keeps. I tossed the boy a silver coin for his trouble. "I'll meet you in the traders' corridor in an hour."

I fought the impulse to roll my eyes at his cold stare. I didn't need to rile Riven up just as he was beginning to leave me alone. Riven nodded before he walked down the alley, disappearing into the crowd of people.

I crossed the circle, repositioning the Blade crest on my cloak. There was a line outside of the merchant house, Mortals trying their luck at a loan to buy a week's rations. The hungry who were too sick to afford one lined the outskirts of the city.

I walked straight through the large door. I didn't need to flash my crest. A young merchant met me at the entrance.

"How can I be of service?" he asked briskly.

"I need gold," I said and passed him a small piece of parchment with the sum.

"This is more than I usually draw without confirming accounts in Silstra," the merchant explained in a quiet whisper. He didn't meet my eyes as he spoke.

"The king cannot wait for Silstra," I said, tossing back my cloak to reveal the collection of blades underneath it. "I'm sure there is someone here who can testify that my account is in good standing." The account was full, even the large sum I was drawing would do little to drain it.

"Very well. I'm sure I can make an exception." He ran down the marble hall without saying another word. A few minutes later, he reappeared with a small wooden chest.

"In the bag is fine." I opened a large leather pouch with a drawstring closure. The merchant slipped several smaller pouches inside, each full of gold. I tightened the bag around my shoulders before covering it again with my cloak.

My next stop was a tailor. The sign that hung over the door was cast in bronze, a spool of thread and a needle cut into the metal. Inside were dresses of every fabric imaginable. Rich hues and intricate lace shipped from every realm. None of the dresses had a price tag.

I walked into the shop. Three women ogled one of the display dresses along the window. They glanced at me, their faces immediately blanching before they turned away in silence. I kept my hood on. I'd rather the women didn't glimpse my face, especially if they were going to attend the celebration we were crashing.

Keeping a low profile was more important than ever.

I meandered around the shop. Wilden had nodded to me when I entered, but he was busy fitting a client. She was a Mortal woman, middle-aged and finely dressed. The dress she wore was laced so tightly she took shallow breaths that made her voice come out weak and airy.

A lord's wife, most likely. They were the only women who wanted to wear the newest fashion years after their bloom.

One dress in the back caught my eye. It was crafted from thin silks of different shades. Deep reds, bright oranges, some as black as night. They were layered on top of each other, forming a tight bodice and long sleeves. The skirt wasn't full like other gowns worn by the aristocracy but followed the curved lines of a female body. The only hint of skin came from the high slit along one leg, ending at the hip.

The result was living flame.

I wanted to wear it, but when I walked around to see the other side, my stomach plummeted. The high neck did not continue along the back of the dress and instead, split completely to reveal an open back that only closed again just above the tailbone.

My scars itched through my tunic. There was no way I could wear the dress without exposing them. Exposing myself.

"Keera." Wilden called my name, coaxing me from my thoughts. My gaze instantly searched for the other women, but they were gone. The entire shop was empty apart from us. The sign on the door had been flipped over.

"Wilden." I nodded, taking off my hood. Apart from the dress I wore in Aralinth, Wilden made every gown I'd ever needed for a mission. "I need a dress."

"I figured as much," he said. His brown curls spooled over his face, and he brushed them back.

"I like this one." I pointed to the firestorm gown. "But . . ." I trailed off. Wilden knew that I liked to keep my back and arms covered. I'd never allowed him to see the scars, and he knew enough not to ask.

He traced a finger along the bodice. "Is it for the Harvest?"

"Yes, so I need something quick," I said with a twinge of guilt.

"You always need something quick," he joked, even though it was true. "I can make this work for you. Do you need a mask as well?" The Harvest Ball was always a masquerade.

"Yes. Something that actually disguises the face." Some women only wore thin strips of transparent fabric. I would need to try to disguise myself as much as possible.

"Ears too?" Wilden asked without a hint of judgment. He didn't care who wore his gowns. He cared only about the beauty of the final look.

I nodded.

"I'll need to get started right away. Take off your cloak. I need new measurements." He pulled out a tape measure.

"Why?" I asked him. He hadn't taken my measurements the last time.

"Because you look better than when I last saw you." His eyes scanned my body and the high cut of my cheeks. I'd noticed small shifts in my body since I left Aralinth, but I didn't realize they were noticeable to anyone else. My body had gotten stronger since I stopped drinking, muscles that had disappeared pulled taut along my clothes. The swelling along my jaw and belly had gone. Even the luster of my hair had returned.

Wilden unfurled his measuring tape and got to work.

I walked down the street, stepping around beggars who slept on the ground. I drew my hood farther down my face. It felt wrong passing the hungry with a bag full of gold, but I was still wearing my black cloak and silver fastener. I needed to keep up my reputation as long as possible.

I slipped into one of the alleyways to cut through the crowd. I walked briskly down the tight corridor when the shape of two figures caught my eye. I turned and saw Riven talking to someone down a branch of the alley.

Both their faces were blanketed in shadow, but I would recognize Riven's brooding mass in the pitch of night. The alley didn't lead anywhere. A few feet behind them was the tall back of a brick building. The only reason to meet someone there was to avoid being seen or overheard.

My instinct was to retreat into the shadows and scale the wall onto the roof of the nearby building. My eyes were already scanning to find a perch. But Riven wasn't a target. I knew we'd never be friends, but something pulled at my stomach at the idea of spying on an ally.

He didn't completely trust me, but I'd gained some favor since we left the Faeland. If he caught me spying, that favor would be forgotten. I watched Riven slip a package into the man's hand before I turned and walked away.

The man had been young, dressed in a burgundy tunic and well-cut trousers. The uniform of assistants at the House of Harvest. But what did Riven need brought in that we couldn't bring ourselves?

I shook off the question. I didn't trust Riven with everything either, but that wasn't what this alliance was. *Need to know.* The words echoed through my mind. Riven had respected that, for the most part. I would do the same. The only thing I needed was for him to help end the king.

For that, I trusted him completely.

I stopped beside a stall selling soaps. Tall glass bottles were stacked in piles along the edge of the cart. Each one of their stoppers was a different pastel color that glimmered in the setting sunlight. I picked up a bottle that smelled of birch and inhaled its freshness. I'd never had a home, but something about the scent brought me more comfort than anything else.

"Did you find something suitable?" Riven asked, materializing behind me. I nodded, taking another whiff of the bottle, my eyes closing to savor the aroma. I offered a small smile to the merchant in payment for his lack of sale.

"Nik found us rooms on the east side of the city."

"The Cornstalk?" I guessed. It was small but clean.

Riven nodded, and we walked to pick up our horses in silence. The suns cast streaks of lavender through the sky. It would be dark by the time we reached the inn.

I followed Riven's horse. The days of travel were starting to take their toll. My body ached where it met the saddle, longing for a night's rest on a soft mattress instead of a thin cushion on the ground.

Riven fetched the keys as I boarded the horses. He came back holding a single black key and a crumpled note in his hand. "Nik and Syrra went to bed already. He says there were only two rooms, so they left us the key to one." He crumpled the parchment in his fist. Apparently, I had not gained as much favor as I thought.

He couldn't bear to share a room with me.

I froze with a saddle in my hands. I'd been so excited to sleep in a room, in a bed. A night spent not worrying about Shades or traffickers stumbling upon us. But mostly, sleeping without worrying about my clothes shifting and revealing my scars.

Riven had only just stopped looking at me like I was a monster. Exposing the endless list of names I'd carved into my skin would only prove him right.

We walked into a room on the second floor, and I realized why

Riven was so upset. The room was tiny, only wide enough for a small bath and bed.

One bed.

It was large enough to fit the both of us, but barely. We would be too close to ignore each other's bodies. I'd have preferred to sleep on a bedroll, but they weren't in the room. There was no space for one anyway.

My pouch was sitting on the dresser. I picked it up and unbuckled the top. The only thing inside was a change of clothes and my nightgown.

My body turned to ice. I hadn't shared a room with anyone since my Trials. While sharing a bed was less than ideal, that wasn't what stopped my breath. We weren't camped outside, under the cool light of the moons, wearing layers of clothing under our coverlets to keep warm. We were in a heated inn.

I didn't have anything to sleep in that hid my scars.

Riven turned around and noticed my rigid stance. "I can sleep on the floor," he said, crossing his arms. His low rasp was less harsh than usual but still annoyed.

"No," I replied too quickly. "It's fine." There was no way his hulking frame would fit on the floor.

I busied myself by unpacking my bag onto the bench. The nightgown was a soft orange, shiny and smooth to the touch. It was glorious to sleep in but left most of my body exposed. I tossed it onto the bench, not caring to refold it.

The rest of the clothes were layers of daywear. I settled on a linen tunic that was thick enough to hide my scars. Riven would have questions if he saw what I worked hard to keep hidden. There were too many stories inscribed along my skin. Stories that I'd tried so hard to forget. I wasn't strong enough to see the revulsion on Riven's face when he realized just what kind of creature the king had made me. That was *my* secret. One Riven didn't need to know.

I disappeared into the bath, using the small basin of hot water to clean the dirt off my skin. It was barely a bath, but I didn't care. If I smelled of horse shit and sweat, maybe Riven would give me more space on the bed.

I came back out wearing different clothes, but still a tunic and trousers. Riven glanced at the rumpled nightgown on the bench, but he didn't say a word. He left me in the bedroom as he washed.

I climbed into bed, taking the side pressed against the wall. The mattress was soft, coaxing the ache out of my limbs. I closed my eyes, willing myself to fall asleep before Riven returned. I counted my slow breaths, but the dreams didn't come. I faced the wall, readjusting myself to try again. It didn't work. I just lay there, listening to the mumbled sounds of Riven splashing water from the basin.

I heard him damper the lamp next to the door and settle onto the side of the mattress. It buckled under the weight of him. He took a single gulp from the waterskin and pulled himself under the blanket we had to share.

His elbow briefly touched my back and I yelped. I turned, flattening my back against the wall so he couldn't touch it again. My chest rose and fell in shallow breaths. I could still feel the press of his skin along my spine, hot and pulsing like a burn.

"I didn't mean to scare you," he said softly. With my heightened senses I could see the furrow of his brow as he studied my face. He bit the inside of his cheek, staring at me with wide eyes. "Are you okay?" he whispered, sliding his face closer to mine.

"I don't like having my back touched," I said, placing a hand on my chest. I could feel my heart hammering against it. It beat so hard I thought it would shake the bed.

I took a deep breath as I pressed myself harder against the wall. Even with my eyes closed, I could feel the weight of Riven's stare. It bore down on me, pressing me into the mattress, anchoring me to his side. My skin rippled with that familiar spark, an electric current pulsing down my spine, urging me closer to him. I opened my eyes, facing him.

Did he feel it too?

I'd thought it had been some trick of his, some power the Dark Fae had to influence those around them. But Fae powers drained; they needed time to recover. This feeling between us was always there.

You don't feel it? Isn't that what he said all those months before. Right before he kissed me.

I hadn't noticed it then, but the same feeling had flooded my body the moment Riven pinned me against that pillar.

I glanced at his lips, thinking of how my body had responded to their touch. I'd written it off as a ploy, a distraction, but Riven was angered by it. He wanted to pretend that it had never happened at all.

I thought it was because of my title, because of what I'd done. Perhaps he resented what had happened between us that night. But the more time I spent with Riven, the more I realized that behind his brooding mask was a Fae I barely understood. He'd hidden in the shadows. And now he hid in his secrets. Maybe he only wanted me to *think* he resented that kiss.

Whatever thoughts he had were cloaked in the storm raging behind his eyes. He was staring at me, but I could see his mind was elsewhere.

"What are you thinking about?" I whispered. The words tumbled out of my mouth without permission. I braced myself for his scowl.

Riven answered immediately, his voice a velvet whisper cutting through the dark. "I'm thinking that after tomorrow, there is no turning back. Once we steal the key, it will only be a matter of time before the theft is discovered."

"Are you having reservations?" I asked, holding my breath.

Riven shook his head. "I'm *relieved* to be doing something. I feel like all I do is plan and never—"

"Never accomplish enough," I finished for him. I knew the feeling well. No matter how many Halflings I saved, how many people I helped, there were still countless more I couldn't.

Riven nodded, biting his lip.

I realized I was staring at his mouth when he tossed my question back at me.

"What are you thinking about?"

"I'm wondering why you kissed me," I answered truthfully. I didn't have the energy to lie.

Riven's shoulder flexed hard enough the mattress groaned. His eyes darkened. He opened his mouth to speak but shut it again. I could just make out the indentation of his fangs along his lip.

"I wasn't expecting to feel . . . I never should've done that," he said after a tense silence. "It won't happen again."

"Why not?" I yawned. I was too tired to stave my curiosity.

"You *want* it to happen again?" Riven asked, shifting his chin toward me. His voice was free of his usual sarcasm. His gaze flicked between my eyes and my mouth.

"Why do you think you shouldn't have done it?" I said, evading his question. My cheeks burned. "I agree with you, but I'm interested in your reason."

His violet eyes cut to mine. They weren't angry but firm. "I surprised you," he said. "And you made it clear to me in Aralinth that you hated it." He pushed his long hair out of his face and rubbed his neck. I could smell the scent of dew and birchwood on his skin. "I've never touched anyone that way who didn't want me to. I regret putting you in that position. Even if you had been trying to kill me."

My heavy lids widened at his admission. He'd never been so honest with me before.

"It was a bit unorthodox," I said with a shrug. "But everything is fair in a fight, Riven. A fight that I asked for, you should remember." His mouth twitched into a tiny smirk.

"And I wouldn't say I *hated* it," I added with a yawn, nuzzling my head into the softness of the pillow.

I expected Riven to scowl or say something smug in return, but he didn't. His wide eyes fluttered at my words before he turned onto his back. I watched the rise and fall of the blanket on his chest for what felt like centuries. My body relaxed into the mattress to the steady rhythm. Just as I closed my eyes, finally feeling sleep wrap around me, I heard him whisper one last thing.

"Good night, Keera."

It was the first time he'd used my name. I fell asleep with a soft smile on my face. Maybe I was gaining more of Riven's favor than I thought.

CHAPTER THIRTY-ONE

I LEFT RIVEN WITH HIS CREW the next afternoon. I told them that I needed longer to get ready for the ball, which was mostly true. I wanted time alone.

There was a chance we would be discovered tonight. I'd stretched over the line many times before, used my position to funnel help to the Halflings, but nothing as daring as this. Once Lord Curringham's key was stolen, it would only be a matter of time until the theft was discovered. The lord would search the stores immediately and find them empty. Grabbing the key was the first part of the plan, but it would set a timer on our backs. And if we didn't blow a hole through Silstra before time ran out, then we would be dead. Or worse.

I wouldn't let that happen. We would succeed. I would make sure of it. Lord Curringham was an oaf. Stealing a pendant from him was nothing in the face of everything I'd done as Blade. No mistakes. No changes to the plan and we would leave Cereliath with our heads.

My dress was waiting for me when I arrived back at the inn. The nosy wife of the innkeeper seemed much too interested in why a package from Wilden's Threads had been delivered. I didn't give her the courtesy of an explanation and pulled my gray hood lower over my face. Irregularities were the easy details to remember. And they'd be the first thing the Shades sought out if we didn't slip through the night unnoticed.

I ordered hot water to my rooms and left the woman at her desk, mouth hanging open. I tossed the package from Wilden on the bed, not ready to open it, and began drafting a letter to Victoria.

It took me longer than usual, since I had to write in code, but I wanted to ensure she would have access to funds for the Halfling refuges even if our plan failed. I left her the location of three burial spots where I'd hidden contingencies. Chests of gold and jewels that would buy the safety of hundreds of Halflings. I knew Victoria had the connections to fetch them and the network to make sure the other refuge houses stayed open. At least until the money ran out.

If I failed, there would be no one left to fund them.

Dark ink stained my fingers from where I had pressed too hard against the quill. I didn't notice until I looked down at my tunic and saw that the sleeve was full of ink. I had been tracing the scars on my forearm again. Over and over, like I was carving them anew.

I couldn't stop thinking of *her*.

I hadn't dreamed about her again. Not since that night Riven woke me.

But thoughts of her filled my head at every waking moment. I saw her face in the strangers we passed. Someone laughing in the distance would sound like her. A glimpse of blond hair and I couldn't help but turn, hoping somehow she'd be there.

Maybe she was.

I was finally doing what I'd promised. Taking down the king and his kingdom just as we had sworn to do together. But now I would do it *for* her. I'd fulfill the oath I had spent so long running from, so long trying to forget.

And if I didn't, I would join her.

These were the thoughts that filled my mind as I bathed, scrubbing off the dirt from my hair and body, the ink from my hands. When I was done, I brushed my hair and let the air dry it in soft waves behind my back. I borrowed some hair oil from Nikolai. It smelled like a faegarden. I recognized a hint of dew rose, but also the myriad floral tones that wafted through Aralinth. Something in me longed to return to the Fae city.

Nikolai pulled up in the coach shortly before the seventh hour. He was dressed in the plain garb of a coachman, his disguise to get close enough to the House of Harvest to keep watch for trouble and act as our escape if things went awry. Beneath his uniform, I spotted the chain of his glamour pendant. It would keep the Mortals from noticing him as long as everything went to plan.

Nikolai jumped down from the bench of the coach. His eyes traced over my body in confusion.

"Please tell me that isn't your dress?" he asked, his lip raising slightly.

Wilden had given me an overcloak to shield the dress during the journey to the manor. It was black, finer than my usual cloak, and trailed down the entire length of my torso to the floor. I held the mask in my hand. There was no need to put it on until we exited the carriage.

"I was willing to be the driver and have you distract the lord," I reminded him. Dressing up as a plaything for the wealthy men of Elverath was the least appealing part of the plan.

"Yes, but somehow I think they'll find *you* more eye-catching. Even if *my* outfit would've been superior." He opened the carriage door with an exaggerated bow.

I stared into the empty cabin.

"Where's Riven?" I asked. We were meant to enter the party together. He was the Dark Fae emissary able to pull rank with the lords. Without him or an invitation, I'd be interrogated the moment I stepped through the doors.

"Slight change of plans," Nikolai muttered. He sounded annoyed.

"What kind of slight change?" I asked through my teeth.

"Nothing big," Nikolai said, holding up his hands. "He just went to the manor early to scout some things out. He'll meet you at the door."

I wanted to protest but there was nothing to be done. Riven was already there, having changed the plans without letting me know. If we made it through the night, he'd be getting a taste of my wrath.

I stepped into the carriage without saying a word and closed the door.

"This'll be fun," I heard Nikolai murmur from outside.

I watched out the window as we rode up the sandstone drive. The manor looked different from the ground. I was so used to perching on the roofs and garden walls, I forgot how beautiful it was. Like the rest of the city, it was built in circles. The drive cut through the circle moat that surrounded the grand house and was flanked by stone walls on either side.

Small circle islands, covered in trees that bloomed red and orange, were sprinkled through the water. The manor itself was erected from sandstone. The second story encased by an open-air terrace. From its perch on the highest hill in Cereliath, the terrace held the most beautiful views in the entire city. Grand pillars of yellow stone held the roof and sunstone tower above it.

Nikolai steered the horses to the small queue of carriages that had formed at the main entrance of the manor. I sat patiently as we creeped forward, searching for Riven through the window of the carriage. I didn't see him.

It wasn't a good sign for how the rest of the night would go.

After several minutes, Nikolai hopped down and opened the carriage door, holding his arm out for me to use. For the briefest moment, I didn't take it. Servants did not offer their arms to the king's Blade.

But tonight, I wasn't the king's Blade. I hadn't been for weeks, truly.

All they would see was another Mortal woman in a spectacular dress.

That is, if they ever got the chance to see it. Riven was our only ticket in. It was safer than exposing my hand as Blade. Not many would question a Dark Fae emissary to his face. They would be too frightened to protest even if they wanted to. We were counting on it.

Just as I was counting on Riven to show up to collect me.

Nikolai shut the door behind me and gave a courteous bow. I could see him stop himself from bowing too low, acting too extravagant for a lowly coachman. The point was for him to be innocuous. A hard task for Nikolai on any day.

I pulled my hood forward. I toyed with the gold bracelet along my wrist. Syrra had crafted it, and Riven had infused the metal with a glamour. It would keep people from seeing me completely. Even if my mask slipped, my ears would appear Mortal to anyone inside. The silver color of my eyes would be a normal shade of brown to anyone who didn't know who was behind the mask. Just like the glamour we had passed through in Aralinth.

Without Riven, I was drawing too much attention to myself, standing in the middle of the entryway without an invitation or a date. Women were not invited to the House of Harvest; they accompanied the lords who worked there.

Riven appeared along the garden path, walking briskly. I sighed, my anger fading into relief. He was cloaked in black. He wore long boots that were cut at his knee and gave way to tailored trousers in the same hue of nightshade. His jacket was long and closed by several buttons along his chest, a gold chain connected the top button to a gold crest of three Elder birch leaves.

The crest of the Fae.

If his garb and towering frame weren't noticeable enough, he wore a mask of dark teal that did nothing to hide his Fae ears. It emphasized the color of his eyes and the sharp angles of his face. His black hair was braided along the sides of his head, the top pulled back into a gold clasp before cascading down his back.

He was more than handsome. He was striking. Even I couldn't help but feel a pull toward him. There wasn't a Mortal man here that could compare to Riven. Which was the point. Our presence was meant to be so obviously distracting that no one noticed when we lifted the key right off Lord Curringham's neck.

Riven dipped his head, offering me his arm.

"You changed the plan." The words ripped through my stiff smile.

"It's all the same from this point forward." His breath warmed my neck.

I grabbed his arm, my eyes narrowing along the sharp bridge of Riven's nose. He turned away, unwilling to meet my gaze. My gut plummeted through the white tile floor.

I didn't care that Riven was keeping secrets. I only hoped they didn't get us killed.

The hall was scattered with people. Some were guests, some Halfling servants of the house. All of them stared as we walked by—not at me, but at Riven.

It'd been decades since any major house in Elverath had hosted one of the Dark Fae. Everyone's eyes bulged when they realized who—*what*—Riven was. One of the lords' wives fainted as Riven walked past.

There was no turning back now. News would spread to the Shades of Riven's presence within a day, hours if someone wrote to Silstra. Thankfully, they had all been called to Volcar.

At the end of the hall was the cloakroom. Two Halfling servants stood outside the small room, greeting guests as they passed off their outerwear. "I need to drop off my cloak," I told Riven, pointing to the room.

He nodded, eyes surveying the face of each masked guest. "I'll meet you by the balcony," he said before continuing down the hall. I watched his head crane back and forth as he searched for our mark.

I walked past the servants, telling them I'd like to hang the cloak myself. I wanted some privacy to adjust the mask. I stepped between the rows of hangers and coats until I found a large mirror. I pulled one of the clothing racks close and hid behind it. I didn't want the servants to glimpse my ears, glamour or not.

I pulled the mask onto my face. It covered most of my brow in gilded lacing that fanned outward like wings catching flight, fanning the smoke and flame of my dress. A thick ribbon of crimson secured it around my head. I pulled my hair upward as I tied it, adjusting the ribbon over each ear. I dropped my hair and was relieved to see that my ears were completely hidden beneath the ribbon and hair.

With the glamour disguising my eyes, I could be anyone.

Mortal. Halfling. Maybe even an Elf.

The guests would whisper about it all night, wondering who hung on the arm of the Fae. I didn't care what they said as long as Curringham joined the chatter.

I took off my cloak and handed it to one of the servants as I left. His eyes widened, trailing along the hem of my dress. Wilden had outdone himself.

I walked down the hall to the large ballroom. I stepped through the grand doors that opened out onto the balcony. Riven was standing in the middle of it, peering over the edge at the crowd below. I could hear the hushed conversations of the guests already gathering on the dance floor. Ladies whispering behind their silk fans, their lords gossiping over gulps of wine.

I took a deep breath and made my way to Riven. A group of ladies gawked as I walked by, their arms freezing midair, holding their fans. A servant dropped a tray, but no one heard it. Every face lining the hall was turned on me. Their wide eyes stared, unblinking, as I walked toward the balcony.

With every step I took, the fabric of the dress shifted, crimson turned to marigold before revealing the layers of charcoal and smoke beneath. I was dressed in living fire. I felt uneasy under their gaze. I'd spent so long lurking in the shadows, avoiding attention at all costs. Dreading the looks people gave me when they recognized my black cloak or the sword at my neck. But these looks were different.

There was no fear or revulsion in their faces. There was only awe. I raised my chin a touch. I wasn't a monster tonight; I was a prize.

The whispers of the guests caught Riven's attention, and he turned around to face me. I felt the release of his breath when his eyes landed on me. His gaze caught at the swirling layers of fire, catching the skin of my bare calf and slowly trailing upward. My breath hitched when he reached the slit showing the slightest hint of my hip. His eyes flashed like a swirling, violet storm as he took in the tight cut of the bodice.

That familiar flicker of electric current coursed down my skin. His eyes cut to mine. There was no hatred there, but something else. Almost feral. I glimpsed his fangs before I took his hand and pulled him against my side.

"You're staring," I whispered.

Riven blinked and cleared his throat. "Sorry," he said, leading us down the left staircase. His hand glided along my back and nestled on my waist. It set a fire to my skin that felt much more real than the illusion of my dress.

Lord Curringham was standing at the bottom of the stairs. The gold pendant hung over his black jacket. It shifted along his chest each time he breathed.

Lady Darolyn stood behind him, her mouth set in a straight line as she glared at me. She'd noticed the hunger in Curringham's stare.

Riven's hand tightened on my waist.

Curringham gave the tiniest bow to Riven, completely ignoring me at his side.

"I apologize for not greeting you at the door. I didn't realize Lord Feron was sending a delegate to our festivities," Curringham said diplomatically. His cheeks were flushed and there was a dewy sheen along his brow.

I smirked, hoping he thought Riven would shapeshift into a direwolf and eat him whole. It was much more fun watching Curringham in the open than lounging on his roof.

"Thank you, Lord Curringham, for your warm reception," Riven said with a small bow of his own. "My uncle sends his regards and hopes this year's harvest is even more plentiful than the last."

"I hope you and your . . . lady . . ." Curringham's eyes glanced over me, trying to discern what kind of creature I really was. I was tempted to flash him my fangs out of spite. "I hope you will honor us by taking part in the first dance."

Riven opened his mouth to refuse, but I wanted to shock Curringham a little further.

"It would be our pleasure," I said, reveling in his surprise of being addressed by a woman. Or female. I knew it bothered him that he couldn't tell. I grasped Riven's arm more tightly and led him across the room.

"We need to create an opportunity to steal the pendant," he whispered harshly.

"We're not going to win any favors by refusing to dance," I said without moving my lips.

Riven looked down at me, unconvinced. His shoulders hunched as he scanned the dance floor filling with couples.

"You can dance, can't you?" I asked. My stomach tightened. We'd planned for weeks to attend a *ball* and I'd never thought to ask Riven if he could dance. I had just assumed he would have learned as an immortal.

"Of course I can dance," Riven spat back. He paused in the middle of the floor.

I smirked. "Good, because I can't lead like I usually do."

The string band started to play, and all the couples readied themselves for the dance. The slow tempo of the music drifted through the room. Riven grasped one of my hands in his and settled the other on my waist. My skin was set ablaze where he touched me.

Riven pulled me close to him. Our bodies touched with every breath as we started the waltz. I leaned my head back as we circled the room. Riven's eyes drifted to my exposed neck. My stomach tightened at the thought of how warm his lips would feel pressed against my racing pulse. Riven's fingers pressed harder into my skin as we turned with the other couples.

The cellist increased the tempo and our steps quickened to match it. The other pairs of dancers flitted about the room, content to turn as one, synchronous wave. Riven grinned and grabbed my waist with both hands. My eyes widened as he lifted me off the ground as if I were nothing. He spun around with me above his head as I tried to catch my breath. The faces around us blurred, violet eyes steadied me as we spun.

The layers of my skirts swirled through the air, threatening to set the room ablaze. Riven lowered me slowly, my body sliding against his until my feet hovered just above the ground. Riven rejoined the dance again, turning with me still pressed against him, my feet only grazing the stone floor. I threw back my head and laughed as we spun faster. With Riven holding me, I looked like I was dancing, but I felt like I was flying.

The music slowed, and Riven let my feet touch the ground. He stretched out his arm and I spun across the floor once more, engulfed in flame. He tugged on my hand and pulled me into his chest. The other couples bowed as the final crescendo rang through the ballroom, breaking into applause for the band, but Riven kept a firm hold.

I looked up to see him staring at me. His face held the same admiration as the guests in the hall, but his was sweeter. He wasn't gazing at the face of a mystery woman but staring at my silver eyes knowing it was me behind the mask.

He lifted his hand and gently caressed the high point of my cheek.

"You're always beautiful," he whispered. "But you're *exquisite* when you laugh."

He kissed my hand and I forgot to breathe as I blinked down at him. All words escaped me. The electric current flowed through my limbs, leaving every inch of skin exposed and raw.

Someone grunted behind me, and the moment broke. I clenched my jaw, turning around to see Curringham standing there.

He held out his hand in front of my face, his eyes on Riven. "May I have this dance?" he asked.

Riven's hands turned to fists. His violet eyes flashed, and I could taste something tangy in the air. "You have to ask her," he said through clenched teeth.

Curringham paled, noticing the shift in Riven's violet eyes. I grabbed Curringham's hand, pasting a smile onto my face. "Of course, my lord," I said with a bow. "It would be my pleasure."

Curringham's hand dropped low against my back. I pulled it up, making sure to pinch his skin as I did so.

"The Fae like their women wild, then?" he whispered in my ear. He couldn't see my scowl over his shoulder.

Riven was standing behind a group of lords, cloaked in shadow from the balcony. He watched as Curringham paraded me around the room like his prize. I wanted to vomit, but I hadn't gotten the pendant yet.

Riven and I had wanted to distract the lord over drinks, but this worked just as well. I didn't dare look down as we danced, but my fingers inched along his shoulder waiting for an opportunity to grab the chain. Curringham bumped into another couple, and I lost my chance. He glared at them like it was their fault. I fought the urge to roll my eyes. No amount of Curringham's fortune could teach him to dance. He tramped along the dance floor and my skirts without care.

The song ended and I cut away from him, lowering myself into a low bow. "Thank you, my lord," I said, walking over to fetch myself a glass of water. Lady Darolyn pounced on her lord, pinning him to the dance floor.

I tossed back the entire glass, dousing my rage as Curringham left Lady Darolyn in the middle of the dance floor and joined a group of four lords. They were laughing loudly, their goblets of wine splashing onto the floor.

I took a step toward them, but another lord materialized beside me. His face looked vaguely familiar from my weeks staking the manor, but I didn't remember his name.

"Shall we?" he asked, holding out his arm. Apparently, I had agreed to another dance while I trailed Curringham from across the room. The lord's brows were crossed, his arm hanging in the air as he waited for me to clasp it. I reluctantly let him sweep me into another dance.

I kept my eyes on the lords with every turn about the room. Riven was standing behind them, waiting for his opportunity. I continued to swerve about the dance floor as I waltzed with the nameless lord. I widened my step, redirecting us toward the lords.

We were only steps away from Curringham; I could feel his eyes thirsting after me. I twirled out of my partner's grasp, holding his hand to make it look like he had initiated it. If Curringham and his lords didn't move, I would crash right into them.

It worked.

The lords stepped back, shouting in their surprise. Curringham didn't even notice when Riven slipped the dummy pendant around his neck. All he had to do was cut the chain holding the real one and it would be done.

I held my breath as I watched him reach out with a knife only I could see. He gripped the golden chain, pulling the blade underneath to make the cut. Curringham lurched forward, reaching for a champagne flute as a servant walked by. Riven's blade missed as the chain yanked free.

The servant hadn't noticed and kept walking across the room. Curringham left the lords where they stood and marched after him.

Leaving Riven standing with a knife and no key.

How long did we have until Curringham noticed that he now wore *two* of his one-of-a-kind pendants?

I needed to do something. Fast.

"I'm getting lightheaded," I said to the lord as we danced. He dropped his hand, asking if he could help find me a seat, but I refused.

I scanned the room, looking for Riven. He was stalking Curringham along the curved walls of the ballroom. I caught his eye and nodded once. He flung the knife toward me as I walked past. I snapped the handle from the air and tucked the blade against my wrist.

Curringham was standing next to the servant near the staircase, his howls about poor service booming off the marbled steps. I slid the knife up my left sleeve and pretended to reach for a drink on the servant's tray. I feigned a slip on my skirts. My body fell against Curringham, my hands flat against his chest for support.

"My apologies, sire," I said in as sultry a voice as I could manage. My left hand rested on his shoulder as my fingers moved against the first chain. I had no way of telling the fake from the true pendant.

"That's all right," Curringham said in a hungry tone I didn't care for. His hand wrapped around my waist, squeezing the flesh on my hip. "I would never let such a beautiful creature fall to her knees, no matter how lovely the sight." I hated him even more.

My fingers laced around one of the gold chains, but I still wasn't sure if it was the real pendant or the fake one. I tried the other. It felt different. Almost heavier, like it was gilded in something the other chain was not.

Magic.

How could I sense it? I didn't have time to wonder. I sliced the metal through with the small knife, pulling it free. It snagged on the other chain.

Curringham stiffened under my touch. His eyes started to shift down his chest.

"There you are," a dark voice called from somewhere behind me.

Curringham's eyes followed Riven as he stalked across the floor. Riven pulled me into him, catching my hand and the pendant in his own. He tucked them between our chests as he leaned in and kissed me.

The simmering electricity between us exploded. Something tore through my chest as the air left my lungs. Riven pulled back for a moment, his eyes wide, and I knew he had felt the same explosion rocket through his core. I didn't turn as Curringham walked away.

All I saw was Riven. His violet eyes bore into my own, heating my skin until I wondered if my dress was truly made of flame. His tongue flicked across his bottom lip, as if tasting the brush that mine had left behind.

I wanted more. I wanted to taste him again, feel that current soar between us.

I pulled him closer, stretching up on my toes to reach him, but I didn't have to. His body melted into mine, arms swooping behind my back and pulling me against him so forcefully that there was no air left between us.

When he finally kissed me, it was not soft, but hungry. He longed to feel that current ripple through us again too. My free hand found its way into his hair. I pulled gently. Riven groaned into my mouth, nipping my bottom lip so I could feel the sharpness of his fangs.

He tasted like spring morning, fresh and wooden. I relaxed into it, into his warmth. His hand grazed over my arm and nestled beside my cheek. He ended the kiss, eyes swimming with hunger before pressing a gentle peck to my forehead.

"I'll take the key to Nik," he whispered into my ear. I nodded, unable to say anything in return, and watched him walk up the stairs. My vision blurred as he disappeared down the hall.

I needed to sit down.

I took one of the small seats usually reserved for older Mortals. *What was that?* I wondered, bringing my hand to my lips. I could still feel the ghost of Riven's touch like a burn on my skin. I knew he kissed me to distract Curringham, but he didn't need to kiss me like *that*.

I looked up at the stairs. My skin longed for Riven's touch, ached for it now that I couldn't see him. I took a swig of a water glass, my eyes refusing to leave the balcony.

"Where's George?" a tall man asked two of his peers. They were nestled at a table along the wall.

"I'm not sure," a short, round man answered. "I haven't seen him since we were speaking with the prince."

The prince?

My body turned to ice. The water glass cracked in my hand.

Damien. He never missed a party. Even when his father had ordered him to stay in the capital. My stomach churned violently as I scanned the room looking for the prince. The scars on my back burned.

We needed to leave. Damien was proud, too proud. He wouldn't leave without trying to flirt with the date of a Dark Fae. One look at my dress, one whisper of me on the lip of some lord he didn't like, and I'd become his next challenge.

I couldn't let that happen. I trusted the glamour to keep me hidden from the lords. People who didn't know my face or my name. Damien was different. He would corner me, trying to learn my secrets to seduce me. But what if he recognized me? My voice? All it would take was one moment of questioning, a fleeting thought, and the glamour would shatter.

He would see me.

A glimpse of silver eyes, and Damien would know it was me. That I was the Dark Fae's date. That I was traveling with a band of criminals. That the king's Blade had betrayed her king. Everything we had done would come crumbling down because of Damien and his foolish pride.

I took a deep breath. I needed to find Riven now.

I stood up so fast my chair fell, bouncing off the floor and splintering its back. I didn't care. I rushed up the staircase. Riven wasn't on the balcony. I scurried down the hall, scanning the thin crowd. He wasn't there.

I peered into the cloakroom.

Not there either.

"Keera?" a voice called behind me. I felt my body relax with relief. Riven was the only one here to know me by that name.

"Riv—" I said, turning around to face him.

But the Fae behind me did not have violet eyes or dark hair trailing down his back. He wasn't a Fae at all.

He was a man.

A prince.

Just not the one I'd been expecting.

CHAPTER THIRTY-TWO

I BOWED A LITTLE TOO LATE. "Your Highness," I said, glancing at the floor.

"I thought that was you," Killian whispered, taking a step toward me. His green eyes surveyed the hall to make sure no one was listening. "I saw you dancing earlier with a Fae, but your eyes . . ." He trailed off and I felt his gaze trail along my body. Not piggishly the way Curringham had or cruelly the way his brother would. He looked like he was trying to piece together a puzzle.

He knew too much. I was caught. My hand wrapped around my wrist, hiding the glamoured bracelet from view.

"That's ridiculous," Killian said, breaking into a soft smile. "Your eyes are the same as they've always been."

"How did you recognize me?" I asked, pointing to the mask and dress. Not to mention the glamour that was supposed to make me unrecognizable.

Killian paused, taking another step toward me. A loose curl fell over his face, grazing his high cheeks. He ran a hand through his hair, pushing the blond curls back. He was close enough that I could smell the parchment on his skin.

"Silver eyes," he said. He leaned in and his breath fell on my cheek. "Your beauty has no equal, Keera," Killian whispered against my ear. "Especially in that dress." He leaned back and gave me the same mischievous grin he had in Koratha. One side poking his cheek so high a dimple appeared beside his mouth.

Prince Killian had recognized me on sight? I let out a breath and pasted on a stiff smile of my own. He didn't realize he'd shattered the glamour then. He still had no idea my face was disguised to everyone else. But how?

I'd only seem him a handful of times at the palace. How could he see through the glamour so easily when we didn't know each other? When he didn't know I was here?

"Your Highness?" A lord poked his head out of the grand doors of the library.

"I will join you momentarily, Duke," Killian said with a smile. "I'm taking a tour of the dance floor." He raised his arm to me.

My shoulders tensed. I couldn't refuse him; he was the prince. I scanned the hall for any sign of Riven, but he was nowhere to be found.

"Shall we?" Killian said. His gaze dropped to his arm, still suspended in the air. I smiled and nodded. If Killian didn't know that I was glamoured, then maybe he didn't know I had arrived with a Fae. I could use the dance to my advantage. Set the narrative for the night so I could control the version I told to the king.

I took a deep breath and grabbed his arm. I could feel the soft warmth of him under my hand. With his lineage, I thought Killian would feel different than other men. Stronger and sturdier, like a Halfling, but no. Killian felt completely Mortal. His pale skin flushed the same color as his blood. Red.

"I want to know what's going on," Killian whispered in my ear as we descended the stairs. His lips barely moved, keeping the soft smile he wore in front of the lords and their guests. I guessed that was the first mask a royal learned to wear.

"Sire?" I asked coyly. I wanted more information before I answered any of his questions.

"I know you danced with a Dark Fae," he murmured, pulling me against his chest as we started to dance. "I'm assuming it has something to do with the Shadow?"

My feet scurried across the floor, following his practiced lead. He still thought I was working on my assignment. I could work with that.

I nodded slowly, taking time to craft my answer. I couldn't completely lie, but too much truth and Killian would know enough to expose me.

"I traveled to Aralinth as planned," I said. He pushed me away from his torso in a spin. My skirts flickered like flame around me as he pulled me back into him. His scent was earthy and Mortal. I could hear his heartbeat as I looked up at him. It quickened when I put my hand on his chest.

"I spent a fortnight in Aralinth, but found no leads," I continued. Killian spun me again as we danced, wearing fake smiles as I whispered to him. "I heard of a Fae emissary leaving for Cereliath. I *thought* the Shadow would meet him here."

"You don't think this Fae is the Shadow then?" he asked, tensing as he considered the options.

"If he is, I haven't seen any evidence of it," I lied smoothly. Nothing shifted in Killian's face at my words. His pulse didn't quiver. He merely nodded. A curl fell loose from behind his ear, but he didn't let go of me to fix it.

"Do you think the Dark Fae are launching an attack against my father?" he asked, the tight smile he wore shifting to a frown for the merest of seconds.

I pretended to contemplate his question before I answered.

"No. Lord Feron seems completely disinterested in Elverath." That much, at least was true. "The Fae I followed here is his kin. I don't think he's seen much of the kingdom, if any. Lord Feron had even been upset at his departure." A slight exaggeration, but one I hoped would help.

"You think it's a journey of rebellion against his lord?" Prince Killian's eyes were hard as he considered who else the Fae might turn against.

"In the mildest of senses," I said, redirecting Killian's thoughts. "I've not heard much about this Fae, not from my contacts nor the Shades. I think he is young, perhaps even the youngest of them. I haven't seen anything to indicate this is any more than a vacation of sorts. Plus, the Fae and their people do not long for the kingdom. I'm beginning to doubt they and the Shadow are connected at all." I twirled once more. I didn't break my gaze with the prince. I needed him to trust my lies.

Killian bit his lip. "So you *don't* believe the Shadow is here?"

I feigned a sigh, pretending I'd been grappling with the same questions. "The Shadow is smart. I don't think it was a coincidence that I believed him to be connected to the Fae. I think he encouraged it, planted the rumor even."

Understanding fell across Killian's face, his brows rising until they were hidden under the cut of his hair. "A ruse."

I nodded. "Exactly," I said, feigning a defeated tone. "One I'm not sure the Fae even realize he created."

"The Shades have been following nothing but dead ends," Killian said. He bit the inside of his cheek and scoffed.

This was my chance. The stakes had changed now that I'd been seen. I couldn't rely on my anonymity to help me survive the king's rage. I needed him to realize I was valuable. Too valuable to kill. And that would start with feeding part of the truth to the prince.

Riven wouldn't like the game I was about to play, but Riven wasn't here.

"I think the Shadow has been hiding in plain sight," I said as we turned along the dance floor. I took an ominous glance about the room that Nikolai would be proud of.

Killian's eyes did their own scan across the room before cutting back to me. "You think he's here?"

This was it. I needed to expose just enough of the truth to set up the lie I would tell in the capital.

"With no true leads," I started with a shrug, "I thought the House of Harvest would be a good place to continue my search. The Shadow has targeted it before, and being so close to Harvest . . ." I trailed off. My stomach clenched into knots so tight I lost my breath. Had I given away too much?

It was a gamble. One Killian could come to trust me completely for. Or one to doom me entirely.

Killian's furrowed brow released. "You think he will attack the trade routes?" he asked, his mouth hanging slightly agape.

I nodded once, keeping my face neutral.

"I think it'd be the most efficient way to launch an attack against the king," I said honestly. I hoped it was just enough of the truth that Killian would realize while the rest of the Shades had their eyes on Volcar, I had been closest to catching the Shadow. When the dam was blown, the king and his son would have no choice but keep me on as Blade. I had been the only one to see the Shadow's moves for what they were.

I would appear to still be the spy they made me into, instead of the traitor I'd become.

Killian's eyes stared over my shoulder, unfocused and thinking as we made our final steps. The music fell into a soft decrescendo and the dance came to an end.

"My father must be informed," Killian said with a stiff jerk of his head. His mouth was set in a straight line. "I need to send a message to Koratha right away."

I nodded but my stomach plummeted. A bird would make it to the capital in three days. Two if the prince sent a hawk. Any Shades in the capital would be dispatched immediately along the trade routes. We would be racing the news to Silstra.

It would be tight, but still doable.

I bowed. "As you see fit, Your Highness."

He grabbed my wrist. "We both need to travel to the capital. Once my father hears the news, he'll want his sons and Blade nearby." I sensed the slightest hint of exasperation in the prince's tone, but it was gone in an instant.

"I'll see you soon," he said, his voice suddenly a low rasp. I lowered my head again, expecting that was all we would say in goodbye, but Killian held on to my hand. In a swift tug he pulled me closer to him, just a single step, and leaned in.

My breath caught in surprise as I watched his face lean into mine. I closed my eyes, unable to move away from the prince, and waited for the brush of his lips I knew was coming.

But his lips didn't meet mine. Instead, they pressed against the thin skin of my neck. My pulse fluttered under his touch. He'd bid me farewell like I was a lady at court.

It was strictly forbidden for a man to do so with a Halfling. Not that anyone in the room knew me to be one, but Killian certainly did. And he had done it anyway.

Killian didn't say anything else. He pulled away from my neck, eyes tracing the lines of my mask before settling into my gaze. His skin was flushed, and his hair fell in front of his eyes, but he didn't move it out of the way. He just looked at me, soaking in the length of my dress and the silver of my eyes. Then he turned around and disappeared into the crowd.

CHAPTER THIRTY-THREE

I WAITED FIVE MINUTES before rushing back up the stairs myself. I needed to find Riven.

The prince and I had danced for one song and talked for longer than that. Riven had said he was only going to return the key to Nikolai. Had something happened to him? To them?

I didn't fetch my cloak. Instead, I marched directly outside, looking for the black coach Nikolai had hired. I found him lounging, half asleep, on the front bench. Riven was nowhere in sight.

"Where is he?" I asked, shoving Nikolai so hard he had to grab the carriage to keep from falling to the ground.

"Who?" he asked, picking up his hat.

"Who do you think, Nik?" I shot back, waving an arm in the air.

Nikolai rubbed his eyes. His mouth hung open when he saw my dress. "You're full of surprises," he said with a smirk.

"Not the time," I said through my teeth. "Where. Is. Riven?"

Nikolai scanned across the courtyard. "What happened? Did you get the key? Did Curringham spot you? Are you hurt?" Nik's voice was higher than normal as he launched his fury of questions. His eyes raked over my face, wide and worried.

"You haven't seen him?" I asked, moving to the other side of the carriage. I glanced over my shoulder to make sure no one was watching us. My eyes scanned the roof, all the perches I knew so well. No sign of any Shades. No sign of anyone.

I hid in the shadow of the coach with my back pressed against the door. Nikolai was smart enough to face forward in his seat and lower his tone.

"No," he answered. "Not since you left."

My stomach churned as I twisted my fingers into knots. It wasn't like Riven to disappear. "He has the key. He said he was bringing it out to you, but he never came back."

"How long?" Nikolai asked.

"Fifteen minutes."

"Maybe he saw something that piqued his interest," Nikolai said, leaning against the carriage bench. "He may just be spying."

This wasn't a time for assumptions. Why would Riven disappear minutes after we snatched the pendant? What could possibly be more urgent than securing the key?

"That's not all," I whispered, barely moving my lips. My leg shook against the carriage door. I wasn't used to working with anyone. I only ever had to take care of myself. Worry about myself. My chest tightened as I tugged at my hair.

Nikolai turned his head. "What else?"

I closed my eyes, wishing everything that had happened since that kiss was a dream. "The prince is here," I said in a heavy breath.

Nikolai swore, pulling on the reins enough that the horses

jerked. He lowered them back on the rail before speaking again. "Which one? I thought you said both princes were accounted for." He glanced down the drive as if the prince would materialize out of nowhere. My cheeks heated at his words. I *had* told them the princes were accounted for. Damien had been ordered to stay in the capital and Killian was meant to return to Volcar. I'd have to discover why he changed his mind after we survived the night. *If* we survived.

"Killian, thank the gods," I said. Nikolai's shoulders relaxed. I tilted my head, wondering if he knew about Damien's cruel nature, when a figure moved behind me.

My hand lashed between my legs, pulling out the parrying dagger I had holstered along my thigh. I almost pressed it into the stranger's chest when I caught that familiar scent of birchwood and dew.

"Easy now," Riven purred.

"Where the *fuck* were you?" I demanded, pointing the blade to his throat. I could see the mist his breath left along the thin steel. I didn't care. I wanted answers.

"I got held up," he said, leaning against the carriage door away from my blade.

"Held up?" I spat. Rage boiled my blood until the sides of my vision blurred. Maybe I should cut him, just a little.

"I'll tell you about it in the carriage, but we need to go," Riven choked against the steel. "Now."

"What's going on?" My voice softened, catching the worry in his tone. What had happened since he'd left me alone?

"We've made too large of an impression tonight," he said as I dropped my blade. "We need to leave now. Pray some lord becomes a drunken scandal and our presence is forgotten by morning." He opened the carriage door and gestured for me to get in.

I laughed. Genuinely laughed. I didn't even care how loud I was. Riven was kidding himself to think that our presence would be forgotten. A message to the king was being drafted as we spoke.

"You're too late for that," I huffed between breaths as Riven stared down at me, his brows fused together. He shot a look at Nikolai, who had an arm slung over the driver's bench.

"The prince is here," Nikolai cut in. His voice was hard. A look passed between him and Riven that I couldn't read.

"Do you think he saw you?" Riven asked, lifting his hand to my bracelet to feel if the glamour was still intact. I knew it was.

"He did more than see me," I said, pursing my lip. Everything had managed to go wrong.

"Did he recognize you?" Nikolai asked.

"We danced," I said, raising a brow at Nikolai. "I had to tell him that I was here in disguise. Tracking the Shadow." My eyes cut to Riven but he didn't meet my gaze.

"He knew it was you?" Nikolai blinked. "Even with the glamour?" He shot a second look to Riven. I could decipher the concern in that one.

I tugged on the ribbons of my mask and pulled it off.

"Yes," I answered, my shoulders falling. "But I don't think he realized I was glamoured. He knew who I was *before* I turned around." My stomach fluttered at the memory of his eyes trailing over me. I lifted a hand to my neck. Riven scoffed beside me.

"Oh, really?" Nikolai said, his tone mocking as his eyes flicked to Riven again.

"Am I missing something?" I demanded.

"No," Riven said as Nikolai shook his head.

"No, of course not," Nikolai said sarcastically. "Only that a member of the royal household who is supposed to be in *Volcar* was here without our knowledge. And *somehow* could identify Keera on sight."

I'd never seen Nikolai look at Riven with anything worse than mild annoyance, but now his nostrils flared and his brow hung low over his eyes, casting dark shadows over his cheeks. His soft, friendly face was menacing.

"Our intelligence must've been bad," Riven said, his voice as hard and cutting as the sharpest steel.

"So this is *my* fault, is it?" Nikolai barked, throwing his hands into the air. One of the horses shifted and Nikolai grabbed the reins to steady them.

"We don't have time to decide whose fault it is," I interjected, placing myself between them. Whatever had Nikolai so angry would have to wait. "The prince is sending a letter to his father right now. We have to get the others and leave immediately. We'll be lucky to arrive in Silstra before the Shades start patrolling the trade routes."

"We can't rush something like this," Nikolai said, shaking his head. "We'll make a mistake. Someone will get caught. At worst, we'll all be hung." Nikolai's voice was cold. He was right. Rushing would lead to mistakes, but we couldn't help that now.

"We don't have another choice," I told him.

"I disagree—" Nikolai started.

"No. We don't," Riven finished in a commanding tone. "I agree with Keera. We need to leave now."

Nikolai opened his mouth to protest but Riven stared him down with those piercing violet eyes. I could see the power stirring behind them, a warning, and a reminder of who held the higher rank between them.

After a moment, Nikolai conceded, turning back toward the horses. I jumped into the carriage and Riven followed behind me. I refused to look at him, anger shaking through my bones.

"I'm sorry I left you stranded," he said after several long minutes. His eyes were cast along the floor.

"That's an understatement." I folded my arms across my chest. The parrying dagger was still clenched in my fist. I wasn't afraid to stick him with it if he angered me even more.

"It's not as if I think you can't handle yourself, Keera," Riven said. "You've been the Blade for thirty years. I'm sure this isn't the first time you've had to work your charm over one of the king's sons." He didn't even try to cover his meaning, the usual venom that laced his words was back.

"What is that supposed to mean?" I said, twirling the dagger over my wrist to distract myself from the blow his words racked against my chest.

"Nothing, other than I'm sure you handled yourself." Riven's jaw pulsed.

"You're concerned about what I said when I was with the prince?" I shook my head, gripping the handle of my blade even tighter. How many times would Riven question my commitment to our plan?

Riven had the grace to look guilty.

"It wasn't me who changed plans and disappeared, Riven," I said, jamming my blade into the wood of the carriage wall. "But if you insist on playing by different rules, then you should know I didn't tell him *anything* about you. Or Nik, or any of the rest. Just the opposite. I gambled with *my* life. If the prince does have any doubt or need to cast blame once the dam is blown, it won't fall on you. *I* will be the one who will answer to the Crown. *I* will be the one who will lose her head."

I faced out the window, watching as the elegant hedges of the manor turned to stone and we left the grounds behind.

"How can I believe you?" Riven whispered.

"You're a prick, you know that?" I barked, pulling my blade from the wall. "I don't know how many more times I can spin the same words with you, Riven. Why would I implicate any more people than necessary? My life is not worth any more than yours or any of your Elverin." My chest heaved against the tight bodice, wrapping me in a fire that flared my rage.

Riven's brow relaxed as he weighed what I said. I straightened against the seat. I was tired of carrying my part of the mission *and* Riven's doubt of me. I tossed the blade onto the tufted bench and crossed my arms. It was time he made his choice.

"I'm sick of this," I said, steadying the anger in my voice. "You need to decide right now if you trust me. We're not going to live long enough to carry out the plan if you don't. I thought after Caerth you'd have realized that, but no—you go gallivanting off in the House of Harvest without telling me where or why and expect me to clean up the mess. And then you have the gall to call *me* a liar." Hot air steamed from my nose. I didn't know what angered me more, Riven's accusations, or my disappointment that we had not grown as close as I thought. The memory of Riven's lips on mine replayed in my mind. Had I imagined his expression as he looked at me, *saw* me, on that dance floor? How could he be so tender in one moment and think so little of me the next?

"You're right," Riven said, pulling me from my thoughts.

My eyes fluttered in shock.

"I shouldn't have left without telling you what I was up to," he said, pushing a strand of hair out of his face. "It's the reason Nik is angry with me too. I know you noticed."

I nodded but didn't interrupt him. Not when I was finally getting some answers.

"Nik learned that Curringham has been wanting to invest in an alternate trade route," Riven continued, leaning his head back against the wall. "He wants to build a road from Cereliath to Volcar. I decided it was too good of an opportunity to miss out on, so I made sure his assistant knew I was interested."

"Nik didn't agree?" I asked, raising my brow. I would buy that Elf a drink when we made it to Silstra.

"Yes." Riven nodded. "He thought it was too dangerous to add something else to the plan. He especially didn't like when I left without telling you." Two drinks. More, I'd buy Nik an entire pub.

"Why didn't he explain this to me when he picked me up?" I asked, biting my lip. If Riven had ordered him not to say anything, I didn't think I could be trusted with the blade sitting beside me.

"You should ask him," Riven said with a shrug. "But knowing Nik, I'd guess he didn't want to needlessly upset you. I was supposed to be done with the trade investment by the time you arrived, but his assistant caught me on the way out. He wanted to have another conversation in Curringham's office. That's where I was."

"That's everything?" I asked.

Riven nodded.

"Truly?" I pushed. "I'm not in the mood for *need to know*."

"Everything I told you is true," Riven replied, his voice softer now. "I've never lied to you, Keera." His violet eyes pierced through me until I forgot to breathe. The air crackled with that same electricity that scattered across my skin when we touched.

I leaned back against the seat. I was too angry to touch him, even though I wanted to. "Do you trust me?" I asked, picking up the blade again. I needed to hold something, or I would reach out for Riven.

He bit his lip. My fingers clenched the dagger. I was sick of his tests.

"I trust you want to bring down the king. That you'll sacrifice whatever is needed to achieve it," he said, drumming his fingers along his knee. "And I promise I won't make any changes going forward without discussing them with you. That's the best I can do."

I sighed. The adrenaline in my blood was fading. I was exhausted from fighting. All I wanted was to get on the move to Silstra.

"At least you no longer hate me," I muttered, leaning my head against the carriage wall.

"I wouldn't say that," Riven replied with a smirk. His violet eyes were daring, but I was too tired to take the bait.

"I'd like to remind you I'm holding a blade, and I'm not above cutting you," I threatened, not entirely sure I was joking.

"Keera," Riven said, looking at the dagger in my hands and then gazing out the window. "You could cut me worse than any blade."

We didn't say anything else to each other. Our plan was still intact, but barely. Yet somehow, I felt like we had won, or at least I had. Riven had promised to keep me informed from now on. It was a small step, but a meaningful one to me. Riven guarded his trust even more than I did. I knew the weight a promise like that carried.

CHAPTER THIRTY-FOUR

Syrra and Collin were waiting for us outside the abandoned storehouse. Her arms were crossed, her marks shining in the warm light of the last setting sun. She wore leather cuffs on her broad shoulders, towering above Collin's thin frame. She was ready for the next part of our mission.

Syrra shook her head as Nikolai pulled the carriage through the wide doors of the building. The scent of stale grain and mold filled the carriage as I opened the door and jumped down before we'd come to a complete stop.

Her eyes trailed over my dress and my back stiffened. Syrra raised a brow and gave me an approving nod. "You are late," she said in way of greeting.

"Take that up with Riven," I told her, not hiding my annoyance.

Riven stepped down behind me and tossed the pendant to Syrra, who caught it in one hand. "It is done then—no surprises?" she asked. She twisted the center of the pendant and it cracked open like an egg. Inside was a golden key. Not the wrought iron ones used at taverns or pubs, but a circular piece of gold. An Elven key.

Syrra tossed the useless casing to Nikolai. It bounced from one hand to the other before he finally caught it in the crook of his elbow. Syrra couldn't help but smirk.

"Nothing *but* surprises actually," I said, still staring at the round key. "But we'll have to tell you on the road." My eyes flicked to Syrra. I needed her to understand the urgency. "We need to leave tonight. Now."

Syrra looked back at the horizon, the last sun was almost set. Dark violet streaks painted the sky as stars started to flicker in the west. "My team is already waiting to grab the explosives. Once I bring them the key, we will be back here in under an hour," she said, tucking the gold key into a hidden pocket in her leathers. "I'll have someone ready the horses. Collin, load the saddlebags—"

"I don't think we have the time to ride horseback," I said. "We'll be quicker by coach." I cut a look to Nikolai and Riven, who were whispering to each other at the front of the carriage. Nikolai rolled his eyes at something Riven said. I thought they hadn't heard me, but then Nikolai took a step toward us.

"A coach can't move nearly as fast as we can on horseback," he countered, turning away from Riven.

"No," I said, my gaze bouncing between them. "But we can't ride through the night on horseback either. I want to get to Silstra as soon as possible. No stops other than to switch out the horses."

Riven moved beside me. I could feel the heat coming off his body and fought the urge to lean into it. Whatever had happened between us at the Harvest had been a mistake. A distraction. We couldn't afford any more distractions now.

"We're more likely to get stopped by Shades if we take a coach.

We'll have to stay on the King's Road. There will be no way to hide," Riven said, crossing his arms. I could feel the weight of his violet eyes on me, but I didn't meet his gaze.

"Luckily, you're traveling with the king's Blade," I replied. "*If* we get stopped, I can pull rank. No one will question or search the coach if I reveal myself."

Nikolai shook his head. "There's no reason to take such risks with your identity. Better to not rush and stay hidden." He pulled off the driver's cap, black coils spilled over his brow.

"That option flew out the window when I was forced to dance with the prince," I snapped. "We don't have time. I've already been spotted—with a Dark Fae no less. Anything I risk will be meaningless if we don't make it to Silstra in time."

Nikolai gave Riven a pleading look. "We don't need to rush this, Riv," he pushed, throwing his hat on the ground.

Riven didn't speak, his eyes shifting from Nikolai's to mine. I stood my ground with my arms crossed. Riven's jaw flexed, his long hair drifted on a breeze blowing in from the large door, but he didn't break his stare. Nikolai was his friend, his best friend. But I was right. Whatever we were—allies, accomplices, rivals—I needed him to side with me. I needed him to agree in front of everyone else. That was the only way they would concede to changing the plan.

"Keera's right," Riven said with a nod. "We leave tonight."

I breathed a sigh of relief before I started issuing orders.

"Nikolai, can you fit the explosives in the undercarriage—is there enough room?" I asked. He nodded. "Good, you and Collin can work on that while Syrra steals the bags." Syrra slipped out of the storehouse and disappeared into the night. "Everything else is packed," I continued. "Riven and I will map the route and plan our shifts. I reckon we can take five. Who do you want to be the fifth?" I looked to Riven.

"Collin," he answered. "He knows explosives almost as well as Nik."

"Do I get a say in this?" Collin asked. Everyone in the room froze, their eyes falling to the Halfling. No one questioned Riven's orders.

"Do you have an issue with the plan?" Riven asked. I saw the shift in his eyes, the darkness swirling beneath them. The muscles in his back tensed, preparing for a fight.

"Actually, I do." Collin stood straight with his arms pinned against his sides like a recruit in the King's Army. The pulse at his throat quickened, but he didn't turn away from Riven.

Riven took a step forward, his large frame towering over Collin. His long hair left tendrils of shadow where he walked. Whether his power was oozing out of him in a show of dominance or a lack of control, I didn't know. Either way Collin wasn't going to last long.

"Go on then," Riven said. He enunciated each syllable so Collin had a full view of his fangs. It wasn't a command; it was a dare.

Collin finally broke Riven's gaze to glance at me, his nose and brows wrinkled as his eyes trailed over my face.

"Are you sure we can trust her?" Collin asked in a slicing tone. "What if this is her plan? Force us all together in a carriage, unable to run anywhere, just to turn us in to the Shades. Maybe even the king himself. She helps us get *one necklace* and suddenly we change the entire plan because she said so? She's spent her entire life killing people like me. She's the king's killer *and* his whore."

Anger coursed through me like a flash fire. My fingers tingled as they tightened on the parrying dagger in my hand. Collin had already thwarted our plans once because of his insolence. It had cost two Shades their lives. I lifted my dagger, ready to tell Collin exactly what I thought of his trustworthiness, when Riven snarled so loudly the walls shook.

The Halflings along the back of the room stopped what they were doing and stared. Riven towered over Collin, his sharp teeth only inches from Collin's face. The air crackled and I tasted that familiar tang on my lips. The shadows around Riven seemed to bend, creeping along the floor toward Collin's shaking legs. Riven had said his powers were extremely limited, but whatever powers he had, he was using them now. His violet eyes were anchored on Collin, silver rings glowed around his pupils.

He was terrifying and beautiful.

I thought he might attack Collin right then, but Nikolai grabbed his arm. Riven turned on him, his lip pulling tighter against his teeth. He raised an arm above his head, preparing to strike. Nikolai didn't waver, his eyes staring into Riven's. I took a step toward them, ready to push Nik out of the way, but something in Riven's rage shattered. His eyes softened, and the shadows rescinded back along the wall. He blinked once, and I knew this time he saw Nikolai as a friend and not a threat.

Riven took several deep breaths, his shoulders curving toward the floor. When he looked up, his mouth was set into a straight line. I could see the pulse of his jaw and the red dot along his lip from where his own fangs had pierced it.

Whatever tension bubbled between us exploded. I was scared to touch my own skin from the heat coursing through me. I shifted my legs, realizing the only touch I wanted was Riven's. He looked up at me, his nostrils flaring, like he could scent the desire on my skin. I twisted my fingers behind my back. I didn't know what that feeling was between us, or what it meant, but I knew we both had to stay focused.

Riven nodded, as if reading my thoughts. He turned toward Collin and the group of Elverin standing behind him.

"I want to settle this now, in front of everyone," Riven shouted. "I know I haven't been encouraging you to trust Keera . . . or even see her as one of us at all." His eyes cut to me, lighting a fire in my belly.

"That's my fault," Riven continued. "I had my own reservations about Keera because of her title—a title that was forced upon her." He snarled at Collin. "I never should have let it color your own sentiments toward her. If anyone has felt uneasy because of my failing as a leader, I apologize. To you all and, especially, to Keera." My throat tightened at his words. There was no sarcasm in his tone or hardness in his face. His apology tore at my chest. He had listened to what I said in Caerth. He had listened, and trusted I was right. The faces of those two Shades flashed across my mind. Thinking of them stung, just as it always did, but the pain was easier to bear knowing Riven understood the weight of their deaths too.

"We have to trust each other," Riven continued, "if we want to survive long enough to bring the Halflings the justice they deserve. Keera put herself on the line the moment she offered an alliance. We didn't have to take it . . . *I* didn't have to take it, but I did. And I do *not* regret that decision. She's already risked her life twice—saved Nikolai's and Syrra's too—and tonight, she was able to finish the mission on her own. A mission that was only put in jeopardy because I couldn't trust her enough."

He looked right at me, pulling his hand to his chest. He took a step toward me without breaking his gaze. "I will not make that mistake again," he finished in a low rasp.

All the air escaped my lungs and my chest tightened. I kept my mouth in a straight line as I nodded. I didn't want to show everyone how deeply Riven's words affected me. In some way, I'd been waiting weeks for Riven to say them, but they made me nervous. Everyone who cared enough about me to show it ended up hurt or dead. I didn't want to be responsible for whatever happened to Riven.

I leaned forward, about to take a step, when Collin shifted on his feet. Riven turned so quickly I thought he had completely turned to shadow.

"There's no place for you here," Riven told Collin, stalking toward him yet again. This time his shoulders didn't slump forward in a crouch and his lips covered all his teeth. He was deadly calm, the peace of a predator standing before its prey.

Collin's eyes widened, glancing between Riven and Nikolai, pleading with the latter to step between them again. "I'm sorry, Riven," he whimpered.

"You will lead the Elverin heading to Mortal's Landing. Syrra will send word of how to resupply there, and which villages you will stock first. Is that understood?" Riven commanded, his deep voice booming from the walls.

Collin bowed his head and left without saying anything else.

The rest of the group busied themselves with packing. Two Halflings unhitched the horses and took them away. Nikolai bent down to inspect the undercarriage of the coach.

"I'll be in the front room when you're ready," Riven said to me, heading toward the door without waiting for a reply. I took my cue from Nikolai and the others and decided to give him some space. I grabbed my saddlebag and popped into the carriage to change. I peeled off the dress and relaxed into my usual trousers and tunic. I wrapped my cloak around my neck, feeling like myself once again.

I hopped out and leaned against the carriage. Nikolai was underneath, back against a rolling board. He said he'd invented it to help him build his creations that were scattered about the storehouse. I could hear him hammering something against the metal of the undercarriage. After a few more swings, he rolled out and looked up at me.

His brows were furrowed, and his eyes danced from mine to the undercarriage. He bit his lip, and I could see a question swirling behind his eyes.

"What, Nik?" I asked, putting him out of his misery.

He tilted his head, holding a wrench. "Something happened between you and Riv in the manor." It wasn't a question.

A rush of heat flooded my cheeks as he slid back under the carriage. I was grateful he couldn't see the guilty look on my face. I didn't know how to answer him as he rolled back out, so I shrugged, hoping he wouldn't ask for details.

"That explains why he's on edge then," Nikolai murmured as he twisted at something under the carriage.

"He's always on edge around me," I said. "I think he hates me."

Nikolai's chuckle was dampened by the coach sitting over his head. He rolled back out and raised a single brow at me. "Did you not hear that speech?" Nikolai's mouth split into a mischievous grin. "Riven doesn't hate you, Keera. And we both know why you put him on edge."

I rolled my eyes. Nikolai and I were not having *that* conversation. "The only thing I know is that you need to get to work. I reckon we have five days until the Shades begin patrols. Which means we have four days to blow up the dam."

The hours passed in a haze of uncomfortable sleep lying across the coach benches, while the uneven road jostled me awake every few hundred feet. When the horses started to slow, I searched for an easy trade. Each time I gave a small pouch of gold worth three times the value of two horses. We didn't have time to barter. We stopped for only a few minutes before we were on the road again.

Some stolen explosives were tied to the bottom of our carriage. Some were tucked under the bench I sat on. The rest were stuffed into the false roof Nikolai had designed. His work was so seamless I don't think anyone would notice the hidden compartment unless they knew it was there.

The days were cut into four-hour shifts. One would drive the coach and one would keep watch. The other two would try to rest inside before switching places again four hours later. I partnered with Nikolai, not trusting myself with Riven. We all needed to focus on the dam. One mistake and our mission would fail.

Nikolai barely slept. He stitched long sheets of fabric together for hours. I didn't understand what he was constructing other than it would hold the explosives. Nikolai moved too quickly to answer my questions, his eyes red with a lack of sleep.

We hardly spoke. Everyone was too exhausted for words, but there was also a creeping tension building between us with every mile we gained on Silstra. Questions swirled in my head, keeping me from sleep. Would the Shades stop us before we even got to Silstra? Would the explosives be enough to damage the dam? Would the damage be enough to destroy the canals entirely? Every moment felt like we were dangling over a cliff's edge, one strong breeze from falling into oblivion.

On the second night, I whispered the questions aloud, too tired to keep them in my head anymore. Nikolai looked up from his work, a cutting blade tucked behind his ear and a spool of thread sitting between his teeth. His brows crossed, and he plopped the spool onto his lap.

"The dam will blow, Keera," he said with wild red eyes. "I've done the math. Once I fill the detonators, these belts will be strong enough to bring down the palace at Koratha if we wanted to." He dove back into his stitching, muttering to himself. All his flirtatious energy had drained away, leaving a Nikolai I barely recognized.

Nikolai the inventor, who had an eye for nothing but his work.

We made it to Silstra in three days. A miraculous speed I hoped I never had to achieve again. My entire body ached from the journey. My throat burned from thirst. I was too tired to know if I craved water or a drink, but I pulled out the vial of *winvra* elixir anyway, dropping a taste of black liquid on my tongue. The scratchy feeling faded along with the stiffness in my neck, but the exhaustion still pulled at my limbs as I dragged them out of the coach.

I grabbed the saddlebags tied to the back of the carriage. Riven came up behind me, grabbing his own bag and mine. "Leave them for the others to grab," he said softly as three Halflings appeared out of the safe house. "You need rest, Keera."

It was the first time we had spoken since leaving Cereliath. I nodded and stepped into the house, wanting nothing more than a warm bath and bed. Riven greeted the Halfling who waited for us inside. She wore a sturdy dress, her skirts covered by an apron. She held out two keys.

She passed a black key with a gold label to Riven but he shook his head. "Give that one to her," he said, gesturing to me. I raised a brow, taking the key from the Halfling's hand.

"It's the only one with its own bath," Riven explained, his eyes soft. I stilled, touched by the kindness, and he disappeared up the stairs with a key of his own.

I took my time in the bath, washing off every minute of the last three days. I savored the bed, grateful that I could sleep in my nightgown rather than the clothes I'd been wearing for days. My body relaxed into the soft mattress, ready for sleep, but my mind couldn't help but wonder if that night's rest would be my last.

CHAPTER THIRTY-FIVE

CHAOS HAD ERUPTED when I came downstairs the next morning. The tables in the dining area were pushed against each other to make a space large enough to hold Nikolai's belt chain of explosives. The chairs were stacked along the windows, curtains drawn so no one could see inside. People were scattered about the inn, preparing weapons and food.

Nikolai and a Halfling I didn't recognize were busy measuring explosive powder and triple-checking fuse connections. By tonight, both chains he'd constructed would be rolled into large spindles for us to unspool along the base of the dam. Once set, we would light the fuse lines and have just enough time to get out of the blast radius before it blew.

If Nikolai's calculations were sound.

And if we managed to dock the explosives to begin with.

"We've been watching the dam for two weeks. There are guards posted at each tower, and threes Shades who shift between them," another Halfling reported to Riven, who stood beside the innkeeper's desk. His ears were clipped, and he wore the clothes of a butcher. Another Halfling hiding in plain sight. Riven's network was larger than I'd realized.

"There aren't three," I said as I took my place beside Riven. He wore no cloak, just his tunic. Half his hair was pulled back in a single braid, the rest tumbled past his shoulders in soft waves. I studied the sharp lines of his jaw and cheeks. He so rarely showed his face, preferring to hide it behind his hood or hair.

Riven turned to catch me staring and raised his brow. "How do you know there aren't three?" he asked, not in his usual harsh tone, but in the same way he spoke to Nikolai. Curious and calculating, hungry for all the information.

"Shades work in pairs. If you've seen three, there must be a fourth." I picked up an apple from the bowl on the desk and bit into it. Its flesh was soft, but its sweetness made up for it. My stomach grumbled as I chewed, I'd not eaten before going to bed.

I stared down at the map on the table; the dwellings rose from the parchment in my mind like I was flying over the city, seeing all its detail from above. Silstra was split in two by a long river. Banks of brick had been built along its edge: on the west were the stone dwellings of the old Fae city and on the east the haphazard constructions of the Mortals. The houses scattered outward from the river but all came to a stop at the edge of the dam.

Silstra was built beside a cliff's edge that towered over the ports below. Once, the river that cut through the city had roared over the rockface in a monstrous waterfall, but the king had stoppered the water when the canals were built. Now a large stone wall jutted out from the rockface and hung the inner city in its shadow. On either side of the dam stood two watchtowers, peering over the crenellated edge. Slow waters churned on the inner side of the dam. The outer side held a small patrol bridge at the base of the dam, almost two hundred feet below. Usually, it was barely visible in the mist of the release spouts tumbling into the bay far below.

"Have you checked the rooftops?" I asked the Halfling.

He nodded. "They're clear. Have been every day this week."

I suspected as much. "Then the fourth is inside the dam." I took one last bite of my apple and tossed it into the burning hearth across the room. It sizzled against the log.

"Inside?" Riven echoed, his voice a hoarse whisper.

"The *other side*," I said. "I'm guessing you haven't been trying to get eyes on the exterior side. You'd have to take out a guard to get a vantage point. It would give away our position." It was a guess, but the Halfling nodded with wide eyes.

"But why have only one on that side?" Riven wondered. "Don't the pairs stick together?"

"They're probably working as a unit." I shrugged. "The same two pairs always working together. That, and I doubt the walkway at the bottom is very wide. An attack would more likely come from the ridge, so it makes sense to prioritize the Shades there. I assume they rotate the person on patrol below. Doesn't sound like a fun job."

"It always seems to be the same three," the Halfling said, running a hand through his brown curls.

"It's meant to be," I replied. "Shades are meant to look the same, our partners and units are selected to enhance that. The Shades are all the same height, aren't they?" The Halfling nodded, biting his lip. "Exactly, they've been trained to have similar gaits too. They could've been rotating every night and your scouts would never notice the difference."

"That doesn't bode well for our distraction," Riven said, crossing his arms as he stared at the map. "We can't wait for the fourth Shade to climb out of the dam. It will waste too much time."

"We're still setting the town house ablaze?" I asked. Riven and his Elverin had purchased a property along the Silstra River. A team of four would light it on fire just as the suns were setting, providing us with the cover we needed to lay the blasts.

"Yes." Riven nodded. "But with the added Shade—"

"Leave the Shade to me," I cut in. "I'll displace her quickly enough."

"You intend to kill her?" Riven asked, his brows lifting. I'd been the one adamant that we draw the guards and Shades away. It was safer for us, but it also meant fewer lives were caught in the blast.

"I will if I have to," I said darkly, my shoulders bowing under the weight of that possibility. "But if I can incapacitate her before she sees me or anyone else, there's no reason for her to die. She will witness nothing." I readied myself for Riven to disagree, but he didn't. His eyes traced over my face for a moment and then he gave an approving nod.

"And you're sure the guards will disperse?" Riven mapped a route with his finger from the dam to the town house that would burn in a matter of hours.

I nodded. "Yes. They'll see the fire as a threat, especially once its big enough to threaten the Crown's merchant house. That'll be reason enough to abandon their posts." I paused. "The guards are trained too rigidly. They're too predictable. The Shades won't help with the blaze, but they'll search for the arsonists. Your team needs to be ready."

To die were the words I left unsaid.

Riven's back tensed. He chewed the inside of his cheek, eyes darting across the tiny streets of Silstra laid out on the table. "They know what is being asked of them," he said in a grave tone. "They've mapped out the fastest route to the tunnel system. If they make it there, they have a good shot of getting out." Riven's wide eyes pleaded with mine. He didn't want to face the fact that he might be sentencing his recruits to die.

"If they make it there, then they do." They would need to move fast once the Shades started their hunt. We were trained to know every shortcut and every passage—not to mention we were faster than Mortals and most Halflings. Even with a few minutes head start, the Shades were likely to win their pursuit.

I felt someone approach on my right. Syrra was dressed in pristine leathers that held her curved blades and holstered a bow and quiver on her back. Her eyes were painted with black ink, the same color as her irises, that dripped below her lashes onto her cheeks and covered her forehead.

Elven warrior paint.

She wore it well. I couldn't help but smile when I looked up at her. We might be able to do this after all.

"Everything is ready for tonight," Syrra told Riven, nodding and finishing her report.

Nikolai sauntered up to us, powder caking his face, his clothes as wrinkled as I'd ever seen them. "The explosives are ready too. No one touch them or we might very well blow up this inn and ourselves with it." I waited for his usual laugh, but it didn't come.

"What now?" Nikolai asked, brushing the dirt from his forehead.

"For you?" I wrinkled my nose. "A bath and nap. In that order." The dark circles under his eyes worried me. He hadn't slept at all since we'd arrived.

"And for you?" Nikolai asked with a yawn. He covered his mouth before looking up the stairs to where his bed still waited for him.

I placed my hands on the map, leaning into the table as I stared at the miniature version of the dam inked into the paper. I raised my head and saw everyone looking at me. "We wait until dusk. And then we move against the king."

We worked in two teams. Riven sent four scouts to set the town house ablaze, armed with crude oil and a vial of liquid fire. The dwelling would be engulfed in the blaze in a matter of seconds, smoke burning a hole in the sky as tendrils of flame reached for the clouds.

That was the first team.

The second comprised us. Riven and Syrra would infiltrate the dam along the west bank, and Nikolai and I would enter at the east. We'd only have minutes to set the charges, light the fuses, and get ourselves away from the blast.

Nikolai and I left first. He carried the large spool of explosives on his back while I hid my weapons and scalers under my cloak. We walked in silence through the back alleys we'd mapped only hours before. Hiding in the shadows as carts rolled by, merchants and peasants filling the street. The fewer who saw us the better.

We reached the east embankment and waited behind in the shadows of a narrow alleyway, watching as the orange skies faded to dark blue. The suns finally set behind us. I turned south and saw the stone barrier that lined the cliff edge. It was tall enough that no child could climb it, but was meager beside the dam that sliced the sky beside it.

The first signs of smoke billowed into the air. Small puffs grew to large clouds, casting charcoal streaks into the sky as the wind blew across the dam. I watched the guards along the top edge point to the smoke, their shouts muffled by the raging flames that burned crimson against the night. The guard closest to me abandoned his tower and ran along the ridge to the west side of the dam, joining the other guard. They left the dam behind, running in the direction of the burning town house.

Three hooded figures stood watching the blaze, sharing quick words with each other before scaling the edge of the dam. Each one jumped deftly from merlon to merlon before disappearing into the smoke-filled neighborhood on the far side of the river.

The Shades had been set loose. It was time for me to scale the wall.

I slipped out of the alley, leaving Nikolai alone.

A horse reared in the lane, and I leaped out of its way. I pressed my back against the wall of the tall embankment, my chest already rising and falling in heavy breaths. I closed my eyes and took three breaths to center myself.

My eyes flashed open with sharpened focus. I pulled out my bow and loaded the grapple arrow. I aimed directly above my head at one of the crenellated busts of the watchtower. It anchored itself securely with only the tiniest crack. I tugged on the rope to check its latch. It didn't budge.

My cloak swayed in a soft wind that carried the scent of oil and smoke as I climbed the rope. I could hear the panicked screams of people all over the city now. Good. With everyone distracted, we had just become invisible.

I slid over the edge, landing on the stone ridge the Shades had just abandoned. I kept low as I peered down the outer base of the dam. Even in the dark, I could sense how high we were over the bay. The lights of the port houses looked like the smallest of stars against the night. The only structure that existed between the smooth wall of the dam and the ports below was the narrow patrol bridge, wide enough for one person to march back and forth. I glimpsed a dark hood facing toward the smoke that now filled the sky.

I grabbed the blowpipe tucked into the holster at my side and launched the dart at her right shoulder. It hit. The Shade turned her head and fell. She would sleep for hours.

I pulled out the small vial Nikolai had given me and shook it. A bright blue light erupted in the glass. I bounced the glow off the steel of my blade, sending a streak of blue light across the sky. Too quick to catch the notice of anyone, except for Syrra and Nikolai, who were waiting for the signal.

I looked down at the Shade's body. Her limbs were splayed out at odd angles, completely unconscious but alive. She hadn't seen me. She hadn't fallen off the edge. I'd be able to spare her life in this.

I moved back toward the wall as Nikolai climbed over the edge. People lined the street, staring up at the black mass of smoke and flame. No one noticed the Elf and his large pack scaling the dam. I hoped it would be the same for the others.

"The Shade?" Nikolai asked, pulling off his pack.

"Unconscious." I helped him set the large metal clasps he'd designed. They anchored around a merlon in a perfect fit. Nikolai pushed the bundle attached to the clasp over the edge. It tumbled down the wall, transforming into a rope ladder that rested inches above the stone walkway below. I hoped all his measurements turned out to be just as exact.

Riven and Syrra appeared at the other side of the dam. Riven stood tall, even with the heavy weight of our supplies clinging to his back. He turned his head, checking in on our progress. I raised a hand and he nodded before unfurling the pack and casting their ladder down below.

I descended first, not bothering to use the steps but trailing down along the wall in freefall before catching the ladder at the last moment. I stepped onto the walkway without any hesitation.

"Show-off," Nikolai muttered. He stepped down the ladder with the chain of explosives. They were bulky, packed on top of one another, protruding from his shoulders. I stood below ready to catch him or a bag if they fell.

But they didn't.

Nikolai winked as his foot touched the bottom of the dam.

"I'll be right back," I told him, pulling the fallen Shade up over my own shoulder and climbing the ladder. Her body was light. She was smaller than most Shades, short like Gerarda. Though I couldn't see her face, I knew she wasn't the Dagger. Her long chestnut braid had fallen around my arms. I left her leaning against the top wall, out of sight from anyone below. Ready for me to grab her as we left.

I caught movement at the edge of my vision. A figure dressed in a black hood was running along the dam, racing toward the rope ladder with a bow and arrow drawn.

The Shade's partner.

I unlatched my own bow and nocked an arrow. I aimed the shot, my gut plummeting to the bottom of the dam as I did what needed to be done. I loosed the arrow, tears falling from my eyes as it flew at the Shade. It hit her square in the chest.

Instant death. It was the only grace I had to give her. She'd seen too much. She'd seen me.

Her body fell into the ravine, crushed by the thunderous spouts of water that churned the canal below.

Her bow lay on the walkway, discarded and forgotten, but not her arrow.

A groan echoed against the dam. Nikolai had fallen, holding his thigh where the Shade's arrow had pierced it.

"Don't touch it!" I shouted, scanning the skyline and riverbanks for any more visitors. There were none. At least not yet.

I slid back down the ladder, barely using it to stop my fall, the stone echoed with the impact of my landing. I got to Nikolai just before Syrra, his hand clasped around the shaft of the arrow, moving to pull it out.

"Leave it," I barked, my hands pushing against his chest. My heart hammered against my ribs so hard I could barely breathe. I grabbed Nikolai's hand and removed his fingers from the arrow, one by one.

"I don't think it's hit the bone." Nikolai grimaced. "If I pull it out, I can still get the job done."

"If you pull it out, you'll die," I warned him. Fear crashed through me like the dam had already burst. I could scent the poison in the blood that oozed from his leg. It was sweet and welcoming, a disguise often worn by death.

"The arrowhead was laced with honeyshade," I said, shaking as I gripped Nikolai's hand. I tried to cover the fear in my words. "If you pull that out, you'll only let more leech into your blood. We need to get you to a healer." I looked at Syrra, who nodded, understanding her new task.

"This is not a two-person job, Keera," Nikolai countered through clenched teeth. Sweat already pooled along his brow, the whites of his eyes beginning to yellow.

"It is now," I said with a ragged breath. I would not let another person die, especially not Nikolai. "Riven and I are the quickest. We'll make sure it's done." I looked down the walkway to where Riven worked. I knew he was listening to every word, tormented that he couldn't help Nikolai himself. He needed to finish installing the detonators.

"Riven will help you get him up to the ridge," I told Syrra. "Do you need help to get him down to the streets?" Nikolai was nowhere near as bulky at Riven, but he was still tall.

"No," she answered, pulling Nikolai to his feet. She threw his arm around her shoulder, and they hobbled down the pathway. Riven spiked his last explosive as they reached the ladder.

I moved as fast as I could. Resting a bag of explosive powder every three feet, a detonator pinned to the wall between each. I had thirty more. I raced, placing two bags at a time while slamming the pins into the wall in one stroke. Each time the stake drove into the stone, I heard Nikolai's scream ring in my ears.

Riven dropped back down into the chasm and installed the last two detonators. I pulled out the fuse lines from Nikolai's pack and handed one loop to Riven. We had to carefully braid the fuse along each of the chains, connecting bag after bag, detonator after detonator. We started at the edges, bringing the fuse to the middle before doubling back, laying the fuse line on the ground. Once we lit each line, we'd only have minutes to scale the ladders and find cover from the blast.

I looked up, holding a match in my hand. Riven's eyes were already on me. Waiting and soaking me in. My hood had fallen back, and I watched his gaze trail from my eyes down my braid, slowly, as if he was memorizing every detail.

Finally, his eyes settled on the fuse, and he nodded.

We lit our matches, bringing them to the fuse in perfect unison. The ends lit and started carrying the smallest of flames along the extra fuse line toward the middle of the dam. A spark that would ignite complete eruption.

I climbed my ladder and Riven climbed his. Halfway up I looked down to check the fuse lines. Riven's was still sparking, a trail of blue-and-red flickers, moving along the stone walkway, just as it was meant to.

But mine had gone out.

The fuse was dead with only a few feet of charred line from where I'd dropped it.

Nikolai had emphasized to me so many times in that godsdamned coach that it was paramount the explosions were synchronous. That was the only way to ensure that the blast was big enough to bring down the entire dam and send a flash flood through the canals.

I saw Riven's cloak soar over the top of the dam and he began running toward me. He didn't realize that the plan had failed. I had failed.

No, not yet, I thought.

I let go of the ladder and landed back on the hard stone. I ran toward the center of the dam watching Riven's fuse. I had to relight mine in exactly the same place.

I raced ahead of it. I grabbed another match and waited for Riven's sparks to catch up. I was less than fifty feet from the first explosion. There was no way I'd be able to clear the blast in time, but I didn't care.

Riven was safe.

Syrra and Nikolai hopefully were too.

If one of us had to die, I was glad it was me. It should be the worst of us.

They were the ones with a legion of Elverin willing to save the Halflings. They would carry on.

I lit the match and took a breath.

All my nerves vanished and were replaced not with fear, but relief.

This was the best I could do to keep our promise, I thought as I lit the fuse.

A grappling arrow landed behind me, anchoring itself in the pathway of the dam. The rope hung taut; Riven had tied it to the merlon. He peered out of the bust, hoisting my rope ladder along the wall.

I didn't have time to call to him. To tell him to leave me to my fate. Arguing would mean the death of us both.

I ran as fast as I could. I sprinted across the rope for seven strides before I jumped.

Too low, all I could grasp was smooth wall.

Riven reached down, his large, calloused hand folding around my wrist as the rope ladder swept against the dam. He had pulled the ladder high enough to use it as a swing. Riven pulled me onto his back and climbed over the edge.

I slid off him onto shaking feet. Riven turned and ran to the edge of the wall, leaping over it without a second look.

I only had seconds.

I saw the Shade leaning against the wall and knew I had to leave her if I was going to have any chance of surviving the blast.

But I couldn't. She wasn't just a Shade; she was a Halfling.

I couldn't take another innocent life. I wouldn't be blown to bits knowing I left her to die as well.

I bent down as I ran, pulling her onto my shoulders in stride.

The first blast exploded behind me as I ran along the top of the dam. Human-sized pieces of stone were launched into the air as the second set of blasts went off, and then the third.

Boom! Boom! Boom!

I only had ten feet left. I ran with everything I could. I used my last stride to leap off the edge of the dam onto the street below. My legs circled through the air, propelling us forward.

My cloak caught the wind beneath me. My grip on the Shade's body loosened. I could see the gravel on the ground, bouncing and shaking with each successive blast.

The landing would be hard. I prepared myself for impact, for broken bones, but then the last blast sounded and all I could feel was heat as my body flipped through the air. I shielded my face from the fevered blast and felt my flesh burn.

Then everything went black.

CHAPTER THIRTY-SIX

My entire body ached. I was bleeding everywhere. Tiny bits of shrapnel had ripped through my clothes and embedded themselves into my flesh. I tried to stand up, but my head split open in agony as the ground spun underneath my hands. I collapsed back on the ground. I rubbed my temple, as if that would quell the throbbing in my skull. I pulled my hand back, feeling something wet. My fingers slowly came into focus as I blinked. They were sticky with amber blood.

I need to leave, I thought to myself. Guards would be on us in moments.

Us. Where was Riven?

Did he get caught in the blast? I thought. I tried to scream for help, but I choked on the blood trickling down my throat.

I turned and saw a face.

It wasn't Riven's. Her hood had fallen off in the blast, but I recognized the long braid. Her eyes were open, amber blood dripping onto the dirt from one brow, the topaz hue of her irises just as piercing as they would've been in life.

The Shade.

She looked vaguely familiar. I may have trained her at the Order or crossed paths with her. But I didn't know her name and now I never would. The only thing I knew was that she was young. I could see it in her skin, her hands. She'd been one of the Halflings chosen to take her Trials before her time.

And now she was dead.

My stomach lurched as I vomited blood across the dirt. My eyes stung. I'd come to save the Halflings, and now I was staring at one. Dead. Immeasurable pain coursed through my body, worse than any of the wounds I'd sustained.

I had failed her. I'd tried so hard to keep her alive and I still failed. I retched again, feeling hollow inside as my pain blanketed me in oblivion.

I had failed her, but I wouldn't live with it much longer. I closed my eyes, ready to succumb to nothingness. Ready for the pain I'd carried for years to fade away with my last breath. My shoulders relaxed against the ground.

A shape appeared in the smoke.

Riven jumped off his horse and knelt beside me. His eyes raced over my body, assessing the damage. I saw his lips move, but my ears were ringing too loud to hear him.

I reached out for the Shade, grabbing her broken arm. Recognition fell over Riven's face. He gently closed her eyes and looked down at me. "There's nothing more we can do for her now," I think his lips said.

Riven picked me up and sat me on the horse. I toppled over in pain, but he slid in behind me, cradling my stomach. I was soaking his arm in my blood as we galloped away from the scene. Pain flared with every step. I leaned back into Riven, my head hanging loosely on his shoulder.

"Did we do it?" I asked him in a whimpering breath. I couldn't see the damage with all the smoke. I hoped I wasn't in so much pain for nothing. I hoped those Shades had not died for nothing.

He nodded stiffly, looking down at my face and biting his cheek. I started to tilt my head down, wanting to see the state of my body, but Riven stopped me. A gentle hand, softer than the first flakes of snow, held my chin. He didn't want me to see. It must've been as bad as it felt.

My mind swirled with cloudy images. Nikolai's leg. Riven grabbing me along the wall. The first bits of shrapnel burying themselves into my skin. My head bounced against Riven's shoulder, even his thick scent of birchwood and dew couldn't clear my mind. I tried to steady myself by focusing on my breath, but each inhale tore into my lungs and each exhale was a weak whistle. The buildings beside us blurred together. Riven was riding too fast, and I was seeing too slow to know where we were. My heavy lids closed. When I opened them, the buildings had turned into a blur of moonlit beige.

A field? I thought, unable to tell. I blinked again, and we were surrounded by trees. My head lolled into Riven's jaw. He pressed his cheek against my hair or maybe his lips. I couldn't tell. I wanted to sleep. Fall into oblivion so I didn't have to feel the pain anymore.

My eyes were heavy. I didn't care where we were going. I knew what Riven was too scared to admit. I was dying. The pain in my legs had already begun to disappear. I couldn't feel them any longer. Soon I wouldn't feel anything at all.

I could hear Riven's heart hammering in his chest. His heavy breaths pushed into my back. I lifted a hand to my chest, expecting to feel the same rapid pulse, but my heart was slow. Calm.

I was ready.

Riven must have seen my eyes closing because he shook me with his arm. "Stay awake, Keera," he said loudly in my ear. I flinched. The ringing had died down enough for his shouts to hurt.

"I'm tired," I whispered.

"Just a little longer," Riven urged, digging his heels into the horse, trying to make it run faster.

"Riven. I'm *tired*." I was pleading with him. Begging him to let me fall asleep. Leave me on the side of the road in peace. My body was broken. I'd already lost so much blood, and I was sure my legs were shattered. I tilted my face to look at him, but my vision blurred. Red spots covered Riven's face. My heavy lids fell, and I was too tired to fight it.

"No!" Riven shouted, shaking me until my eyes opened again. "You can't sleep, Keera. Stay awake. I'm taking us to someone who can help you."

"I don't need help," I argued.

"Now is not the time for your pigheaded independence," Riven teased, though his voice carried a hard edge.

"That's not what I mean," I slurred, my eyes focusing on the arch of his nose. Riven turned to look at me, his eyes wide and glazed. I tried to lift my hand to his cheek, but my arm fell limp at my side. "Just let me die. *Please*."

The admission broke whatever resolve I had left. My chest loosened as my limbs went slack. I was tired of fighting. Tired of killing. My body was searing from my wounds, but it was nothing like the decades I'd spent trying to forget faces of people, of children. The innocents whose names I took, as if that was a true penance.

I didn't want to do it anymore.

"I'm tired," I said again, hot tears rolled down my face leaving amber streaks. Riven stared at me, the line between his brow deepening as he shook his head. I felt his hand squeeze my waist even tighter, as if he could hold me to life by sheer will. His arm shook my torso as we rode through a wood. My eyes would not stay open wide enough to see the trees. I could only smell the damp earth and the scent of my blood.

Riven let out a deep breath, his voice cracking against my hair. "I will tell you anything you want to know, but you need to stay awake, Keera." It was a bargain.

I peered through my lashes at his face. His jaw twitched and his eyes were framed in red. An amber circle covered his cheek from where his face had touched my head. Why couldn't he see how broken I was? Why didn't he realize I wasn't worth saving?

"I can't," I whispered.

He swallowed so hard I felt it against my head. "You have to," he said, his voice splitting. I looked back up at him. His head was cocked to one side as he focused on the road. I didn't see any blood on him other than my own, but Riven was breaking too.

I could play his game for a little while if it meant he didn't break completely. "How old are you?" I asked, too weak to smirk.

Riven inhaled a shaky breath and chuckled against my hair. "I was born just over ninety years ago. I am the youngest of our kind, born of a Fae named Laethellia Numenthira."

The name stirred something in my memory, but my head ached too badly to retrieve it. I let my face fall forward, bouncing with the gait of our horse, until Riven pulled me in to the crook of his neck.

"She was beautiful," he whispered, eyes flicking down to make sure I was conscious. I tried to smile but my cheeks hurt, like the skin around my lips was raw. "She was a wonderful singer and archer. Her favorite flowers were dew roses and that is why Aralinth is littered with them. Feron made sure his gardens were full of them each time she visited. Now he keeps them year-round in her memory."

I nodded, closing my eyes as I remembered the fresh scent of the navy roses. It was the same dew that covered Riven's skin.

"She was gifted," he continued, jostling me awake. "Even for a Fae. They say she had the ability to turn herself into an owl."

I blinked. Still able to feel shocked through the pain. "A shape-shifter?" I murmured.

"Yes," Riven answered. "A rare gift, even among the Fae."

Riven tapped my cheek lightly, coaxing my eyes back open. I struggled to peer at him through my lashes. The pull was stronger now. I really was dying. All I needed to do was let the darkness claim me.

"She was also a healer," Riven cut in, shaking his shoulder underneath my head. "Not just elixirs and potions, though she was a master alchemist too. She had the healing gift. The ability to weave together torn flesh or cure the sick on the brink of death."

Too bad she isn't here, I thought.

"Your father?" I breathed, trying to stay conscious. My lungs burned, sending excruciating waves of pain through my body with every breath. The metallic tang of my blood coated my tongue. I didn't have much time.

"I don't have a father," Riven said, chewing his lip as he stared down at me. "Hold on, Keera. We're almost there." Panic coated his words. His pulse hammered in his neck. I could smell the adrenaline coursing through his blood. Riven was scared. More terrified than I'd ever seen him, but he didn't need to be.

Death did not scare me.

Death is the only certainty in this life. Those were Riven's words. The Shadow's. The Fae who clung to me, willing me to live.

But I was ready for that certainty. I closed my eyes and did not open them again.

Voices. I heard voices.

"What happened?" someone shouted. A gruff voice. Not its usual confident candor. It was Nikolai.

"The detonators malfunctioned, and Keera decided to ignite them herself." Riven's hard voice. It sounded close. I could feel his breath on my cheek. He was carrying me in his arms.

I opened my eyes a sliver. I was in too much pain to widen them anymore. We were in a room. No, a cave. The ceiling and walls were made of dark stone, but there was light. Lots of light. I spotted a large faelight in the corner of the room.

"Bring her in there," a hoarse female voice commanded. Through the crack in my lashes, I saw a small, gray-haired woman walking in front of Riven. "Put her on the table," the same voice said, though her words were muffled like she was far away.

I peered through my lashes again. She was close. Someone else spoke, but their words were muted, like I had been plunged underwater and could only hear the cadence of their speech.

Riven put me down with overwhelming gentleness. The hardness on my back hurt. I missed the weightlessness of being cradled in his arms. I tried to speak, but an unnatural sound escaped my throat. I think I was screaming.

"How did she expect to survive the blast?" the hoarse female voice asked. "There's so much blood. It's a miracle she made it here still breathing." My arms bent uncontrollably as I moaned. I felt hot. Like I was on fire from the inside out.

"I don't think she was planning on surviving." Riven's voice cracked. I felt someone grab my hand and squeeze my fingers.

"A hero complex and a magnetism for death. It's a wonder she hasn't died already." It was that same hoarse voice I didn't recognize.

I heard the sound of steel rubbing together. "Her clothes are useless to her now. Quicker if we cut her out of them."

Someone grabbed my arm, tugging at the sleeve caked in blood. They lifted it above my wrist, and I felt a cool piece of metal touch my skin. They were going to cut the sleeve.

They were going to expose my scars.

My eyes snapped open, and I shook my arm away. I panted as I searched for whoever was cutting my tunic. A woman with curly gray hair peered down at me with yellow eyes.

"What is it, child?" she asked, holding a pair of shears in her hand.

"Don't—" I started, but my voice caught in my throat. "Don't let him see me," I told her, looking up at Riven. I grabbed her hand holding the shears, my fingers clasping around the blades.

"Don't let him . . . anyone. Just you," I whispered. My head spun, and my breaths grew faint. I leaned back on the hard table. Her yellow eyes studied my face, snapping the shears open and shut. She gave me a firm nod and rested the shears beside me.

"Out!" she shouted at Riven.

"But what about—"

"I said out!" Muffled footsteps echoed against the stone walls and faded away.

Yellow eyes appeared above me once again. I blinked, thinking I was in a dream. "I won't let anyone see," she said. The first slice along my tunic felt like the pierce of a blade. The second was a hard punch to the jaw. I wrestled against her, not wanting her to see the truth written on my skin.

"Hush now," she whispered. I felt a prick on my bared arm and my eyes closed once again.

CHAPTER THIRTY-SEVEN

I WOKE WITH A DULL ACHE all over my body. I was no longer in pain, but I was tender. My head was heavy as I came into consciousness. My body was stiff, rigid like I'd been lying still for hours. Days. I tried to sit up, but something held my body to the table.

No, not the table.

There was no longer anything hard against my legs. Instead, I was floating. I opened my eyes, blinking as they adjusted to the soft light from a nearby torch. I was in a small pool, my legs and torso wrapped in a moist plant.

The coolness of it soothed my skin. I lifted one of my arms out of the water. It too was wrapped in thin strips of the turquoise plant. I reached out to touch it. It was tacky and soft. Purple liquid oozed out and onto my finger. My fingertip tingled before dissipating into a soothing chill.

I pulled back the layers on my arm. Small red marks dotted my skin where the shrapnel had pierced the flesh. They had already closed and lay flat. I doubted I'd have any scars from the explosion.

Scars.

The names on my arms looked the same as ever. Thin lines swirling along my skin. None of them had vanished. Even in the places where shrapnel had sliced the skin, the scars remained. Shining through the redness like nothing had happened.

I pulled at the ribbons of plant, tugging them off my other arm. Then legs. Then chest. Every name I'd ever carved remained. Pristine, like the explosion had never happened at all. I sighed and leaned back in the pool, floating in my relief. One attempt at sacrificing myself did not make up for the lives I'd taken.

My back bumped into the side of the pool. A thin sheet of the plant slid off. I didn't remember getting hit on my back, but the healer would have checked my entire body. She must have seen those scars too.

I stripped back each layer until nothing was left. Just my skin. There was no mirror to look in, and even then, the torchlight was too dim. I wrapped my arms around myself, my fingers stroking my skin as I felt the familiar grooves along my back. I checked my hip and sighed. All my scars were accounted for.

I dipped back into the water. The discarded ribbons sat in a heap at the edge of the pool. Their sticky residue still clung to my skin.

I spotted a bottle of soap next to the pool and grabbed it, eager to wash off the remaining tackiness from my bandages. I pulled out the glass topper encrusted with a blue jewel. I held it under my nose, closing my eyes as I inhaled the scent of birch. I could just make out the tiny lettering along the bottle. I recognized it from the merchant cart in Cereliath. I smiled as I poured the liquid over my shoulders. Riven must have purchased it without me seeing.

I doused my body and hair in the bubbles, reveling in being clean. I rinsed, studying the room. If it even was a room. It had no door and was merely another part of the cave, but it felt private with the single, narrow entrance.

There were two other pools of water besides the one I was in. Each were empty. I hoped that meant that Nikolai and Syrra were safe and healthy. There was a chair next to my pool with a book sitting on the seat. A burnt torch handle was holstered in the wall behind it. Someone had been watching over me while I rested.

Next to the chair was a blanket and some clothes. Presumably for me. But I wasn't ready to get dressed yet. Once I stepped out of this room, I would be focused on the next part of the plan: ensuring that the Crown fell.

I still wanted the Crown to fall. But after—after a moment of peace for myself.

I pulled my arms to the edge of the pool and rested my head on them. I could just touch the rocky bottom with my toes, back curving out of the water. The cool air felt refreshing on my skin after being wrapped for so long. The coolness stroked my back as my breaths slowed against my arm.

I was drifting back to sleep. Perhaps I did, and that's why I didn't hear him approach.

Riven gasped, holding a torch in his hand.

He had full view of my back and shoulders.

I didn't move to cover myself beneath the water. The usual panic didn't pound against my chest. Instead, a wave of relief washed over me, bringing with it a strange sense of peace. Now he knew. I didn't have to hide anymore. The truth was in the open. The proof that the king had turned me into a monster.

"Now you know a secret of mine," I said with more vigor than I felt. I didn't turn my head to meet Riven's gaze. It'd been so long since

I had let anyone see my full body. Years. Decades. And in that time the scars had creeped from my back over my shoulders and down my arms in winding spirals. I didn't just feel naked. I felt exposed.

I pulled myself out of the pool and turned to face him. Water poured down my body, covering the rock edge. I didn't try to conceal any part of myself. Showing Riven my scars felt much more intimate than showing him my nakedness.

He stood a few feet from me, his hair loose and unkempt. "What are they?" His voice was barely a whisper.

I squared my shoulders and fought the urge to cross my arms. "Names."

"Names?" he echoed, his brows knotting together. I lifted my chin, forcing myself to meet his gaze. His violet eyes were tracing over my limbs, my chest. Taking in every line I'd etched into my skin like he was reading me.

He held the torch above his head, devouring the swirls of names over and over like I was a letter he needed to understand. An excerpt of prose he cherished. "Why names?" he asked, taking a step forward.

The answer caught in my throat at the softness of his voice, the gentleness in his eyes. I'd always seen my scars as something terrible, but Riven stared at my skin like they were a thing of beauty.

"They're the names of every innocent I've ever killed." I swallowed. "I cut them into my skin, so I carry them with me always." Riven closed the space between us. I surprised myself by standing my ground. I didn't pull away from his touch as his finger gently traced the wave of tiny names that started on my right shoulder and crested over my chest. His touch left behind a trail of fire along my skin that hitched my breath.

"They look like waves," he whispered, tracing his finger back along the same path. "And here . . ." His hand moved down the length of my arms. "These look like flames."

I nodded, overwhelmed that he had noticed the pattern so quickly. "I cut them like—"

"Elven armor," he finished for me. My stomach lurched when I realized that he wasn't looking at me in disgust but wonder. He took a step closer, so our bodies were only a breath apart. "They're beautiful. You're beautiful," he whispered, pressing a gentle kiss on my shoulder. My chest split open at the sincerity of his words. He saw the scars. He knew the meaning behind them. And still he found beauty in the darkness of it, in my light *and* my shadows.

Riven's hand caressed the length of my arm, casting shivers across my skin. My breath caught when he grabbed my right wrist.

"And this?" He lifted my hand so the name on my forearm was pulled into the torchlight. My body stiffened as Riven's eyes traced the lines along my arm.

I pulled myself out of his grasp and turned toward the chair.

"Some names are bigger than others," I answered before scooping up the clothes, leaving him alone in the dark.

It must have been the middle of the night because I found everyone asleep in a small cavern lying on their cots. I didn't wait for Riven to follow me in, so I grabbed a cot and found a different room.

My head was spinning with thoughts so fast I could barely grab them. So many lives, so many stories in which I was the villain. Each of them written on my skin. I wouldn't be able to repay those debts in a thousand lifetimes.

But now I was doing something about it.

I'd been prepared to die. Thrusting my body toward those explosives, I knew that someone would carry out the rest of the plan. Riven. He would take down the Crown even if I couldn't.

How long had I wanted just that? And now it was in my grasp.

I traced the name on my arm. My head full of memories of her. The vow we had made so long ago. The one I had tried so hard to forget.

One person was not enough to break the Crown. But now, it was more than just me.

Somehow, I had found myself surrounded by the people I needed. Maybe even people who were my friends. I felt that usual hardness pulling itself around me, reminding me to keep everyone out. To keep me safe.

Keep them safe.

But people died regardless. I didn't save any more lives by closing myself off. If anything, I had only caused more death. Maybe there was a path forward where I could let some people in and still keep my vow. But I would have to be strong enough to do it.

Revealing my scars had been a step. The flashes of faces and names that constantly played across my mind were changing. Still there, but somehow friendlier. As if they too realized that I would avenge them.

That their memory had been shared, instead of just saved.

A tear ran down my cheek. Maybe that's what I had needed all along—to share the weight of them. If only so I could get the job done.

CHAPTER THIRTY-EIGHT

I HAD FALLEN ASLEEP just as light began to pour in from above, thin rays slipping through the cracks in the roof of the cave, casting golden hues along the floor. It was like seeing stars made of daylight. It made the rocky abode feel much more comfortable.

Someone placed a mug of hot tea in front of where I sat, asleep in a chair. I woke with a start and saw the healer looking down at me with her piercing yellow eyes.

"You heal fast," she said, stirring her drink with a twig.

"Thank you for helping me," I said, taking a sip of the tea. It tasted of cedarwood and lemon, a healing elixir.

The woman nodded. She had a curved body that once was tall but now slumped with age. Her face was creased and weathered, but her eyes were observant, watching every flicker in my face. Her hair was braided down her back, entirely gray except for the ends that faded into a dark brown. Her hands were strong, but her fingers were beginning to bend in different directions, her knuckles swollen from gout. The lines in them looked gray compared to the tan of her skin.

She was very old for a Mortal.

"Yet not as old as you," she said, as if reading my thoughts.

"Excuse me?" I asked, brows knitting together. I was only a few years past sixty; she had at least two decades on me. "I have only lived sixty-eight turns."

"Have you?" she asked, yellow eyes narrowing.

I shook my head. "I think I would know." I was grateful that this woman saved my life, but she was obviously losing her senses in her old age.

"Rheih, I hope you aren't bothering Keera. The poor *ikwenira* just woke up." Nikolai chuckled from the opening in the cavern wall. He smiled at me so wide that his cheeks pinched his eyes. He was leaning on a walking crutch, his leg wrapped in a splint.

"Rheih?" I asked, catching her name.

She held out her hand to me. "Rheih Talonseer."

I shook her hand. "You may call me Keera," I said with a small smile, aware that Rheih's eyes tracked me even as I turned to Nikolai.

"I'm grateful you managed to blow the dam," Nikolai said. "But you didn't need to blow yourself up too." His smile was tight.

"You didn't lose your leg," I said, raising a brow.

Nikolai made a show of placing his full weight on it as he walked over to the table. Rheih muttered under her breath, but Nikolai still managed his usual saunter.

"The splint is just temporary. Rheih managed to patch me up. Though not as well as you, it seems." His eyes raked over my body. I noticed that I was sitting straight and without an ounce of pain.

"It's not me. She was healing before I even touched her," Rheih said, taking a sip from her own mug.

"I was *what*?" I echoed, my mouth hanging open. I would have to thank Riven for getting me here in time, but this woman was obviously mad.

"Healing," she repeated, taking another sip. "Anyone else would have died from your injuries well before you reached me."

"That's ridiculous. Only Fae have healing magic," I scoffed, rolling my eyes. I looked at Nikolai for support, but he was studying me like I was one of his inventions.

Rheih shrugged, pouring more tea. "And yet here you are. Alive."

Syrra walked into the room and took a seat next to Nikolai. He whispered to her in Elvish, catching her up on Rheih's fantastical claims.

I crossed my arms. "Are you calling me a liar?"

"No, I'm calling you *Valitherian*," she said, placing her mug on the table.

Syrra gasped. My head snapped back at her wide eyes. They trailed my entire body like she was seeing me for the first time. "*Valitherian*," she whispered. "Of course."

I held my arms out in front of me. "I don't speak Old Elvish," I reminded them.

"It means *the gifted ones*," Syrra explained, her eyes unfocused as if unlocking a far back memory. "In the early days of the Mortals' arrival, there were children born of Fae and Halflings. It was rare, but they did exist. Sometimes the children would be born with a touch of magic. For most, it was immortality despite their Mortal lineage. For a few, it was communicating with nonspeaking beings, predicting the weather, or . . ."

"Healing?" I finished for her.

"I thought as much as soon as she opened her eyes," Rheih said to Syrra. Syrra's lips twitched as she nodded in agreement.

"My eyes?" I asked. Just then Riven entered the room and raised a brow at Rheih, having heard everything she said. The woman shrugged, and Riven turned his gaze on me. His eyes were soft as he noticed the fading red marks on my face and neck, but his jaw was tense.

He took a deep breath and addressed my question. "Has no one ever mentioned the coloring of your eyes?"

I rubbed my brow. "Some make comments on it. They're a strange color. I've never seen anyone with eyes like mine."

"I don't doubt it," Rheih said into her mug.

I cut the woman a look but Riven continued. "No one has seen eyes like yours in a millennium. Just as violet eyes mark the Dark Fae, silver eyes mark the Light Fae."

His words clanged against my skull, too hard to understand his meaning at first.

"But the Light Fae had eyes of gold?" I thought aloud, biting my lip. Stories of the Fae were told all over the kingdom. The cruel violet eyes of the Dark Fae and the piercing gold of the Light.

Rheih shook her head, but Syrra was the one who answered. Her back straightened as her fingers pressed flat against the tabletop. "There have only been three Fae with golden eyes, child," Syrra said calmly, her eyes shifting to Riven. "And they all died well before the Light Fae disappeared."

I swallowed her words, my mind flooding with questions. My throat tightened as I looked down at my hands. Amber blood coursed through my veins. There was no doubt I was a Halfling, but could I be part Fae?

"The last of the Light Fae died out a thousand years ago," I said, still staring at my hands and the secrets my amber blood kept, even from me.

"Perhaps not," Rheih said with a shrug. "Either some Light Fae remain hidden, or you are over a thousand years old."

"That still doesn't mean I have healing powers," I pushed. My heart pattered harder against my chest.

"I saw it happening, Keera," Riven said, shaking his head. "When I picked you up after the dam exploded, half your face was blasted away. By the time we reached the wood, it had almost healed." Riven's jaw was hard. He seemed angry.

"Then why now?" I asked, standing up. "Why would I suddenly be able to heal after sixty years?" I crossed my arms. If I'd had magical healing abilities my entire life, I would have noticed.

"Have you ever been so gravely injured?" Rheih sipped from her cup. "You wouldn't be a good Blade if you made it a habit to blow yourself up."

I paused. She was right. I'd broken bones before, sliced my skin in sword fights, but nothing life-threatening. I had always healed quickly, but I'd accounted it to the strength of my Elvish lineage. Halflings healed quicker than Mortals, and I had always healed quicker than other Halflings.

"But I have wounds that haven't healed. Not completely," I reminded him. Trying to avoid saying it directly in front of Nikolai and Syrra.

"None that haven't been done with a mage pen," Rheih answered coolly. "Apart from that your skin is flawless, Keera."

I stared at her dumbly. I had spent so long fixating on all the scars I carried, I never realized that I should've been carrying more. I thought of the Shades, the bodies I had seen through the years. Stab wounds that never healed, burn marks from fire and torture. They all left their marks on their bodies. All but mine.

"How did you know that's what they're from?" I asked Rheih, the hair on my neck prickling. I stepped toward her, towering over where she sat.

"I feel like I'm missing some critical piece of information," Nikolai whispered, his gaze bouncing from me to Rheih.

I ignored him, solely focused on the woman in front of me.

"I *am* a Mage," Rheih said, still sipping her tea. "My daughter and I are the last of the Talon bloodline."

I sat down in disbelief. Mages were magic wielders—*Mortal* magic wielders. Stories of their kin were whispered around fires and haunted the bedside of frightened children. But they had been nothing but stories. Cautionary tales to keep children out of the woods. I stared at the frail woman in front of me, wondering how much magic she held beneath her skin.

"I knew what made those scars before I saw the pen myself. I reckon a mage pen is the only thing that could leave a mark on you." Rheih peered down my arms, as if she could see the swirls of scars under my sleeves.

"You went through my things?" I asked coldly. She might have saved my life, but that didn't mean I liked her.

"I went through them," Riven said, casting his eyes down the table.

"Riven told me that he saw you with one," Rheih said. "I didn't believe him, so I made him fetch it from your things. Those were rare, even at the height of the magic folk. It very well may be the last one in existence. How did you come across such an item anyway?" Rheih's pupils tightened. I realized now that her eyes were that of a bird's. An eagle, the symbol of her bloodline.

"I stole it," I admitted. There was no point in hiding it.

Riven and Nikolai grinned. Rheih just stared at me, trying to discern something in my eyes.

"I have no answers for you," Rheih said. "But one thing is for certain: you were born of Fae. Perhaps the Light Fae are truly gone, but one was alive the day you were made." She left the room without another word.

The next day, we split up. My presence was needed in the capital. There was no way to avoid the king's wrath after what we pulled in Silstra. He would want his Blade at his side more than ever. Or my head, if he had any knowledge that I was the one behind the explosion. Plus, Prince Killian already thought I was on my way back.

Riven saddled the black horse beside me. We left the other one for Nikolai and Syrra. They would stay behind long enough for Nikolai to heal. Riven would send word where to wait for us once I met with the king. For now, our only goal was to make it back out of the capital with our heads—and hopefully, for me, with the king's trust.

"We will meet again," Nikolai said as I buckled in the last saddlebag. "And hopefully not in matching dungeon cells," he added, pulling me into an embrace.

"Heal fast," I whispered, squeezing him tightly. "I'll need your humor when Riven gets into one of his moods." Nikolai laughed before pulling Riven into their own embrace. If he whispered any warm goodbyes to him, I did not hear them.

Syrra placed a wrapped bundle into the bag beside me. "Some rabbit for the journey," she said, pulling me into her stiff arms. I let out a breath of surprise but curled my arms around her. "Do not be reckless in the capital, child," Syrra whispered so quietly no one else would hear. "Do what you need to survive, and I will help you find the answers you seek." She pulled back and gave me a warm smile, patting my shoulder before taking her place next to Nikolai.

I mounted the horse and waited for Riven to slide in behind me. I picked up the reins. If we had to share a ride, I would be the one to steer it. I waved at Syrra and Nikolai as we trotted down the path toward Koratha.

Riven didn't say anything as we rode. His grasp on my waist was light, and he leaned back like he was trying to put as much distance between us as he could. After an hour I felt compelled to say something. He would be useless in a fight if his back cramped.

"If you're scared of hurting me," I said, turning my head over my shoulder, "I promise I'm healed." I pulled his arm around me when he didn't answer. After a moment, he relaxed against my back.

"I didn't want to make you uncomfortable," he murmured in my ear. I had to keep myself from leaning into his breath on my neck.

"I appreciate the thought, but I'm not uncomfortable." I smiled at the truth of those words. The weight of the names no longer dragged along my skin. My shoulders felt light without the secret. I doubted there could be anything that would make me uncomfortable around him again.

We didn't stop until we reached the canal to Koratha. Or what was left of it. The stone walls had been pummeled in the flash flood. The packed dirt the Mortals had used to fill the river had given way. Large patches of earth floated downstream accompanied by pieces of broken docks and barges that didn't survive the flood. The river had returned to its former glory, broken out of the shell the king had forced it into. Flowing to the sea once again.

I hoped the same had happened on the other two canals. Not only because it meant our plan had worked, but because I couldn't ignore the beauty of water as it flowed; the memory of the land returning and reclaiming what was once its own.

We stalked along the riverbed as we traveled. It was midday when we reached the dilapidated port. Its paint had faded from red to gray and nothing had been done to fix the leaking roof. The building rested on a high cliff's edge along what was once the canal. Its dock had washed away in the flood, but there were two grounded barges set beside the building. I bartered with the owner, an old man who slumped over the counter in despair. He had lost three barges and their shipments in the floods.

I tossed him a large sack of coin and asked if he would take us downriver on one of the small vessels. His hands shook as he held the money, his red eyes burning with tears. "I don't know how far I can take you," he said between his whimpers. "There are blockages toward Silstra. It may be the same heading east."

"Take us as far as you can," I said, leaving him to ready the boat.

Riven and I returned at dusk, and the man directed us below deck. We drifted down the river on a small barge that smelled of teas and spices. There was one hammock for us to share. Riven offered to sleep on the floor, but I refused. The hammock was big enough for the both of us, and the floor of the barge was damp. By the time we reached the city, it would leak.

Riven reluctantly agreed, slipping in beside me, careful not to touch my scars. We fell asleep back to back, but when I woke, my head rested on Riven's chest and his arms were wrapped around me. I froze against him; it had been so long since I had slept so closely with someone. Riven sensed the shift in his sleep, his arms pulling me tighter against his chest and his hand stroking my back. I breathed in his scent, letting the birchwood and dew envelop me. I closed my eyes, relishing Riven's warmth.

But there was something else. That same feeling that sparked between us when we fought as Blade and Shadow. The electric pull that never faded. In the quiet of the barge, with only the hum of flowing water, I felt it again. A pull I didn't know how to explain but knew was there.

I wondered if he could feel it too.

As if he heard my thoughts, Riven's eyes fluttered open. He yawned, running his hand over his chest and feeling my own there. He looked down, eyes widening as he realized how entangled we had become. The smallest grin ran across his face. "Good morning," he said, his voice was hoarse with sleep.

"It's not morning," I whispered. The captain had given me an eight-hour candle to mark the time—it still shone, only halfway through its wick. Dawn was hours away.

Minutes passed as I listened to the beat of Riven's heart inside his chest. At some point, he started stroking my hair. I leaned into the small moment of peace we were giving ourselves. It could very well be the last one we had to enjoy. The capital would be overflowing with guards and Shades hunting for clues. Looking for the culprits. And we were going to walk into the capital right under their noses.

I glanced up at Riven, his high cheeks glowed in the dim light from the candle. His eyes stared unfocused along the rafters of the barge. For the first time since I'd woken in that pool, I realized that I was glad I didn't die. I would do anything to liberate the Halflings and end the king. I would lay my life down again if I had to, but I was pleased that I had another shot to see it through. I had never thought of *after* before. I'd always pictured the king's death tied to my own.

Maybe that was still true, but maybe it wasn't.

"What happens after?" I asked Riven, tilting my head toward him. "When the Crown is gone, who will lead Elverath? The Dark Fae? You?" I had never pictured that future before. It had always felt like a dream, so I'd never let myself linger on a fool's hope. That night at the dam, it had felt like a future that didn't belong to me. A future I didn't deserve.

Now? I didn't know what the future was or what it would feel like, but I was curious.

Riven stopped stroking my hair and was silent for a long while. "No, not me," Riven said, a slight edge in his voice. "I'm sure the Fae would help rebuild a system of governance, though I don't think they would want to rule it."

I nestled my head against his chest. "Didn't they rule the lands before?"

"No," Riven said, his fingers twirling a strand of my hair. "Before the Mortals came, before Aemon conquered and sealed his rule, the Elverin governed by council. Light Fae, Dark Fae, and Elves altogether. There were representatives from each of the territories and all the clans . . . I think that would be the best for Elverath too. A council representing each of the peoples left on her lands. Fae, Elves, and Halflings."

"Shared rule?" I pondered the idea. How different would the world look if more people had a voice in decisions? How different would it be for the Halflings who were considered nothing more than property under the king's law? My chest tightened at the idea. A continent where no one had to hide themselves or pretend their blood was a different color.

"It would be a beautiful thing to see," I said against his chest.

Riven pushed a stray lock of hair out of my face and I looked up at him, leaning into his touch. His eyes were dark in the dim light, swimming with something he wasn't saying.

"Just ask," I whispered, not breaking away from his gaze. His expressions were getting easier to read.

"I'm not sure I should," he said, his mouth set in a straight line.

"I don't know anything about my parents," I replied, raising a brow. "And I'm not sold on Rheih's theory."

Riven chuckled, his breath warming the crest of my cheek. "I'm not sure I am either. I'll have to ask Feron when we return to the *Faelinth*." He tucked a finger under my chin, pulling my gaze to his. "That's not what I wanted to ask," he whispered. His eyes were soft. The hand on my face gentle, testing.

I froze. If it wasn't about my lineage, there was only one thing he would be reluctant to bring up. His hand stroked my back, his fingers tracing along the thick ridges of the scars. My jaw snapped shut, but I didn't stop him. Sharing the names with him had alleviated part of the burden I carried. Maybe sharing another story would do the same.

"These scars are different," he said, biting his lip. "Than the names, I mean."

I nodded, swallowing to loosen the tightness at my throat. It didn't work.

"You didn't cut them, did you?" Riven asked, his voice turning hard, but the hand stroking my back was as soft as ever.

"No," I said, forcing myself to meet his gaze. "They're from my Trials. It's the symbol of my most impressive test."

Riven took a deep breath, understanding starting to register on his face. "Aren't they usually given as tattoos?" he asked. The hand on my back stilled and his breath stopped in his chest. I could feel his heartbeat rising as he waited for me to answer.

"Usually," I said, turning my head toward the rafters. "But my Trial was different than most. It was thought that a different kind of marking was needed."

"Thought by whom?" Riven's hand grasped my waist. His voice was ice, hard and close to shattering.

I plucked a loose thread from his tunic, avoiding his gaze as I answered. "That would be the prince."

Riven's chest heaved under me. The hand on my waist clenched, catching part of my tunic with it. The shadows in the cabin started to swirl along the candlelight. The air tasted tangy against my tongue. Riven's eyes were feral. I lifted a hand to his face, caressing his cheek, bringing him back to me and away from whatever images filled his mind.

"It was a long time ago," I reminded him. The scars were the least gruesome part of that tale.

"Why would Damien do such a thing?" Riven asked, stroking my back again.

"He said it was a lesson," I answered, echoing the words the prince had whispered over and over again as he cut my back.

Poison coated Riven's voice. "What kind of lesson?"

"One I never learned," I said, pulling myself up into the crook of Riven's neck and closing my eyes. Riven's arm stayed wrapped around me as I slept, keeping the nightmares at bay.

CHAPTER THIRTY-NINE

The old man dropped us off outside of a village, only a day's ride from the capital. The suns were too high in the sky to start the journey by the time we disembarked the barge. The wood creaked under my feet as Riven jumped off first. He landed on the floating dock with an easy grace, not bothering to hold out his arm for me. He knew I could manage.

Down the river was a set of rapids blocked by pieces of broken wood and chunks of earth that floated downstream in the floods. It would take weeks to clear. Even then, there was no way for barges to cross now that the walls of the canal had washed away. No ship could sail over the sharp rocks and steep falls. All trade into the capital would have to happen on horseback. In a few weeks, the first snows would fall, and trading would slow almost to a stop.

Just like we had wanted.

We walked through the tiny town, hoods drawn over our faces, but the streets were empty. Almost everyone had run to the capital as soon as the floods came, seeking out stores and rations before winter. My stomach churned seeing the elderly and children left behind. How many of them would survive? I doubted the king would make feeding the hungry a priority now. The truth of that tasted bitter in my mouth. I knew we would save more people in the end, but it didn't make sacrificing the few any easier.

We found food and board at an old tavern. A shutter along the front of it was loose, laying crooked on one hinge. We sat at a table near the hearth, the dust caked along the edge from lack of use.

There was no one else in the tavern besides an old Mortal who had fallen asleep in his chair, hair spilling into the bits of food left on his plate. The innkeeper's daughter only came out to bring our meals. I could hear her giggling with the kitchen staff behind the set of swinging doors.

If there were any other guests, they were gone or in their rooms.

Riven and I ate in an easy silence. The stillness before we ventured into the capital. If we managed to breech its walls at all. I set down the last of my duck bones and wiped my fingers on the cloth napkin beside my chipped plate. Riven took a sip of his wine. I could smell the robust aroma of oak and berries but refused my own. I sipped from a goblet of water instead.

I watched Riven finish his meal. He cut the lamb steak into perfect pieces before savoring each bite. "Glad it's not rabbit?" I asked with a smirk. Riven nodded, swallowing his laugh with another bite.

The fire was hot beside us. I'd already taken my cloak off, but even without its weight, sweat pooled along my skin. I scanned the room, making sure we were alone, and rolled up my sleeves. The longest flames of scars peeked past the rolled sleeve, too small for anyone to notice. The only scar that was completely visible was the name etched along my forearm. My fingers traced over it again and again as Riven ate.

Riven swallowed the last of his lamb and set down his fork. His eyes followed my fingers.

"Was that the first name?" he asked gently. I knew it was a question he didn't expect an answer to. One he wouldn't ask again if I didn't want to speak of it.

But I did.

I'd been thinking of her so much lately it hurt, burning through my flesh like the scar was newly branded with every passing thought. Somehow, Riven seeing my scars had eased the pain of them. His acknowledgment had started to drain whatever poison I carried beneath my skin. Maybe telling him of her would ease that burden too.

"It was," I answered after a moment. I traced the name once more.

"Whose name is it?" he asked in the same soft tone. Offering the same choice.

"Brenna," I replied in a whisper that fought against my throat. I hadn't said her name aloud since that day. The day I had carved it into my skin and vowed to fulfill our promise. "She was my roommate in the Order. We didn't like each other much at first, but eventually we became friends, the best of friends . . . and then something *more.*" My lips burned from saying her name, like opening a festering wound. It hurt, but it needed to be done.

Riven cleared his throat. "You were lovers?" His expression was hard, but I saw no judgment in his eyes.

I nodded. "Yes, I guess we were," I said. I bit my lip as I thought of her face. Those blond curls and honey eyes that had haunted me for so long. That word didn't seem big enough to describe all the ways Brenna existed in me. "But it was more than that," I continued, my eyes cutting to Riven. "We were all the other had. Friend, family, lover, *hope*. Most don't find any of those at the Order, let alone all."

I thought of the Shades who had died already. How many more would never get the chance to find a bit of hope to hold onto? My eyes stung as their faces played over in my mind. The Shades from the dam I didn't know. Alys. Elinar. *Brenna.*

"What happened to her?" Riven's eyes were gentle and inviting, but again, I knew I didn't have to answer. Riven didn't need that piece of me to trust me. To *see* me. I was Keera with or without my secrets. That made them easier to tell.

Riven's hand reached out and settled on the crook of my elbow. He traced along the skin of my unscarred forearm.

"She was a fiery person. Always striving to outdo herself and everyone else," I said, my lips perking up to one side. "She entered the Order later than most, but eventually became one of the best. Not through natural talent. In truth she had very little of it, but she succeeded by sheer will. To her, nothing was impossible, and to say so was to issue a challenge." I laughed, leaning on my hand as I laced my fingers through Riven's. I never let myself think of the happy memories. I had kept her wrapped in darkness. Bringing her into the light eased the weight on my chest, the burning in my throat.

"She was the one who made me see what the king had done, what he still does. Imprisoning our people, letting them die for him, starve even though their labor sustains his kingdom. *She* was the one who was determined to stop him. To break the Crown until there was nothing left. She wanted to do it from the inside, as a Shade. The both of us." The words came so easy now, spilling out of me like a dam had burst inside my chest. The memories flowed out, crashing through the walls I'd built around me. Riven didn't say anything, but he squeezed my hand so gently I thought I might cry.

"I don't know if it was love or naïve righteousness, but we swore an oath—a promise. That we would work together and wouldn't rest until the king was dead and the kingdom gone." My throat tightened against the words I didn't say. It was the only promise I had ever made, and I had broken it so quickly.

"Did you try to take down the king? Is that how she . . ." Riven didn't finish his thought, but I understood his meaning all the same.

"No. We never got that chance," I said in a heavy whisper. "Brenna was good. The best in our class after me, and better than many initiate classes before or since. But I . . . I was something different. I don't know if there has ever been someone so . . . naturally skilled in each of the pillars as me. Then or in the history of the Order." I sighed, leaning back in my chair and letting go of Riven's hand. He placed his palm flat against the table and waited for me to continue.

"We didn't realize how dangerous we were, being that talented. We didn't realize how closely we were being watched . . . We trained all our lives to be the best. To be stronger, faster, and smarter than any enemy we came against but"—I took a deep breath, meeting Riven's gaze—"we were just girls on an island. We didn't understand the threat we posed. We never even tried to conceal the depth of our feelings for one another. All the instructors knew we were the best of friends; I suspect many of them guessed it was more than that . . ." I trailed off, staring at the flames in the hearth. I couldn't feel their heat on my body. I rubbed my arms to keep from shivering.

I turned my head back to Riven, his black hair shining in the light of the fire as he stared at me. I took a deep breath, readying myself for the truth I hadn't seen as a child. "Two skilled Shades can be a powerful weapon for the king, but only if he can be sure to wield them." I stopped to touch the bumpy edges of her name. "We were called forward to the same Trials, which excited us. Brenna had been at the Order for just over fifteen years. She'd always expected to be called."

"But not you?" Riven asked, his voice a hushed whisper.

I shook my head. "I hoped I would be when they announced them. But I'd already been training for twenty-five years. I'd seen nine Trials called and was never asked to any of them. Even as good as I was. But that year the mistresses decided that it was time for both of us." I bit the inside of my cheek and crossed my legs, thinking of that day. How excited I had been. How naïve.

"Since my Trials had been so long-awaited," I said, staring at the flames again, "the Crown was in attendance for all of them."

Riven's eyes were wide and his voice unsure. "The king was there?"

I nodded slowly, thinking back to that first Trial. "And Prince Damien too."

"Is that when he cut you?" Riven's hand balled into a fist on the table.

"Yes, after my last Trial," I said, biting my lip. "He saw to it himself."

A feral look flashed across Riven's face before settling back into the calm mask he had worn before. Soothing and patient. Just what he knew I needed.

"They watched every Trial. Then I was called to my last, the Trial of Loyalty." A cold shiver passed down my back at the words. Recognizing the symbol carved across it.

"No one knows what the Trials are until we take them," I said. "We train for them, knowing that our skills must be perfected, but Shades are forbidden to speak of them, so initiates often only have an *idea* of what to expect.

"I don't even know if the Trials are always the same or change from year to year. It's all kept very secret." I rubbed my head as I slumped against the chair. "I suppose I could learn now. As Blade, I'm allowed to know. But I've only attended one set of Trials since my own. And since then, I've refused to participate." My throat burned at the thought of that year. The month I spent dousing my memories in wine and ale. I reached for the vial of elixir in my pocket out of habit, but it wasn't there. It was still stashed away in my bag.

Riven cleared his throat, leaning on the tabletop until it creaked under him. "Did Brenna speak of hers? Is that why she—"

"Died?" I finished for him. He nodded, patting my hand. "No, she wasn't executed for treason . . . She didn't survive the Trials. The Arsenal tries to avoid it—they usually expel initiates they know won't survive—but it still happens. The Trials are meant to test your limits. If you fail, you die. Brenna's death was . . . unexpected."

A darkness fell over Riven's face, as if the light from the fire could no longer touch him. "I didn't realize it was so severe," he whispered, staring at the tabletop. His eyes cut back to me. "Doesn't the king want as many Shades as possible?"

I scoffed. "No, he wants as many *obedient* Shades as possible. The competitive edge, the chance of failure and death . . . It's all part of the design. Shades graduate feeling lucky to have been chosen, to have survived. The king uses that to his advantage." I tried to swallow my disgust, but my mouth was too dry.

Part of me wanted to tell Riven all of it. Tell him exactly how Brenna had died. What Prince Damien had done to her. Done to me. But the words didn't come. It had taken me thirty years to finally say her name out loud. It might very well take another thirty before I was ready to tell the rest of that sordid tale.

So I summarized it instead.

"It was Prince Damien," I said, my voice breaking as I said his name. "He took a . . . *liking* to Brenna. He thought she'd bested him, before she came to the Order, and he never forgave her for it. He had a habit of reminding her"—I grimaced as the prince's face flashed across my mind—"even with the protection of the

Order. But that doesn't mean much when the crown prince has an interest in an initiate." Heat flooded through my skin. My heart pounded in my chest like Damien was sitting in front of me instead of Riven.

"Damien eventually caught on," I said, folding my arms. "That we were more than peers or friends. He convinced the king that it was dangerous for any Shade to love something more than the Crown. That it tainted our abilities, made us unusable. The king realized that he would rather have *one* talented Shade he knew would obey than two he couldn't trust." The words caught in my throat, and I wiped the tears from my eyes. Riven reached across the table and held my hand in his.

"Damien made the decision," I continued when I caught my breath. "And then carved that mark in my back so I would always remember I was the one who lived, while Brenna was the one who paid the price. She was the cost of my loyalty to the Crown." I slumped back in the chair. I was tired but also relieved. Brenna was no longer a ghost between us, one only I could see. She was no longer forgotten or ignored. I had breathed life back into the memory of her with my words and found that I felt better. Lighter.

Alive.

Riven's body was stiff and his breathing had stopped. The only hint of life was the warmth of his fingers still holding my hand.

"If you ever get the chance, kill him," he said through clenched teeth, his voice dark and dangerous. "And if you can't, I'll kill him for you." His eyes narrowed to violet slits, the feral look returning to his face.

"I carved her name because of that," I said, tracing the scars again. "The way Damien scarred me . . . He said it was an homage to the scars the Fae and Elven warriors would wear. Like Syrra's . . . Hers are a mark of her power and skill. But he made mine into something cruel." I traced my hand along Riven's skin, enjoying his warmth under my touch.

"He left the mage pen he used behind. I took it. I didn't want his scars to define me. So I cut her name into my sword arm and told myself it would be the arm that struck Prince Damien down." My voice cracked again. "It was a reminder that I wouldn't be the Shade they thought I was . . . I would be a warrior, like the Elves who came before me. I carved the names into my skin as a tribute to them, reclaiming that part of me that was lost. Stamped out by the king. Brenna's name was the first. A way to keep her and my promise alive."

"You have," Riven said, squeezing my hand. His jaw pulsed as he laid a gentle caress along my cheek. "You have kept her alive. And you will see your oath through, Keera. I know you don't make promises, but I will make one to you. As long as I live, I will work to take down the king. For the Halflings, for Elverath . . . and for Brenna." His eyes stormed as they pierced through me. He squeezed my hand and a tear rolled down my cheek. I knew he meant every word of his promise. And that he knew what those words meant to me.

CHAPTER FORTY

RIVEN LEFT ME ALONE so I could bathe in our room. I soaked in the hot water until my skin wrinkled, covering myself in suds from the soap Riven had bought me. When I was done, I studied myself in the mirror. There was no sign that just a few days before I had been on the brink of death. Just the opposite. I looked to be the picture of health. The redness around my eyes from nights drinking and morning hangovers had faded along with the dark circles. My hair was soft and bright against the candlelight. I looked better than I had in years. Felt more alive than I ever remembered feeling. My body was stronger too. I had definition along my arms and legs again that had disappeared decades ago. I was sturdier. I breathed easier.

Because I finally have something to live for, I thought. It was true. Going after the king gave me the purpose I had been missing. The purpose I had left behind and tried to forget. All the years I'd spent running away from my demons had almost killed me. Facing them head-on might prove to kill me too, but at least I would feel like a person while I did it.

Even my scars looked better. The scars along my back weren't red or swollen and no longer hurt to touch. Rheih's bandages must have healed some underlying infection. Had I been carrying poison under my skin for three decades? It didn't shock me. For two of those decades, I had been actively poisoning myself.

I always thought the pain of those scars was my punishment. What I deserved for what Damien did to her. But now, I wondered if it was my unwillingness to let go. Like the pain kept Brenna alive somehow, kept me thinking of her always. As though I wouldn't remember her until my last breath.

I riffled through my saddlebag looking for a hairbrush. I found it, along with the nightgown that I usually wore on missions. For weeks, I'd been sleeping in my clothes to keep my scars a secret, but that was pointless now.

I put on the nightgown. It hung over my chest from two thin straps that slid down the back and met again just above my tailbone. The edges were lined with a soft lace that complemented the deep red of the garment. I had purchased several from a tailor in Koratha. They were the only sleeping style that didn't itch my scars.

I heard Riven return and close the door. He walked past the bath without glancing in and set his bag on the desk. I was suddenly nervous to leave the small room. I thought about braiding my hair to stall myself, but I liked the way it had dried in soft waves that floated along my waist. If I was determined not to hide myself anymore, then I didn't need to keep my hair pinned back.

Riven leaned against the desk, both of his hands gripping the edge. He wasn't looking at me, but the floor. Pondering something. I closed the bathroom door with a quiet snap of the latch. He looked up at me and I caught my breath.

His eyes were a scorching violet that radiated from under his dark brow. The entire room was lit by a single lantern, casting a warm glow against his skin. I followed the path of the shadows down his neck to where his tunic was slightly open.

I swallowed as a flush of heat ran through me, building at the crest of my thighs. I hadn't felt like this in so long.

I hadn't been *looked* at like this in so long.

Riven wasn't just looking at me; he was devouring me. His gaze trailed along my legs, pausing at the hem of my nightgown before moving upward toward my neck. He somehow looked at my scars in a way that didn't feel like he was noticing *them*, but me. He was seeing all of me, all at once, and couldn't turn away.

I took a step toward him. A strand of my hair fell in front of my face.

His grip tightened on the desk, and the scent of birchwood and dew crashed through the room. I thought the smell was intoxicating, but Riven looked like he wasn't breathing at all.

"Are you okay?" I asked. I wasn't sure I wanted to know the answer.

Riven shut his eyes, still gripping the desk.

"I have another question for you." His voice a hoarse rasp.

I took another step forward. "What is it?"

We were in arm's reach of each other.

"You've never taken another lover, have you?" His jaw throbbed and his grip on the desk was so tight that his knuckles bulged. Like he was trying to restrain himself. But there was understanding in his eyes. What it had meant for me to tell him about Brenna, for him to see my scars. It wasn't something I had let anyone do before.

It felt hard to breathe. "No."

"If you were . . . to take another"—his voice was a rough whisper now—"would they be another *ikwenira*? Or a woman?"

I blinked in shock from the question. I had never thought of that before. There had only ever been Brenna. Nothing else had mattered.

"Why?" I asked, unsure how to answer.

Riven's eyes opened and cut to mine. They no longer looked violet, but almost black. His wrist twitched at the desk, but he didn't move.

"Because the only thing I want right now—the only thing I ever want—is to kiss you. But not if you won't enjoy it." His expression was hard, but there was a gentleness in his eyes. Caring. The same caring that had been there the day he carried me to Rheih. Or when he had seen my scars. The same caring he had shown only hours before, when I shared the worst of me and he had called it strength.

I wanted him. There was no denying that. But I cared enough that I also wanted him to know I craved him too.

"Riven." I took another small step toward him. His stare bore into me, dark brows casting a shadow over his face. He bit his lip, the sharp point of a fang peered out from underneath. Hunger. He was hungry for me. My stomach tightened as I took one last step. "You should kiss me," I whispered.

His lips were on mine before the last word was out. The desk groaned when he finally released his hands, gripping my waist instead. His lips were soft and testing. Slowly tasting mine, tracing the edge of them with his tongue.

An invitation and a message. That he would only take things as far as I wanted. I was in control of this.

I wanted more.

I balled his tunic in my fists and pulled him against me. Our bodies pressed together so tightly I could feel his pulse on my chest. I lifted one hand into his dark hair and pulled. He groaned and nipped my lip before picking me up off the floor.

I wrapped my legs around him, feeling the hardness at his hip. The need between my thighs grew and I caught his bottom lip with my teeth. He responded by trailing kisses down one side of my neck and up the other. I whimpered at his touch and dug my fingers into his shoulder.

"Beautiful," he whispered into my ear before kissing the scars along my chest. The compliment sent a shiver down my skin. I could feel it in the way he kissed me, the way his hand gripped my back, my thighs, that he meant it.

"Keera," he whispered after several minutes of trailing kisses along my skin.

My eyes fluttered open as if waking from a dream. Riven grinned wickedly and leaned in to kiss my lips once more. "Can we take this to the bed?" he asked, caressing my cheek with his thumb.

My body froze. I wasn't sure if I was ready.

"Not for *that*." He pressed a kiss to my forehead. "I want to kiss you until you fall asleep." His grip on my waist tightened. "And for that we need a bed."

I tossed back my head in a laugh. I nodded, smiling at the ceiling.

When I looked back at him, he was staring. His mouth opened, eyes wide as he cupped my face in his hand. "I could spend centuries listening to that laugh." He grinned as he leaned me back onto the mattress.

My skin prickled as I looked up at him. His legs were straddling mine and his arms framed my face. One hand was playing with a strand of my hair. He kissed my cheek and then my forehead, fingers tracing along the side of my neck.

"I could kiss you everywhere," he said, looking at me in awe.

"You should do that then," I said, raising a brow. Riven gave me another wicked grin before descending upon me.

His kisses were no longer soft, but hungry, as he tasted every inch of my skin. He started at one shoulder and kissed down the length of my arms. When he reached my hand, he pulled it to his face so I could touch his cheek before he kissed each finger slowly. The look he gave me while he did so made my thighs press together.

He kissed my chest, following the waves of scars until his lips met unmarked skin. He didn't try to move the nightgown, but instead kissed over it. It was so thin that I felt every brush just the same. He licked my breast and my back arched up into him as I let out a soft moan.

Riven kissed my body with even more heat, palming my breast through the gown as he did so. My chest rose quickly as the need inside me grew. He kissed down my legs, his hands trailing upward to my hips, balling the fabric in his fists so he could nip at the top of my thigh.

His hand dipped below the hem of the gown for the quickest moment, but it was enough for him to feel the wetness there.

"I can take care of that for you," he growled into my ear. "If you want me to."

I quivered as his breath warmed my neck. "I don't think I'm ready for . . ." I trailed off, too shy to say it.

Riven pulled himself back to my lips, his thumb caressing my face as his hand settled along my jaw.

"Then I'll wait for when you are," he whispered before bringing his lips back to mine, pulling my body into his. I tangled my fingers in his hair and hitched my leg over his hip, deepening the kiss. It felt like we spent hours in the fervor of each other's bodies before our passions tempered and we lay holding each other.

I don't know how long we lay there, entangled in each other's limbs. We were entirely content with breathing in the same air and saying nothing. Eventually, a thought crossed my mind that I couldn't shake.

"Was I such a terrible kisser that you kissed me not once, but twice, and were still convinced I couldn't fancy you?"

Riven chuckled against my hair and kissed my head. "No, the exact opposite actually. I could barely sleep after that first kiss. I hadn't meant for it to happen, it just . . . did. And then when I kissed you in Cereliath, I knew I wouldn't be able to stay by your side without it happening again," he admitted. I pressed a kiss against his neck.

"It was Syrra that put the idea in my head. It was something you said to her on our way to Cereliath. She figured you were carrying a broken heart from your time in the Order. She made a joke about growing up surrounded only by *ikwenira* . . ." Riven shrugged. "It would make sense if that's where your attraction lies."

"Not just *ikwenira*," I said, tasting the word for myself. It was so much better than calling Halfling's females.

"Syr had me worried after that." Riven pulled me closer to his chest. "You were healing in that pool for days and I was annoying everyone, pacing around. I couldn't sleep, I didn't eat. I just needed to know you were okay. When Syr asked if I was sure you had the same . . . longing, I second-guessed myself. Wondered if it had all been in my head. The first time you had tried to stab me, and the second could have just been part of our cover."

"It wasn't," I said truthfully. I was tired of hiding, and each confession was easier to share with him.

"Thank fuck for that," Riven said, pulling me to him for another kiss. Eventually our lips parted, exhaustion finally covering both of us in sleep. I slept the whole night through in Riven's arms—no dreams, or nightmares. Just peace.

CHAPTER FORTY-ONE

THE NEXT DAY, we rode to the outskirts of Koratha but could go no farther. At least not together.

I wore my black cloak and hood, the sword clasp shining from the polish I had given it that morning. I would be entering the capital as the Blade, but Riven would need to find his own passage.

"I'll wait for you at the cavern, just like we said," he murmured against my ear. We let our horses graze along the tree line as we said goodbye. I breathed in the scent of him, the birch and dew relaxing me.

I nodded, my back still tight. We would only meet again if both of us fooled the guards, and I fooled the king.

If the king decided to keep me at all.

The ability to plan our next attack rested on how well I could manipulate Aemon. How much information I could glean during our audience.

Riven's arms wound around my waist under the cloak. I rested my head against his chest, his heartbeat as steady and solid as the rest of him. We didn't speak. There was nothing left to be said that hadn't been whispered to each other the night before. Now, we were savoring the last moments before we parted, unsure if we would come back together again.

I was the first to break away with a soft kiss to Riven's mouth. He pressed his hand against my face; I could feel the roughness of his calluses on my cheek, proof of the years he had spent training. I lifted my hand to his face so he could feel my own.

He smiled before kissing my brow in a light caress, letting me mount my horse.

"Maybe I'll be the one waiting for you," I said, my tone lighter than I felt, before steering my ride toward the city and leaving him to wait for nightfall to follow.

The city was in chaos. I rode through the first gates, left open for anyone to enter. Only two guards stood watch in the towers. Inside the walls, people were shouting and yelling at one another, bartering over scraps of food and clothing, fighting in the streets as guards tried to corral the crowds. It was only worse in the next ring. Merchants stood at their carts with bemused looks as their tables sat empty. News of the blast had reached the capital and, panic-stricken, people had bought out all the goods. An empty cart was usually the heart's delight of any merchant, but now they stared at the emptiness not knowing when their next shipment would arrive. If it ever would.

I couldn't help but feel guilty as I passed more crying people. We had known what we were doing, the chaos and strife it would inflict.

All I could do was acknowledge their pain, their worry, and make a silent vow that I would try as hard as I could to ensure their suffering was worth it.

The guards standing outside the palace walls waved me forward. I entered through the wrought iron gates, creaking as they opened. The white stone of the palace looked gray against the overcast sky, as if it knew the people wept below.

Two Shades waited for me at the servants' entrance to the palace. I didn't say a word to either of them. I had expected the king would want to see me the moment I arrived in the capital.

Inside the palace, servants buzzed about, too engrossed in their whispers to even notice the Blade passed them by. I preferred the hum to the usual silence, even though I knew they were speaking of Silstra. Wondering who was responsible for such a blatant attack on the king, not even realizing that the culprit had just walked by them.

Even with my hood on, I kept my face neutral. I didn't know what I was walking into, what the king had heard, what the Shades had learned. I could be walking to my death, but I suspected they would have sent more than two novice Shades to collect me if that had been the case. As long as my wrists were free of shackles, I would take it as a good omen.

I trailed behind the Shades up the wide marble staircase and into the windowed wing. I looked up to see the first droplets of rain hit the glass ceiling. The clouds began to swirl and darken. I suppressed my smirk. Added rain would only slow the establishment of trade by land. The rain would muddy the roads and leave the carts slow, or even stuck. A favor from Nature herself.

I stood at the towering doors to the throne room and took a deep breath. The doors swung open, and I left my two escorts in the hall behind me. I bowed my head as I approached the throne. There were two smaller chairs sat on either side of the king, not gilded in gold like his, but ornate and beautiful. The princes sat in them.

I tried to keep my breath steady as I removed my hood. I had not expected Prince Killian to make it to Koratha so quickly. Even at a healthy pace, he shouldn't have been in the capital for days. He must have rode through the nights, like we had to Silstra, knowing that his father would need him.

I bit my cheek. I would have to be even more careful in what I told the king.

"Rise," King Aemon spat. I could see the anger etched in his face, deepening the few lines that marked his eyes and forehead. His hands were clenched in fists against his throne, so tight that his knuckles were white, his cheeks a flaming red.

"I send you to take care of the Shadow, and you return with my dam blown to bits! My trade routes in shambles!" I didn't need to pretend to flinch as the king's words struck deep into my chest. I had failed by not attacking him sooner. I let that failure rise and rest along my face.

Damien was hunched over the armrest of his chair, fingertips pressed together as he watched me. I could see the hope dancing in his eyes, wishing his father would take his rage out on me in a more physical way. Or even let him attend to the lesson.

The scars on my back did not burn as they usually did under his gaze. My muscles didn't tense. Whatever hold Damien had kept on me for the past three decades had broken. Had it been the day I brokered an alliance with his father's enemy? The day I laid down my life to ensure the dam was blown? The healing bath that leeched out the infection I'd carried in my back?

Or maybe it had been a slow shattering. Cracks in glass that grew like branches of a tree, unremarkable until the pane burst into pieces so small the glass could never be made the same. Since I'd left the capital, I had changed. I couldn't recognize it as it happened, but standing in front of the throne—facing the people who had enslaved my kin, molded the Shades, broken me—I couldn't deny I was different.

I was no longer the Blade they had forged. I was something else entirely.

Damien scoffed as if he could sense I no longer trembled under his gaze. "The kingdom is in complete disorder," he spewed, leaning forward from his seat. "My hunt at the Rift was canceled. Even Killian felt compelled to return from Volcar." He glanced to his brother and waved his hand dismissively.

"Volcar?" I echoed, glancing at Killian. The prince never could have journeyed there and back, then north to Cereliath since we spoke at the library all those weeks ago. When I saw him at the Harvest, I assumed he'd never left for Volcar at all.

Killian was hiding something. That much was clear.

"I never quite made it to Volcar, as I told you, brother," Killian answered, his eyes glancing across his father's throne to his brother. "I paused my journey outside of Wenden and heard a rumor that the Shadow had been nearby, planning an attack on Silstra."

A rumor it must have been, since Riven had been with me the entire time. It was too convenient. Too perfect for me to accept it was a coincidence. Prince Killian didn't want his family to know about our encounter in Cereliath. It was either the greatest stroke of luck or an ominous sign.

"I learned as much as I could in Wenden and then returned to the capital. I only just arrived when we heard that you had landed as well," Killian finished. His eyes were daring, urging me to play into his ruse.

Like I had any choice in the matter.

"I expect you found no trace of the Shadow in Aralinth?" Killian asked. It was the perfect setup. The king would never doubt my tale when one of his sons backed it. But why? What good did it serve Killian to deceive his father? What truth was he hiding?

I shook my head, committing to our shared narrative. "No, Your Highness, I did not," I lied, willing my face to remain flat despite the knots forming in my stomach. "I spent my time in the Faeland surveilling the Dark Fae. I investigated everyone living in the city as well as their kin. There were no indications that they've been supporting the Shadow or rallying any sort of defiance against the Crown. Once I was sure that the Shadow was not there, and likely never had been, I journeyed home. I suspected the Shadow would target the trade network. Unfortunately, I didn't make it to Silstra until the dam was blown, and by then I thought it would be best to return to the capital immediately."

"As you should," the king said, somewhat mollified by Killian's address and my explanation. "I need my Blade more than ever now. But perhaps that Blade isn't you." The king's eyes pierced through mine; his mouth set into a hard line. He lifted his chin, daring me to protest his decision, beg him for my life.

I would not give in to another one of his orders. Even if he slipped a noose around my neck. I stood tall, hands clasped behind my back, and met his stare head-on.

"Father," Killian cut in, "we cannot punish Keera for faulty information. She went to Aralinth for you and returned with her head. That, in itself, is a victory." I lifted my brows in shock. The king pursed his lips to one side, drumming his fingers against the throne.

"And further," Killian pressed, "she just admitted she suspected the Shadow was planning on attacking the trade routes. She is the only one who saw this attack coming. She may be the only one to see the next." Killian gave me the slightest smirk that made my chest tighten. I didn't know if he was toying with me, but I knew the choice was play or die.

The king paused, mulling over his son's defense. I stood still, not wanting to disturb the king as he weighed the value of my life. After a tantalizing moment, he nodded. "This threat against me shall not stand. I expect you to put out the brush fire before it sets the forest aflame." His eyes were hard as he surveyed my face. Watching for any flicker of weakness.

"I think the fire is already ablaze," Damien muttered from his chair. His father ignored him.

My face was a stone. "I will not rest, Your Majesty, until the menace is stopped," I replied, staring straight at the foot of his throne.

"Good. Your assignment still stands." The king gripped the edge of his armrest, his voice caked in venom. I bowed my head, expecting to be dismissed.

"Father?" It was Killian, his brows raised and eyes round as he addressed the king.

"What is it?" the king barked.

Once, Killian would have recoiled from his father's impatience, too timid to push him any further. But in his years away, he had changed. His shy disposition had evolved into confidence. His presence radiated beside the throne, listening and evaluating. His words, while few, carried a weight they never had before.

Decades of travel and study had molded Killian, the Bastard Prince, into more of an heir than his true-born brother.

"I don't think we should send the Blade to hunt the Shadow," Killian said.

Damien scoffed, throwing his leg over the side of his chair.

"Would you rather wait, brother? Until the Shadow cuts us down in our very seats? What good is a Blade if she can't cut him first?" He looked to his father for his usual nod of approval, but none came. The king turned to Killian.

"No, brother," the younger prince replied. "This Shadow is a menace. A threat not only to the kingdom, but the monarchy—your legacy, Father," he added, glancing at the king and his crown. "We cannot simply send the Blade to hunt him and expect that to be enough. She is not just a sharp edge, but a sharp mind. I think we would be best to put her to full use."

"What are you suggesting, Killian?" his father pushed, his tone less aggressive than before.

"The Blade is the commander of your Arsenal, so let her be," he said. "Call in the Arsenal. Call in the Shades. See what she can do when she has the entire Order at her disposal. Keera did not rise to her position to be an executioner. Any skilled killer could do that. She is the Blade because her skills are equally matched by her wit. Let her put them *both* to use." Killian barely looked at me, but I stared at him in disbelief. My stomach churned so violently I couldn't tell if I wanted to vomit or interrogate the prince.

I would have to pay closer attention to the younger prince moving forward.

The king gave his son a long, considering look. Like he'd only just noticed Killian was no longer a boy, gangly and weak, but a man. After a long pause, he gave a single, slow nod.

"Call in the entire Arsenal," he ordered, turning to me. "You'll meet with them and devise a plan. I want *all* the Shades reassigned to hunt the Shadow. I want to know how big this threat is, and then I want it snuffed out. I expect my Blade to lead them accordingly. Leave us."

I gave a low bow and exited the room, leaving the princes with their father.

Killian had not only saved me from the king's wrath, but he had orchestrated the perfect vantage point for me to manipulate events moving forward. Direct access to the Arsenal and the Shades, as commanded by the king.

I would have to give myself time to determine how I would use this against the Crown, but for now I had a singular mission ahead of me—learn what Killian was planning before he took me down with him.

CHAPTER FORTY-TWO

I HEADED STRAIGHT to my chambers with my hood covering my face. Thoughts of Killian and his motives filled my mind. I could only come to one conclusion: the Bastard Prince of Elverath wanted the throne.

He'd spent most of his life out of his father's reach. I'd always thought it was to avoid the whispers of court, his own brother's taunting. Life was easy for the second prince in the libraries of Volcar, hiring tutors to teach him history and language as he traveled. The luxuries of a prince who knew he would never be king.

But what if that had all been a ruse? Had Killian been buying his time, plotting against his father in hopes of overthrowing the king? I'd heard stories of the Mortal realms; their bloody histories were filled with regicide and rebellion. It was only a matter of time before the same stories were inked into the pages of Elverath's history.

I would not be used as a pawn for the son to replace the father.

My mission wasn't to move the Crown from one head to the next. I wanted it gone. Destroyed as completely as the Halflings and the Elves had been.

I wouldn't hesitate to kill Killian if he tried to stop me.

I entered my chambers, hoping for some time to think, but I was crushed against the door the moment I stepped through the threshold.

"Keera!" Gwyn squealed, pulling me into a tight embrace.

"Can't breathe," I whispered, but Gwyn only pulled in tighter. "Gwyn, I can't breathe," I rasped again.

"What?" She pulled back and saw me wheezing. "Goodness, I'm sorry." She held a hand up to her head, cheeks pink as she held in her laughter.

"You're surprisingly strong for a chambermaid," I said with a laugh of my own.

Gwyn gave me a radiant smile and shrugged, tugging at her skirt while she swayed back and forth. "So how was Aralinth? Did you see any Elves?" Her eyes widened in anticipation.

I plunked down onto the bed and pulled off my boots.

"A few." I smirked when Gwyn squealed even louder.

"What did they look like? Were they beautiful? Terrifying? Magical? Did you see any Fae?" she rattled on.

I chuckled. "So many questions."

Gwyn bit her bottom lip to keep more from spilling out. "I'm just a little cooped up, I guess," she said, her voice no longer light and airy.

"What do you mean?" I asked, my back tensing.

"Nothing really," she said. I raised a brow and she caved. "Prince Damien had planned for a hunt last week. The king forced him to cancel it when the news of Silstra came. He didn't want his heir gallivanting in the woods while a resistance was forming only a few hundred miles away."

"The king was right," I agreed, but that didn't have anything to do with Gwyn.

"Damien was upset. He called me to his rooms and kept me there. It wasn't all bad. He was out most of the day. And grew tired of me after a few . . . sessions. But I wasn't allowed to leave his chambers and he doesn't like having the staff in and out of his rooms, so it's been a while since I've had anyone to speak to." She rubbed her fingers in her lap.

My teeth clenched against the inside of my cheek. I needed to find a way to get her out of the palace, but that would be impossible until the king was dead.

"So . . ." Gwyn interrupted my thoughts, eyeing the saddlebags on the bench at the end of my bed. "Did you *find* anything of interest while you were away?"

"Is that why you were waiting in my rooms?" I laughed. "I see. You make me feel like you missed me, but really you just want your presents."

Gwyn looked appalled. "I did miss you! I can't believe you—wait, did you say pre*sents*? As in more than one?" Her mock hurt was completely forgotten as she ran over to the bags, bringing them to me.

"I did visit a few other places along the way," I said, pulling out a package wrapped in dark blue silk. A dew rose petal was pressed into the wax seal, only a little ruffled from all the travel.

Gwyn sat back down, her feet tapping excitedly from where they dangled off the bed.

"What is it?" she asked.

I cocked my head, playing into our usual rapport. "You have to open it." I dropped the package into her lap.

She was too excited to finish her line and pulled at the silks with deft fingers. She let out a soft gasp when they fell away to reveal two beautiful sapphires. They were small, even for earrings, but brilliant and encased in the finest gold the Faeland had to offer.

"They're beautiful!" Gwyn held them up to her face to inspect each one closely. The clasps were also made of gold, carved into the shape of a dew rose.

"They're more than beautiful," I said, undoing one clasp and placing it through Gwyn's ear. "They're enchanted with Fae magic." Gwyn leaped off the bed holding her ear as if it burned.

Fae magic, even items infused with it, was banned in Elverath. For a Halfling, it would mean death if they were caught.

"Don't worry. It's not an enchantment anyone will find," I reassured her. I had made sure of it before I purchased the gift. "When you wear them, they will let you know if the person you fear most is nearby. You—and only you—will hear a soft ringing that will get louder the closer you get. If you lose them or someone takes them from you, it will not work for them." I had taken a vial of Gwyn's blood with me to Aralinth to ensure it. I doubted she remembered the day I took it from her. She'd been a child, but I wanted to be prepared in case I ever made it into the Faeland.

Enchanted artifacts were hard enough to find in the kingdom. Custom-drawn enchantments were all but impossible now.

Gwyn slipped the other one into her ear and checked her reflection in the looking glass. They contrasted with the color of her hair in a way that would tarnish most, but on Gwyn the color made her glow.

"I love them. Thank you so much, Keera." Gwyn smiled but her tone was heavy with understanding. For now, earrings were the best protection I could offer.

"The other gift is in that bag," I said, pointing to the large leather satchel that held my clothes.

"A mask?" Gwyn said as she pulled out the gilded lacing I had worn in Cereliath.

"I had to disguise myself to attend a fancy party," I said with a shrug. "I have no use of it now, and I know you appreciate pretty things. I thought you'd like to keep it."

"Did you wear this to spy on the Fae?" Gwyn asked in an excited whisper.

A laugh bubbled in my chest. "I wore it to dance with one," I answered in a matching whisper.

"Really?" Gwyn's eyes widened in disbelief.

"The Fae are beautiful dancers," I said, describing the dinner at Lord Feron's and the ball at Cereliath. In the story I weaved, they were the same event, held in Aralinth. I couldn't risk Gwyn knowing my secrets.

An hour later, I had divulged everything I could to Gwyn, who lay across my bed. Her head dangled toward the floor with the gold mask tied to her face. She reminded me of when she had been a girl, so curious and silly. Gwyn had not just grown, she'd aged. Left to experience how cruel the world could be to Halflings.

The dinner chime filled the hallway, and she jumped up. Gwyn would be needed to bring up my meal. She took off the mask and held it in her hand as I opened the door.

"I'll see you in—" Gwyn was cut off by the man standing at my doorway.

Prince Killian stood with his arm raised like he'd been about to knock.

His eyes widened as he registered Gwyn's features, pausing on the mask she held in her hand. A flash of recognition streaked his face and then vanished.

I stood, protective of Gwyn with the prince. Whatever plot he had tried to rope me into, I wanted her to have nothing to do with it. I refused to let the wrath of the king—or his son—fall onto her shoulders.

"Your Highness," Gwyn said, bowing and leaving the room. Behind Killian's back, her mouth hung open in shock.

"Is there something amiss with the king?" I asked once Gwyn had cleared the hallway. I knew that Killian was here to explain himself for our audience earlier.

"My father is currently fine. Safe and well," he said casually, as if his words did not veil a threat against his own kin.

"How can I be of assistance, sire?" I asked with a small bow.

Killian shook his head as he smiled. "No need for the niceties, Keera. It's just us." He stepped into my room.

I blinked at his daring, shutting the door behind him. The last thing I needed was to be spotted with a prince who wanted to commit patricide.

"What do you want?" I asked plainly.

Killian chuckled, a dimple appearing on his left cheek.

"Nothing other than to thank you. For *not* revealing to my father that I had been in Cereliath," he said, crossing his arms behind his back.

"I didn't have much of a choice." I glanced at my blades across the room.

Killian shrugged. "I guess not, but I'm grateful all the same." He walked back toward the door and turned the knob.

"Is that all?" I asked in disbelief. I didn't expect the prince to care at all, let alone come to thank me in person.

"For now," he said, opening the door. "Until we meet again."

CHAPTER FORTY-THREE

THE ARSENAL ARRIVED the next morning. I couldn't remember the last time we'd all been in the same room together. Years. A decade even. I hated our meetings almost as much as I hated being the Blade.

I left my chambers before the suns had risen and crossed the unfinished bridge. I leaped from post to post over the churning waters beneath, salty air filling my lungs. I felt stronger than the last time I touched the island's shores. I was ready to take command the way I should have done thirty years before.

The Order was hardly safe territory with so many spies in one place, but I preferred it to the palace where the king and Damien could insist on overseeing our meeting. The small castle nestled across the channel from Koratha was the only place we could be assured of enough privacy for frank conversation.

Though hopefully not *too* frank. I couldn't risk exposing myself to the Arsenal. They had too many connections to one another and the Crown. It would be impossible to know where anyone's loyalties truly lay. But I could use them against the king either way. Tiny maneuvers that would cut at the base of the throne without notice until it toppled completely.

I stalked up the long path to the Order, a cool breeze blowing through my hair as the suns rose. The clang of steel rang through the air. A small group of initiates was practicing their sword work on the grounds. I spotted the two initiates I had paired together during my last visit. They circled each other like lions, dodging the other's strikes and laying blows of their own. Their steps formed a dance along the grass, leaving mirrored footprints on the morning dew. I smiled, knowing they were lost in the trance of it all. Nothing existed for them other than their partner and two blades. The rest of the world had faded away.

Hopefully, the world they found waiting for them would be different by the time they left the island. I rubbed Brenna's name along my arm and continued up the steep path toward the white castle.

I did not speak to anyone when I entered. The halls were mostly empty so early in the day anyway. I walked up the large stone staircase and came face-to-face with the statue of the Fae warrior. I had passed her face thousands of times, her full mouth and the curls that circled around her head in a fierce mane. She wore no cloak, but the same leathers Syrra wore carved with the elements. The same patterns I had cut into my skin.

Her eyes were closed, and I couldn't help wondering if she had silver eyes like mine. Eyes like the Light Fae who had abandoned me at the bottom of a chasm. I needed answers to those questions. I chewed my lip as I gazed at her face. Rheih's words echoed in my mind. Had the Light Fae truly been hiding all this time?

If any lived, I would find them. And convince them to help us end the king.

A group of initiates passed me along the stairs, stirring me from my thoughts. Each bowed her head as she walked by before scurrying down the steps. I walked down the hall to the war room and waited for the other members of the Arsenal.

The large wooden table had no head. I took the seat with my back against the window, overlooking the rolling waves of the sea. I'd already spent too much of my life stuck here, staring out at that view. I would not force myself to do so for another moment.

Myrrah was already in the room when I arrived. She sat beside me; a large map spread out in front of her. Its edges splayed out over the circular table, tickling the wheels of her chair.

Myrrah had been injured on a mission when I was still an initiate. Though she would never walk again, it hadn't stopped her from becoming the Shield. Elverath's defenses had improved in the years after her injury, every weak point had been rectified, and every threat nullified.

At least until the Shadow.

And now me.

"Good morning, Mistress," I greeted. Myrrah carried no last name of her own either. She held the same hatred for the name *Kingsown* as I did.

"Long time, Keera," she said with a raise of her gray brow. Her eyes trailed over me in disbelief, like she was seeing me back from the dead. In some way, I suppose she was. I'd spent years surrounding myself with nothing but ghosts. Now, I had chosen to fight for the living instead. Myrrah gave me an approving nod and returned to her maps. Small wooden pieces were placed across the continent, just like the pins Hildegard had marking the Shades in her office.

Myrrah pulled her long sleeves onto her lap. She didn't wear the black hood or cloak. With her chair she was too distinguishable for a hood to be useful, and the cloak was an impediment when she moved about the castle. Instead, she wore a long black robe with her silver shield pinned against her chest.

"Was your journey from Volcar quick?" I asked to fill the time.

She nodded. "The seas were clear," she said in a soft rasp. "We made it back just as the floods washed through." She didn't offer any more details than that. I knew better than to ask. Myrrah had always been a Halfling of few words.

Hildegard entered the room with a hooded figure behind her. Even with her hood drawn, I could tell from the breadth of her shoulders and the way she towered behind Hildegard that it was Mistress Moor. The silver arrow glinted in the sunlight as they took their seats. The Arrow lowered her hood, uncovering the gray braid down her back. Her eyes were black and framed by purple circles that hung low under her lashes; even her skin looked gray. I glanced at Hildegard, sitting next to Myrrah. They both looked just as tired.

I took a breath, rubbing my fingers under the table. The chaos was already beginning to wreak havoc on my comrades. A twinge of guilt pulled at my stomach, but I ignored it. I couldn't let myself be distracted by short-term issues. The long-term goal was freedom for everyone.

Halflings.

Shades.

Us.

That is what I needed to stay focused on.

Gerarda was the last one to arrive. As expected, she took the seat directly beside mine. A not-so-subtle reminder that she was the second-in-command.

"Why did you call this meeting, Keera?" Hildegard asked.

I took a deep breath. There was no use in talking around the issue.

"The king has requested the Arsenal go after those that attacked Silstra. That means the Shadow and whoever we find to be his conspirators. He wants us to reassign every Shade as well." I laid my hands on the table, ready for the complaints.

"*Every* Shade?" Myrrah echoed, her brows grazing her hairline. She tapped her fingers against the armrest of her chair.

I nodded.

"Some Shades are as far west as Volcar. It would take weeks just for them to receive the notice to return, let alone step foot in the capital," Gerarda said, her chin lifting. She loved pointing out any mistakes of mine, even when requested by the king.

"I'm aware," I said, glancing at her. I'd been thinking the same since the king set his orders. "Call in anyone we can spare within a fortnight's ride of the capital. Everyone else will have their missions adjusted to provide surveillance of the Dark Fae borders and reconnaissance of anyone we suspect of being associated with the Shadow."

Gerarda raised a brow. "I thought you told the king that the Dark Fae were unconnected?"

I fought the urge to roll my eyes. I wasn't shocked Gerarda had spied on our audience. She liked having all the information, even when I tried to cut her out of it.

"I did," I said with a stiff nod. "I saw no proof of their involvement while I was in Aralinth. But on the *off chance* that I'm wrong, do you want to tell the king that we left their border completely unsupervised?" I raised my own brow back at her. She straightened in her seat but said nothing.

"A job like that explosion takes manpower," the Arrow cut in. "It's remarkable they were able to do it without the Shades catching wind of anything, but that can't last forever. The Shadow must have dozens of men working for him."

"My thoughts exactly, Rohan." I nodded. "Have we received any reports from Silstra?"

"The fire was set with a powerful accelerant," Myrrah cut in. "My contacts believe it was liquid fire, which indicates that the group is well-resourced or well-connected with the black markets. Probably both. One team set the town house ablaze, and another took out the dam. No one was apprehended by either the Shades or the king's guard."

I pretended to consider this information, my bottom lip protruding slightly.

"A ten-person job then?" I asked, pretending that I didn't know exactly how many of us there had been.

Myrrah nodded, adjusting the shield pin at her chest. "A dozen at least. There were over sixty charges set along the base of the dam to bring it down. Whoever they were, they moved quickly."

"And they're only going to get quicker," I added.

Gerarda didn't hide her eye roll as she twirled a throwing star in her fingers. "We don't know that."

"We do," I countered, snapping my head at her. "In every sense of the matter, the Shadow won his first attack. He'll be preparing for another soon and we would be foolish to not take that threat seriously."

"I agree," Myrrah said. "They drew first blood. We need to make sure we end the fight before everything is wiped away in the blows."

Silence settled across the room, each weapon of the Arsenal considering which sector of the kingdom the rogues would strike next. It was time to take charge.

"Until we receive better intel, we need to be optimizing our defenses," I cut through the silence. "Myrrah, I want you to work alongside the king's guard to schedule rotations across the capital, as well as Mortal's Landing. You will be responsible for determining the rations of our food stores and how long the city can be held if the trade routes are attacked again."

The Shield nodded.

"Mistress Hildegard," I said, "is the king still insistent on holding the Trials?"

She nodded slowly, her mouth a straight line. "Yes," she said, clearing her throat. "Though I think he could be convinced that hosting an event that large would be a poor use of resources with the Shadow lurking about."

Good, I thought. The initiates were safe for now.

"I would prefer to spare the initiates as long as possible," I said, gazing out the window to where they practiced below. "We don't need to worry about adding to our numbers until we have a better idea of the size of the threat we're facing. Do you agree?" I asked the room.

Everyone nodded, including Gerarda. At least we agreed on something.

"Hildegard and Rohan will maintain their teaching posts at the Order," I said, receiving nods from the Bow and Arrow. "As for the rest, I am assigning them to you, Gerarda."

"Me?" she echoed, leaning on the table.

"Yes." I nodded. "You will serve as my eyes and ears in the capital and assign the Shades as you see fit. Everyone else will funnel their intel through you. I expect regular reports."

"Isn't that your job?" Gerarda said, slumping back in her chair.

I gritted my teeth. Everything had to be a fight with her. "When I'm in the city it is," I said. "But I won't be after tomorrow."

"Why not?" Gerarda asked, standing up from her chair. "You're going to abandon us while the largest threat in recent history looms over the kingdom?"

"No." I stood up from my own seat. "I am going undercover in Mortal's Landing."

"Mortal's Landing?" she scoffed, crossing her arms and looking to the others for support.

I took a step toward the window. Gerarda may be second in command of the Arsenal, but I was the head of it. I would not stand for her complaints. Even if she had a right to them.

"Yes, Mortal's Landing." I raised my voice as I turned toward her. "And while the *Blade* does not need to explain herself to the *Dagger*, let alone anyone else, I will. The Shadow didn't just attack the trade routes. He targeted the food supply. If I were trying to overthrow the king, my next move would be to attack the textiles, especially on the eve of the winter season." A hush fell over the room as the Arsenal raised their brows as one.

"Mortal's Landing is the next logical target," I continued. "And considering I found no sign of him in the north, there are only so many places the Shadow could hide while remaining so well-connected. Mortal's Landing is the perfect cover and the ideal location to stage a quick getaway if needed."

Gerarda opened her mouth to respond but no words followed. She sat back down in her seat.

"Now that you've had your little tantrum," I added, "I was serious about you being in command while I'm away, Gerarda. I thought I had selected the right person for the role, but please correct me if that is not the case."

Gerarda didn't say anything, eyes focused on her boot.

"I didn't think so," I said with a final nod. "As I said, you will lead the Shades and determine their stations while I'm gone. I will arrange for us to meet once a month, and you can provide me with any information that cannot be sent by coded message. Until I return, you will serve as my mouthpiece back to the Arsenal."

"For how long?" Gerarda whispered.

I smirked. "Until I bring in his head."

There was only one head I intended to bring in, and that was the king's.

CHAPTER FORTY-FOUR

I LEFT THE CAPITAL before first light the next day. The Arsenal would see to official matters while I planted seeds of rebellion throughout the kingdom and searched for answers. I pulled out the map Riven had given me. An ancient scroll of parchment, creased so thoroughly down the middle I thought the wind would break it in half.

The suns rose over the western horizon, casting warm light over the map. It was what Riven had told me to wait for. I halted my horse and held the map up to my face, letting the sunlight soak through the thin paper. The moment it touched the light, symbols appeared across Elverath with names I couldn't read or recognize.

It was a map of hideouts left by the Light Fae. Riven and his crew had been using them for years. The one I was looking for was a cavern hidden at the edge of the Dead Wood. It made for the perfect meeting place while we devised the next stage of our plan.

I found the small dot marking its location in blue ink and set my course. It was a full day's journey following the river and crossing into the Dead Wood. I'd be lucky to arrive before sunset.

I folded the map and placed it back in my pocket. The skies were clear as I rode. I crossed paths with people carrying their life's belongings on their backs—citizens of the Crown who had lost everything in the floods. My chest tightened each time I passed a family along the riverbank. I only hoped we would succeed and their suffering wouldn't be wasted.

Hours later, I reached the edge of the Dead Wood. Bent trunks curved around burnt branches, oozing black sap from their bark hot enough that I could feel the warmth on my legs. I checked the map. The path was set right next to the large gray stone beside my horse. I jumped down, holding the reins as I stepped onto what looked to be blackened, smoking earth.

The glamour shattered. The dead trees pulled back to reveal a clear path through the wood, stones lining the way over a small hill. I pulled on the reins, but my horse didn't want to step forward. I took another step, disappearing beneath the glamour before she followed.

The cavern was nestled between thick trees as black as night. I tied my horse to a stump outside the cave. A twig snapped behind me. I only had time to turn before I was swept off the ground.

"I told you I'd be the one waiting," Riven growled in my ear as he spun me around. His warm breath tickled my neck as I laughed. He held me, feet not touching the ground, pinning me against his chest. "I missed that laugh," he purred before bringing his lips to mine.

My body exploded, shivering with the heat of his touch. I wrapped my legs around his waist and nipped at his bottom lip. Riven grunted against my mouth, trying to pull away but I didn't let him.

It had been too long. The days spent without his hands on me, his scent wrapped around my skin, were excruciating. I wanted to taste every part of him, steal his breath for my own, and never let him go. I pulled at the nape of his neck, his hair spilling through my fingers. Riven's hands trailed down my back, lifting me higher into the air.

"Keera," he whispered against my neck. I groaned in response as he licked under my ear. He wanted to taste me too. "If we don't stop now, I might not let you go until morning."

I smirked against his mouth as I pulled him into another kiss. "I don't see the issue with that," I teased, trailing my lips down his jaw. It tensed under my touch, and I scraped his skin with my teeth. Riven's fingers dimpled my thighs as he cleared his throat.

"We have things to discuss," he choked. "And I know you're hungry."

As if on cue, my stomach growled loud enough to scare the horse. Riven chuckled, pressing a soft kiss to my lips before lowering me to the ground. He grabbed my saddlebag and walked me into the cave.

I gasped when I saw what he had done. A straw mattress lay on the floor with a sheepskin blanket. The soft hum of flowing water filled the room from a small stream cascading down the rock wall. The water pooled along a waterfall, creating a small basin sprinkled with dew rose. Drops of water clung to the petals, almost sparkling in the soft warmth of the faelights that floated at the top of the cave.

It was like Riven had transported us back to the Faeland. Our own private hideaway.

"Did you do all this?" I whispered, looking up at the floating orbs.

Riven shrugged as he watched me. "I had some time to kill," he said. He grabbed my hands and pulled me toward the mattress. A small basket sat beside the gray cover. Riven opened it as we sat. It was filled with salted meats, cheeses, and fruit. I bit my lip as my stomach grumbled in anticipation. I had ridden all day without food to get to Riven as quickly as I could.

He grabbed a large leaf to use as a plate and set a sampling for me. I devoured the food before Riven had started on his own. He smiled at the empty leaf as I loaded another helping. "Wine?" he asked, uncorking a small wineskin. The rich scent crashed through me.

My throat burned. "No," I said a bit too loud, shaking my head.

Riven set down the wineskin, his brow raised. "Is something wrong?" he asked, reaching for my leg. His large hand covered the entirety of my thigh.

I swallowed. Part of me had hoped Syrra had lied and told Riven what happened in Caerth.

"I used wine—any alcohol really—as a crutch for a long time," I said, heat rising to my cheeks. "I spent the better part of two decades drinking the days away, trying to forget. Trying not to care. I don't think I will ever trust myself to drink it again." My eyes widened as the last words fell out of my mouth. I had never said that before, but I was surprised it felt right on my lips. Even the craving at my throat faded as I looked at Riven.

His hand squeezed my leg as he put the wineskin back. "Thank you for telling me," he said, his violet eyes piercing through me as he caressed my cheek.

"But you can. I don't mind—"

Riven shook his head. "To be honest, I don't much care for the taste of Mortal wine."

He pulled me against his chest as we ate. He told me of his days meeting with contacts in the capital. The black markets were volatile after the floods. Merchants all over the kingdom were trying to find supplies to sell. The price of grain had already tripled.

I told him about my meeting with the Arsenal and how I would be able to keep a close watch on the Shades while we worked. I mentioned the audience with the king and his son. "You don't think Prince Killian is making a move for the throne?" I asked.

His body was stiff behind my back, his dark brow low over his eyes as he stroked my hair. "If the prince kills his father, that makes our job all the easier," Riven said. There was a cold edge to his voice that I didn't understand. Or like.

"But if he—"

Riven cut me off with a kiss. "I can think of *many* things I'd rather be doing than talking about the prince," he said with a smirk. His eyes never left mine as he pulled the string along the neck of my tunic. It fell open and he trailed a line of kisses down my neck, biting my skin.

My breath caught. Riven's fingers trailed along the scars etched into my arm, inching my tunic over my shoulder. I tensed as his thumb moved along a swirl of names. "Keera," Riven whispered against my ear, kissing my scars. His gentle fingers pulled at my jaw, lifting my head to face him. "You're as beautiful as you are strong." He pressed a kiss against my ear. "And you're the strongest person I know."

He held my face in his hand, his thumb trailing over my cheek before he kissed my lips. Warmth pooled at my belly. I reached up behind me, my hands tangled in Riven's hair as I deepened our kiss. He groaned against my mouth.

I turned around, straddling Riven's lap in one fast motion. His eyes fluttered as I smiled down at him, pulling him in for another kiss. I could feel the hunger in Riven's touch. He pulled at my lips with his teeth until I moaned. His hands squeezed my hips, pulling me closer to him. Something hard pressed against my thigh.

Riven's hands wrapped around my back. I arched against his strong hold as he trailed more kisses down my neck. He pressed his lips against my collarbone as his fingers grazed along the open line of my tunic. Waiting for permission. Giving me control.

My heart burst as I lifted Riven's face to mine and kissed his forehead. He closed his eyes against my touch, and I smiled down at his face. He wore no hood or mask. The faelights cast golden streaks along his skin. He was Riven. Cloaked in nothing but his hunger for me.

I nipped at his bottom lip. "Take it off," I said—no, demanded. Riven's eyes flashed open, and he grabbed the neck of my tunic, ripping it down the middle.

Riven caught my gasp with his mouth. "You can have mine," he said between kisses, his voice a hoarse rasp. His lips warmed my jaw and then my neck. He bit my shoulder, his sharp fangs sending shivers down my spine. His hands roved along my torso, stopping over my breasts and pushing the tunic off my shoulders. Leaving me and my scars completely bare.

Riven leaned back, drinking in the view of me. His tongue swept across his lips once before he descended upon my skin. His hands palmed my breast, coaxing a soft moan from me. My breath caught when his tongue flicked against my nipple. My fingers clenched on his shoulders as he tasted my skin.

"I spent so long trying not to want you," he whispered against my chest, pressing a kiss between each word. "But when I watched you plummet from that dam"—his hands tightened around me—"I knew I would never need another the way I need you." My chest tightened at his words. I blinked down at him, unsure of how to tell him I had wanted him too. That charge had hung between us as Shadow and Blade, and now as Riven and Keera. Unmasked and unbroken.

His fingers teased along the edge of my trousers, casting shivers along my belly. His thumb dipped into my waistband and my back arched, waiting for his hand to travel lower. I looked down and was met with a wicked grin as Riven unbuttoned my pants without moving his eyes from me. His fingers skirted along the edge of the fabric, taunting me. I shivered. He did it again.

"Please," I begged. Riven's smile widened, and his hand plunged between my legs. He snarled against my neck at the slickness he felt, his fangs scratching against my skin.

He licked my nipple as his fingers pressed against me, releasing a wave of tension. I tugged the hair at Riven's neck, pulling him tighter against my chest. His fingers teased me, brushing against my skin everywhere except for the one place I wanted.

Riven tugged at my nipple with his teeth just as he pressed against that untouched spot. My moan echoed off the cavern walls. I shifted my hips. He flicked his thumb and I arched against the touch. I felt the weight of Riven's stare on my skin as he played with me, building the need between my thighs.

"More," I pleaded in a ragged breath. I gripped Riven's shoulders and ground against his hand. Riven swore. He slid a finger into me and groaned at the wetness he found waiting for him.

He plunged his finger in and out of me. Hard strokes that stole my breath. Riven pulled me to him, filling my lungs with his hungry kisses. I rocked my hips against him, quickening the speed. Riven matched the tempo and slid a second finger into my core.

I gasped. I couldn't focus on anything but the tightness. The scent of dew and birch that wrapped around me as Riven pushed me closer to the edge. My eyes fluttered and I saw him watching me. His eyes locked on my hips, unable to look away from where our bodies joined.

My thighs tightened and I pressed against the hardness at his thigh. "Fuck," Riven coughed. His eyes cut to mine. "Keera," he sighed. My name on his lips was a release. I cried out his name in return, clutching him against me as waves of pleasure rocketed through my limbs. Riven caught my moans with his lips, calming the climax with each kiss.

"Beautiful," he whispered against my cheek.

I moved my hand to the hardness I felt but Riven grabbed my wrist and shook his head. He lowered us against the mattress. My brows furrowed as he laid a kiss between them.

"We don't need to go any further," he said, tucking a strand of hair behind my ear. "I'm in no rush, Keera."

"But I want—"

"Oh, I know." Riven grinned, kissing my wrist before letting it go. I inched forward, trying to pull his mouth back to mine. "I'm serious, Keera." He laughed. "I *want* you. More than I care to breathe. But when that day comes, I don't want it to be rushed or in a cave. I want hours, *days*, to coax my name from your lips again and again. I don't want the weight of tomorrow's goodbye between us or the weight of . . ." He bit his lip, his eyes flicking down for a moment.

"When we share that with each other, Keera, I want there to be nothing pressing in against us. Nothing but you and me," he said, his eyes swimming with resolve. I could see the weight of what we'd done, what we still would do, on his face. The strain it took to keep his fear in check.

I pressed my hand to his cheek and nodded. Riven pulled me against his chest and stroked my hair. We lay there, tangled together beneath the faelight, memorizing the feel of each other. When the suns set, Riven braided my hair as I washed my face in the small basin. I went to bed with his tunic hanging at my knees, wrapped in the scent of him with his arms wrapped around my waist.

It was still dark when I opened my eyes, moonlight filtering through the entrance of the tiny cave. The only reason I woke at all was the coolness at my back. Riven was no longer sleeping beside me but packing his bag a few feet away.

"I know you said you needed to leave early, but it's barely tomorrow," I slurred, grabbing the pillow he was trying to pack.

"I need to get going if I hope to make it to the Rift." Riven gave me a slow kiss and wrestled the pillow out of my hand.

"Do you need your tunic?" I asked coyly. I sat up and started sliding it off my body, hoping it would entice him to stay a little while longer.

"Keep it." He pulled the hem down and grinned against my neck. "You can wait two weeks." He nibbled at my ear, making me doubt that was true.

"You look better in it anyway," he said, his eyes trailing down my bare legs.

"I do, don't I?" I teased, biting my bottom lip. I looked down, scanning the length of my body, before looking up at him with a wide grin. I winked.

Riven shook his head, but there was laughter in his eyes. "You've been spending too much time with Nikolai, I think." I shrugged. That was probably true.

I pulled him on top of me. I loved the weight of his body on mine, his warmth and scent. How had I lived so long without touching another this way? Now that I had it again, the thought of going without felt like living without water.

Riven's large hands closed around my back and turned us on our sides. We just lay beside each other, bodies pressed together, while he gently stroked my back. His violet eyes were discerning as they watched me. I kissed his lips gently, and Riven pulled me closer to him.

His lips scorched mine, unable to get enough of my skin as he trailed his kisses down my neck and jaw. My fingers pulled at his hair, beckoning him even closer. When he didn't relent, I hooked a leg around his back and a soft moan escaped my lips.

Riven softened his bite. His thumb grazed over my cheek in a soft caress before he ended the kiss.

It was lovely, but it felt like goodbye.

"It's only two weeks," I said, echoing his words back at him. My skin already felt cold without his lips on me.

Riven's eyes were hard, his jaw flexed. I could hear the gritting of his teeth as he looked down, away from my gaze.

"You aren't just going to the Rift, are you?" I pulled his head back toward me with a finger under his chin.

Riven's body froze against mine.

"I trust you, Riven," I said earnestly. "If you can't tell me, or think it's better that you don't . . . I trust you. Need to know, remember?" Of course, when I made that deal with him, I never expected us to be wrapped around each other the way we were.

"Need to know," Riven echoed softly, his eyes closed as he nodded. We just held each other, Riven stroking my back, until the first notes of birdsong played from the trees. Their harmonies had almost lulled me back to sleep when Riven broke the silence.

"You were a surprise, Keera," he whispered fiercely. "You were a wonderful, beautiful surprise. I never thought this would happen, but I'm glad it did." His words were urgent and pressing, his grip on my waist tight.

"I'm glad too," I answered. I wasn't one for grand speeches. All I could offer was the truth and hope that would be enough.

He kissed me a final time. I couldn't shake the feeling of farewell as he did so. I pressed my lips to the space between his brows. He pulled me into the crook of his neck and rubbed my back until I fell asleep. When I woke hours later, he was gone.

The suns had already risen above the tree line before I was packed and readying my horse. I had slept well past dawn, later than I remembered doing in a long time. My body felt refreshed. I was even excited to ride all the way to Mortal's Landing.

Our plan was working, and soon the king—the Crown—would topple.

For the first time ever, I was excited by the prospect of what would follow it.

I hummed to myself as I buckled the saddlebags to my ride. She was grazing on the brush at her feet. I took the time to brush the horse's mane. We would have to bond over our five-day journey. I slipped her some oats from my pouch, laughing as her tongue tickled my fingers.

I was still wearing Riven's tunic. His scent lingered on the linen. I pulled up my trousers and tucked it into the waistband. It was much too large for me, but I didn't care. No one would be seeing me for days anyway.

I lifted a boot into the stirrup but caught a flicker of the mare's ears. A twig snapped behind me.

I turned but it was too late.

I felt a prick on my arm. When I looked down there was a small red dart sticking out of my skin. My vision began to blur, and my legs gave out.

The last thing I saw before I passed out was someone walking over to me and placing a bag over my head.

CHAPTER FORTY-FIVE

I WAS IN A CARRIAGE, thrown in beside stores of food and grain. I could hear people outside riding on horseback. Several voices. Men. I tried to count how many, but my head was cloudy. It was like I was listening to them speak from underwater. My head ached from the strain until I gave up.

I could smell the scent of rosewood, damp earth, and fresh water. The ground beneath the carriage wheels was soft but laced with hard roots and gravel. We were in a wood, but I had no idea which one. I felt like I'd been asleep for weeks. My arms and legs were bound in rope. My back was stiff from lying in the same position as I struggled to sit up.

Something itched on my neck. I reached to scratch it with both of my bound hands. I pulled something out of the skin. A red dart. The same kind that I had used on the Shade at Silstra.

Sleeping draught.

But the dart that pricked me outside that cavern had been in my arm. Whoever had taken me had been keeping me unconscious for days. Maybe longer. I could be anywhere by now.

I fought against my bindings. The tight rope burned my flesh as I rubbed my wrists together trying to loosen the knot. I made no progress other than splitting the skin around my fingers until they bled. I knew my captors could hear me cursing at the ropes, but no one came to sedate me again. I didn't know if that was a good sign or a bad one.

My body flung forward as the carriage came to a halt. I fell onto my bound wrists with a heavy jerk. Footsteps. Someone was approaching the doors to the carriage. I leaned back on my knees right beside the doors. I lifted my hands above my head, ready to strike.

The doors flew open, white light from the suns blinded me as I launched myself into whoever opened the door. It was a Halfling, only a bit taller than me. I used his shock to my advantage and shoved my elbows into his face. He fell with a scream, and someone knocked me to the ground from behind.

"Don't hurt her," a voice called out from nearby.

I froze. Not because the voice scared me, but because I recognized it.

Nikolai.

Someone held my shoulders down as Nikolai walked in front of me. His usual warm demeanor was gone, replaced with a stoic mask I had never seen him wear.

"Keera," he said with a slight bow. I spat at him. He winced but did not move to strike me. He bit the inside of his cheek when he noticed the raw skin around my fingers and wrists. Nikolai held a hand to me, but I jerked backward. His arm stilled. There was a sadness in his face as he watched me, but I knew it was a lie.

Everything had been a lie.

Nikolai pulled me off the ground and held me from behind. He placed a bag over my head as I hurled every insult I knew at him. He ignored me and pushed me forward. We walked in small steps; my gait bound by the rope at my knees. I leaned back into his shoulders and grabbed his torso with one hand. I pinched. Hard. He sucked in a breath as he pushed me off him, but he didn't say anything.

I hoped it hurt. He was a traitor. Had sold me out to whoever it was he was bringing me to. Riven would be livid when he found out.

A cold wave of realization crashed through my body, settling into my blood.

Riven. What if Nikolai wasn't a traitor at all?

What if Riven had ordered this?

He knew exactly where I had been. He left before I woke that morning. I thought he'd been leaving to enact his part of the plan, but perhaps he needed me alone. Gave Nikolai the opportunity to catch me unaware.

I didn't have time to think through the implications of that because we stepped into some sort of building. The floor under my feet was hard and uneven. It was made of wood. I could hear the faint crackling of a fire and a breeze brushing against a windowpane.

Where in the gods am I? I thought bitterly.

Someone opened a door and we walked through it. My ears picked up the added heartbeats, too many to be sure. Maybe five? Plus, the three who walked in with me.

I didn't need to guess any longer because Nikolai stopped, halting me with his arm. He removed the bag.

A man sat in front of me in a large wooden chair, not unlike a throne. Behind him stood Syrra and Collin. The man had blond hair that emphasized the thin, golden band circling his head. His eyes were a fierce green, like spring leaves fading into amber at the center, the same as his brother's.

Prince Killian.

The ground swayed underneath my feet. Nikolai's grip tightened on my shoulder, keeping me steady. Killian raised his chin, assessing the state of my bindings. His eyes paused on the redness around my wrists. His lips pursed for a second and then broke into a cruel grin.

"Please, forgive the impolite nature of this audience, Keera," the prince said, casting a dark hush over the room. "It was for your safety as well as the safety of my comrades."

"Capturing me? Or holding me hostage?" I bit, not even trying to conceal the ice in my voice.

"Both," Killian said. "I couldn't risk freeing you until we spoke. And I couldn't risk revealing myself until we were well out of my father's and brother's reach."

"And for what exactly?" I snapped. I thrashed against Nikolai's grip and took a step toward the prince. Nikolai made to grab me, but Killian held up his hand.

"Keera is our friend, same as always," he told Nikolai. His hard gaze swept over the rest of the people in the room. Some nodded their heads. Most stood silently with their hands latched around the hilt of a blade.

"Bullshit," I spat. Syrra lifted her hand to cover a smirk.

"But, Keera," Killian said, his lips twitching to one side, "we've been friends the entire time. Your surveillance in Aralinth, your mission in Cereliath, blowing up the dam in Silstra." Killian listed off each city on his fingers. Every tick landed like a hard blow against my gut.

"You know about that?" I didn't believe it.

Nikolai scoffed behind me. Killian sent him a warning look.

"I devised it," the prince answered.

"But Riven . . ." My breath hitched. It was starting to make sense.

"Yes, my Shadow has kept me well-informed of your missions," Killian said, waving his hand.

His Shadow? It couldn't be true. Riven would have told me. He couldn't have kept this alliance from me for so long. Not after I proved myself in Silstra. Not after we . . .

Need to know. The blood drained from my face and my body fell limp beside Nikolai. I wasn't the only one who had been keeping heavy secrets.

"Where is Riven?" I asked. "I want to speak to him now!"

Killian's mouth fell into a straight line. Exhaustion flooded my bones even though I'd been sleeping for days, my knees straining to hold me.

"Riven is indisposed at the moment," Killian said, standing up from his chair and walking toward me. "He knows where you are and will be back soon. As soon as he arrives, you may speak with him. But you'll have to make a choice first."

I scoffed. "A choice?" What choice did I have bound and unarmed?

"Yes," Killian said, taking one last step toward me. He was close enough that I smelled the scent of parchment wafting from his clothes. I could see the faint spots of ink on his hands.

"Our secret alliance no longer serves either of us," Killian said. "The king will move quickly. If we have any hope in defeating him, you need to know who you've really been dealing with."

"You want me to join your ranks?" I shook my head in disbelief. "Why would I trust you?" I lifted my bound wrists. They were only one example of how Killian—how Riven—had betrayed me.

Killian smirked. "You already have. You just didn't know it. I need you to recommit yourself to the mission, Keera. Knowing your Riven answers to me. If you can't, then I'm afraid—"

"You'll have to kill me?" I guessed.

"Truly, I'd rather not." Killian lifted his hand to his chest. "I think you and I will become great friends."

"Do you make a habit of lying to your friends?" I asked. "Binding their hands?"

"Not unless I have to." He shrugged. "Keera, you know better than most that secrets are dangerous things to share. Your wounded pride was not worth risking all my men by revealing myself." His voice was hard and unmoving. I hated the part of me that understood what he meant.

"Why reveal yourself now?" I asked.

"For starters," Killian said with a grin, "I reckon someone willing to get blown up wants to defeat my father just as much as I do. Maybe even more." He tilted his head, studying me.

My skin prickled under his gaze. Why did the prince want to defeat his father? How long had he been working against the Crown? I scowled at him. I wouldn't give him the satisfaction of asking my questions in front of all his accomplices.

"More importantly," Killian added, "I think you would be of better use beside me in the fight to come."

I scowled. "You mean you don't trust me." The bindings on my wrists felt tighter, like they would never be undone. All those people I had killed trying to escape the weight of the Crown, trying to end the reign of the king, had been for nothing. I had freed myself of one set of shackles only to find my hands tied to another instead. My stomach lurched. If I was going to vomit, I'd make sure it landed on the prince.

"I *do* trust you, actually," Killian said, his expression softening. "And I will have to keep doing so for us to succeed. I think you're an even better strategist than you are a weapon. I have others that will kill for me; not as many that can see which pieces need to be moved to topple a monarchy."

He had said something similar that day in the throne room. My cheeks heated as I remembered how grateful I had been for his support in front of the king. Now his words left a bitter taste in my mouth. He'd been playing me all along, and I'd been too dimwitted to catch it.

"I wanted to end the *Crown*," I said, my voice hoarse against my throat. "Not work to place yet another king upon the throne."

"We want the same," Killian answered evenly. I raised my brows at the gold circlet on his head.

Killian took it off, his eyes not leaving mine as he did so. "This crown is nothing more than a tool, Keera. Like your blade. Or better yet, your hood. It helps us move without being seen. It protects those who trust me." He looked around the room at the Halflings and Elves who stood watching us.

He took a step toward me. "But once we succeed, I will take it off. I have no interest in being king. In ruling a land that was never meant to be ruled to begin with." He dropped the crown and it bounced against the floor. I didn't trust his words, but when I looked over his shoulder, I saw Syrra. Her lips were set into their usual straight line, but her eyes were locked on me.

She nodded once. A sign that I could trust the prince. Or at least that *she* trusted the pretty things he said.

Killian took my hands in his. They were gentle and unmarked. He had no callouses from fighting or training, but his skin was rough. Dry like the scrolls and parchment he spent most of his days with.

He pulled a blade from his belt. The thin steel glinted. It was short but long enough to pierce a heart.

"I meant what I said, Keera," he whispered, so close his breath warmed my cheek. "I want you to be my ally. But I also want you to be my friend." His eyes bore into mine, daring me to take one last chance. I sucked in a breath, unsure if I could trust them. They were so much like the cruel ones of his brother.

I nodded.

Killian thrust the blade through my bindings.

"Now," he said as the thick rope fell to the floor. "Let's kill my father."

It wasn't a joke. It was a promise.

Acknowledgments

So many hands held the various versions of this book and many more held me up while writing it. I would like to say thank you to my family and friends who listened to all my excited tangents, stressful tears, and anxiety-ridden thought spirals while I published this book.

To my sister, Emma, for reading multiple drafts and spending several car rides talking it out. To my friend, Marissa, for reading various drafts and believing that BookTok would love this book as much as I do. To my mom, Cheryl, for giving me pep talks when I needed them and tough talks when I spiraled. To my brother, Eric, for helping me pick a cover even though I ignored your advice completely. To my dad, Greg, for accepting that this book would have to cut into our *Dexter* rewatch. To my brother, Sag, for taking me out to dinner and distracting me from all my edits. You didn't know it then, but I needed that. To my friends, Abby and Emily, for always being a phone call away and never doubting that I could actually publish this thing. I hope I did you all proud.

This book had two amazing teams of people behind it who made this dream come true. Thank you, Hannah VanVels, for your edits and feedback. These characters were carved out, in part, by your watchful eyes. Thank you, Colleen Sheehan, for turning my manuscript into the first book I ever published. Karin Wittig, thank you for drawing Elverath so readers could follow along. And thank you, Kim Dingwall, for your incredible cover design. You brought Keera to life in a way I never thought possible.

This version of *A Broken Blade* wouldn't exist without the team at Union Square & Co. I would like to thank my editor, Laura Schreiber, for believing in this book and helping it shine even brighter. Thank you Stefanie Chin for catching plot holes I would have never noticed. And thank you Hayley Jozwiak for perfecting this story and navigating my questionable comma use. I am so excited that Keera's story made its way to all of you.

My last thank-you is to the BookTok community. I wrote this book midway through 2021 after seeing videos on book series I'd never heard of and the insightful discourse that pulled me in. I wrote this book for you, combining all the things BookTok loves, with all the missing parts I craved. This community has been so lovely to be a part of, to learn from and explore, to escape into again and again. I hope you found some escape between these pages too.

Turn the page for a special bonus chapter from Riven's perspective . . .

CHAPTER SEVEN
RIVEN

I LED NIKOLAI THROUGH the sandstone buildings of Cereliath. We passed the port where the city canal system merged into a small bay, and where we had found the boat left in plain sight. The shipment of goods Curringham's assistant was meant to get out of the city. Rylan had flashed the lord's seal dozens of times, steering stolen food down the tiny man-made waterway toward Silstra. He had never had a problem.

Until *her*.

We arrived at the outskirts of Cereliath, our hoods drawn so no one could see our faces. Nikolai stepped through the ruined temple, his boot shifting on shards of broken glass that were once a window. His gaze scanned along the beams shrinking with rot and the damaged pews time had left behind. Nikolai's tongue prodded the inside of his cheek as he took another step inside, then lowered his hood.

"You want me to lure her *here*?" Nikolai's finger swiped along the pulpit. He flitted the thick layer of dust onto the floor. "Of all the places you could pick to die Riv . . . is this truly the last room you want to see?" He raised a brow at a patch of mold on the wall.

I ground my teeth. "I won't die," I repeated for the seventh time that day. "And if I do, you know what must be done."

We didn't have time to argue. Nikolai needed to leave before the suns finished setting.

Any remaining humor hardened in Nikolai's eyes as he turned to face me. "I know I made a vow to you Riven, but I did not think I was agreeing to follow you *and* your stupidity."

"It's not stu—"

"It is absolutely ludicrous, and you know it." Nikolai took out a piece of linen from his breast pocket and rubbed the dust off a pew. He sat down slowly, wincing as he did so. "Playing into the Blade's game. Accepting her invitation to kill you . . . ridiculous," he mumbled to himself.

I cleared my throat and he stopped grumbling. "I wish Syrra was here." He sighed, looking up at the bend in the ceiling. "You wouldn't dare *suggest* this to her, let alone go through with it."

I held back my smile. "Why do you think I sent her to Myrelinth?"

Nikolai's head snapped back to me. His eyes narrowed, but then softened as he rubbed his brow. "Rylan is dead, Riven," he said gently. "There is nothing that we can do to change that. Sacrificing yourself to avenge his death will not bring him peace. Accomplishing what we promised him, what we've promised the Halflings—that needs to be your focus."

I leaned against one of the pillars. The plaster that had once decorated the beam was beginning to crack. "It is my focus."

Nikolai's lips transformed into a stern line across his face.

"Am I just supposed to forget that a young man is dead?" I spat. "A man who helped us for months? Who helped feed hundreds?"

"Riven, we're at war—"

"I will not use those who follow me as pawns in a game," I yelled. Heat flooded my body. A brutal mix of rage and fear that stirred my magic. "Their lives have meaning. I won't forget that. I *can't* forget that . . . I thought you of all people would understand." The power ripped against my skin, like daggers poking through flesh. I took a deep breath and closed my eyes. My magic had been harder to control since we reached Cereliath. Now it spiraled through me with enough force that my vision blurred from the pain. I hadn't felt this unsteady in years. Not since Syrra and Feron had started training me.

Nikolai waited patiently for me to get the surge of emotion under control. I cleared my mind like Feron taught me—pushing my magic back into whatever depths existed inside of me. A moment passed. Then another. Finally, my breath settled. I gave a small nod to Nikolai, signaling to him to continue.

His eyes lingered on me before he resumed his argument. "Riven, if you die tonight, who will be there to protect the next Rylan from Aemon's wrath?"

I folded my arms, still aware of my breathing. "*She* is not the king."

Nikolai shook his head. "No, she is not. But even if you manage to kill her tonight, Aemon has a line of Halflings ready to take her place. You would never stop avenging Rylan—or the whichever innocent life Aemon sets his new Blade on."

My anger flared again. Small shadows swirled against the sunlit wall, casting intricate patterns made of darkness onto the wood. I took another breath. "If I have to kill every member of the Arsenal—every Shade—then I will."

Nikolai crossed his legs and opened his mouth to continue, but I cut him off.

"She's the best of them. She would be replaced in title alone." I took another breath. "She's a monster, Nik. Aemon's monster. When she dies tonight, it will be weeks before the Arsenal recovers. We can use that to further our cause. We can be better. *I* can be better." The last words caught in my throat as I thought of Rylan crying over his brother's grave. I'd promised him I would change Elverath for the better. That he would see a world without hungry children. Halfling or Mortal.

But he was dead. And I, a liar.

I turned back to Nikolai. His eyes were already on me, wide and defeated. "If she is as monstrous as you say, I just hope *she* doesn't kill *you*." He pulled up the hood of his cloak and disappeared into the setting sunlight.

All I had to do was wait.

I watched from the shadows as she climbed through the second story window. Unexpected point of entry—Syrra would have approved. The Blade earned her name, cutting through the night air like a sharp edge. She landed on the decaying pulpit brandishing her dual blades. A quarter turn and she would see me. My chance to deny her invitation had flown out the window as she jumped through it.

Magic flared inside my chest. I pushed it back, keeping my breath even and leaning against the pillar. I wanted to appear calm. Collected. The Blade needed to know I had planned this. And I planned on leaving.

I spoke into the darkness. "I heard you wanted a rematch." She turned in one fluid motion. Her shoulders were lax, but ready. Her feet shifted almost imperceptibly, feeling the uneven tile beneath her boot. I kept my eyes on her torso, learning the balance of her body just as Syrra had taught me.

The Blade was dressed in her normal black garb. I smirked.

I wondered if she knew I had designed my own clothes after the Shades' uniform. After her uniform. Aemon hadn't noticed my mockery yet, but the Blade wouldn't be able to ignore it now. We weren't fighting on that rooftop, limbs spiraling in every direction. We were standing in the peace before the inevitably deadly storm.

Her face was veiled behind the shadow cast by her hood. My power flickered. I was tempted to use it, to split that shadow in two and push it apart, revealing the face beneath.

I couldn't. This would be easier to do if I didn't have to see her face.

"Glad to hear my message was received," she answered. She twirled her left blade, testing its weight. The left wrist didn't shake, but I noticed a quiver in the right. I would attack that side first.

I shrugged. She may have requested the meeting, but I arranged it. She was not in control here. "It would be impolite to ignore a request from the king's Blade," I replied, my gaze never leaving the line of her shoulders.

She cracked her neck. I was hit with the thick scent of stale wine. The Blade was on edge. Maybe tonight would end in my favor.

"You're eager to die?" she asked. I could hear the smugness in her voice, but it didn't match the quick beats of her heart. She was nervous. I could use that.

I chuckled.

"Are you sure you *can* kill me?" I pulled my sword out of its holster, remembering the first lesson Syrra had taught me. *Rage is a catalyst; it can be your weapon, or it can be your downfall.* How many taunts would it take to stoke the Blade's downfall?

I stepped forward. Her left foot shifted against the uneven wooden floorboards.

"Are you so sure I won't?" she asked from underneath her hood.

Nikolai and Syrra flashed through my mind. The Halflings. The

Elverin. I took a breath and prepared myself for what needed to be done. "May the worthy win," I whispered.

Then I charged.

She was quick, dodging my blows and throwing her own. I attacked her right side, but the shakiness had vanished. Her right blade protected just as well as her left.

I needed to change tactics.

I smirked, hoping she heard it in my voice. "It's been more than a minute and you have yet to draw blood."

"Again, you're so eager to die," she snapped. Her voice was a little winded.

I switched my sword hand. I would play defense while she tired herself out. "Death is the only certainty in this life," I replied. It was one of Syrra's favorite lines in training.

She stepped back, noticing my change in maneuver. I could feel her eyes burrowing into me. Waiting for my next move.

Rage. I needed to provoke her. "I expected more from the king's Blade. I was dodging blows like yours as an apprentice."

A snarl broke free from under her hood. She pounced like a fire lion, slashing at me with her blades. I blocked every swing, knowing her energy was draining faster than mine.

We cut across the floor in a blur of flashing metal, our breaths keeping the tempo as each of our blades tore toward the other's. Her arms lowered slightly, like her weapons were getting heavier.

I had her.

She backed into a pew. I swung. She dodged it by stepping onto the bench.

I readied another swing, but she was soaring over my head. She kicked the hilt from my grasp. The sword slid across the floor behind me. I couldn't reach for it without turning my back to her.

That would be instant death.

I leaned toward her as she landed, grabbing her wrist. I twisted hard. My mouth twitched when I heard the metal clank against the floor. Another flash of metal cut through my sight line. I caught her arm in my hand, stopping it midair.

I was bladeless. I needed to recover my sword before she had time to stab me from behind. I closed my eyes and kneed her in the stomach. Hard enough that I felt her gasp for air on my neck. My magic pulsed, pounding against my chest. I ignored it and ran toward my sword.

I reached out; my fingertips brushed against the handle. Then there was a flash of searing pain. Red blood dripped from my hand from where her dagger had cut me. My magic blazed around the wound, igniting the pain again and again as the blood dribbled out. I snarled.

"Any requests for how I kill you?" she taunted, but her voice was raspy. She was buying time to recover.

She wanted time and I needed to distract her as I grabbed my weapon.

"No," I answered. "But I would like to know *why* you want to kill me." In truth I didn't care. I needed to watch her. See where her body was hurting, where she was weak. I shifted ever so slightly toward the blade on the floor.

"The king commands it," she replied, almost automatically.

The answer wasn't what I expected. The Blade was a menace to the entire kingdom; her bloodshed was unmatched. Surely some part of her enjoyed it, or at the very least enjoyed the pleasures life as the Blade awarded her. "You don't dream of *not* serving the king?" I asked, trying not to sound too interested. I needed to find her weakness. Her reasons for killing would be meaningless once I avenged Rylan's murder.

"That's the thing about crowns," she whispered. "When one head falls, they're placed on another."

I paused. Those words. I had said something very similar to Nikolai all those years before, convincing him to join me in taking down the king. Did the Blade know? My heart rate fluttered and so did my magic. Sharp stings of worry jabbed at my skin. The shadows around us grew darker. My magic pushed against my control, threatening to burst out into the open.

I needed to end this. Before others got hurt.

My hand inched closer to my sword, while I still faced the Blade. "Only if you leave a crown to claim," I whispered. Metal met my fingertips.

She lunged, sliding across the floor and kicking the sword out of reach. I leaped to my feet, readying myself for her attack. The Blade flipped off the floor and I swung at her. This time with my fist.

She ducked. I swung. I punched. She dodged.

We circled each other like caged beasts. Only one of us could leave the victor. My magic tore at my skin. My hands tensed, trying to keep it contained until this was over. I swung again, but she stepped to the side with a feline quickness.

I ducked as she levied a kick. I straightened and swung once more, aiming for her left. She stepped to the side again, but this time I expected it. I hurled myself at her, pushing us both against the pillar.

A loud crack echoed against the rotting walls. I looked down and saw a dark braid spilling out of her pinned hood. Then I saw her eyes. Silver pools of light encased in the shadows my magic had darkened.

An electric shock blasted through my body. It was warm and radiant, like basking in the sunlight of a long summer's day. Magic. My magic. It radiated from me, trailing down my arms toward . . .

Her.

She was calling my magic forward. There was no coldness or pain, only warmth. I could see the magical glint in her irises. Silver mixing with violet.

"It's not possible," I whispered. I had heard the stories. Feron had explained it to me myself. Could that really be what I was feeling?

She said something, fighting against my hold, but I couldn't hear her. All I could hear was the deep pulse of magic matching my heartbeat. Our heartbeats.

I blinked, trying to focus on her words. Her brow was furrowed. Anger. She was angry. How could she be angry wrapped in such lightness?

"You can't feel it?" I realized in a whisper. She tilted her face toward mine, bringing us a fraction closer. My magic responded with another pulse of warmth.

She was drawing me in. Magic and body. I'd never felt anything so strong. I focused on her face, cut and bloodied, but beautiful. Radiant. Her silver eyes blinked, and I lowered my face to hers. Succumbing to whatever magic existed between us.

Her lips were soft. Like a breeze at dawn, gentle but with the threat of growing into something dangerous. I kissed her again, pressing my body against hers, feeling the warmth of my magic flood through both of us. My hand tightened on her hip as my tongue memorized her taste. Her mouth was seductively sweet, like a poison that consumed me fully.

She pulled me closer, biting my lip. Any control I had disappeared. My hand climbed to her neck, pulling at her hair as I bit her back. Anything to get her closer to me. I would devour her all night if she let me.

A small moan escaped her lips. I blinked. Could she feel the magic too? Did she feel the same intoxicating rush?

One kiss and she'd ruined my plan. One kiss and I knew I could never kill her.

Her shoulder shifted. My magic sensed the dagger before I could see it. My hand reached, grabbing the wrist plunging a dagger into my chest. I felt a sharp prick before pushing her back against the pillar.

The pain sobered me slightly. My shadows still whirled between us, but I could control them now. I looked down at her. She wasn't radiating with magic and warmth.

She was just the Blade.

The enemy.

Had this been some kind of trick?

She thrashed against my chest, trying to break my hold. "You make a habit of kissing people before you kill them?" she snapped. She thrashed again before looking up at me. I thickened the shadows in my hood. If she noticed, she didn't show it.

I leaned forward, hiding my face as it swept her cheek. "It won't happen again," I murmured, trying to find the strength to walk. I took a breath of her scent. She smelled of dawn and cedar. I took one more breath and then I left her there before she killed me.

I flew through the back alleys of Cereliath to the small inn where Nikolai and Collin were waiting for me. My heart raced and I could still feel the rush of power in my veins. Like an aftershock. Warmth pulsed through my body, electrifying my skin. It was intoxicating. I stumbled through the back door.

"You're alive," Nikolai said, deadpan, peering over his magnifying spectacles. He was holding a metal contraption in his hand.

I slapped my hand on the counter of the empty kitchen and took another ragged breath. All I could feel was my magic. The coldness hadn't returned, but it still felt familiar. No sharp point of a dagger clawing down my limbs, instead my power caressed my skin. Gentle and waiting. For once, it was fully at my command.

I didn't trust myself to use it.

"What's wrong?" Nikolai stood, his metal ball falling to the floor. "Did she stab you? Are you hurt?"

I waved Nikolai's worried hands off and stumbled toward the table. Nikolai took a seat beside me, one knee bouncing as placed his spectacles on top of his curly head. "Is she . . . dead?" he whispered, needlessly looking around the empty room. It was just us. Collin would be keeping watch from the roof.

"No." I held my face in my hands, trying to ignore the magic stirring in my veins.

Nikolai gasped. "She escaped?"

"Not exactly." I lifted my head just enough to look at him.

Nikolai pursed his lips, waiting for an explanation. I took another deep breath and leaned back in the chair.

I rubbed my brow, replaying that moment over again in my head. Her face. My magic. Her lips. "I kissed her," I answered, still in a daze.

Nikolai's eyes widened before his face broke into a knowing grin. "Not the best time to get swept up in the moment, my friend." I huffed a laugh. Nikolai thrived on the unexpected.

"What did she do when you kissed her?" Nikolai's smirk grew.

I coughed. "She tried to stab me."

Nikolai blinked once. Then again. Suddenly he slapped his knee and doubled over in laughter. "Promise me I can meet her before you try to kill her again," he rasped between laughs.

"I'm not trying again. . . . At least not yet." I stood up, the magic finally cooling along my skin. I took a normal breath. "We need to leave."

Nikolai stood without question. "To where?"

"Aralinth," I answered. "I need to see Feron. *Tonight.*"

About the Author

Melissa (she/her/kwe) is an Anishinaabe-kwe of mixed ancestry living on Turtle Island. She splits her time between Treaty 9 in Northern Ontario and the unceded territory of the Algonquin Anishinaabeg in Ottawa, Canada. She has a graduate degree in applied linguistics and discourse studies, loves movies, and hates spoons. Melissa has a BookTok account where she discusses her favorite kinds of books including Indigenous and queer fiction, feminist literature, and nonfiction. *A Broken Blade* is her first novel.

Find her on TikTok @melissas.bookshelf